The Pagoda Tree

by the same author

THE ACHILLES AFFAIR
THE PASS BEYOND KASHMIR
THE ROAD AND THE STAR
THE GOLD OF MALABAR
THE SPRINGERS
THE BREAK IN THE LINE
THE TERMINATORS
SNOWLINE
THE WHITE DACOIT
WITH EXTREME PREJUDICE
THE MEMSAHIB

The Pagoda Tree

BERKELY MATHER

CHARLES SCRIBNER'S SONS
NEW YORK

To Juliet O'Hea, who has guided, encouraged and launched more authors than Helen has ships — from one of the former, in affection and gratitude.

B.M.

A quest for quick money drives two orphaned brothers, Neil and Ross Stafford, across thousands of miles of strange lands as the two pursue their elusive dream from England to Australia and through the Orient.

PAGODA: In China, a temple – in India, a gold coin – in both, the *Plumeria acutifloria*, which bears yellow flowers. Hence to seek one's fortune in the far places is to 'shake the Pagoda Tree'.

Chapter One

I was born in Cumberland in 1833 but what part exactly I've never found out, because I've certainly not been back there to make enquiries. I remember hearing my father once say that his family originally came from Lincolnshire and that my mother had been Scottish, which latter may have accounted for my Christian name of Ross, and my brother's of Neil. I can't remember her, but Neil, five years my senior, told me that she was a large red-headed woman who stormed out of the house one night after beating the very devil out of Father for coming home drunk three times in as many days. She never returned, so Father was able to hiccup his way to a drunkard's grave in peace, literally, because he was Curator of Kensal Green Cemetery. His stipend was sixty-five pounds per annum – little enough no doubt for a man of his prodigious thirst – but there were certain perquisites which helped out considerably. A house went with the post, yellow brick and cramped, with mean little lancet windows which gave it a pseudo-ecclesiastical appearance, and it was overshadowed by dank yew trees. I hated it, although I was well aware of the social cachet it imparted to the family when viewed in context with the even smaller dwellings of the Head Sexton and his eight gravediggers, all of whom had to call my father Sir. A further consideration was that of the education of my brother and myself. We were entitled to free places at the nearby Church of England parish school, which cost the unprivileged a daily penny per head which had to be handed over to the master on arrival each morning. The ultimate guerdon was free burial for all employees who died in service. This my father claimed one bitter winter's night after falling into an open grave on his way home from his favourite tavern, and drowning. Neil and I were sent off to St Caldbec's then by the Parish Council. I was eight and Neil thirteen.

St Caldbec's, or, to give it its original name, The Sir Thomas Kyle Asylum for Indigent Children, had originally been founded and endowed by a benevolent brewer who had ironically died penniless shortly after receiving the accolade with which his charity, plus a sizeable donation to Whig party funds, had been rewarded. It had then been taken over somewhat grudgingly by the Church Commissioners as a refuge for orphans too young to be admitted to the adult workhouse, and they were boarded, clothed and educated up to the age of fourteen for a Poor Law fee of five pounds per annum, which was, at least, an improvement on the parish orphanages, most of which turned their charges out at a much earlier age. All this my brother and I learned as we sat glumly listening to the cemetery managers and the parish clerk discussing our future after the funeral.

The school lay in marshy country between Colchester and Harwich, and I was at the damned place for six dragging years, only the first being made bearable by the protecting wing of Neil. We wore shapeless suits of fustian, flat caps of the same material and ploughboys' boots, with, on Sundays, clerical 'bands' of coarse white calico that chafed our skinny young necks like the deuce. There were girls there also, but these we only saw in church, out of the corners of our eyes, because looking at them directly across the aisle which separated the sexes was taken to indicate incipient lechery, punishable, in official jargon, by 'six strokes of the birch upon the untrousered breech'. Fortunately the temptation to ogle wasn't overwhelming because the poor little wretches were as drab and miserable as ourselves. They were destined for domestic service, we for any trade in which a vacancy could be found and where the employer was willing to forgo an indenturing fee in the sweet name of Charity, or, when all else failed, the Army. Neil gained his quittance on his fourteenth birthday and was bound to a monumental mason near our former home, and thereafter I saw him only on such Sundays as he could raise the fare on the recently built railway from Liverpool Street to Colchester, and then only clandes-

8

tinely because visits from friends or family were viewed with suspicion by the school authorities as a possible prelude to running away. Even at a fiver a head we apparently still showed a profit. Actually I did run away, three times, in the year after Neil left, but was caught within a matter of hours on each occasion, ignominiously returned, and soundly flogged. Neil wisely talked me out of further attempts.

How I looked forward to his visits. Sunday was the one day on which we had a free and relatively unsupervised period – four hours after our midday dinner, until evensong. In the summer we were permitted to walk and talk in groups in the muddy playground, provided that voices were kept at a seemly level. In the winter we huddled together in the cold and barnlike assembly hall. Walking and talking were forbidden in the latter because the superintendent's quarters adjoined it, and if disturbed from his afternoon nap he was apt to emerge like the bull of Bashan, laying about at random with an inch-thick rattan cane.

Neil and I had arranged a drill before he left. He would make a chalk-mark on a railing at the back of the orphanage grounds when he arrived, and then repair to a nearby wood where there was an abandoned shepherd's hut, and I would slip out and join him there, and we would make a fire and roast the saveloys and potatoes he had bought in the Aldgate market. His apprenticeship carried no wage, so these visits were financed by the theft and resale of flowers from fresh graves in the cemetery. The fare alone was two shillings, and the food he brought cost at least as much, so his floral depredations at a penny a bunch must have been considerable. It was he who first aroused in me a love of reading, and wide and varied was the literature he brought me – all stolen from secondhand stalls in the market – Penny Dreadfuls of the Springheel Jack and Dick Turpin type, copies of *Household Words* in which Dickens was then serializing his novels – and later, heavier fare – *Tom Jones, Roderick Random, Robinson Crusoe, Arabian Nights, The Vicar of Wakefield* – all grist to my insatiable mill, to be read covertly in odd corners, often by the light of scraps of candle filched from

9

the church. That was the foundation of such education as I possess, because from the wretched schoolroom of St Caldbec I took away nothing but the bare three Rs and a hatred of *The Pilgrim's Progress*, the only book recommended and allowed for light recreational reading by the ecclesiastical starvelings who mistaught us.

By the time my own fourteenth birthday approached, Neil was out of his apprenticeship, a deliverance he had celebrated by getting his employer's wife with child, a feat the mason himself had not accomplished in fifteen years of marriage – or so Neil boasted. He had accordingly abandoned the chipping of headstones and obtained employment as a 'starter' at a hackney cab office in the Haymarket. The wages were only a pound a week but, as in our father's case, there were 'perks'.

'The footmen come from the big houses,' he told me. 'A cab's wanted here – a brougham there – we even handle post-chaises, although the railway's knocked the bottom out of that business nowadays, but whatever it is they want, I handle it. I send who I wish – and the driver concerned has to show his appreciation – that's if he wants to be kept busy. As much as five bob to be made on a good day. Call it half-a-crown on an average and multiply that by six. Fifteen bob on top of my quid! I'm doing better than ever the Old Man did, and I've yet to reach my twentieth birthday.'

But he wasn't stopping there, he went on. He had plans – plans that included me. 'In business on our own. Just wait until I've got a bit of capital behind me. We're going to jump the moon, young Ross.'

And I didn't doubt him for one moment, because he represented for me everything that was fine, noble, brave and accomplished – a shining paladin in an otherwise very dim and dingy world. His looks matched his disposition. He was very fair, with blue eyes that could be as soft as summer skies when he was cajoling a woman, but as hard as arctic ice when he was angry. He was strong and well built, as indeed we both were in spite of wretched feeding since infancy, which was particularly fortunate in his case because some of the drivers and ostlers round the hackney stables were very tough characters indeed, and his fists and muscles, hardened and strengthened by six years of humping marble slabs and carving sorrowing angels, stood him in good stead when dealing with the dissatisfied or recalcitrant.

I travelled up to London the day after my birthday, clad in the 'going-out suit' that was the Foundation's last largess to young hopefuls being launched on life's uncertain sea, with a small carpet-bag containing a change of underclothing, a pair of socks and a Bible. My treasured library, retrieved from various hiding places in the grounds, had been taken up for me by Neil on his last two visits. The suits were supplied to the school in one size by a contractor, and mine was therefore short at wrist and ankle and tight under crutch and armpits. In my pocket was a letter addressed to the chief clerk of Messrs Willoughby and Doddington, Shipping and Forwarding Agents, at Cloak Lane, Blackfriars, and the sum of five shillings.

'You are a very fortunate lad,' the superintendent had told me on leaving. 'This is an opportunity that can lead to many things. They want an office junior who writes a clear, well-formed hand for copying duties. You will be on probation for twelve months. Board and lodgings are found and you will receive an honorarium of two shillings a week.' Then followed the homily that I already knew by heart. It was about Idleness, Drink, and worse – much worse. Loose Women, Music Halls and Public Houses, Flesh, and the Devil who lay constantly in wait to ensnare and drag down to Hell the unwary and the vicious. It was delivered to all of us on leaving and it never varied by one syllable, and the about-to-be-free used to retail it to the rest of us, obscenely paraphrased, in the dormitories at night.

Neil met me at Liverpool Street, looked askance at my procrustean suit, and took me off to a Jewish tailor in Aldgate who dealt in rejects and misfits. Both terms were misleading as the garments he sold were basically of good cloth and workmanship but had failed to meet the individual tastes of more discriminating customers, and very shortly I was arrayed in what was then the uniform of the City of London – black jacket and grey trousers, with white shirt, cravat, top hat and gloves. And to my awe and amazement, he paid the two guineas it all came to with coins from a magnificent sovereign case on his watch chain.

We went off then to Messrs Willoughby and Doddington, I with great trepidation, but Neil as coolly self-possessed and easy of manner as the President of the Royal Exchange itself.

It was now nearly six p.m. and the office was about to close, and Mr Creswick, the chief clerk, seemed a little put out at being delayed in his passage home to deal with a lowly probationary junior clerk, but Neil's suggestion that we should take a little refreshment while discussing my future mollified him greatly, so we went off to a public house in Cannon Street, where they drank brandy and water and I a whole pint of light beer. My lodgings, apparently, were to have been in Mr Creswick's house in Finsbury, which he shared with a wife and seven children, an arrangement that we gathered had been rather forced upon him by Mr Doddington, the head of the firm.

'A Quaker,' Mr Creswick explained sourly. 'Philanthropist. Bloody office is full of orphans – no offence. Farms 'em out on the rest of us for eight bob a week, because he doesn't like juniors to be on the loose in London. I'm afraid this youngster will have to bunk in with my two eldest boys.'

My heart sank. A room of my own had been a constant dream. Neil caught my eye and winked reassuringly as Mr Creswick buried his nose in his brandy and water.

'I could fix him up at my lodgings,' he suggested helpfully.

'Good of you,' Mr Creswick said. 'But I'm afraid Mrs C. is counting on the eight bob. The firm ain't so damned philanthropic when it comes to wages.'

'You needn't tell them – so you'll be that much up on the transaction each week,' Neil said.

Hope gleamed for a moment in Mr Creswick's eye, then faded.

'Much as my situation's worth,' he said sorrowfully. 'If the old skinflint ever found out he'd sack me without a character.'

'No need for him to find out if we all keep mum about it,' Neil assured him.

Fear fought with avarice until after the fourth brandy and water, and then the latter won, and Mr Creswick nodded and tapped himself on the nose with his forefinger and we solemnly shook hands on it and I was sworn to discretion over another pint of beer, which I threw up in the hansom cab on the way back to Neil's digs. They were in the Waterloo Bridge Road – two rooms over an ironmonger's shop, for which he was paying half a sovereign a week. The sheer prodigality of it appalled me.

'Cheap at half the price,' Neil said airily. 'Don't you worry about money, young Ross.'

'But I'm only to get two shillings a week until I come out of my time,' I told him.

'I'll let you have another five bob on top of that. Didn't I tell you? We're going to be all right.' He aimed a mock punch at my head and grinned widely.

But I was genuinely worried. 'You can't do all this,' I protested. 'Not even on thirty-five shillings a week. That money you spent on my clothes – then you paid for all the drinks – and the cab. Ten bob a week for this place – and there will be money for food – '

But he refused to be serious. And then Caerwen entered.

Mine had been an entirely male world up until now, and the arrival into it unannounced of this strange female creature stunned me. She burst in without knocking and stood for a moment with her hands on her hips, regarding me intently – then she smiled, and something of the panic that was threatening to engulf me receded.

She said, 'So this is Ross? Like you. Better-looking though. Going to be a big lad when he fills out a bit. How are you, cariad?' She threw her arms around me in a bear hug. She was tall, almost as tall as I, and comfortably buxom with it. She smelt nice and, to my unaccustomed eye, she was magnificently dressed in, I think, a red floral gown, with bustles and hoops and puffed sleeves. She had a lot of red curls cascading from under a beribboned straw bonnet, and her cheeks were the rosiest I had ever seen – and her lips the deepest red.

Neil said, 'For God's sake, Caerwen! With that lot on you'll be run in for a whore on the prowl. And you've been drenching yourself with that damned patchouli again.'

'Well, there's nasty of you!' she said indignantly. 'Done myself up special I have, just to welcome your young brother. Asked me in for supper you did – if you remember.' She held up a basket. 'Got it all here – pork sausages and real Welsh lamb chops, and some kidneys – and cheese and a loaf of what these Cockneys call bread – and a flagon of stout, and still with sevenpence change left out of what you gave me.'

She was shedding her outer garments, with never a check in her spate of words, until she was down to her petticoat and a very scanty bodice thing that revealed far more than it hid. I tried to focus my eyes on the fire, but she moved round into my field of vision and set up a dutch oven in front of the grate. I looked fixedly at a picture on the wall of a blind fiddler being led by a little girl then, but again she moved – this time to get a white cloth and some plates and knives and forks from a cupboard. She was obviously familiar with, and quite at home in, these quarters. I caught Neil grinning impishly at me.

'You're embarrassing the boy,' he said to Caerwen.

'Embarrassing my foot,' she scoffed. 'What's to embarrass in this? You should see us in the fields at home at harvest time. Down to our shifts and drawers then, and sweating like Dafydd Owen's bull. Healthy, it was. Damned skinny, bloodless English women, covered from neck to ankle even when they go to bed. No wonder their husbands come looking for a bit of bare flesh when the old dander starts to rise. You'll never catch the Welsh wasting their money on sly miggy. Kept too busy at home, they are.' She turned and looked at me in the guttering gaslight. 'By damn, you're right,' she agreed. 'He *is* embarrassed. Scarlet, he is. Never mind, cariad. Don't take any notice of me. It's only my old talk.'

Quickly and dexterously she cooked our supper and placed

it on the table, then, relenting, covered herself more decorously before sitting down with us to what, looking back, was the most delicious meal I had ever eaten in all my short life.

Warm, replete and very tired I dropped off to sleep in my chair. I remember half waking as she and Neil got my splendid new clothes off me and tucked me into the big double bed in the next room. Neil was arguing with her.

'There's the couch in the other room,' he muttered.

'What if he wakes up and catches us?' she retorted. 'Shame on you! You said yourself, he's only a boy. *Mochyn budr*!'

She had gone when I awoke next morning. My head was aching dully from my unaccustomed beer-swilling of the night before, but the walk across Waterloo Bridge with my brother helped to clear it. We breakfasted on tea and batchcakes at a stall, and since I still had an hour free before having to report to the office at eight o'clock, Neil took me for a short walk along the Embankment and pointed out some of the landmarks – the new Houses of Parliament, much of its carved mock-Gothic stonework still sheathed in scaffolding at that time, Nelson's Column, seen in the distance from the bottom of Whitehall, the Metropolitan Police headquarters at New Scotland Yard from which a detachment of frock-coated, top-hatted constables was just emerging – 'peelers' they were called, Neil told me.

'Quite safe,' he said. 'You can tell them a mile off in that uniform. It's the ones that wear ordinary clothes you've got to be careful of. Right bastards some of 'em.' He looked at his watch. 'You'd better be getting along now. Just keep on the Embankment until you reach Blackfriars, then turn left for Cloak Lane. You'll remember it when you see it. Good luck, old cocker. See you back at the digs tonight.' He winked at me, tilted his hat at a jaunty angle and went off up Whitehall whistling.

There were ten of us altogether in the office, not counting Mr Doddington, who was always referred to as the Guv'nor. Apparently there was no longer a Willoughby with the firm.

Mr Creswick, the chief clerk, in spite of his apparent friendliness at our initial meeting, was an unpleasant little man who lived in mortal terror of losing his 'situation', as he invariably called it, and seemed to think that his best assurance of keeping it was to make the lives of the rest of us as miserable as possible. Under him came Keddle, the bookkeeper, then two 'tide waiters' or clerks who stood by at the entrance to the East India docks ready to be rowed out to incoming ships in order to collect bills of lading and mail and convey them to the office. Their names were Turvey and Santos respectively, and we juniors were firmly convinced that they each made a fortune smuggling contraband from the ships they boarded. Then came the juniors, four of them 'established', which meant that they were each paid twelve shillings a week and were free to make their own arrangements in respect of board and lodgings, and another probationer, like myself, an orphan from a charity school, named Merridew who was living with the Turveys. I shared a dark corner under a staircase with this youth. Keddle conducted me there and pointed to a pile of letters and bills.

'He'll show you what to do,' he told me, rapping Merridew sharply on the back of his head. 'Copying. No smudges or blots or they'll be docked out of your two bob at a penny a time. Get on with it.' Merridew muttered 'Bollocks' under his breath and made a rude sign behind his back.

We worked from eight until six on this deadly monotonous task, six days a week, the pile never seeming to diminish, because the others kept bringing more documents by the basketful. Mr Doddington was a stickler for orderly records, so a copy of everything that went through the office, however trivial, had to be painstakingly engrossed word for word into big ledgers which, when filled, were stacked in racks on the upper floor, thereafter to gather dust and provide nesting places for the huge river rats that infested the old ramshackle building. Merridew, a thin, consumptive youth of about my own age, gave me a vitriolic account of the firm that first day, in a muted undertone.

'The Guv'nor's a proper sod. Mean as catshit and twice as

nasty. We handle all the shipping business here that other firms won't touch – at two-and-a-half per cent, against the market rate of five. Getting crews for hell ships that decent seamen won't sail in – victualling the convict transports for Australia – that sort of thing. He makes his profit by starving us poor bastards – then sings and prays his bloody head off on Sundays. Creswick stuck a barmaid at the Boatswain's Rest in the family way and has to pay her half-a-crown a week. That's why he takes in boarders. Keddle's been cooking the books here for years. The Guv'nor knows it but he can't do anything about it because Keddle's got something on him. Santos grinds Turvey's missus when Turvey is on overnight duty on the tide. I can hear 'em in the next room – ' and much else of a sensational and no doubt slanderous nature.

But if the days were long and the work tedious, the nights of that first year in London were a delight. With my brother I must have visited every music hall, assembly room, dancing 'academy' and other low haunt in the West End of London. When Caerwen was free of her current gentleman friend she often came with us. She was a creature of contrasts, bawdy and rough of tongue, but with a certain gentleness and even delicacy at times. She could fly into rages with often disastrous consequences to anybody within range of her whirling fists and clawing fingers, and the next minute kneel on the muddy cobblestones to comfort a slum brat that had fallen and hurt itself. She might sing a dirty song in a gin mill that would bring a blush to the cheek of a Thames waterman, then follow it with a Welsh hymn that would hold a drunken audience in hushed silence, both in a clear, sweet soprano. She would dress garishly one day, with her face a painted mask, and a mass of false curls pinned unnecessarily into her own abundant tresses, and the next, usually after Neil had made fun of her, she would wear a simple gown, and no paint and powder. On these occasions she looked her proper age, which was seventeen – when bedizened, at least ten years more.

'Why does she do it?' I once asked Neil. 'She's pretty without all that stuff on.'

He shrugged. 'Why does a peeler wear a frock-coat with brass buttons and a dirty big top hat?' he said. 'A uniform, to tell the world what she is, and so attract business.'

'You mean she's a – a – ?'

'A whore? Yes, in a sort of way. She's never actually had to go on the batter in the streets at a bob a time, but that will come in the end. It does for all of them.'

'But *why*? She's such a nice girl when she likes.'

'Niceness has got bugger-all to do with it,' he said. 'She's got to make a living like anybody else.'

'But she could do it another way – '

'Could she?' he said drily. 'Without a character from her last situation? Not a chance.'

'Why didn't she get a character?'

'She came up from Cardiganshire to a situation as nursery maid in a gentleman's house in Belgravia. The butler tried to get across her the very first night. She fended him off, because she came from a religious home – and she held out for a week, which was bloody good going considering all the circumstances. He was a bit drunk and noisy the night he did manage to get there, and the mistress heard and sent her husband up to the attic to find out what was going on. Caerwen was bundled out, bag and baggage, on the instant.'

'What about the butler?'

'He'd have got a good talking-to, no doubt. Well-trained butlers are hard to come by. Skivvies are ten a penny.'

'So what did she do?'

'A peeler picked her up and was going to run her in for "wandering abroad at night without visible means of support". That's a crime in this town. She must have looked a bit pitiful, because he relented and gave her some good advice, and took her to a swell knocking-shop. She didn't need a character there. Pretty as a picture, as you've remarked yourself. She was there a year, and learned an awful lot about life. They didn't want to let her go. She damn nearly had to fight her way out. Some smart young cockchafer set her up in furnished lodgings in Marylebone then. He had a few peculiar tastes that she didn't like, so she left one night after putting her mark on him with a broken glass and helping herself to a couple of fivers out of his wallet while he was shrieking the place down. She worked the promenades at the Lyceum after that and was taken up by the old gent who is keeping her now. He's a lawyer – a QC – and he goes on circuit with the Assize courts a lot. That's when she's free to please herself.'

'Where did you meet her?' I asked.

'A rough tried to maul her one night in Drury Lane. I thumped him and we went and had a drink together. It grew up from there.' He was silent for a while, and I tried to find words to frame my next question, but it wasn't necessary. 'I want to break things off,' he went on. 'It's not because I don't like her. I do – very much – but I'm not ready to settle down yet – not by a long chalk. But I think that's what's in *her* mind.'

But the break certainly hadn't come at the end of the first twelve months. I would have been very sorry if it had, because I had come to look forward to those nights when she came and cooked our supper for us, and we went out to a theatre or a music hall or to dance at one of the assembly rooms afterwards. My elevation to 'establishment' hadn't come either, although my probation was to have been for this period only.

'Why don't you see the Guv'nor?' Merridew asked me. 'That bastard Creswick won't put you up – not unless you shove him.' He, Merridew, had been promoted and had shaken the dust of the Turvey household from his heels. He was now technically my superior in the firm although I knew, without undue conceit, that I was the better clerk of the two and had lately been entrusted with more responsibility. But at last I plucked up courage to beard the chief clerk in his den, and met with scant success.

'Think yourself lucky to be still employed here,' he told me sternly. 'I haven't been altogether satisfied with your work. Do you know how many competent clerks there are without situations, *starving*, in the City of London at this moment? No? Well, I'll tell you. *Two thousand*. Two thousand young men who would give their eyeteeth to be where you are now – on the threshold of what could be a comfortable and respectable career – *if* you give of your best. Go back to your desk, Stafford, and think of these things. Come and talk to me again in six months' time.'

Neil grinned when I told him glumly of this interview.

'You know the reason,' he said. 'He loses eight bob a week when you go up. Don't worry, old cocker, I'll think of something to stir his bloody stumps for him before long. He's right about there being a lot of unemployment in the City at the moment though. Don't give him an excuse for sacking you, and maybe selling your vacancy to some poor fool for a premium. There's a lot of that being done.'

'For a job worth two bob a week?' I said incredulously.

'*And* keep. Yes – there's plenty who would raise the wind, just for a start at *nothing* a week. While you're out of a billet, without a character, you have no chance of getting another. Hang on. My job's sound enough, and we're doing all right.'

'But you're keeping me and giving me five shillings a week on top of that,' I protested. 'I can't go on sponging on you like this.'

'Sponging be damned,' he said. 'We stick together, you and I. Hang on. Something will turn up before long – you'll see.'

And it did. Much sooner than either of us expected.

Other than Christmas Day and Good Friday there were no statutory holidays at that time. Most employers, however, gave their people Whit Monday off. It fell that year in May – a glorious gold and blue day, with the trees along the Embankment in full early leaf and the gardens fronting on to the Thames from the Temple and Somerset House a blaze of spring flowers. We had arranged many weeks before to spend the day at the Greenwich Fair, which was held annually on Blackheath Common. I was free of the office, although Mr Doddington thriftily stopped us all a day's pay for the privilege, which amounted in my case to fourpence, but Neil and Caerwen were playing truant.

'They will be yelling for me round the stables,' Neil said, 'and that old devil of yours is back in London, isn't he, Caerwen? But to hell with all of them.'

'He can give his wife a treat for a change,' Caerwen grinned. 'Not that he can do much for either of us these days, poor old dab.'

We went by omnibus, riding on top, eating whiteheart cherries and singing and pelting pedestrians with the stones, Neil and I in shirtsleeves and wearing straw hats, Caerwen as fresh as the morning itself in a green gown, her bonnet hanging by the ribbons and her glorious red hair blowing free in the wind.

The omnibus was packed to capacity with junketing Cockneys – sixteen inside and twelve on the narrow knifeboard seats on top – a murderous load for the two straining horses. It distressed Caerwen, a farm girl with a genuine fondness for animals, and she protested to the driver when he stopped on a hill and the conductor tried to squeeze another two fares on. The driver, a huge red-faced lout in a blanket greatcoat and a billycock hat, gave her a mouthful of abuse, and Neil leaned forward and held a bunched fist under his roseate nose and said softly, 'Say all that again – to *me* – or apologize to the lady.'

'Sorry, guv'nor,' the driver mumbled. 'No offence meant.' And he shouted down to the conductor not to take any more aboard, and even stopped, at Caerwen's suggestion, to allow the horses to drink at the next trough. They worked on bonus, the busmen, and it was no uncommon sight to see their overworked animals drop from exhaustion and die in the shafts, even though the Queen, on her Accession in 1837, had given her patronage and the grant of 'Royal' to the newly formed Society for the Prevention of Cruelty to Animals.

I shall never forget my first sight of the fairground. A square mile of tents and booths lapped by a moving sea of people, and a blast of noise that deafened one until the ears became accustomed to it. Gypsies, horsecopers, showmen, barkers, buskers, all bellowing the merits of their wares. Food of every type and variety – mussels, cockles, oysters, jellied eels, pease pudding, saveloys, parkin, gingerbread. Fairings and favours of coloured ribbons and pinchbeck jewellery. Cockshies, dolls and coconuts. Dwarfs and freaks. The Wild Man of Borneo, The Bearded Lady, The Two-headed Boy. Strong Men and Acrobats. Performing Animals. Fortune Tellers and Doctor Cure-'em-Quicks with an infallible specific for every known and unknown ailment. Three Card and Pea and Thimble riggers. Dancing and Drinking Booths, and Prize Fighters – these last officially illegal but tolerated on fair days.

Neil had given me four half-crowns, double his usual weekly largess, and had threatened to thump me when I demurred about taking it.

'Keep it clenched in your fist, and your fist in your pocket,' he told me. 'The dips here are artists.'

We pushed through the crowd, three abreast with Caerwen in the middle linking our arms, seeing everything, joshing with the magsmen and duffers who tried in vain to coax us into their tents to show us goods that had but that morning been smuggled ashore under the noses of the Customs, so they assured us.

'Sprinkle some scent on the back of your hand, then switch a bottle of coloured water on you,' Neil explained. 'Or give you a good cigar and lumber you with a parcel of brown paper and horse shit. Trust nobody, young Ross.'

But it was he who was the first victim. We had intended to see a play – *The Soldier's Return* – 'guaranteed to bring tears to the eyes of a brass tiger, ladies and gen'men' – in one of the bigger tents. It started at three o'clock, and he felt for his watch to check the time – and it was no longer in his pocket, nor the chain and the sovereign case that he wore on it. 'Solid silver it was, all of it,' he mourned. 'Bought it cheap off a fence for three guineas – and there was four quid in the case. Oh, my Christ! I ought to be pole-axed for a mug.'

I had a little of my ten shillings left, and Caerwen had a guinea secreted in a safe place, but he was not to be comforted. The day was ruined for all of us, or so it seemed until we fetched up outside a boxing booth.

'Roll up, gen'men all and admirers of the fancy. A fi'pun note for any lad who goes three minutes with Jemmie Aldrich, the Seven Dials Gamecock,' the showman was calling, and, not surprisingly, there were no takers, because the battered pug who stood, arms akimbo, glaring balefully at the crowd, looked very formidable indeed.

'Come on, lads,' the showman wheedled. 'Where's your spirit? Jem never hurt no amateur gen'men yet. He stops the moment you drop your guard – and if you don't drop it for three minutes, then it's a lovely crisp fiver. No, dammit, seeing as it's my birthday, we'll make it *two* fivers.'

There was a ripple of excitement in the crowd, but still no takers, although a large but lethargic-looking youth in a Sussex smock was being urged by a couple of 'friends' to take up the challenge.

'A plant,' Neil muttered. 'He'll go forward in a minute and the mob will go in to see the slaughter, at sixpence a head, and the yokel will stop a couple of clouts, but manage to stick it out and collect the tenner, which he'll come out waving over his head and capering like a clown. Then some genuine mug will fancy his chance and throw his hat into the ring, and get his bloody head knocked off for his pains. Well, not this time, cully.' And before we could stop him he had thrown his straw hat through the entrance to the booth.

The showman looked at him speculatively, then glanced towards the bruiser who grinned indulgently and nodded.

'So we *have* got some pluck left in Blackheath after all, gen'men,' the showman called. 'This way! This way! – Roll up! A little sixpence, that's all, to see the fight of the season. Your name, sir?'

'Battling Bunko of Battersea,' Neil told him, and shook off Caerwen's restraining hand. 'Take her away, for Christ's sake,' he muttered to me.

'Neil – you can't,' I begged. 'Please – that blackguard will kill you –'

Caerwen was screaming and clinging to him, which was excellent for business as the crowd seemed to sense that this was going to be a proper contest and was pressing forward to the entrance.

'Bugger off, both of you,' Neil ground through his teeth. 'If I can't go three minutes with that windblown old hack I'll pick up my hat and eat the bloody thing.'

'This way, sir,' the showman beamed. 'Lovely, lovely – the best house of the day – and they're all behind you.'

And so were we, because Caerwen had pulled away from me and followed Neil into the tent and I had perforce to go after her. We sat on a rough bench as far from the ring as the space allowed. Caerwen was hiding her face in her hands and sobbing. The bruiser was already in his corner, flexing his muscles and shadow boxing, and Neil was stripping down to the waist below the ropes. He was big and well set up, but beside the brutish bulk of the other he looked pitifully slim.

The showman was calling the conditions. 'Three minutes, ladies and gen'men, with bare knuckles – on his feet and on his guard – not lying down or with his hands dropped – three minutes between Jemmie Aldrich and – what was the name again, sir? – oh yes – Battling Bunko of Battersea – the well-known middleweight. If, of course, the challenger knocks the champeen out in *under* the three minutes he will be deemed to have won, and will collect his ten pun. This way, sir – if you please.'

Neil climbed through the ropes and came up to scratch in the centre of the ring.

'Shake hands, gen'men,' the showman said. 'That's right. Now, a good clean contest. No biting – no gouging – no hitting below the belt or bringing the knee up into the orchestra stalls in the clinches. *Time!*'

They came up into the stiff-postured stance of the day, long since altered by Marquess of Queensberry rules, and Neil led with a left, which the bruiser didn't attempt to counter. It landed lightly on his cauliflowered right ear and he looked comically surprised, but the blow did as much damage as a sparrow alighting on a slate roof. I was not a little dismayed. Much as I dreaded this whole wretched thing, I would have wished my brother a better showing than that. This brute was obviously going to make a farce of it for the amusement of the crowd. Neil led again, feebly and uncertainly, and the bruiser didn't even block the punch. He merely reached out and grasped Neil's shoulder and gently turned him round, then smacked him open-handed across the rump, like a nursemaid dealing with a naughty child. And Neil reacted like a child. He sulked and pouted and it looked as if he was going to drop his hands and quit, which didn't suit the crowd at all. They were booing and catcalling now. The bruiser crouched forward and pointed to his own chin and closed his eyes, then rested both his hands on his knees in an open invitation to Neil to do his worst. And my brother accepted the invitation. His right fist swept round and up in a perfect parabolic haymaker that landed fair and square under his opponent's chin and lifted him a good foot clear of the floor, and then crashed him down like a falling tree. The poor devil didn't even twitch. He just lay there, out to the wide, and Neil had to do his own counting, because the showman was stunned and speechless. The crowd howled its appreciation as Neil turned and held his hand out for his money.

There was a little acrimonious disputation after he had dressed.

'Be reasonable, guv'nor,' the showman whined. 'A hundred and twenty-two in the house at a tanner a time. That makes three pounds – and you're expecting me to give you a tenner?'

'I'm expecting you to give me what you promised,' Neil told him. 'Do I get it, or does this tent come down round your bloody ears?'

'Call it a fiver,' the showman begged. 'I'll still be two quid down and me boy is buggered for the rest of the fair. Live and let live, guv'nor.'

'Ten pounds, God damn you,' Neil swore – and got it.

We rode back to London in a four-wheeler behind a smartly-trotting horse, and Neil insisted on a real smack-up supper at Kellner's. Caerwen was aghast at the very suggestion.

'Three of us?' she protested. 'It would cost you a good two guineas, what with wine and tips and all. Supper, yes indeed, but somewhere cheaper, boyo.'

'I was seven pounds to the bad,' Neil said. 'Now I'm holding a lovely tenner. Three pounds up! Kellner's it is.'

And Kellner's it was, and by the time we had dealt faithfully with oysters and turtle soup and guinea-fowl and baron of beef followed by iced pudding and Turkish coffee, with a magnum of hock and a bottle of claret, with port to top it all off, the bill came nearer to four pounds than two – and Neil paid for it with a five-pound note and a magnificent flourish, and tipped the head waiter a whole five shillings, then we sat back, too replete to dance to the splendid German orchestra, while Neil smoked a cigar and I tried to, but I had to dash for the cloakroom to be sick.

It was while I was thus engaged that the peelers arrived.

There were four of them. They said nothing. They just pounced on my brother and Caerwen and lifted them bodily from their chairs. Caerwen reacted instinctively and hit one of them between the eyes with the claret bottle and then Neil was into them with flying fists.

I came out of the cloakroom into the lobby and saw them being bundled into a black maria and haled off to Bow Street, so I ran frantically in their wake on foot, and slipped into the police station behind them, in time to hear Neil being charged with uttering a counterfeit five pound note. Then he was searched and they found the other, which was also snide. Caerwen was accused of aiding and abetting him, and both incurred a further charge of assaulting the police. The cashier and the head waiter arrived then and noticed me skulking in the background, so I was arrested also, and we were taken off to separate offices for questioning.

They finished in the early hours of the morning, with me firmly sticking to my story, from which they could not budge me, and since it happened to be the plain unvarnished truth and agreed with that of the others, they decided to accept it, albeit reluctantly, and I was turned loose.

I didn't go home. I just hung about Covent Garden, dozing uneasily in the shelter of a pile of vegetable baskets until dawn, then I bought a cup of tea and a bun from a porters' stall and waited until the police court opened at nine o'clock.

I found a seat in the public gallery and sat through a string of cases – whores – pick-pockets – drunks – footpads and similar criminal small fry until, just before midday, Neil and Caerwen were brought up from the cells to the dock, and I heard Neil give his story almost word for word as I had been reiterating mine half the night. It seemed to impress the stipendiary magistrate, and the police didn't press the uttering charge.

'It would appear that you accepted the prize money from this rascal in good faith,' the beak told Neil. 'But that in itself was illegal, since prize fighting is against the law. However, I will give you the benefit of the doubt, in view of the fact that I believe you have been of previous good character. But that does not excuse your murderous assault upon these constables. For that you will go to hard labour for six months, and the woman Morgan to the House of Correction for two. Take them down.'

I hurried down to the foetid passage below the courtroom in an effort to see either of them before they were taken off, but a turnkey barred my way and told me to make myself scarce unless I wanted to join them, nor would he even tell me to which jails they had been consigned, but in this latter point an old lag hanging about the entrance to the court helped me.

'Six months hard for the bloke and two for the donah? He'll be for the cockchafer at Millbank and she'll be booked into Coldbath Fields, poor bitch,' he told me. 'Get in to see them? No chance. A boot up the arse for even asking, more like. Only them as is for hanging can have visitors as a right.'

Disconsolately I went off to the office, there to be told in an awed whisper by my fellow juniors that Mr Creswick was waiting for me, in a hell of a bate apparently. Lateness, let alone absence, was a cardinal crime for which no excuse was ever accepted. At best it incurred the docking of one's pay – at worse, the sack. I went in to him inwardly cringing, with an unconvincing story about an early morning high fever ready on my lips, but I had no chance to deliver it.

'This is a generous employer's reward for a day's holiday,

is it, Stafford?' he thundered. 'Look at you! Still pallid and shaking from your debauch instead of refreshed and eager to resume your duties. And you were the one who had the effrontery to question your lack of advancement here. Well, now you know the reason, don't you? I have a nose for these things, my lad. I can sum up *your* kind in a glance – Why I haven't sacked you before this I just do not know –'

But I had had enough. Something snapped, and instead of breaking down into tears, as I had feared I was going to, a red mist seemed to rise before my eyes, and the accumulated spleen of nearly eighteen months poured forth.

'You miserable little penpushing bastard,' I spat at him. 'Who are *you* to preach to me? You've been diddling the Guv'nor out of eight shillings a week ever since I came here, and by God I'm going to tell him so – and what about your bloody situation then, eh? *You* sack me? Like hell you will. You'll finish up in – in – in *Bow Street*, with all the other rooks and gonophs –' and much more in the same vein, including a reference to the barmaid at the Boatswain's Rest.

He sat back in his chair, a pale shade of green, with his mouth opening and shutting like that of a landed codfish.

'There's no need for that sort of thing,' he mumbled when he was able. 'I was merely giving you a well-deserved reprimand for your own good. Listen to me – *please* –'

But I had sensed my advantage now, and I pressed it to the full.

'What about my promotion? I should have been established long since,' I shouted.

'Keep your voice down,' he begged. 'Yes – your promotion. Actually I have already recommended it to the Guv'nor. I think you can count on it coming through this very week.'

And it did. So out of a major catastrophe came a minor victory, and I was able to pay the rent of our rooms in Neil's absence though it left me with but two shillings a week for food.

I was desperately hungry one night some weeks later when,

wearily climbing the stairs, I was greeted by a smell of cooking that had the drools running down my chin. Caerwen turned from the dutch oven and smiled at me as I burst into the room.

'Sit down, boyo,' she said, as if she had never been away. 'All ready it is. Lamb chops, kidneys, new potatoes and spring greens – with an apple dumpling and cheese to follow. You look as if you could do with it. Famished as a workhouse cat you must be. Not a scrap of food in the cupboard.'

'They've cut your hair,' was all I could manage to say.

'It'll grow again,' she laughed. 'Better than being lousy. You can look out of the window after supper. I'm going to have a bath in front of the fire. Now no more talking. Sit down and eat.' And I needed no second invitation.

Her two months in the House of Correction had been hard, she told me – 'But no harder than working on a bloody Cardigan farm. It was the dirt I couldn't stand. Filthy, some of those whores and beggars.'

Actually, outlandish as any other woman might have looked with cropped hair, in her case it only served to make her more beautiful, because it had formed into tight curls that fitted her head like a copper helmet. She was certainly thinner for her holiday, as she called it, but that had fined her down – and it had not taken any of the mischievous sparkle from her blue eyes.

'Have you heard anything about Neil?' she asked anxiously. 'Never mind,' she went on when I said I hadn't. 'I'll go to the Mill tomorrow and blag a door screw.' Which, when translated, I found to mean that she would go to the Millbank Prison and bribe a turnkey at the gate to give her news of my brother, and even smuggle some food and tobacco in to him.

'We were lucky to be in front of a decent beak,' she told me. 'Shofulling snide usually pulls a lagging or a boat.'

I said, 'Caerwen, for God's sake keep to English.'

She grinned. 'Passing counterfeit money can earn you penal servitude or even transportation to Botany Bay,' she said.

She went on then to tell me of her own vicissitudes. She

29

had been lucky in that she had been employed in the laundry.

'Fourteen hours a day, wet through all the time, dollying dirty bed linen from the hospitals – blood, pus, and worse,' she said and shuddered. She was now sitting quite unself-consciously in our tin bath in front of the fire, luxuriating in hot soapy water. 'But at least one could keep clean there. In the ragpicking sheds and the sewing rooms one was lucky to get enough water to drink, let alone wash.'

She had come out that morning, she told me, and fortun-ately her gentleman friend was absent on circuit, so she was at liberty for some weeks and she intended to spend the days in our rooms, cleaning and furbishing them, because she hated dirt and disorder above all else. I accordingly came home each evening to a beautifully cooked meal, and my clothes were overhauled, washed, ironed and mended, and I was generally cosseted and pampered. She would go off at night, and although I offered more than once to see her back to the discreet apartment overlooking Regent's Park that her gentleman had taken for her, she would never let me. I sug-gested one very stormy night that she should stay and she stared at me open-mouthed, then burst into laughter.

'Oh! Growing up, are we?' she rallied. 'Cheeky young devil. Get along with you.'

I told her indignantly that I was thinking only of her welfare, and had no ulterior designs upon her, but the more I protested the more she made fun of me, until I was beside myself with rage.

'Go to the devil then,' I shouted. 'Get soaked to the skin and catch your death of cold for all I care.'

'Better that than lose my virtue, and be cast out by your brother,' she giggled.

'You can't lose what you never possessed,' I told her. 'And as far as my brother is concerned, he doesn't give a damn where you sleep.'

The laughter ceased and the mischief went out of her eyes.

'No, I don't suppose he does,' she said quietly. 'Good night, Ross.' She went, and I felt as if I had kicked a friendly dog.

But she was back the next night as if nothing had happened, and she was in high good humour because at last, after many attempts, she had been able to make contact with Neil.

'Unloading coals from the brigs at Chelsea Pier they are,' she told me. 'Their gang comes out of Millbank at six every morning and they march along the Embankment, and I dropped the screw five shillings, and he passed a parcel to Neil – bread, cheese, a piece of boiled beef and some tobacco – and a sovereign wrapped in a bit of rag. I walked beside the gang the whole way. I couldn't talk to him, of course, but I saw him get the parcel – and he waved to me. Quite cheerful he looked, but, *pobl anwyl*, he's thin. Still, I know what to do now.'

'But, Caerwen,' I said uneasily, 'all this is costing money. How are you managing?'

'Tut! Don't bother your head about that, boyo,' she laughed. 'Got a bit put by, I have.'

'Yes, but we can't go on taking charity from you like this,' I said.

'You'll do as your brother says,' she told me firmly. 'The last thing he whispered to me before they took us off from Bow Street was to look after you.'

'I'm not a baby,' I said angrily.

'No indeed you're not,' she said solemnly. 'Quite a man now. Trying to get me bedded, no less. Eat your supper, you silly, and don't talk such nonsense.' It was never any good trying to talk sensibly to her.

And so things went the even tenor of their way until the day that Neil was released.

Chapter Two

He put up a game front that first day, but he had obviously been through the mill. His clothes, in which he had always taken such pride, were crumpled, damp and stinking from the prison storeroom in which they had been bundled for six months, and they hung on his gaunt frame like a scarecrow's rags. His hair was cropped to the skull and his face was bruised and he had a black eye. Caerwen stared at him for a long moment, and then she started to swear filthily about the turnkeys and the police, cursing them and the whores that bore them, right to the first generation, but I could see that her anger was merely holding back her tears. We got him into a bath, that panacea for all ills in Caerwen's book, and she gently bathed his face and the wounds in his shoulders and back that had become tattoos from the coal dust that had worked into them. His battered face, he explained, was due to a fight he had with another prisoner a few days earlier.

'Tried to pinch some food from me, the bastard,' he told us. 'That will do, old lass – give me the towel. I want to dress and go out and get drunk.'

'Not a damned step,' Caerwen said firmly. 'You'll stay here in bed, boyo, if I have to throw your trousers out of the window.' And she had her way. She fed him and fussed over him all that day and between whiles laundered, ironed and pressed his clothes back to their pristine smartness. Then, to crown her efforts, she triumphantly produced a watch, chain and sovereign case and presented them to him. He stared at them open-mouthed, then at her.

'For God's sake! Where did you get this?' he gasped.

'Well, there's a nice thing for you,' she said indignantly. 'I give you a present, and all you can say is "where did you get it?" I bought it off a swagman. To make up for the one you had lifted.'

'That was silver,' he said. 'This is gold – solid gold – with a monogram in *diamonds. Where did you get it?*'

'I told you,' she said sullenly. 'I bought it.'

'What do you think I am?' he demanded. 'A bloody gull? This lot would have cost you two hundred quid off the greenest fence in London. Twice as much off a straight dealer.' He was really angry now, and it saddened me because I could see that once again she was near to tears. This was the day we had been waiting for, and it was being spoiled.

'All right, old boy,' I said soothingly. 'There's no need to fight about it. Caerwen only meant – '

'Shut your mouth,' he snapped. 'Listen to me, my girl. You've been feeding young Ross, paying the rent, blagging the screws and sending me baccy and grub inside, and keeping yourself at the same time. Do you think I don't know what it all cost?'

'What the hell does it matter what it cost?' she screamed. 'Anyhow, Ross paid the rent – and kept himself. Yes – I was on the game, if that's what you're getting at. What's so odd about that? Did you get so high-stomached in prison that a bit of cunny cash offends your principles? It's water off a duck's back as far as I'm concerned.'

'You thick-headed little trull,' he said through set teeth. 'Where and how you got your money is your affair, not mine. It's this watch I'm concerned about. You never earned enough to buy it honestly – not if you were charging five pounds a lay – therefore you must have hooked it off some swell. Jesus Christ! Don't you realize what it means? A thing as valuable as this is bound to be on the peelers' Hue and Cry List. We've got records now – both of us. If we were found with this it would mean a lagging – transportation even. Well, *I'm* not catching a boat to Botany Bay for the sake of a watch.' He threw it to me. 'Here, chuck it over the bridge into the Thames,' he said, but Caerwen caught it in mid-air between us.

'No, by God you don't,' she spat. 'If you won't have it I

know plenty who would. To hell with you both. I never want to see either of you again.' And she stormed out of the room, slamming the door behind her.

I started to go after her, but Neil shook his head. 'Leave her be,' he said wearily. 'She'll come back – or she won't. There's nothing you or I can say that will make any difference one way or the other.'

And for the first time since I was a small boy in St Caldbec's, I actually cried.

I woke next morning, which was a Sunday, to the glorious smell of sizzling bacon and the strains of 'Cwm Rhondda' in a clear soprano. I sat up and stared, and Caerwen turned from the fire and laid her finger across her lips, because Neil was still deep in sleep. I crept out of bed and joined her and she put her arms round my neck and smiled at me.

'There's sorry I am, cariad,' she whispered. 'It was seeing him so beaten and sore that upset me. You know I didn't mean any of those dreadful things I said to you both.'

'Of course not,' I assured her. 'And neither did he.'

'I don't know,' she said doubtfully. 'He doesn't like me earning money on the bash. Silly boy. It's a job, like any other – and all a girl can get in London without a character. My gentleman had locked the place against me while I was in prison.'

'It wasn't that. It was the watch that worried him,' I said.

She shook her head. 'I know him – better than you. Better than he does himself. He hates me working the streets. I'm glad. It shows he must care *something* about me,' she finished wistfully.

Neil woke then, and the row was forgotten and after a hearty breakfast we spent the day on Hampstead Heath. Winter had come early and there had been a fall of snow and a hard frost, and people were skating on the frozen pond, and the air was crisp and clean and it brought the colour to our city-pallored cheeks, a sparkle to our eyes and a lift to our hearts, and we pelted each other with snowballs and laughed and sang, and bought roast potatoes and chestnuts and drank hot rum punch – and rode home on an omnibus in the evening, tired and happy.

Caerwen moved in with Neil then, quite openly, and I was relegated to the sofa in the living-room. I think they were happy in those first weeks, though things were desperately hard. Neil's job at the hackney office had, of course, been filled, and the best he could find was occasional casual labour – portering at Covent Garden – cleaning stables behind the houses of the gentry in the West End – or carrying luggage at the newly built railway stations – never earning more than sixpence or so a day. How Caerwen managed to keep two healthy males fed was a miracle of economics. She was no longer 'working' except for some shirt finishing – sweated labour that brought her twopence per dozen for buttons and buttonholes – four hours' work even for one as manually dexterous as she, plus a five-mile walk to and from the cellar workshop in Seven Dials. Bit by bit Neil's treasured possessions were pawned – his best suit, his greatcoat, then the furniture, all but the barest necessities. My library, which had grown to some fifty volumes from the stolen nucleus of my childhood, paid for a sack of coal and a few potatoes. Everything Caerwen had formerly possessed except for one gown and a change of underwear had long since gone the same dreary way to the sign of the three brass balls.

I finally plucked up the courage to beard Mr Creswick again and ask for a modest increase in my pay, which was still twelve shillings a week, but the threat of exposure to the Guv'nor had now lost its immediacy and therefore its terror, although he still treated me with a certain circumspection and even civility. He held out no hope of advancement in the near future but he did at least offer me the opportunity of understudying Mr Turvey, the tide waiter, whose colleague, Mr Santos, had recently been haled off to the Marshalsea Prison for Debtors.

'It will mean extra work for you, Stafford,' he informed me ponderously. 'It will sometimes call for the sacrifice of your Sundays, because time and tide, literally in our case,

35

wait for no man – but on those occasions you may draw an extra shilling in addition to your normal salary.'

And glad enough I was to do so, because quite apart from the financial gain, the excitement of being rowed down the Thames to board an incoming Indiaman, swift clipper or lumbering transport was its own reward. Our boatman, an old sailor, was one of a very rare and select coterie – an ex-convict who had served a seven-year sentence in Botany Bay and lived to be repatriated to England on ticket-of-leave.

'Couldn't do it now though,' he told me one day as we waited for our ship to drop anchor in the Pool. 'Only fourteen-year laggings get transported these days, and if you're unlucky enough to cop the road gangs when you've finished your year in the stone jug which everybody has to do on arrival, you can kiss yourself goodbye. Twelve hours a day, in chains and under the lash, feeding on pig-swill, and little enough of it, Gawd knows, and you're a dead man before your time's half up.'

'You mean everybody who gets sent there dies?' I asked, awed.

He shrugged. 'Nearly everybody, although there's some fortunate bastards who've landed in the shit of New South Wales and come up smelling of violets. A good strong carcass, a bit of education which can get you a job indoors, in a store or a Government office, and you can still make it. There've even been fortunes made there by liberated convicts who've had a face that fitted, a gift of the gab, an eye for the main chance and, above all, a bit of capital. They've opened stores and such. And there'll be a lot more, I'll wager, now that gold has been struck out there. Blast me bloody eyes, there's times back here, especially in the cold of winter and me rheumatics is playing me up, when I wish I'd taken me ticket out there meself.'

We talked a lot after that first day – I, now bereft of my books, agog to hear more of this strange and terrifying yet fascinating land, he, glad of a listener. A lot of what he told me was obviously arrant nonsense, but there was much besides that had the ring of truth – and all of it was interesting.

But at home things were going from bad to worse. Even when I worked on Sundays the most we had left from my wages after the rent had been paid, was three shillings a week. Neil had walked his boots through to the uppers in search of work, and Caerwen, who I was certain was starving herself to keep us fed, was thin, fragile and waxen, and she had developed a hacking cough that robbed her even of the solace of sleep at night. That winter was a bitter one.

But the longest lane has a turning. Ours came one night as Caerwen and I sat over a guttering candle as she struggled to complete her last dozen buttonholes, which I was to deliver before going to the office the following morning. She snapped the cotton viciously as she came to the end, and said, 'Dammo! That's it. No more of it. I'm going back on the game.'

'You know what that will mean,' I warned her. She had tried it once before and Neil had taken his belt to her.

'I'm not going to be fool enough to let him know this time,' she said.

'He'll find out. Don't, Caerwen – *please*,' I begged.

'What am I to do?' she asked hopelessly. 'The two of you, not getting enough food to keep a cat alive. And this place, as cold as a workhouse grave. What sort of life is this for a man?' Her face was hard and bitter. 'We need a fire, some decent food in our bellies – and a couple of hours out there in Windmill Street would get it for us. I know the ropes – none better.'

I said, 'Damn it all – allow us a little pride, Caerwen. A man who ponces off a woman is the lowest thing on God's earth. Yes – I know – *I* did it for months before Neil came out – but I didn't know what you were doing then.'

'Tut! As if it mattered,' she said impatiently. She jumped up from her chair and reached for her bonnet and shawl. 'Keep your mouth tightly closed, boyo. If he wants to know where I am when he comes in, tell him I've gone to Camden Town to collect some sewing.'

But then we heard him on the stairs, and for a moment we could not believe our ears, because he was singing lustily – a ribald music hall song. He burst into the room with his arms full of parcels, and he was followed by a grimy urchin staggering under a sack of coals. He dumped the parcels on the table and tipped the boy a whole shilling, then as the door closed behind him, he turned to us, grinning all over his face. 'Still corn in Egypt,' he said. 'Come on, lass! Smack it about! Here's beefsteak, spuds and all the trimmings, bread, butter, a plum cake and a couple of bottles of something warming. Move your bloody self, young Ross, and get a fire going that would roast an ox.'

'*Arglwydd mawr!*' breathed Caerwen. 'But where – ? Where from – ?'

He flexed his arm and smacked himself on the muscles. 'From here,' he boasted. 'One straight left, a right cross, my knee in his balls, because it was no holds or punches barred, and then an uppercut – and the bastard was flat on his back – out to the wide.'

'You mean – a prize fight – ?' I said. 'But there isn't a mark on you –'

'No bloody fear!' he laughed. 'They're all on *him*. He never laid a fist on me. It was all over in the first round – just like at Blackheath that time.'

'But where did it take place?'

He was opening a bottle. 'Don't ask so many questions,' he said. 'Come on, Caerwen – get that grub on the go. I'm hungry enough to eat a dead horse. No, it wasn't a properly arranged fixture. There was a main – you know, cockfighting – out at Hounslow, and the birds were all finished in the first hour, and the swells and bloods were angry because they'd wasted a whole day for nothing, so some nobber put up a pug for all comers. Ten quid in the bucket – winner take all. I'd gone out in the hope of picking something up, because there's damn all on in Town here – and I chucked my hat in the ring.'

'I hope for your sake it isn't snide, like last time,' said Caerwen, already busy with her pots and the dutch oven.

'Gold, lass,' Neil said. 'I've spent a sovereign of it on this lot and the omnibus – but here's the rest of it.' He pulled

38

nine sovereigns from his pocket and laid them on the table in high good humour. 'Here you are – three each – and you can spend the damn lot. There'll be more of the same where this came from.'

'*Perhaps*,' Caerwen said, and pounced on them. 'There'll be no chucking it around while *I* have anything to do with it. We want to get some of our stuff back from Uncle's first. And as for fighting again, oh no, my boy. I don't mind cooking and cleaning for you, but I'm not nursing you if you come home again cut to ribbons.' Neil winked at me and buried his face in his tankard.

We fed to bursting point that night, and when I came home the following day it was to find all our previous comforts restored – furniture, bedding and the modest household goods which were Caerwen's pride and delight, and there was a roaring fire in the grate and a heart- and belly-warming smell of cooking.

Our luck seemed certainly to have changed for the better because Neil then found a job as doorman at a gambling den. He was paid only ten shillings a week, but once again there were perks – tips for calling cabs, and presents from fortunate players after a lucky run at the tables – and on more than one occasion he went to the rescue of departing clients who fell victim to the footpads who waited in gangs for the unwary, receiving on one occasion twenty-five guineas from a grateful sprig of nobility who was being badly kicked by a pair of bullies. I saw little of him in those days, because the gaming rooms opened only at night and he had usually left for work by the time I got home, returning each morning at dawn to tumble, dog-tired, into bed – but he was granted an occasional Sunday off and when it coincided with a free day for me the three of us would go to Cremorne Gardens or Hampstead Heath, or take a train into the countryside of Kent, and thoroughly enjoy ourselves. There was certainly no shortage of money, and we were well dressed, fully fed, sleek and very happy indeed.

But once again the halcyon days had to come to an end, although this time not disastrously, since it meant advance-

39

ment for me in the firm. The Guv'nor decided to open a branch office downriver at Gravesend. Mr Turvey was placed in charge of it, and I was sent with him. This new plan enabled us to board incoming ships at the pilot station twenty miles short of London, and come ashore with our papers the minute we moored at the docks, and thus steal a march on our competitors of anything up to a day. But, of course, it meant that we had to live in Gravesend. It saddened me to leave home. Caerwen cried bitterly and even Neil looked very glum, although he teased me and said he would be easier in his mind each night now that I was no longer in a position to cuckold him.

My salary leapt in one bound from twelve shillings to twenty-five, and I was allowed a shilling a day subsistence when travelling up and down the river. I found comfortable lodgings with a pilot's family for ten shillings a week, and became more prosperous than I had ever been in my life before, and, for the first time, no longer dependent upon my brother's bounty. I tried to repay them a little, but it was indignantly refused by them both.

'Save it, boyo,' Caerwen advised me earnestly. 'You'll find in this life that your pocket is your only real friend – and that only when it's got something in it.'

'How can you of all people say that?' I said indignantly. 'You and Neil have gone short to look after me for as long as I can remember.'

'That's different,' she said. There was never any logic in Caerwen. Only kindness and gentleness and love.

She was worried about Neil, she confided to me, after I had been in Gravesend for six months or so. 'These gambling dens are sewers,' she said. 'Even the swell ones. I don't like him being there.'

'Neil can look after himself,' I assured her.

'Yes, I know,' she agreed. 'But they are often raided by the peelers, and when that happens everybody that works there is taken up before the magistrates and charged with helping to run a disorderly house. Neil has a record now, and it would go hard with him.'

'It would have to be a very smart peeler who felt our Neil's collar,' I said.

'Don't talk silly,' she snapped. 'Smartness doesn't come into it. If he's arrested there one night and taken up to Bow Street, he'd get at least twelve months' hard labour.'

I could see that she really was anxious, so I didn't argue with her further. I did take it up with Neil, however, next time I came to London, as we were drinking in the Hero of Waterloo.

'Oh, for God's sake, don't *you* start now,' he snorted. 'I get enough of that from Caerwen.'

'She's worried, Neil,' I said. 'Surely now you're on your feet again you can find another job.' And for the first time in his life, or mine, he was angry with me – really angry.

'Don't lecture me, my lad,' he told me grimly. 'I take that from nobody – not even my brother.'

I must have looked hurt because he relented almost immediately. 'Don't you fret,' he said, and clapped me on the shoulder. 'We're not going to be raided. Our guv'nor has got the peelers and the beaks squared. He must be paying out a hundred quid a week at least. You mustn't take any notice of Caerwen. She's only bellyaching because she thinks I'm keeping secrets from her. Actually she's right there, but it's not going to alter things.'

'What secrets?' I asked.

'If I told you they wouldn't be secrets any longer, would they?' he laughed. He regarded me for some moments. 'All right then. I'll trust you, but if you let me down I never will again.'

'You know perfectly well I wouldn't,' I said.

He took a deep breath. 'Capital,' he said. 'Remember me telling you something in the past? I had plans, I said, plans that included you – provided I had a bit of money behind me. They include her too – or will, if she stops nagging me. It might even run to a wedding ring. I've almost got the money together now.' His voice dropped to a whisper. 'Two hundred and fifty jimmy-o-goblins, boy. I need another fifty, and I'm *there.*'

I stared at him, my breath taken away. 'Two hundred and fifty *pounds*?' I squeaked unbelievingly. 'You've got *that*?'

'That's what I said. Three hundred's the target, and I reckon to have that before the year is out.' He drained his tankard and called for more beer. 'Drink up,' he said, 'and don't look at me as if I were a liar.'

'I don't think you're a liar – but two hundred and fifty! Where in the name of God did you get it?' It was too much to believe. 'Look, Neil, you're not – I mean – '

'Getting it on the ramp?' He shook his head. 'No – it's all honest – more or less.'

'But six months ago we were all but starving!'

'That's right. But things changed about then, didn't they?'

'Two hundred and fifty in six months.' I made a rapid calculation. 'That's damned nearly ten pounds a week – and you've been living like a lord – and yet you said your wage was only ten bob – '

'If you'll stop interrupting I'll tell you where it's all come from,' he said. 'I've had four fights – at twenty-five pounds a purse, since then. That's a hundred of it. I had ten pounds on Jamie Lad at Newmarket at nine-and-a-half to one – that's another ninety-five. The other fifty-odd has come in various ways – tips – a few bob at cockfighting – twenty-five off a gull I stopped from getting a kicking – and so on. And I've still been able to let Caerwen have two pounds a week for the housekeeping. I told you I was going to do it, didn't I?'

'You did,' I said. I took a deep breath and exhaled it slowly. 'But where is it? That sort of money should be in a bank.'

He shook his head. 'No banks for me, little brother. I prefer to look after it myself – although I must admit that it has been worrying me a bit lately. I've changed all of it – gold and silver – into banknotes, and I've got it in a leather wallet under the floorboards at home, but I'm scared that either Caerwen will come across it when she's on her eternal scrubbing and cleaning, or the bloody rats will chew it up. I've been thinking for a long time of asking you to keep it safe for me.'

'*Me?* Look after that amount of money?' The very idea appalled me. 'Suppose it was stolen from me?'

'Why should it be, if nobody knew you had it?'

'But where would I keep it?'

'You've got your Saratoga trunk, haven't you?'

I nodded. 'Yes, I got it back out of pawn before going down to Gravesend.'

'The lock and keys are all right? Good. Then my advice would be very carefully to slit the lining right down in the bottom of it and put the notes in there – flat – then repack it with your clothes and such.'

I was still frightened, although the eternal schoolboy that lurks in us all, both young and old, was stirring my sense of adventure. Me, Ross Stafford, who had never handled more than a few shillings at a time, holding a secret hoard of this size. Neil was watching me closely. I took another deep breath, and nodded.

'Good boy,' he said softly. 'That's a load off my mind.'

'But the plans?' I asked. 'What are they?'

He looked dreamily up at the ceiling. 'Something like this,' he said. 'A pub – a good one. Out of London. Say on the Dover Road – somewhere between Rochester and Canterbury. I've gone into the matter very carefully. You put up a bond for three hundred in the first place, and then get some big bug to give you a character – '

'Could you do that?' I asked doubtfully.

He winked and tapped the side of his nose with his forefinger.

'The swell I saved from the bruisers,' he said. ' "Any time at all," he told me. "You want someone to speak up for you, Mr Stafford, you just call on me. Proud and happy to do it," he said. That part of it is all right, old lad. All we've got to do now is to find the right spot. Just think. Nice little place – taproom and a snug – with a dining-room, and Caerwen doing the cooking, or rather overlooking the cooking, with a brace of wenches doing the dirty work. Half a dozen bedrooms. You and I doing the liquor side of it. The *Guv'nors*. A gentleman's life. Never another worry again in all our days. See what I mean, laddie? This is something I've dreamed

43

about all my life. All the stinking misery we've been through – that bloody workhouse of a school – then starving most of the time up here in London – Caerwen and me in chokey – for doing sweet fuckall except arguing with a peeler about being arrested for something we hadn't done in the first place.'

'That and chivving him with a bottle,' I reminded him.

'Well, Christ, if a peeler can't take a poke in the chops now and then, he should be in another business,' he said defensively. 'The point I'm trying to make is that if we'd had a bit of standing it just wouldn't have happened. "Some low person stick you with a snide tenner, Mr Stafford? How unfortunate. I'm sure it was no fault of yours. Constable, you had no right to interfere with this gentleman." That's what it would have been.'

We went back to the rooms after that, and Caerwen was out shopping, so Neil lifted a section of boarding under the bed and drew a leather wallet forth, and I put it in my satchel.

I felt as if I was carrying a fused and smoking bomb on my way back to Gravesend that night, and even after I had secreted the twenty-five ten-pound notes in the Saratoga. I still remained a prey to anxiety, and I used to hurry home from the office every day for weeks to assure myself that it was still there.

I was now deemed experienced enough by Mr Turvey to go out to ships on my own, so as my duties increased, my turn-round time in London was accordingly shortened, and instead of waiting for the evening paddle-steamer after reporting to Cloak Lane, I was obliged to return to Gravesend each trip by the first available train. This meant that I was seeing less of Neil and Caerwen, and sometimes a month or so would go by without our meeting. I was very lonely at first, but I was young and resilient and my new life was full of interest. I knew my way about a ship, and I had learned the intricacies of bills of lading, cargo stowage lists, manifests and customs regulations, and I often thought wistfully of my brother's fortune. If only I had half as much as that I could start modestly in business on my own, as a shipping and forwarding agent, handling the small vessels that this firm disdained. I was on the point of suggesting this to him more than once, but I put it aside. He wanted to be guv'nor of a cosy little pub, and Caerwen, whom he had now taken into his confidence, was even more enthusiastic about the project than he. No, I had no right to persuade him to abandon something they had both set their hearts upon.

I came up the Thames one dark and foggy evening on a big barque that had taken convicts and mixed cargo out to Port Jackson and had brought back wool and a strongroom of gold. I leaned on the poop taffrail with the supercargo as we were warped into the dock, and he looked at the grimy skyline above the City and chuckled.

'There you are, my old lovely,' he said. 'London – the bonniest sight a sailor's eyes ever lit on.'

'Mud, fog, soot and horse dung,' I said. 'You call that bonny?'

'I do,' he answered. 'Though it's not in London I'm going to settle when I leave the sea. I just want one final fling here.'

'And where *are* you going to settle?' I asked.

'Port Jackson – Sydney, as it's known now,' he told me. 'That's where the money is.' He looked around swiftly, then lowered his voice, 'Whitebirding, they call it.'

'*White*birding?'

'Quiet!' he warned. 'Yes, whitebirding. When labour is short the *black*birders go out into the bush and round up niggers and ship 'em down to the sheep and cattle farms. It's illegal, of course, but it's winked at. Blackbirding means running *black* men *into* the colony. Whitebirding, on the other hand, means running *white* men *out* of it. You follow me?'

'I don't,' I said.

He shrugged. 'You wouldn't. The ignorance of some of you longshore lubbers about Australia astounds me at times. It's gold at the bottom of it all. My God! They're digging it out by the shovelful round Bendigo and Ballarat. The gutters are bloody well awash with it in Sydney. If a convict manages to get his hands on a bit he'll pay up to a hundred quid for a passage out.'

'But is he allowed to leave before his sentence is up?' I asked.

He spat into the water. 'Of course he bloody well isn't. He's *smuggled* out. The whitebirder makes a deal with the skipper or mate of an American clipper – there's a regular run across the Pacific now, between New South Wales and California – with gold at both ends. Fifty quid to the whitebirder, fifty to the ship, and the jolly jailbird is in San Francisco a couple of months later as perky as you please, smoking a big cigar and rooking the Yankees, and cocking a snook at Her Majesty's Convict Administration.'

'Don't they send them back if they find out they're escaped prisoners?' I asked.

'Not as long as they keep out of fresh trouble. They've got too many dark horses of their own swarming across by land and coming round Cape Horn by the shipload, to bother about a few of ours sneaking in through the back door. They're striking it as rich in California as they are in Australia, and when gold fever's raging nobody gives a damn about anything else.'

I stayed on board listening to further tales until long after office closing hours. I left my papers with the night-watchman and then half decided to spend the night with Neil and Caerwen and catch the early train next morning, but I knew there were at least two ships waiting on the tide, and Mr Turvey would be wanting me back urgently, so regretfully I went off to London Bridge station and dined off a sandwich and a glass of beer, then I bought an *Evening Standard* and settled myself comfortably in a corner seat of a third-class compartment of the last train, and promptly went to sleep.

We were more than halfway to Gravesend before I awoke. I opened the newspaper and glanced through it idly, and my eye caught the report of a burglary the night before.

'Desperate Chase Over West End Roofs,' I read without particular interest, and then waded on through half a column of turgid journalese about a man being disturbed while rifling a strongbox on the premises of a jeweller in Regent Street. The police had surrounded the building, and the man

46

had made his way through a skylight on to the roof, where he had been cornered and arrested after a fight. It was a commonplace enough incident, Lord knows, and I almost turned the page in search of something more riveting when I saw his name at the end of the item.

– the miscreant was then brought down in handcuffs and taken to Bow Street, where he was charged. It is understood that his name is Neil Stafford, an unemployed day labourer, residing at 72 Waterloo Bridge Road. He was remanded to Newgate and will appear before the Bow Street magistrates tomorrow.

I arrived at their rooms in the early hours of the morning. I cannot recall to this day how I managed it, because there were no more trains back to London that night. I remember walking along a seemingly endless road by the Rotherhithe Docks, and then being given a lift part of the way by a Covent Garden vegetable wagon, but most of the time I was moving in a dream. There was no answer to my knocking, and the key was not on the ledge above the door where they usually left it, so I sat on the stairs and dozed, and at daylight the ironmonger who was our landlord arrived to open his shop. He sniffed disapprovingly when he saw me.

'The place has been swarming with police since yesterday morning,' he told me. 'They found some stolen property in that woman's trunk – valuable stuff worth hundreds of pounds – and they've taken *her* off too. It's not right, Mr Stafford. I thought I was letting these rooms to respectable people, and now *my* name is being dragged in the mud also. They searched my place and turned my stock over – and there's this week's rent owing. I'd be obliged if you could settle up on your brother's behalf, then I'm giving him notice to quit – and I'll thank you to move his furniture – '

But by this time I was already walking towards the bridge. Caerwen too? My thoughts were in a turmoil and I was moving through a vacuum of misery. I had to see them. Would they let me? Where did one apply? Bow Street? 'Kick

47

up the arse even for asking,' the old lag had said. But that was two years ago. I was a boy then. I was a man now, or so I thought. Should I go straight to Newgate itself? I'd been past it often. The grimmest prison in England, outside which public hangings regularly took place. Yes – that would be best. I was known at Bow Street.

I found it was surprisingly easy to get in. I knocked at a small wicket door set into the huge main gate, and a turnkey looked out through a peephole.

I said, 'My brother's in here. Would it be possible to see him, please?'

'Lagged or pending?' he asked, then seeing me look blank he translated. 'Sentenced or remanded?'

'He certainly hasn't been sentenced,' I said. 'I understand he hasn't even been before the magistrate yet.'

'Name?' the screw asked.

'Stafford – Neil Stafford,' I told him, and he consulted a list.

' 'S'right,' he confirmed. 'On remand. This way.' He opened the wicket.

He led me into an office and handed me a card on which a list of prohibited articles was printed.

'Haven't got none of them things on you, have you?' he asked, then answered himself. 'No, of course you haven't. Respectable gent – I can see that with half an eye. No guns, knives, files, explosive substances, poisons or spirituous liquors? No? Well, remands are allowed refreshments from outside, but they have to pay for them – and we don't allow them to be passed money. Small amounts – say anything up to half a sovereign – can be left here, unofficially, if you take my meaning, and I'll see that he gets anything he wants – '

I took the hint and gave him ten shillings and he winked and passed me over to another warder and I was led along a dark passage into a small yard across which were set two parallel rows of iron bars about six feet apart. A woman was leaning on them on my side, talking to a man on the other in an undertone, and as far as they could get along the bars from the first couple were some more whisperers.

48

'Visitors' yard,' explained my guide. 'Wait here and I'll have him sent down.' This one winked also, so I parted with a further two shillings, and after a wait of some ten minutes Neil appeared through a door in the side wall and stood shielding his eyes against the light. He came up to the bars and peered through. Once again his face was battered, and his clothes were dishevelled and torn. He grinned ruefully when he saw me.

'Sorry, old cocker,' he said. 'Bit of a do, this, isn't it?'

I found myself swallowing hard. I said, 'Oh, Neil – for Christ's sake – *Why?*'

He shrugged. 'Lost my job,' he said. 'The bloody place changed hands and the new guv'nor put his own man in.'

'But you had enough put by without – ' I started, but he silenced me with a gesture.

'Not a word about that,' he muttered. 'You understand? *Not a word – to anybody.*'

'We'll have to get a good lawyer,' I said, and he laughed drily.

'Caught on the job? Don't be silly, old lad. All a lawyer would do would be to skin you of every stiver – for nothing. No – I'm going to plead guilty. I'll get off with seven then. If I put up a fight it would be fourteen in Botany Bay for sure.'

'You know about Caerwen?' I asked.

He nodded miserably. 'Yes – I got the whisper from a screw. She's in here – in the women's wing. We'll be going up together – me for burglary – she for receiving. It was that bloody watch. The silly bitch couldn't bring herself to get rid of it. I'm going to tell them I planted it on her for safe keeping, and she knew nothing about it. She might get off lightly then. Try and see her and tell her to back me up in court. Then get away from here and don't come back. Do you hear?'

'Of course I'm coming back,' I said indignantly. 'I'm standing by you both. What the devil do you think I am?'

He was gripping the bars so tightly that his knuckles were showing white through the grime of his hands. 'Listen to me,' he said tensely, 'and listen carefully. That damned landlord mentioned you to the peelers, and they were on to it like a shot. I was questioned about you. I said you'd gone away and I hadn't seen you for months. They didn't believe me, but I stuck to the story. If you're seen hanging around here and are recognized you'll be dragged in as sure as God.'

'But *I* haven't done anything,' I said.

'That wouldn't worry the bastards. They'd find something to fit —'

'You're not going to plead guilty — and I'm going to get a lawyer for you both,' I insisted.

'God damn you!' he raged. 'Will you listen to me. Down there in Gravesend you're out of the Metropolitan Police area, and you're safe, as long as you keep your nose clean. Up here you're asking for a pick-up. Even if you weren't convicted of anything you'd be held in this shit-hole on remand — maybe for weeks. Pending investigations, they call it. You'd lose your job — and what damned use would you be then — to yourself, me or Caerwen? You've got to stay out — and look after her — and hold that bit of money safe for when *I* come out.' He was pleading now. 'Do as I say, laddie, *please*. I know what I'm talking about. Seven years isn't a lifetime — I can do that on my head, as long as I know you're both waiting for me. Caerwen and I will get spliced then — and that pub is still going to be ours. *Please*, Ross. Promise me you'll do as I say.'

So I promised. What else could I do?

But try as I would I wasn't allowed to see Caerwen because the regulations governing the women's wing were stricter than on the men's side, and one had to prove relationship with the prisoner before a permit could be issued. So I waited a long dragging month watching the Newgate Calendar, which was put up each week outside all police stations in the country, until their names appeared, with the date of their trial. I broke my promise then and begged a couple of days off duty from Mr Turvey, on the excuse of a sick grandmother, and went up to London and waited all night outside the public entrance to the Old Bailey, which was next door to

Newgate, and so got into the gallery with the motley crowd of morbid spectators who habitually haunted such places for the free entertainment they afforded.

They came up late in the afternoon – first Neil, who was quickly disposed of on his guilty plea.

'Anything known?' asked the Clerk of the Court after the formal evidence of apprehension and arrest had been given, and a detective officer was ushered into the witness box and sworn.

'Attempting to pass counterfeit banknotes, m'lord – ' he began, and by the worst possible fortune Caerwen, who was waiting out of sight on the steps leading up into the dock, heard him and bobbed up like a fiery-headed jack-in-a-box.

'Lying bastard!' she screamed. 'He was cleared of that, and you know it. It was some damned rogue on the fairground who – '

Unseen hands dragged her down and the officer continued unperturbed. 'Of which he was given the benefit of the doubt, but he was found guilty of a murderous and unprovoked attack upon the police with an offensive weapon and sentenced to six months' hard labour.'

'Which apparently failed as a deterrent,' the judge said sternly. 'Stafford, you have pleaded guilty and thereby saved the Court a great deal of time and trouble, but I cannot but take the gravest view of this type of felony, which is unhappily becoming more prevalent by the year. You will go to penal servitude for a period of fourteen years – with the strongest recommendation that it should be served in an overseas convict establishment.'

'Jesus!' breathed a man behind me. 'Transported, the poor bastard. That's *one* that won't be coming back.'

A turnkey tapped Neil on the shoulder, and he turned, plainly dazed but still game enough to attempt a jaunty wave to the Court, and he disappeared down the steps. I could hear Caerwen screaming.

'You swine! Bastards! Whores' gets! He was promised seven if he pleaded guilty – and me a year if I kept my mouth shut about where I got that watch!' She had come up into the dock again, fighting every inch of the way against two beefy matrons who were trying to hold her down out of sight. 'Well, I *won't* keep it shut. Given to me by Julius Anderton, Esquire, Queen's bloody Counsel and barrister-at-law, the dirty old sod – when he was drunk, which was most of the time he was keeping me in rooms near Regent's Park. Bring him here and put the bastard on oath – and ask him – '

They had got her down by this and were evidently gagging her, because her screams ceased. The gallery was in an uproar, and the judge, visibly shaken, was hammering with his gavel and calling for the court to be cleared, so we were herded out and were not allowed back. I waited in the street with the rest of the hilarious crowd which had, today at least, got its full mete of excitement, until a grinning usher came out and announced her sentence.

'She's copped a boat, too,' he said. 'Fourteen years over the briny!'

'Bloody shame!' somebody yelled. 'Fourteen for just nicking a ticker?'

'Ah, but *whose* ticker?' the usher said waggishly. 'God Almighty! Old Randy Andy! – the bloody judge's brother!'

And the mob roared its appreciation of this exquisite jest.

I found another usher in the inn across from the court, and bought information from him.

'Kept here in Newgate overnight, until jail delivery to-morrow,' he told me. 'They'll be taken by wagon to Millbank then, and sent downriver to the hulks at Chatham. They'll be held there until the next transport.'

I had got over the initial shock and grief that had well-nigh overwhelmed me immediately after the trial, and by the time I arrived back in Gravesend I was trying to think constructively once more. The first thing was to make contact with them both I decided. Chatham was only a short train journey from Gravesend, so I went there on my first free day.

The hulks, old demasted and decaying ships, swung at anchor half a mile offshore in the Medway, but even at that distance, when the wind came from the east, the stench from them was putrid and offensive. They had come into use at the turn of the century to ease the pressure on our regular prisons, which were invariably overcrowded, but they, in turn, were now full to overflowing, particularly when there was a longer than usual interval between transport sailings.

As I arrived at the jetty that served the hulks, I saw a large draft of convicts come in from Millbank by tender. There were about a hundred of them, all men, clad in shapeless grey clothes besprinkled with broad arrows, and with heavy leg-irons clamped to their ankles so that they were only able to move in a lumbering, flatfooted shuffle. I searched their faces as they were herded down into the ships' boats from the tender, but Neil was not among them. There was a detachment of redcoated Marines in charge of them, and I saw the sergeant hand a list to a functionary in a watchman's shelter at the end of the jetty, so I approached him when the boats had rowed out towards the hulks, rubbing my nose absently with a half-sovereign, because I had become wise in my generation by this time and I knew that when dealing with subordinate officials nothing could be gained without a bribe.

I said, 'I come from a solicitor's office, and I have been wondering if you could help me with a little information.'

'Always willing to help, guv'nor,' he said heartily, with his eye on the coin. 'That is if I not being suborned from my duty. What's the lay?'

'Two convicts sentenced at the Old Bailey last Friday – a man and a woman? Would you be knowing if they were here or not?' I asked.

'Friday? Friday?' he mused. 'They'll have come down on Monday then. Yes – there *was* women amongst that lot. A dozen of 'em if I remember right. Let's have a look at the lists.' He reached for a ledger. 'All names are kept here. What's theirs?'

'Stafford – and the woman's is Morgan.'

He riffled through the pages. 'Smith, Smith, Spencer, Solomon – yes, here we are – double-two, nine, eight, five – Stafford N. Good – now the judy –nine, nine, three – Morgan

C. Unmarried. They'll be for the next ship, thank God. They're packed in on them hulks like bugs in a workhouse blanket – and they keep sending 'em down from Millbank by the boatload, doesn't matter what we say about being full up.'

'Could I get out to see them?' I asked, and he looked shocked.

'Not a chance in the wide world,' he said. 'They've got to have a half company of Marines standing to with shotted muskets and fixed bayonets to keep strangers from being scragged on the rare occasions when any *have* to go out. Even us officials have to be leery about things since they chucked the parson overboard a couple of months ago.'

'Couldn't I hire a boat privately anywhere?' I persisted.

'You wouldn't get a waterman to risk it – not for a ten-pun note. The Marine sentries would put the first shot across your bows, and the next *into* you.' He held out his hand. 'Sorry, guv'nor. I've done all I can to help.'

But I withheld the coin. 'The next ship, you say? What would that be?'

'The *Cambrian Queen*,' he told me.

'Sailing when?'

He shuffled uneasily. 'Look, guv'nor,' he mumbled. 'We're supposed to keep mum about things like that – ships and sailing dates and such – or we'll be having relatives and the bloody Quakers and God knows who around when the prisoners are being transferred from the hulks, then the bloody Reformers start making trouble. I've got me job to think of.'

'*When?*' I demanded. 'Or do I have to go to your superiors to find out?'

'On the tide on Thursday,' he growled, so I gave him the money and returned to Gravesend and set about trying to find some valid excuse for boarding the transport, with the object of taking a few small comforts with me and bribing a member of the crew to pass them on to them during the voyage. But it was hopeless. The *Cambrian Queen* was lying in midstream off Wapping Wall, and, in keeping with the

Government's policy of secrecy in everything to do with Transportation, no unauthorized member of the general public was allowed aboard under any circumstances whatever, and since no sea captain in his right mind would dream of letting any of its crew ashore so close to sailing day, all chance of communication was stillborn.

I borrowed a telescope from my landlord, the pilot, and went back to Chatham at dawn on Thursday and watched the ship's boats plying between the hulks and the *Cambrian Queen*, which had moved round the day before, and although I could not distinguish Neil from the others as they came down the gangway, Caerwen was unmistakable among the women, her glorious red hair shining like a bright beacon.

How in heaven's name they crowded them all into the transport I do not know. There must have been a thousand men at least, with, I estimated, a hundred women, plus, of course, a strong detachment of Marines – the officers, crew, and possibly a few official passengers. She was a large ship, of over two thousand tons or more, and I knew that in addition to her human freight, she carried general cargo in her holds, which meant that only the 'tween decks would be available for the convicts. I shuddered at the very thought of it.

Sadly I saw her warp out, making sail as she dropped down-river on the ebbing tide. I watched until her topmasts were out of sight round Queensborough, then I snapped the telescope shut, and with that decisive action came a new resolution. They were not going to rot and die out there. *By God* they weren't! Somehow I was going to free them.

I lay awake all that night recalling every scrap of information I had ever gleaned about Australia, both from reading and from conversation with people who had first-hand knowledge of it. The old boatman, the supercargo, officers and sailors on the ships I'd had business with, a Marine corporal I'd talked to who had served a tour of duty there as a guard – a lecture by a Quaker philanthropist at the Guildhall. I had read and listened purely for the interest the stories afforded, but now I began to sift and analyse – to separate possible fact from storytellers' fancy. To collate points on which they coincided, and discard the rest.

Firstly: there were three main convict settlements – Western Australia, New South Wales and Van Dieman's Land, or Tasmania as it was now called. New South Wales was the largest and most populous – so much so that it had recently been divided into two separate colonies, the southern part now being called Victoria. Secondly: all convicts on arrival served a year in enclosed prisons. At the end of this period they were either retained on Government labour – road building, public works, bridge construction and such tasks – or assigned to private employers as farm workers and general labourers. Women, I had read somewhere, formed only a small proportion of the convict population and were much in demand by the more respectable section as domestic servants. They were, in fact, often excused the first year in prison for this reason. Thirdly: when their sentences had been served, convicts were entitled to a passage back to England, or, if they were skilled in a trade and had been of good behaviour, they were free to accept employment and continue to live in the colony as ordinary citizens. The death rate was appallingly high, particularly among those who were unlucky enough to be retained on public work, or were assigned to a bad employer. None but the strongest and most resolute of these latter were expected to survive a fourteen-year sentence. Fourthly: though escape attempts were frequent, few, if any, succeeded, for the simple reason that a convict without money had no means of getting out of the country – unless, of course, as my friend the supercargo had told me, he could steal enough to pay a 'whitebirder'. A hundred pounds a head, he had said.

I was holding two hundred and fifty pounds of Neil's money, I reflected.

I got out of bed as the sun rose, and stood at my window and looked at the river. There were three ships waiting to go up to London on the next tide, and three outward bound. I watched them with mounting excitement. Sailings to Australia since gold had been discovered averaged two or three a month. Passages were at a premium, and a cabin ticket could cost as much as fifty pounds – and steerage not much less – but, on the other hand, the merchant service had such a bad name that captains were often at their wits' end to find a full crew before sailing, even with the aid of the crimps and shanghaiers who infested the waterfronts of every port. It should be easy enough to talk, or buy, my way into the fo'c'sle of a Port Jackson bound ship. Easy or not – that was it. *I* had to go there. There was no other means of getting the money to them.

But once there, I asked myself? What then? Wouldn't I be hunting for a needle in a haystack? Three settlements scattered across a country bigger than Europe. How was I to know to which they had been sent?

I shrugged these doubts off impatiently. First things first. Just get there. Port Jackson was the main receiving station, and that was where the *Cambrian Queen* was bound. Even if they had been sent elsewhere on arrival, there was bound to be a record of it somewhere, in some Government office, in the charge of some official penpusher or other – and, as I had already found out, they could all be bought.

Yes – two hundred and fifty pounds I had. A hundred a head for their freedom and a passage to California, and fifty for incidental expenses. I must keep that intact come what may. I overhauled my own resources. I had seven pounds and some odd shillings, and a handful of possessions on which I could raise another pound or so. Little enough to finance a project the size of the one I was contemplating, but with care I could manage.

I found I was in very bad odour indeed with Mr Turvey, as I had by now absented myself for another two days without leave, on top of that which he had granted me, but I humbly apologized and promised to mend my ways in future. And indeed I did. I put my nose to the grindstone and worked voluntarily on my days off, thereby saving him many a trip that he would otherwise have had to undertake himself, which suited him very well indeed, as he had now formed an alliance with his landlady in Gravesend, which he found more congenial than the bonds of matrimony in his London residence. I took up, in short, every ship that I saw from the lists would be sailing for Port Jackson on her next voyage, and I assiduously made the acquaintance of each bosun and gave him to understand that I had contracted a bad case of sea fever, and was willing to forgo my pay, and even add a couple of pounds to it in return for a berth in the fo'c'sle. Several took up the offer, but there were many unforeseen hitches. In some cases the sailing orders were changed at the last minute, and the ship was sent elsewhere, in others the mate refused to take a green hand aboard, and once the bosun took my two pounds in advance, and was shanghaied himself aboard another ship the same night.

But meanwhile I was not wasting my time. I was selling my possessions, and saving every shilling from my salary after paying for my board and lodgings, thus increasing my working capital considerably.

The safeguarding of the two hundred and fifty pounds during the voyage had been worrying me. Fo'c'sles housed some pretty rough characters and the very thought of my luggage being broken into and the money stolen was enough to bring me out in a cold sweat. I mulled long over this problem, and at last the solution came to me. A skinbelt. These were reputedly made from the inner skin of the cobra, and great store was put on them by the superstitious. They were supposed to ward off rheumatism, consumption and a host of other ills, and were a certain safeguard against drowning. Sailors used to buy them in Japan and could sometimes be persuaded to sell them when they had run out of money. They were as soft and supple as the finest silk, and the inside pockets were completely waterproof. I managed to pick one up for half a sovereign in a Gravesend pub, and I took it back to my lodgings and packed the twenty-five ten-pound notes in it. But the bulk was very obvious, so I took them to a bank in Lombard Street and changed them for five fifties. As a respectably-dressed, top-hatted clerk I attracted no unwelcome attention, and the notes, when folded flatly into the belt and worn next to my skin, might not have been there.

Then, finally, the day came, and I was signed on as an ordinary seaman by the master of the *Boadicea*, a four-masted barque of twelve hundred tons, sailing for Port Jackson at the end of the week, with passengers and cargo, but, thank God, no convicts. I wrote a letter to Mr Creswick telling him I had been offered a post with a firm in Glasgow, thanking him, with tongue in cheek, for his past kindness and courtesy and apologizing for the suddenness of my departure.

I walked up the gangway that night, with a sea chest on my shoulder and the sum of twelve pounds in my peajacket pocket after paying the bosun his *douceur*, and found my way down to the dark and stinking fo'c'sle.

Chapter Three

I had been travelling up-and downriver for nearly three years, and I consequently considered myself very well versed indeed in the way of ships, but I was soon to be disabused of this. We were roused out by the bosun before dawn and assigned to watches. Mine was the Port, or Mate's watch. In theory we worked the ship alternatively with the Starboard – Second Mate's watch in four-hourly periods. In practice it was usually a case of 'All hands on Deck!', certainly in those first few weeks as we tried to claw our way down the Channel and through the Bay of Biscay in the face of a sou'westerly gale which didn't abate for a moment. I shall never in all my days forget the sheer terror of my first trip aloft. It was dark and blowing hard when we dropped the pilot. Someone bellowed from the poop to 'Break out fore and main t'gallants and set main and mizzen stays'ls', which, of course, was so much Greek to me at that stage. My education commenced immediately. It came in the form of the mate's seaboot applied vigorously to my rear end, and I was propelled to the weather shrouds. Some good Samaritan hard on my heels, recognizing me for a greenhorn, yelled in my ear, 'One hand for the ship, one for yourself, sonny. Hang on like bloody hell,' and I went with the others up a flimsy, twanging ladder to a rickety platform which seemed higher than the dome of St Paul's, but which was only the first futtock, and from which soared another and flimsier ladder with ratlines a full two feet apart, to the topgallant yard, where my seafaring career would have ended had it not been for my newfound friend who guided my feet on to the foot-rope and then nudged me out farther and farther into space to the very tip of the yardarm where, under his instruction, with frozen and bleeding hands and torn nails, I cast off various pieces of rope the others called brails, gaskets and buntlines, until the huge sail below us burst forth and bellied into the wind, and the yard bucked like a mad thing. Below me through the darkness I could see the white surge of broken water as the ship got under way. Somehow or other I groped my way blindly inboard to the mast again, and came down to the deck, but not smartly enough to satisfy the mate, because I was driven to another mast and an even higher yard – the main royal – above which, as my mentor informed me, was only heaven. I tried to descend faster from this, sliding like the others down the shrouds, but in my ignorance I gripped the wire rope with my bare hands instead of breaking the contact with a fold of my oilskin, and I stripped my palms almost to the bone.

But all things, however terrifying, come to an end and by the time we had reached warmer, and blessedly calmer, latitudes I could go aloft with confidence if not grace and I was beginning almost to enjoy this new life. She was a splendid ship, clean-lined and well-found, her hull painted like that of an East Indiaman in alternating black and white gunports resembling an older generation of warships. She had a raised fo'c'sle and poop, but in between she was flush-decked with no unsightly deckhouses to break the graceful sweep of her waist. Her holystoned and limejuiced teak planking shone in the sunlight, her lower masts and standing rigging were painted white, her upper hamper was black, and she had a wealth of polished brass. She was, in short, beautiful to behold but a grinding, slavedriving bitch to maintain, because like all ships of the period she was scandalously undermanned, with a crew of master, three mates, bosun, carpenter, sailmaker, twelve able and four ordinary seamen on deck, and a steward, Chinese cook and a couple of cabin boys to manage the interior economy. Her limited cabin accommodation was crowded to bursting point with some twenty male and three lady passengers, the latter being a source of continual ill-will among the crew, because it meant that they had to remain decently clad on deck in shirts and trousers at all times, and bad language, even when the ladies were out of earshot below decks, was punishable by a shilling fine, no small deduction from an able seaman's pay of a pound a month.

When I had got over the misery of seasickness I was sent to the wheel under the instruction of an experienced helmsman. It was six feet in diameter, brass bound, of polished teak, and it stood, together with the dazzling copper compass binnacle before it, on a raised platform in the centre of the poop. Abaft of it was the cabin skylight through which one could catch tantalizing glimpses of the magnificently appointed saloon with its long dining-table, red plush upholstery and bright curtains.

Steering a sailing ship is an intricate art, fraught with peril for the idle and the unhandy. There is a course to be kept to, worked out by the master and the second mate each day before noon, checked and compared and rechecked with sextant and log, then set to the compass and chalked up on a board in front of the binnacle. When running on a fair wind it is simple enough to keep to the course, but when the wind changes, as in some latitudes it does with maddening frequency, the huge fore and aft sail on the mizzen mast becomes the dictator, and the helmsman has to bring the ship up as close to the wind as she will go, while still keeping as near as possible to the course. The sail was called the spanker, and it was set between two huge spars – boom and gaff – and it strained out into the wind on the lee side, and one had to watch the rear edge of it, which was called the leach, for telltale flutters.

'When that happens you've got her too close,' my teacher explained. 'She don't like that, and she bloody soon tells you she don't, and if you don't heed her warning she'll bring you up into the wind, and beyond, and she'll gybe and the spanker goes right over from one side to t'other and you'll have her on her beam ends and demasted. Many a good ship has been lost with all hands through the man at the wheel dreaming of his last woman ashore and not keeping his eye cocked on the leach.' And once again I was terrified, and I concentrated on the task in hand as I never had on anything before, and became fairly soon quite a reasonable helmsman, and my teacher was dismissed to more productive tasks and I was left at the wheel on my own in good weather, for often a whole trick of four hours at a time.

The master was a volatile little Welshman, whose accent put me strongly in mind of Caerwen. He was given to singing hymns in a high tenor while briskly pacing the poop, which my instructor told me solemnly was due to being caught in a harem one night in Constantinople. The mate was a burly Yorkshireman, amiable enough ordinarily, but as I had found, very free with his boot when making or shortening sail. The second mate was an ex-master, broken through drink, and taciturn and vicious. The third was a mere boy getting in his sea time before taking his second mate's ticket. The passengers were mainly officials, the three ladies being the wife and daughter of a surgeon going out to take up an appointment with one of the regiments stationed in Western Australia, and the elderly wife of a Colonial Secretary rejoining her husband after an extended holiday in England.

The girl was delightful. She was about twelve, I judged, or perhaps a little less – certainly still young enough to be able to talk naturally and innocently to one of the opposite sex without the coy simpers and blushes of one of more mature years. She had deep chestnut hair which was sensibly allowed to tumble freely about her shoulders instead of being gathered up in a snood as fashion was dictating in those days, and her eyes were vividly blue. She was tiny and spritelike in figure which gave her an appearance of fragility that was wholly deceptive, because when her mother wasn't in sight to check her she would shin up into the rigging with the agility of an organ-grinder's monkey and remain there, billowing skirts and petticoats notwithstanding, until fetched down by the voice of authority, which she recognized only in those of her father or the master.

Evelike, she gave me an apple once. We were fairly adequately fed on the standard ship's diet of salt beef and pork, potatoes, biscuit, dried peas, and occasional duff, but one's longing for something fresh became at times intolerable. I had come to the wheel at eight bells one Sunday which meant that both watches were allowed below at the same time, the eternal painting, scrubbing and scraping being suspended for the sabbath. Midday dinner was about to be served in the saloon, and I glanced down through the skylight just as the steward was placing a big bowl of apples on the long table, and they fascinated me, and I'm sure that had my arm been long enough I would have stolen one. She came out of a cabin into the saloon and happened to look upward, and I couldn't turn my eyes away quickly enough, so that she saw my face, and no doubt the longing in it. As the steward turned from the table she snatched an apple, but she wasn't quite quick enough and he caught her redhanded. 'There's only one per passenger Miss Judith, so don't let me see you taking another after dinner or I'll be telling your ma,' he told her, and she giggled and ran up the companionway.

She came up to me and held the apple out, and I, speechless with shyness, could only scowl and shake my head.

She whispered, 'Don't be silly. I took it for you.'

But once again I shook my head, so she reached out and dropped it down inside my oilskin jacket and ran off again down the companionway. That was the longest trick at the wheel I have ever done, or so it seemed at the time. I went up on to the fo'c'slehead when I was relieved, and ate the apple to the last morsel, pips, core and even stalk, lingering over every bite.

There were many such gifts after that – a handful of hazel nuts, a small iced cake, a crystallized plum – all unbelievable delights – and not always filched. Often, I know, they were her own legitimate portion that she was sacrificing – for me – a gawky, tongue-tied youth who never dared to speak a word to her, even to thank her.

It was a long and arduous passage to the Cape. Head winds delayed us for days off the north-west corner of Spain. We stood out into mid-Atlantic in order to catch the northerly drift, only to meet with a violent storm that damaged the rudder, so we had to make the best of our limping way into Lisbon, for repairs which took a whole month. The passengers were able to go ashore, but the mates took it in turn to mount guard with a Portuguese policeman on the gangway to prevent wholesale desertion, because now there were grumblings in the fo'c'sle and mutters of her being an unlucky ship, which was unfair. The weather was foul, not the lovely *Boadicea*.

We got under way again, and the doldrums held us becalmed for the better part of yet another month. But at last we crossed the Equator and the occasion was enlivened by the traditional ceremony of Neptune and his court coming aboard, and first-timers were initiated, which meant nearly all the passengers and four members of the crew including myself, and we were plentifully besmeared with grease and tar and half drowned in a large canvas bath, and I was terrified that the money in my skinbelt would be damaged, but I need not have worried, as I found to my relief when I sneaked into the chainlocker to check that the belt had lived up to its reputation, and the notes were quite dry.

I went back to the festivities then and watched Judith and her mother, decorously swathed in layers of old garments, being respectfully handed into the water. I went forward to help them out and the little devil thanked me demurely, then pushed me in again.

We stormed along down the West African coast with a hot, dry nor'easter on our quarter, and I was carrying a dixie of pea soup from the galley to the fo'c'sle one day when I lost my footing on the wet deck and went skittering into the scuppers. I climbed to my feet and a searing stab of pain pierced my shoulder like a cold, sickening knife thrust. I had learned to take the knocks and bumps which were our daily portion with a certain unconcern, but this I knew was something more serious, so I reported sick and the master, who presided over the medicine chest, pried and prodded at the black swelling that was forming, and called for a second opinion from Judith's father. He pronounced it to be a broken collar-bone, and he expertly set it and strapped it into a reasonably comfortable position, and gave me a laudanum pill to overcome the pain of that first night. Thereafter he saw me each day, and since the heat of the fo'c'sle was well-nigh unbearable he got the carpenter to fix me up a small shelter on deck, and he and his wife and, of course, Judith, were kindness itself, spending many an hour talking to me.

Surgeon John Everard Palmer was the first man of intellect with whom I had ever come in contact, and the impression he made upon me was profound. He was a graduate of Edinburgh University and was a Doctor of Philosophy in addition to being a skilled surgeon. His interests were wide and varied, ranging from history through archeology to mathematics and astronomy – a fine balance between the humanities and science – and merely to talk with him was an education in itself. He was kind and patient and never once did he ever make me conscious of my ignorance. In fact he had the reverse effect upon me, because he could discuss practically every book I had ever read, always upon equal terms, drawing from me my opinions as well as advancing his own. He believed, with Darwin, that education and environment had but small effect on the mind of the individual, and that most of our qualities were innate. 'Read, my boy, just as you have obviously done in the past. Read anything and everything that comes to your hand. Your natural intelligence will separate the chaff from the wheat. Read and observe and listen,' he advised, and to that end he lent me book after book from the vast store he carried with him, and I spent every waking minute of my convalescence in a new and exciting world.

I had not returned to duty by the time we arrived at Cape Town and I was standing on the fo'c'slehead as we came into harbour gazing at the wonder of Table Mountain at dawn, with the bustling city clustered round its feet, when he came upon me together with Mrs Palmer and Judith.

He said solemnly, 'I am a little anxious about that break, Ross. I think it is knitting well, but I would like a second opinion. Fortunately a former colleague of mine is in charge of the military hospital here, and I have asked the captain if he will permit you to come ashore with us for an examination.'

I was naturally grateful and delighted at the prospect of setting foot for the first time on alien soil, and we were rowed ashore after breakfast and Mr Palmer, an impressive figure in red tunic, cocked hat and sword, engaged a carriage to take us to the hospital on the shores of Table Bay. I was very self-conscious in my rough sailor's clothes, and I badly needed a decent haircut after the ministrations of our fo'c'sle barber, but I was relieved to see that the style of dress of the Cape colonists was considerably less formal and certainly more sensible than that of London. I could not help but notice, however, that we were very brusquely treated by the officials on the quay when we landed, while the attitude of many people that we passed on our way to the hospital was positively hostile.

As we neared the hospital a stone was thrown which narrowly missed Mrs Palmer, and there were cries from the crowd of *'Verdompt rooinek!'* which I learned later meant in Dutch 'Damned redneck', a term of contempt for British soldiers. But there were also English phrases – 'Bloody hangmen!' and 'Take your filthy convicts back to the damned Queen!' and Mr Palmer, normally the quietest and most courteous of men, was furiously angry, and at one stage he had his sword half drawn from the scabbard and he seemed about to jump from the carriage and face them. But finally we reached the high wrought-iron gates of the hospital and a guard of British soldiers threw them open to us, and then slammed them in the faces of the mob. An officer hurried down the steps of the main building, which was set among pleasant lawns and garden beds, and greeted Mr Palmer most cordially.

'Palmer! My dear fellow! How good it is to see you. I heard that you had been posted to New South Wales, but I hadn't dared to hope that your ship would call here – not since the *Neptune* incident.' He bent over Mrs Palmer's hand. 'Your servant, ma'am. Welcome to Cape Colony – and accept my apologies for the behaviour of this wretched rabble.' He patted Judith on the cheek and then looked enquiringly at me.

'A young friend of ours, making his way to Australia and,

we hope, his fortune,' Mr Palmer explained. 'Mr Ross Stafford. This is Senior Staff Surgeon Mr Burstow. Stafford has sustained a comminuted fracture of the left clavicle, Burstow. I think it is knitting well and there seems no inner suppuration from the splinters, but I would greatly appreciate your opinion.'

'Certainly, certainly,' Mr Burstow said. 'But a glass of sherry first. This way.' He offered his arm to Mrs Palmer and led us through the garden to a small but very pleasantly situated house, chattering volubly the while. 'These damned riots! Terrible – they need a whiff of grapeshot or two – Pity the Iron Duke is no longer with us – By God! *He'd* have shown 'em – '

'But what is the cause?' Mr Palmer asked.

'This convict nonsense,' the other answered, and I pricked up my ears. 'New South Wales is starting to refuse them. They are getting enough voluntary immigrants now, and they are yearning for respectability. Van Dieman's Land is following suit, so the authorities at Home are at their wits' end as to where to send 'em. They tried to dump a load of them in the *Neptune* a month or so ago, and hell broke loose. The colonists, British as well as Boer, were up in arms. They lined the sea walls and threatened to fire on the boats if they attemped to bring the gaolbirds ashore. The army turned out to restore order, so anything in a red coat now, including us poor damned doctors who are attempting to help the local populace, civil as well as military, come in for their opprobrium also. The *Neptune* had willy-nilly to sail on to Australia.'

'So we are likely to see the end of transportation, are we?' Mr Palmer said thoughtfully. 'Thank God for that. It's a foul system.'

'Then what the devil are we to do with them?' Mr Burstow asked. 'The hulks are overflowing at Home, and the taxpayers are objecting to building more prisons. Hanging is for murder only now, so we've got footpads, burglars, pickpockets, rogues and prostitutes – begging your pardon, ma'am – mounting up by the thousand. Can't leave the blackguards loose to continue to prey upon society.'

'We might turn our attention more to the conditions that produce the poor devils,' Mr Palmer suggested. 'Unemployment, bad housing, sweated labour – dear food and cheap drink – '

'Fiddlesticks!' Mr Burstow snapped impatiently. 'That's rank Radicalism. Here, drink your sherry. *That's* not cheap. I had a pipe of it sent out from Cadiz with the last transport. Your health, ma'am – and yours, Palmer – and little Judith here – and you, young man. What are you going to do in Australia?'

This last question was to me, and I stumbled into the mendacious story I had already told Mr Palmer about seeking some honest employment, saving my money and then looking for an opportunity to launch myself into business as a shipping agent in a small way. I had come genuinely to hate the necessity for this, and there had been times when talking to my kind benefactor when I was tempted to tell him the truth, and perhaps even to try and enlist his help in the freeing of my brother and Caerwen – particularly when he expressed sympathy with the underdog. But I firmly put this from me. Mr Palmer was an officer, and his duty and allegiance, whatever his sympathies and humanity dictated, lay towards the authorities. No – I was not at liberty to take anybody at all into my confidence.

We had a delicious meal with our host, who was a bachelor, of soup, lobster, fowl and various varieties of vegetables that were entirely new to me, followed by grapes, nectarines and oranges, impeccably served by black servants, and we drank some of the finest wine I had ever tasted. It was, all in all, a memorable experience. In view of the unsettled conditions it was deemed inadvisable to take a drive round the city or into the surrounding countryside, so we returned before dark to the quayside, accompanied by a military escort, after Mr Burstow had examined my shoulder and pronounced it well on the way to complete recovery.

We sailed the following morning, after taking on further supplies, and made a quick run south on a fair wind, rounding Cape Agulhas and heading into the Indian Ocean a day later. The weather was colder now, and the huge seas, driven by the constant westerly winds that circle the globe in the southern regions, were mountainous and frightening. We stood on into the Roaring Forties and made King George's Sound at the sou'westerly corner of Australia, and the little settlement of Albany that stands upon it, in forty-three days, and here, sadly, I said goodbye to the Palmers, because the regiment to which the Surgeon had been posted was stationed at Perth, the capital of Western Australia, more than a hundred miles' march through wild country to the north. I think I felt that parting almost as much as watching the ship that was taking my brother and Caerwen away disappear down the Medway, and the tender-hearted Mrs Palmer's misty eyes and young Judith's frank blubbering did not in any way make things easier.

Mr Palmer gripped my hand and made me promise to keep in touch with them. 'Port Jackson is the better part of two thousand miles farther east than this,' he told me. 'But distances mean far less in this huge country than in England. It is quite possible that my regiment, the Nineteenth of Foot, will be sent over to Sydney or somewhere else in New South Wales – or that you might come in search of employment over here to the west. One never knows from day to day where one may find oneself – so write to us often, young Ross, and we will do the same. God bless and keep you, my boy.' And he gave me a beautiful morocco-bound copy of Dean Swift's *Gulliver Travels*, on the fly-leaf of which he had written,

To Ross Stafford, from his friends of the barque *Boadicea*, with their affection and best wishes: Jno. Everard Palmer
Surgeon elect to HM
19th Regiment of
Foot and
Emmeline Palmer

and, in Judith's round schoolgirl hand, her autograph also, followed by the place and date, 'Albany, W. Australia, April 26th 1852'. And by great good fortune I was able to give them a small memento in the form of a narwhal's tooth, beautifully carved into the shape of the *Boadicea* under full sail by the carpenter, who sold it to me for a pound.

I stood on the bulwarks returning their waves, until their boat was a speck in the distance, then the bosun's bellow brought me back to the stern realities of the present. Mr Palmer had insisted that I remained on light duty until my arm had fully recovered its strength, but I was no longer a privileged passenger, the bosun informed me, and he was going to work the skrimshanking bloody hide off me – and he did, all the way across the Great Australian Bight, through Bass Strait and up the New South Wales coast until, a month later, we arrived off Port Jackson.

We took a pilot aboard outside the Heads. He came across from his cutter in a gig, rowed by six oarsmen in white ducks and straw hats, and I remember thinking how smart they appeared, until I looked down into the boat as they came alongside and saw the chain that linked them together at the ankles. One of them looked hopefully up at me as the bowman reached for the accommodation ladder with a boat-hook, and mimed the act of filling a pipe and smoking, but I had no tobacco so I shook my head regretfully. He called up softly but penetratingly, 'You miserable bastard. I'll know you again.'

The pilot, in the act of swinging his leg over the bulwark, paused and looked down. 'Cox'n,' he called. 'My compliments to Mr Fisher when you get back aboard the cutter, and ask him to give Number Thirty-eight twelve lashes for attempted tobacco cadging – laid on with a will.'

'Aye, aye, sir,' answered the petty officer at the tiller, and gave the order to push off and bear away, and as the boat swung round I saw the numbers on the backs of their smart duck shirts – and the look of resigned misery in the eyes of the man who had spoken to me. It remained with me for a very long time.

We were towed the length of that magnificent harbour by a smoke-belching, paddle-wheeled tug, and although we were kept on the jump making a harbour stow of the sails, I managed to catch passing glimpses of the bushclad shores, where, in clearings dotted on the slopes handsome houses had been built.

'More of 'em every trip,' a sailor on the yard beside me said. 'The wise ones stay out here when they've made their pile. Fancy living in one of them lurks. Who the hell would want to go back to the Old Country? Not me, by Christ. I'm jumping the ship this time, and staying.'

And he wasn't the only one. We had picked up a few passengers at Albany, in place of those who had landed, and rumours had reached the fo'c'sle, via the cabin boys, of the gold fever that was bringing an ever-increasing rush of men to New South Wales and Victoria from all parts of the world. We had heard that sometimes ships lay at anchor for weeks in Port Jackson unable to sail after their crews had deserted *en masse* and struck out for the goldfields.

'Some skippers are trying to get desertion made a felony now,' my informant went on. 'But the authorities have turned it down because they're only too glad to get people out here who ain't convicts. You've got to watch it though, once you hit the beach, because there's vigilantes here, same as in San Francisco, who'll provide crews at a couple of quid a head, like the press gang used to do for the navy, and they don't give a damn who they knock off.'

We dropped anchor in Farm Cove, within sight of the city, and our passengers went ashore by tender. The master had the crew mustered aft then, and warned us of the perils of desertion.

'You'll be put back aboard if you try it, never fear,' he told us grimly, 'and God help you on the passage home. If any of you have ideas about swimming ashore from here, let me tell you that the sharks of Sydney Harbour are the biggest and hungriest in the world. That's all.'

I watched the shore in a fever of impatience for three days before we were warped into Circular Quay, where the fast-growing city came right down to the water's edge. My friend the bosun came up to me as I stood looking at the shore with a speculative eye, and said, 'Don't try it, sonny. Don't even think of it. We've got a deal, us two. The gangway will be manned by the mates and the police the whole time, like in Lisbon.'

'The deal was that I gave you two pounds at the beginning of the trip,' I said. 'You've had that. Then I was to sign off here and give you my pay – which now amounts to six pounds. I'm keeping my part of the bargain. I expect you to keep yours.'

'The bloody skipper refuses to sign *anybody* off,' he growled, 'so you'll stay aboard and pay me the six quid when we get back to London – or I'll cut the liver out of you.'

'Help me to get ashore and I'll pay you the six quid out of my pocket,' I promised.

He considered this for a while, his little pig's eyes glinting greedily. 'Show us the rhino,' he said.

I shook six sovereigns from the small leather bag that hung round my neck, and held them under his nose.

'Yours,' I told him. 'When I'm safely ashore. Don't try and get your mauleys on it before then, or by Christ I'll do for you.' And I meant it. I was a strong lad, well-muscled and active, and the voyage had toughened me both bodily and mentally to a degree that I would not have thought possible six months earlier.

He raised his hand as if to cuff me. Mine shot out and closed round a belaying pin in the fiferail, and we looked into each other's eyes for a long moment, then his dropped and he grunted, 'All right. We'll see what we can do,' and walked off.

We commenced discharging cargo the next day, sullenly and unhappily, the mates dog-driving us from dawn until sundown, with half the crew below in the holds loading slings, and the remainder manning the back-breaking hand winches on deck. I had hoped that some of us would have been sent ashore to unload the slings, but the master had cannily arranged for this to be done by a stevedoring company, and we were kept on board with armed police at the top of the gangway, and more patrolling the quay.

The cargo had suffered badly during our rough voyage,

and many crates and barrels had been smashed, strewing their contents far and wide in an unsavoury litter of splintered wood, straw, salt pork from a shattered harness cask, and soaked sacking, all of which had to be collected together on a tarpaulin hatch cover and dumped ashore at the end of the day's work. It was a filthy task, but it proved to be my deliverance, because I noticed on the second morning that the tarpaulin was still lying on the quay, unemptied, with the high-stomached stevedores refusing to touch it until a gang of convicts came down late in the afternoon. Hardly daring to hope that the same thing would happen again, I sneaked back to the fo'c'sle and stuffed my pockets with my few personal possessions, and just before we were knocked off for the day, unnoticed by the rest of the weary crew, I climbed into the tarpaulin and covered myself with rubbish. I lay in the stinking morass for what seemed the better part of an hour and I was about to give up and climb out again when I heard the bosun yell up on deck, 'Come on, for Christ's sake, and get that dunnage ashore,' and I felt myself being swayed aloft, swung outboard, and let go with a run down on to the cobbled quay – and as before, the stevedores refused to handle the mess.

I waited until darkness had fallen, my insides heaving in rebellion, then I crawled out and scuttled into the shelter of a stack of cargo, narrowly missing detection by a policeman. I stole across the road that circled the quay and found myself in front of the Custom House. A wide street lay before me, leading away from the waterfront, and I hurried along it, keeping to the shadows of the substantial buildings that lined it. A sign on one of the infrequent lamp-posts showed it to be Pitt Street. It was crossed at intervals by smaller streets, and the four corners thus formed were taken up by public houses, all of which seemed to be doing a roaring trade. I looked longingly at each one as I passed, because I was burning with thirst and ravenously hungry, but in my stinkingly dirty state I knew it would be highly inadvisable to risk going in.

Pitt Street seemed to be interminable but I kept padding onward with no thought other than to put as much distance between myself and the *Boadicea* as possible, until I was literally walking in my sleep, then when I realized I could go no farther, I tripped and fell headlong into the gutter. It at least served to waken me, and I picked myself up and looked around for some dark corner or doorway in which to rest while I considered my next move. But there was absolutely no shelter in this section of the street and, to make matters worse, I could see a police patrol outside a pub a little farther along, so I ducked down one of the side streets and found myself in a market square.

There were stalls all round its four sides, with a fenced enclosure for livestock in the middle, and late though the hour was, business seemed to be in full swing. The place was crowded with people, many of whom were just as unkempt as I, and I no longer felt conspicuous. I made a full circuit of the square and saw a stall that was doing a roaring trade in roast mutton and potatoes, so I pushed through the crowd and tendered one of my sovereigns. The Chinaman in charge carefully examined it in the light of his naphtha flare, bit it and then rang it on the wooden counter before, finally satisfied, handing me four enormous chops and a couple of baked potatoes on a tin plate, which I ate standing, with my grimy fingers. On counting my change I found that the meal had cost me two shillings, which I thought at the time was appalling, but I certainly felt much better for it, and more able to face my immediate problems.

I saw a clothing stall which seemed to be dealing in the universal garb of the crowd, namely yellowish moleskin trousers, rough tweed jacket, flannel shirt, stout boots and the broad-brimmed felt hat that I learned was called a 'wide-awake'. I stood and listened to a couple of obvious miners bargaining with the old woman behind the counter, and from their cut and thrust gained a rough idea of the accepted price of the garments, and then rigged myself out from head to foot for one pound and my foul, but still serviceable, sailor's gear. I changed behind the stall and went on my way, and came to another long street running parallel with Pitt Street, and saw a sign under a guttering oil lamp advertising 'Clean Beds for Single Gents. No Drunks' at one shilling a night. I went in and was shown into a long dormitory by a villainous-looking character who pointed to the one vacant bed left and said laconically, 'You want to use your coat for a pillow, keep your strides on, and put the bed legs into your boots if you still want the bastards in the morning.'

The bed consisted of two planks over trestles, and a straw palliasse covered by a threadbare and evil-smelling blanket, but, after following the attendant's advice, I slept like a log until morning.

I had breakfast in a nearby pub and then set out to explore the town and I was fortunate in finding a public bathhouse almost immediately, where I soaked myself in a tin tub of semi-scalding water and pondered like Archimedes over my next move. I was here – but where in this huge continent did I start my search for my brother?

There was only one way, I decided. First, find a minor official, and then bribe him. I shaved and generally spruced myself up and then set off back towards the waterfront, because it was there that most of the Government offices seemed to be grouped. I felt reasonably safe because I knew that it was highly unlikely that any of the officers or crew would be ashore, and in my new clothes I imagined that I had merged unnoticeably into the background of this bustling city.

I came back down Pitt Street to the Custom House and there by the greatest of good luck I saw a notice that read, 'Convict Record Office Removed to Dawes Point', and I found on asking directions from a passer-by that it was less than half a mile from Circular Quay. Keeping my head well down under my wide-awake, I walked literally under the bowsprit of the *Boadicea* and round the Quay to the battery of guns at the end of the point, and I found the office located in a small stone-built house surrounded by a pleasantly green lawn which a grey-clad man in leg-irons was mowing with a scythe. He paused and nodded pleasantly as I approached, and removed his straw hat.

'Good morning, sir,' he said. 'I suppose you wouldn't be having a stray shred of baccy about you, would you?'

'I'm afraid not,' I answered, and took a couple of shillings from my pocket. 'But if this—' I got no further. He said 'Blimey!' and the coins vanished.

'Could you tell me who's in charge of this place?' I asked.

'A slave-driving son of a whore called Knowles—sorry—' He crossed himself and looked skyward. '*Mister* Bloody Knowles as he likes to be addressed by the likes of us poor downtrodden bastards nowadays. Ticket-of-leave man who was wearing jewellery round his ankles, the same as me, not two year agone, but now you'd think he come out here first-class saloon with the sodding governor hisself. That's him, the red-nosed bleeder, looking out of the window now. Tell him you was asking directions and I give 'em to you respectful like, or I'll be getting me back warmed again.'

I thanked him and walked on up the path and in at the front door. The large room inside was lined from floor to ceiling with racks containing leather-bound ledgers, and an elderly man in seedy clerical black sat at a desk in the window. Typically of government penpushers the world over, he pretended to be immersed in a pile of documents in front of him for some minutes after I entered, then he looked enquiringly at me and said sourly, 'Yes? What is it?'

I had my story ready—one which I had formulated, altered, discarded, readopted and revised for weeks past, until I thought it might sound reasonably convincing.

I said, 'Good morning, sir,' and smiled winningly. 'I have recently arrived out from England, and our vicar asked me to trace, if possible, a man from the parish who was transported a little over a year ago, and see if there was anything we could do for him—within permissible regulations, of course,' I added hastily.

He regarded me speculatively for a moment, pursing his lips and tapping them with a penholder.

'Difficult—very difficult, I'm afraid,' he said. 'You don't know to which settlement he was assigned?'

'Just New South Wales—'

'Of course it would be "just New South Wales",' he said impatiently. 'We keep telling the fools back Home that we're taking no more transportees here, but they won't listen. A year ago, you say? He'd have gone to Van Dieman's Land

– or Tasmania as they call the damned place now.'

My heart sank. 'Then you can't help me?' I said.

He shrugged and examined his fingernails. 'I didn't say that exactly. I dare say I *could* find out for you if you give me his name and, if possible, that of the ship he came on – but it would entail a lot of work, in my own time, and of course I'd get into serious trouble if it were found out that I was disclosing official matters – ' He rubbed his forefinger and thumb together absently.

I took the hint. 'The vicar advanced me a small sum in case there were any expenses attached to it,' I told him.

'How much?'

'A couple of pounds.'

'I hope he didn't have to strain too much. He couldn't go to a little more, I suppose?'

'Maybe three, but that would be the absolute limit.'

'Call it a fiver,' he wheedled, but I thought, correctly as it turned out, that I had got his measure now.

'Three,' I said firmly.

'Four,' he countered.

I turned on my heel and started towards the door. 'It isn't all that important,' I said. 'Good day to you.'

'All right – three it is,' he said hastily. 'What's the gull's name – and the bloody ship?'

'Neil Stafford – and the ship was the *Cambrian Queen*.'

He held out his hand. I ignored it and put three sovereigns on the desk and kept my hand on them. He sneered, got up and crossed to the racks, ran his finger along a line of ledgers and took one down and leafed through the pages.

'Stafford,' he said. 'Yes – here he is. Fourteen years – burglary. They were put ashore here with ship fever – twenty-two of them. The rest were diverted to Hobart – where they should have gone in the first place.'

I said, 'There is another name, while you've got the book open. Morgan – a woman – '

He snapped it shut. 'One name, three quid,' he snarled. 'Think I'm a pie-can? Here – give us the blunt and be off with you.'

'Two names five quid,' I offered.

'Six, you cocky young bastard,' he spat.

'Five – or sweet damn all.' I picked up the three sovereigns and put them back in my pocket.

He cursed horribly but I left in the end with the full information I had come for. Neil had been taken to the prison hospital at Parramatta, and after six months his enclosed prison term had been remitted and he had been sent to the road-building gang at Bathurst.

'He must have been cutting up rough,' Knowles said with malicious satisfaction. 'That's reserved for refractory cases. He'll get the piss and wind taken out of him there, by God. The woman?' He consulted the book again. 'Assigned servant to the District Magistrate at Lithgow, who, if she's good-looking, will no doubt have screwed the arse off her by now. He's a randy old bastard.'

I threw the five coins in his face and left in haste, wanting to vomit, and went back into town and made enquiries at the post office and found that Bathurst was a centre of some importance a little over a hundred and twenty miles to the west of Sydney, while Lithgow was a small town in the Blue Mountains in the same direction. Both places were served by mail coach I was told and they directed me to the Rob Roy Hotel on Brickfield Hill at the end of George Street.

I hurried there in a fever of impatience to be out of this damned town and started on my quest, only to be met with a crushing setback. Because of a series of rich gold strikes in the Bathurst area, every seat on the daily coach had been bought up by shrewd operators for weeks in advance, for resale at murderous profits, and the best bargain I could have made would have been a seat three weeks later for *forty pounds*, which was, of course, unthinkable. I certainly had no intention of cutting into the two hundred and fifty pounds in my belt at this stage, but other than that all I now had in the world was six pounds and some odd silver.

I wandered back to the market, deep in thought, to get something to eat. It was called Paddy's Market, I found, and apart from a few smart and expensive shops in Pitt and George Streets, it appeared to be the main commercial centre of the city although it was ankle-deep in mud, animal dung and rotting vegetables. Most of the stalls were run by pig-tailed Chinese, and the houses overlooking the central square seemed all to be either pubs or knocking-shops, the denizens of both, from their accents, being preponderantly Irish or Cockney. I was standing on the outskirts of a crowd, listening to a cheapjack selling crockery when my hat was snatched from my head and I spun round in time to see a blowzy female running helter-skelter towards a doorway. Furious, I ran after her and had succeeded in grabbing her shawl when I found myself hemmed in by two or three tough-looking characters, one of whom accused me of interfering with his wife! I angrily protested that all I wanted from the filthy bitch was my hat, then I realized that I was being slowly but firmly edged towards the doorway, and I recognized a ploy that I'd often heard of in London. 'Bonneting' it's called – your hat is snatched – you chase after it, and find yourself bludgeoned and robbed down some dark alley. I dug my heels in and tried to resist the pressure, but they were winning, and I could feel panic rising. I started to lash out in all directions with both fists and feet and almost immediately the pressure eased and the toughs were scattering, and I realized that my deliverance was due to two strangers who had taken my attackers in the rear.

One of them, a large bearded man, roared angrily, 'For Christ's sake, George, will you watch what you're doing! That could have been nasty.' Then he peered closely at me and said, 'Jesus! It ain't George. Sorry, mate.' The other man retrieved my hat from the mud and handed it back to me with a grin.

I said, 'No need to apologize. I'm much obliged to you gentlemen.'

The big man laughed. 'Gentlemen? Hear that, Bluey? You been called many things in the past, but I'll bet a deener never that before.'

'Speak for yourself,' the other said. 'There's George over there. We better grab him before the whores do, or he won't be seeing Bathurst again.'

I pricked up my ears. 'That was really kind of you. Would

you care to join me in a drink?' I asked.

'My oath,' said Bluey promptly, and led the way to the nearest pub. The big man had collected George by this time and we breasted up to the bar and I called for pints. I knew I had to husband my money very carefully, but this, I felt, was something in the nature of an investment.

The big man put his hand out. 'I'm Charlie Larkin,' he said. 'This little ginger bastard is Bluey Noakes, and the bloke on the end is George Blanchard. We're down from Bathurst and we're lighting out back at kookaburra-fart tomorrow.'

I gripped his hand and almost slipped and gave my own name, something I'd prudently decided not to do under any circumstances, but I remembered in time and gave the one I'd already chosen for myself. 'I'm William Walker,' I said.

'Glad to make your acquaintance, Bill,' said Charlie, and raised his pint. 'Cheers,' and he sunk it in one draught.

'How are you returning to Bathurst?' I asked, trying to make the question sound casual and of no particular interest.

'Broke,' laughed Bluey. 'I've never known these bludgers to be anything else after a few days in town.'

'We come down with seven and a half ounces,' said George sorrowfully, 'and blew the sodding lot in a week.'

'You'll find it difficult to get back in that case, won't you?' I said. 'I asked about the coach today and found they wanted forty pounds.'

Charlie looked at me in horror. 'Coach?' he said. 'Jesus! You keep away from *them* bastards. You want to come with us – with the bullockies.'

'The bullockies – ?' I said, mystified. 'I'm sorry – I don't understand,' and George and Bluey laughed uproariously.

'Neither did you two jimmygrant bastards, when you first come up-country,' said Charlie angrily, and added to me, 'The bullock carts, son. Bloody slow – in fact it's quicker to walk, but at least they carry your swag for you, and you make camp every night, and most of the coves who use 'em know how to look after themselves, so you don't get worried by bushrangers. It'll cost you two quid, it takes ten days, and you find your own tucker – what you'd call grub in the Old Country.'

'That sounds just what I'm looking for,' I said. 'How do I go about arranging it?'

'Just stick with us,' George said.

'But I'll need camping gear and – what do you call it – tucker – ?'

'Don't worry,' Charlie told me. 'We're all set. You shout the beer tonight and pay your own fare, and we'll shout you the tucker and a kip. How's that?'

I started, insincerely, to protest that I felt I would be taking advantage of their kindness, but they would have none of it, and just roared for more beer.

I remember little of the rest of that evening. Reckoning up later I found I had spent a pound on beer, which, at twopence a pint meant that we had sunk a hundred and twenty tankards between us. I have a dim recollection of stumbling along a country road with the others, and later sleeping under a tree. I finally came to on top of a pile of sacks in the back of a huge springless cart that moved at a snail's pace to the accompaniment of some of the filthiest language I have ever heard in my life. Sitting up slowly, I found that this came from a small wizened character riding a horse and wielding a long two-handed whip over the backs of a string of oxen, yoked in pairs and seeming to stretch to infinity in front of us. Twisting my head painfully I saw my three companions of the night before trudging along in the rear of the cart, with a dozen or so other men. Charlie waved and grinned, seemingly quite unaffected by the mighty marathon, although the other two appeared rather subdued.

Charlie bellowed, 'How're you feeling, cock?' and on my shaking my head feebly he answered his own question, 'Like as if a dingo bitch had littered in your gob, I'll bet. Never mind – get some mutton chops and a dollop of damper down you and you'll be on top of the world again.'

That was all I needed. I hung over the edge of the cart and vomited, and the gentleman on the horse told me that if I spewed on any of the cargo he'd have the bloody ears off the side of my sodding head with his copulating whip like a pair of defecating jug handles in a fair cockshy, all in one breath.

We stopped at mid-morning to drink murderously strong, milkless tea while the bullocks were watered at a roadside creek, but thankfully there was no further talk of food until we halted for the night, by which time I was sufficiently recovered to be hungry.

The country we had been moving through was flat, dry and dusty and made desolate by the skeletons of dead gum trees that gleamed whitely against a colourless landscape.

'They ringbark them,' Charlie told me. 'That kills 'em off and the grass grows better and then they bring in more bloody sheep.'

'What do they do with the sheep?' I asked, because we had been passing flock after flock all day, apparently unattended and ownerless.

'Round 'em up twice a year, get the wool off 'em, then slaughter 'em,' he answered. 'Then they boil 'em down for the tallow and dump the rest. You were dead-oh when we came along the Parramatta road last night or you'd have got the stink of the carcasses.'

'Isn't that a waste?'

'What the hell else can they do with 'em? There's millions of the bastards. Of course a lot of it's eaten – especially by the soldiers and those poor sods.' He pointed to a gang of convicts working at the side of the road.

'How many convicts do you think there are in New South Wales?' I asked casually.

'God knows,' he shrugged. 'Ten – twenty thousand maybe. Transportation to these parts has officially stopped now, so the bloody government is working the hides off them that are here while they've still got the chance.'

I said, 'They seem to have leg-irons on them in Sydney, but the ones we've passed today were all loose.'

'That's just to stop 'em trying to jump a ship. Not many of 'em escape from the inland settlements.'

'What about the bushrangers?' Bluey said. 'Every bloody

one of 'em's an escaped convict.'

'What are bushrangers?' I asked.

'Highwaymen you'd call them back Home. A cove with a gun and a horse and nothing to lose,' George said. 'Often thought about having a go at it myself. Bloody sight better than slogging your guts out at the diggings, for sweet Fanny Adams. Rob the rich and give it to the poor, like Robin bloody Hood.'

'They rob everybody,' Charlie said. 'Rich and poor alike. Some bastard come in to Blayney while I was buying me stores for the month. I only had half an ounce, and it'd taken me a couple of months to get it. I told him so, and got a wipe across the jaw with his gun butt. I hate the coppers, but I hate them bloody dingoes worse.'

And so I learned – day after day – through idle conversation – learned and stored for future reference. So they didn't wear leg-irons inland? That was a relief, because it had been worrying me. If Neil was working with a gang like the ones we had seen today, guarded in some cases by a single soldier dozing in the shade of a tree, it should not be too difficult to slip off into the bush, provided he was unfettered.

We came to a river at the end of the second day. It ran along the foot of a mountain range that rose like a wall in front of us, and there was a small village on the bank – a few wattle-and-daub houses, a pub and staging section for the coaches, and a police station. Penrith it was called, Charlie told me, and explained that the road zigzagged up the mountains from here to the highest point at a place called Mount Victoria, and then descended to the plains on the other side.

We bathed in the river as the sun went down, and George said he had once gone all the way to the coast by boat from Penrith, and Bluey called him a liar.

'I did, for Chri'sake!' George insisted.

'The coast is behind us – east,' Bluey said. 'This bloody river is running north, so how the hell could you?'

'It *bends* east, you drongo,' George shouted, 'and comes out into Broken Bay, about thirty miles north of Port Jackson. Then if you keep going north overland you finish up at the Hunter.'

Bluey winked at me. Baiting George was a favourite pastime of his. 'Doesn't know his arse from his elbow, the poor cow,' he said. 'The bloody Hunter is up at Newcastle.'

'Of course it is, God damn you!' screamed George. 'Newcastle is where you finish up – about a hundred miles up the coast from Sydney.'

'Who the hell wants to finish up at Newcastle? Sod of a place.'

'Bloody sight better town than Sydney. That's where the American clippers turn round now. Best pubs and knocking-shops in New South – and not so many coppers breathing down your neck and looking at your ankles for iron marks.'

'Bigger bloody liar than Tom Pepper. Anyhow, what was you doing up there?'

'Prospecting. What do you think?'

'Find anything?'

'Yes – mud and bloody mangroves. I never saw another soul between here and the Hunter. I nearly went dingbats.'

And so the argument went on, and I garnered the facts that there was a route to the coast other than the busy, police-patrolled one by which we had come. And Newcastle was apparently a freer and more open town than Sydney – and the American clippers turned round there. All facts well worth remembering, and I made up my mind to get hold of a map of this area at the first opportunity.

We climbed steadily for the next three days, and as if in compensation for the dreariness of the coastal plain, the country became beautiful from the moment we crossed the river. The bush crowded right down to the track, thick, verdant and impenetrable, and the air was clear and cool and heavy with the scent of eucalyptus and wattle.

We came to the summit and then began a hair-raising descent to the plains the other side of the range, when several times the huge wagon seemed about to take charge and over-run the bullocks.

And so, on the tenth day, we arrived in Bathurst.

Chapter Four

One of the more attractive traits of the goldminer was his singlemindedness and his total lack of interest in other people's affairs. Nobody in that ten days had asked me my reason for going to Bathurst, nor when or how I had come to Australia, taking it for granted, no doubt, that I was just another young immigrant bitten by the gold-fever bug and about to experience for the first time the toil and sweat and disappointment of that uncertain pursuit. On the other hand, if I asked a question of them, they would answer courteously and helpfully, so by the time we arrived I was considerably less green than when we started.

'If you're going fossicking,' Charlie advised me, 'don't for Chri'sake do it anywhere near Bathurst without a licence. The coppers here are bastards, but that bit of paper will get you through most anywhere.'

'Where does one get a licence?' I asked.

'Government Assay Office, but they'll charge you twenty quid, the thieving cows. If you can't raise that it's best to get a horse and go out into the bush. Nobody will bother you there.'

'What does a horse cost?'

'All depends. You should be able to pick up a decent old brumbie for round about a fiver at the Exchange.'

'What's that?'

'Place along the Blayney road about a mile, where diggers sell their gear when they've learned sense and are getting to hell out of it. Saddlery, camping gear – anything at all – at about a quarter the price you'd pay the Chinks in town.'

We had a final drink together, then they left to walk to their diggings. Where those were situated I never found out, because I had learned by this that it was highly impolitic to appear inquisitive about such matters. I had a much-needed bath and a meal, and then booked a bed in Mother Riley's boarding-house, recommended by Charlie as being less bug-ridden than most of the others, and afterwards set out to explore the town, and I was lucky almost immediately, because I saw a large map in the window of the Assay office on which were marked all the claims in the Bathurst area. These in themselves did not interest me, but the roads, which were also shown, did. There were, in fact, only two main ones – the Sydney road by which we had come, and its continuation west towards Orange, but there were minor ones leading off them to the diggings, and some of these bore legends such as, 'under construction', 'under repairs', and 'projected'. There were seven such off-shoots, at distances I judged to range between two miles and six from the town, so I found a book-shop and managed to buy a school atlas and a pencil, then I went back and made a rough copy of the local map on the fly-leaf.

Now, at least, I felt I had something definite to work upon, so I spent the rest of the afternoon in buying a couple of blankets and a set of clothes that duplicated those that I was wearing, and I rolled them into a swag, together with a billy can, hatchet and a few provisions in a tucker bag, and I started out next morning systematically to explore the roads I had marked.

I found him on the third day.

There were some fifty of them building a rough timber bridge over a small creek that crossed a track leading to Wallerawang. They were chopping down gum trees in the scrub and hauling them to the site, and Neil was straining on a rope not a couple of yards off the road. Two soldiers and a police trooper seemed to be the only guards, and they were sitting under a tree playing cards, while the work proceeded under the direction of a civilian ganger.

I had learnt in the two preceding days that it was not advisable to linger over-long in the vicinity of a convict gang, as it attracted the attention of the guard, and I had been told civilly but firmly to move along on a couple of occasions, so

I walked on without giving the party a second glance, although I confess without shame that I was nearly weeping. He was thin and sunken-cheeked, and burned almost black by the sun, stripped to the waist like the rest of them, and in the one swift scrutiny I had risked I saw the stripes on his back of a flogging – but he was still the same Neil and he was leading the others in a dirty song. They hadn't broken his spirit.

I went on round the next bend for about a quarter of a mile, and then I dived into the scrub that bordered the road, and worked my way back towards the bridge, guided by the sound of axes, and I came to the clearing where the trees were being felled. There were half a dozen men there, working in pairs, and seemingly without supervision, and a tree came crashing down uncomfortably close to where I crouched in the thick undergrowth.

A party came down from the road, but Neil was not among them. They fastened a rope to the end of the felled tree but before commencing to haul it back a couple of them crossed to a canvas waterbag the other side of the clearing and took a drink. I retreated into the scrub again and worked my way round until I was close to the tree on which the bag was hanging, and waited – and hoped.

Neil's party came down after some minutes, and took the next tree to be felled, but although two men came to take water, my brother was not one of them, but he did the next time, and by the grace of God he was the second to drink, so he was on his own for just a moment, with the rest of the party already starting the haul back to the road.

I said, 'Neil. It's me – Ross,' and pushed the undergrowth aside for him to see my face. He looked uncomprehendingly at me, the waterbag poised in mid-air, then he shook his head slowly as if to clear it, and went on drinking.

'You bloody fool!' I raged. 'It *is* me – come on, for God's sake,' and I reached out and grabbed his wrist and pulled him into the scrub. He followed for a yard or so, but clearly the shock had taken the strength right out of him, because he collapsed on to his knees and stared up at me open-mouthed, and although it cut me to the heart to do so, I had to slap him hard across the face to bring his wits back. He nodded then, still unable to speak, and followed me.

We pushed through the bush to where I had left the swag, and by this time he was thinking again.

'Away from the road,' he muttered. 'Downhill to the river.'

'How long before they miss you?' I asked him breathlessly.

'With luck not until lock-up time at the compound – that's at sundown – but there's a squealer in our party who might notice I'm missing, and suck up to the trooper –' He had taken the lead now and was heading quickly down the slope. 'We'll hear a shot and then a bugle when they find out –'

But there was no shot, and after an hour, soaked through with sweat and wellnigh exhausted, we stopped for breath at the top of a hill the other side of the river, which we had waded waistdeep.

'For God's sake,' he clamoured. 'How? *How the hell did you get here?*' His face clouded for a moment as a thought struck him. 'You weren't boated yourself, were you?'

I told him in as few words as possible what had happened, and his first question was, 'Caerwen? Have you heard anything – ?'

'She's in Lithgow – assigned servant to the magistrate, I was told,' I said.

He looked relieved. 'That's the usual thing for women. It needn't be so bad. All depends what sort of bastards she's working for. She saved my life on the ship.'

'How?' I asked.

He shrugged. 'The usual way – for Caerwen. A lot of us were down with ship fever and the sawbones gave some of the younger women the job of nursing us. Caerwen got taken up by a Marine sergeant and she used to get extra food from him – which she fed to me. There were over three hundred cases in the 'tween decks. Twenty of us lived to be put ashore at Port Jackson.' His head sunk forward on to his chest and I could see tears making runnels down through the grime of his face. 'God – I'd give my right arm just to see her once again – to – to tell – her –'

'Stop that,' I said harshly. 'You're going to see her. What the hell do you think I've come all this way for? We're getting out – all three of us.'

He smiled wanly and said, 'Yes, yes, old lad,' as if humouring the vainglorious boasting of a child. 'But have you any idea where Lithgow is – ?'

'Not forty miles from where we are at this minute,' I told him knowledgeably. 'We passed close to it on our way up from Sydney.'

He stared at me. 'And you didn't try to see her?' he said accusingly.

'One thing at a time,' I said. 'Anyhow, I didn't know until we had passed it.'

He jumped to his feet, his gloom dispelled for the moment. 'Then by God I'm going there, if it's the last thing I do,' he said.

'Isn't that what I said? We're going together,' I told him.

He shook his head firmly. 'No – I've had time to think now,' he said. 'If you and I are taken together you'll be in this hell with me for at least a seven-year stretch. You've got to stay out and keep an eye on Caerwen for me – do what you can to help her. You could even marry some respectable woman out here and get Caerwen assigned as a servant. Now that *is* an idea – '

'By God it *is*,' I said drily. 'Stop talking like a fool, Neil. I told you – we're all going out together.'

'How the hell can we?' he said impatiently. 'You need money to have any sort of a chance to make a run for it.'

And only then did I realize that I hadn't mentioned the two hundred and fifty pounds round my waist. I pulled up my shirt and unbuckled the skinbelt and took the five fifty-pound notes out.

'What are these?' I asked him. 'Bloody cabbage leaves?'

I thought for a moment that he was going to choke. His jaw dropped, his breath came in gasps and his eyes bade fair to pop out of his head.

'Holy God!' he breathed. 'We can then – *we can!*' He threw his arms round my shoulders and wrestled with me as we did as children, pounding my ribs and scuffing my hair. 'You clever old laddo. I thought you'd have used it to get out here – for expenses – to live on – Damn and blast it! You're the eighth wonder of the world – you bloody well are. I'm proud of you.'

We went on then, circling north and east in low, densely scrub-clad hills, in the general direction of Bathurst, and late in the afternoon we found a cave in a gully and we screened the mouth with blankets and made a small fire and cooked a meal from the rations I was carrying. We buried his convict trousers and rough wooden-soled clogs, then he bathed in a stream and painfully shaved a month-old beard with my razor.

'They gave us one shave a month – head and face,' he told me, and rubbed the stubble on his skull. 'This will grow quite quickly and when I've got these decent clothes on I'd risk walking through Bathurst in broad daylight. That's why so few escapes ever succeed – or are even attempted. A convict on the run has got to get clothes and money. To get them he's got to break in somewhere. That means he's got to keep near the settlements, and that's where they are watching. He can't get clear unless he's got help – and nobody helps a gaolbird in this country.'

We lay awake in our blankets that night for many hours, exchanging our stories and laying our plans for the immediate future. I was to go back to Bathurst and change one of the notes at the Bank of New South Wales, then buy more stores and rejoin him here.

'You'll be stopped and questioned,' he said. 'But you should be safe enough. We may be brothers but we're not very much alike except for our size – and you haven't got bengallers. That's the first thing they look for.'

'What are bengallers?' I asked.

'Stripes,' he said shortly. 'Like the Bengal tiger. A flogging leaves its mark for life. I've had three, and it's down on my record chitty. Oh yes – they'll know what to look for all right.'

The idea of going to Newcastle appealed to him. We studied the map in the atlas next morning and traced the course of the Nepean River from Penrith to Broken Bay. It was just as George had claimed – a northerly flow bending to the east, and finding the sea some thirty miles north of Sydney.

'A boat if we can get our hands on one,' Neil mused, 'or if

not, make a raft and drift down with the current, always moving at night and laying up in daylight. We'll have to get boy's clothes for Caerwen.' He grinned. 'How the hell we're going to flatten those glorious tits of hers I don't know. Remember to get scissors for her hair – right, off you go now. You've got the best part of a day's march ahead of you. Straight ahead down the hill from the gully here, and you will come to the road about three miles short of the bridge. Make some sort of mark there so you will know where to turn off on your way back. Good luck, laddo.'

I strode off downhill happier than I had been for many a long day, and with a sense of achievement that I had never known before. I had *done* it. I had traversed the globe and fulfilled my mission – or half fulfilled it. I still had to get them out of this beautiful, cruel country. It was not going to be easy, particularly with Caerwen, but I knew that Neil would never leave without her – nor would I have wanted him to. It would probably mean that they would have to go together, and I would remain and follow later, working and saving my fare –

I was deep in thought as I tramped along the road towards Bathurst, and the two troopers who rode out of the bush and held me up with their carbines startled me badly.

'Bail up,' one of them said, then when I didn't understand, he roared, 'Get your bloody hands up when you're told.'

I dropped my swag and held my hands aloft. They dismounted and one of them crossed to me while the other held the horses. He peered into my face and he seemed somewhat disappointed.

'He don't look like the bugger,' he said. 'What's your name?'

'William Walker,' I answered. 'What have I done wrong?'

'Shut your mouth until I tell you to open it,' he snapped. 'Where are you from?'

'Bathurst.'

'Where in Bathurst?'

'Mother Riley's.'

'What are you doing out here?'

'Fossicking.'

'Got a licence?'

'No. I was told at the Assay Office that I didn't need one until I staked a claim and registered it.'

'Ah – we've got a bloody bush lawyer on our hands, have we?'

'Have a look at his fucking back,' the other trooper called.

'Get your shirt off,' the first ordered.

I recalled Charlie Larkin's advice about tactics when dealing with the police. 'Never swear at the bastards, because they can lift you for that. On the other hand if they swear at you, look shocked and ask for their names and numbers and say you want to see the Inspector. It scares the shit out of them.'

I took off my coat and pulled my shirt over my head, thanking my lucky stars that I had left the skinbelt with Neil. But I had one fifty-pound note in my pocket and I was hoping to God that they wouldn't search me.

The trooper motioned to me to turn round. I did so, and he called out, 'No bengallers on the bastard.'

'Pity,' the other one said. 'He wouldn't have been so free with his lip if he'd had the cat round his arse a few times.'

'May I put my shirt on now, please?' I asked meekly.

'Not so bloody fast. Who do you know in Bathurst who can identify you?' This one was reluctant to give up, but his more authoritative colleague was getting impatient.

'Only three people besides Mother Riley,' I answered. 'Charlie Larkin, Bluey Noakes and George Blanchard. I came up from Sydney with them by bullock cart last week.'

That was the clincher. They exchanged glances, and the one in front of me looked furious and said, 'Why the hell didn't you say so at first, instead of wasting our time?'

'I tried to, but you told me to shut my mouth.' I tucked in my shirt and put my coat on. 'And now may I have your names and numbers, please, gentlemen?'

Again they exchanged looks, this time uneasily.

'What for?' the first one asked.

'I've answered your questions correctly,' I said. '*I* have a few to ask now – of your Inspector.'

'Only doing our job, mate. There's a convict on the run.'

He smiled appeasingly. 'No hard feelings.'

'You used filthy language to me,' I said primly.

'Sorry about that. We've been beating the bush since yesterday. No sleep. A bloke gets a bit touchy.' They mounted hurriedly.

'No offence meant, mate,' the first trooper called. 'Keep your eyes skinned for this cove, and don't take any chances. He could be real nasty. Tell 'em at the next post that you've seen us and you won't have any trouble. So long.' And they cantered off up the road.

I was stopped twice again before reaching the outskirts of the town, the first time by soldiers, who were less zealous than the police, and I was allowed to proceed after the most perfunctory of questions, but the troopers at the next post, although not quite as offensive as the first pair, were considerably more searching in their questions. Who had I seen along the road that morning? Where had I spent the previous night? Why was I going in to Bathurst now? My answers came pat enough, and seemed to satisfy them – their colleagues, who had already questioned me and let me proceed – and a military patrol under a corporal. Last night? Camped in the bush at the side of the road. Reason for going to Bathurst? More supplies and to get a fossicker's permit. As George had said, they certainly put great store by this wretched permit. While I was being interrogated, two other men passed without let or hindrance upon showing it. It was, in short, an unquestioned guarantee of *bona fides* in this area, and the possibility of an escaping convict coming by one had apparently never occurred to the official mind. Inwardly shuddering at the thought of squandering so much of our funds, I decided that Neil, at least, must have one. I had an alibi which could be proved, he had not.

I found my way to the Exchange and bought the items we had listed between us. We had kept this as low as Neil had deemed prudent, but even so it made a formidable load by the time I had bought trousers, jacket, shirt and a blanket for Caerwen. Then I went to the Assay Office for a licence. The price wasn't as great as I had been fearing, as it came in two parts. One paid ten pounds for the fossicker's permit, which allowed one to 'scratch' anywhere except on somebody else's claim, and a further ten for the full licence when a strike had been made and registered. I gave considerable thought to a suitable name to go on it, and had decided to stick to William Walker, the one I had already given to the patrols that morning, in case someone asked to see it on my way back. I set out then, loaded like a camel with flour, tea, sugar, oatmeal and clothes plus two last straws in the form of long-handled shovels, without which no self-respecting prospector considered himself properly dressed.

I picked up several intriguing morsels of gossip round the town and in the Exchange. The escaped convict was, apparently, a very desperate character indeed, and in the short time he had been at liberty had already turned bushranger.

'The bastard bailed up the store in Wallerawang last night and then pinched a thoroughbred off the sawbones. He's making up-country to Orange,' I heard one well-informed miner say in a pub.

'How the hell do you know?' somebody jeered. 'He only got away last night – ten bloody miles from Wallerawang.'

'Like hell he did. He was off like a scalded dingo yesterday morning, after scragging a redcoat and swiping his gun.'

'It'll be Mittagong he'll be heading for. Got two mates there he's going into business with – '

'Bet you it's Sydney – '

'Don't talk like a bloody fool. No gaolbird goes back over the mountains. Too many coppers that side. No, it's west for him. That's the way the trackers have gone anyhow.'

And I found that the last view was the generally held one, and going back along the road in the evening, bent double under my load, it looked as if it was the correct one, because I saw no more police or soldiers.

I found the point at which I had come out of the bush – it was marked by a gaunt dead blue-gum and a clump of wattle – and I walked past it for some distance to make sure there were no hidden watchers – then I slipped into the undergrowth and started to climb – and I nearly jumped out of my skin as somebody dropped from an overhanging branch in front of me. It was Neil, and I cursed him angrily, but he only grinned amiably and relieved me of most of my load.

'I heard them pretty close to the gully,' he told me. 'Going hell for leather through the bush and into the hills to the west, so I hid our stuff and came down here where they were far less likely to look for me. The few escapers from this section have always gone west. I could hear the coppers talking on the road before they left.'

'That's what I heard in town also,' I said. 'So it looks as if we were right to decide on the east,' and I told him about the permit, somewhat uneasily, because I expected him to disapprove of such an outlay, but he thought it an excellent idea. Rested and fed and out of his hideous prison grey, he was already a different man and was impatient to get under way the following morning, but I came down heavily against that.

'Let the hunt draw away a bit,' I advised. 'The town is buzzing like a beehive at the moment.' He demurred at that and we argued far into the night, but I had my way in the end and he agreed to wait here another two days before moving.

We decided to march only at night, I fifty yards in advance so that he would have time to slip into the bush if I were stopped. By day we would lie hidden a good half-mile off the road, one watching while the other slept. Lithgow was about forty miles to the east, the atlas showed, and a thousand feet above us in the Blue Mountains. I had skirted it on the way here without knowing it, as it lay some distance off the Sydney road. We reckoned that we could make it in three night marches with anything like luck, and on arrival there I would go into the township quite openly and buy more provisions and find out the whereabouts of the Magistrate's house. Beyond that, at this stage, we could make no hard and fast plan.

'Women servants have complete freedom,' Neil told me. 'They wear prison grey, of course, but they go into the towns to do their bloody mistress's shopping, and look after their brats and everything else – just like a skivvy at Home. The only thing is they don't get paid, they work all hours God sends, feed on pig-swill and get flogged if they don't look grateful. We'll just have to lie up close to the house and wait our chance to talk to her when there's nobody about.'

'Not "we",' I said firmly. '*Me.* You've got to keep out of towns until we get over the mountains.'

'Oh, be damned,' he said impatiently. 'No more skulking once we're clear of Bathurst. In these clothes, with a permit in my pocket, and an Irish banjo over my shoulder, who's to tell me from any other digger humping his swag?'

'Maybe you're right,' I told him. 'But you're not going to take needless chances.' And once again we were arguing furiously.

But things went smoothly for the next few days. We circled Bathurst and swam the Macquarie River the first night, without seeing a single soul, which was hardly surprising since few people in their right senses travelled on these roads after sunset. There was always the odd chance, however, of running into a police patrol because Neil told me that they sometimes set up ambushes when they suspected a bushranger to be in the vicinity, or, as now, an escaper was on the loose.

'Three or four of the bastards lying up in the bush at the side of the road, ready to pounce on anybody passing,' he said. 'But that's a risk we'll have to take, because it's no good trying to move except on the road. The bush is too thick, and you finish up walking in circles.'

We worked out a ploy for this. I was to walk boldly in the middle of the road like a man with nothing to hide, with a roll of chewed gum-leaves distending my cheek, while Neil padded along in the shadows, fifty yards in the rear. If I were stopped I was to let out a startled yelp, then explain to the ambushers that I was being driven mad by an aching tooth and I was on my way to the nearest village to get the sawbones or the farrier to pull it, and Neil, with this few vital seconds of warning, would be able to slip silently into the bush and lie low. It had many imperfections, but it was the best we could do. We hoped fervently that it wouldn't come to that.

Dawn found us an estimated ten miles on our way. We turned off the road and pushed through the thick scrub up an incline until we found a spot well screened on all sides but from which we could overlook a stretch of the road in both directions. I was worried about water because we had drunk what we were carrying with us, but Neil's newly acquired bushcraft came to the fore now, and he collected a couple of quarts in as many minutes from the hollow stumps of fallen trees, and then he showed me how to strip the bark from dead wood until the tinder-dry inner pulp that gave no smoke was exposed, and we made tea in our billies and baked damper in the ashes. He had several useful wrinkles now. He had shown me the night before how to maintain direction from the pointers of the Southern Cross, and he had kept our swags and clothes dry on a quickly-constructed raft when we swam the river – and although we had an adequate supply of matches in a bottle, he took pride in making fire with a pointed stick rapidly spun between the palms, a block of hardwood and a few slivers of tinder.

'You just had to learn or starve,' he told me. 'When they moved the road gangs from one stretch to another, they gave you nothing except a hunk of stringy mutton, a pannikin of flour, and a bit of tea and sugar, and you mucked in with a couple of others and did the best you could. If you were wise you latched on to blokes who knew the bush and its ways.' Expressing my genuine admiration for these accomplishments did much to restore his self-confidence, and a lot of our earlier arguing was forgotten as he resumed his natural leadership and no longer felt the necessity to take foolish risks.

We had a bad scare the following night when, marching in our Indian file, we heard the sound of horses' hooves ahead of us, and we just had time partially to close the gap between us and dive into the bush before a troop of cavalry came trotting down the road towards us, their accoutrements gleaming in the moonlight and steam rising from their sweating animals. The officer leading them reined in and blew a whistle and they halted and dismounted – and my heart missed several beats – but, thank God, none of them left the road. The men stamped about, stretching their legs and easing belts and tight clothing and cursing their horses as they tried to reach odd tussocks of grass on the verges. One, in fact, succeeded in doing so while his dismounted rider was lighting a pipe, and its head almost touched mine before it became aware of my presence, and shied and reared.

It was only a regulation halt on their line of march, and after ten minutes or so I heard the officer order them to mount, and they set off again at a walk that broke into a trot, and when the hoofbeats died away in the distance Neil and I came out on to the road. He was cursing furiously because a soldier had eased himself over him.

'Dirty bastard!' he blazed. 'He came up to the edge of the scrub and pissed all over me, and I didn't dare move.'

'What were they exactly?' I asked.

'Oh, just bloody soldiers moving station. They always march at night to avoid the heat.' He shook himself disgustedly. 'Come on – we're wasting good time.'

We didn't reach Lithgow until the fourth night, because the last ten miles was all uphill. The town lies in an amphitheatre, open to the west and hemmed in on the other three sides by the encircling mountains, and it was served by a track that led off from the main road which by-passed it two miles to the south. We climbed the heights above it and lay on a ledge all the next morning watching the activity in the two bisecting streets and the central market square that formed the place. The view from here of the great western plains was breathtaking, but we were not in an appreciative mood, and once again I was having difficulty in restraining Neil, who wanted to go down to the town and start the search immediately.

'God damn it!' he said angrily. 'We'll attract more attention sneaking along the streets at night than we will in daylight. She'll probably be locked up at night anyhow. I *must* go down now. It's my affair – and only mine.'

'It isn't. I'm in this too, and I'm not going to let you throw everything away just through your damned pigheadedness,' I answered, and so it went on for hours, but in the end I had my way and he reluctantly agreed to wait on the ledge while I went down and made a preliminary reconnaissance.

It was a longer walk than I had anticipated, because from the ledge we had not been able to see the river that lay between it and the town. It came out of the surrounding hills and ran through a deep, sheer-sided gorge in a series of rapids, and, although it was not more than twenty yards across, it was completely unfordable – deep, swift and dangerous, with the banks on both sides clothed with a particularly vicious type of thicket that Neil had told me was aptly named the wait-a-while bush. It took me a couple of hours to reach the one bridge that spanned the gorge, although the distance was less than a mile, so it was evening before I arrived at the market square.

The place boasted two stores, a post office, a police station, a tin church and five pubs, which ranged in descending order from one of some pretension called the Royal Victoria, through the Diggers' Arms, the Nugget and the Miner's Rest, to a ramshackle shed whose roughly painted sign read simply 'O'Donaghue's'. This last was undoubtedly doing the best business, judging by the noise that was coming from it and the number of swags and Irish banjoes, as the long-handled fossickers' shovels were called, that were lined up along the wall outside. I dumped mine with the others and started to push in through the door, partly because I was thirsty after my battle with the wait-a-whiles, but mainly because it looked the sort of place where one might ask a few casual questions without unduly arousing curiosity.

Two or three men squatted in the dust each side of the door, with the unmistakable signs about them that I was beginning to recognize at a glance – the ticket-of-leave men – time-expired convicts – tattered, dirty, gaunt and shifty-eyed – their sentences now served and with the freedom to starve ahead of them, because most were totally unemploy-able. If a farmer wanted a labourer, the authorities were more than willing to assign him a convict who would cost him nothing beyond his food. A 'free' man wanted wages.

The one nearest to me said, 'Garnish, mate?' which was a begging term in convict cant. Neil had strictly warned me against ever giving alms to them, however pitiful the plea, because it inevitably brought others crowding around and was an open invitation to have one's pocket picked in the resultant jostling. I therefore took no notice and pressed on into the low, smoke-filled room, but he tweaked the tail of my jacket and muttered coaxingly, 'I can get you a woman – better than them in there. *They'll* only pox you up – '

I paused and looked at him, because he was still squatting on the ground with his back against the wall, and said, 'Where?'

'Not far,' he said. 'The Magistrate's compound. Lovely stuff – you never saw the like – and clean – ' He had scented business now and was babbling in his eagerness to further the transaction.

'I'd want to see it first,' I said tentatively.

'Sure – sure, mate. I'm not asking you to buy a poke in a poke in a manner of speaking.' He cackled gleefully at his own wit. 'You pays your money and you takes your choice. A choice of four – four real strappers – not like them scrawny cows in there – '

A large red-faced man in a dirty beer-stained apron burst through the crowd from inside and roared, 'If you dirty bludging bastards don't keep away from here I'll have the coppers down to run the bloody lot of you in!' The loungers vanished like startled rats, and the newcomer turned to me apologetically. 'Sorry, mate. I try to keep 'em away, but they keep coming back like flies round a blown sheep. The little swine was after flogging you a woman, was he?'

'Something like that,' I said. 'He was mumbling about the Magistrate's compound but I wasn't interested.'

'I should think not.' He was righteously indignant. 'If you was mug enough to believe him he'd lead you out into the bush for a bunch of his pals to nobble you and roll you for whatever you've got.' He winked confidentially. 'If you're feeling that way there's plenty on tap here – through in the back room. Good beds – short time or all night. Better than up against the beak's back fence.'

'I'll think about it,' I said. 'At the moment it's a pint I want.' I made as if to follow him back into the pub, but then I halted and looked round and heard an urgent 'Phsst!' from the darkness and saw the little man making frantic signs to me round the corner of the building. I went out into the darkness and he sidled up to me.

'What about it, mate?' he enquired. 'Coming? You won't regret it.'

'How much?' I asked.

'Only a few bob – couple for her, couple for me – live and let live – you know – call it half a quid.'

'Lead on,' I told him. I picked up my swag and thrust it at him, but kept the shovel. 'Carry that,' I said. 'And no funny business, or I'll slice your God damned head off with my banjo.'

'No funny business from me, mate. Straight up – hope to die,' he chattered. 'This way – about half a mile. You don't have to worry about coppers. They're all boozing and screwing by this time. You never get a tweet out of them between sundown and kookaburra-fart – not unless some galah starts a fight in O'Donaghue's. Somebody's going to cut that fat bastard's throat for him one night. Hard enough to make a crust as it is, without skrimjaws like him making it harder. Live and let live – that's me name and nature –' He went ahead of me at a Chinaman's trot, with the swag over his shoulder and I had to stride out to keep on his heels, for which I was vaguely grateful, because one can't think too deeply when walking fast, and I didn't want to think just then – certainly not of Caerwen, and of what I was going to see in the near future. 'The bash', she called it, and shrugged it off as of no consequence. 'It's work, like any other – and all a girl can get in London, without a character.' And on the bash she had gone, cheerfully and uncomplainingly, to feed a couple of hungry boys – to keep our wretched little home together – and again on the ship to save my brother's life. Oh God, I was praying, don't let it all have happened again – not hawking herself to the scum and filth of this horrible place for a few coins to keep body and soul together – let her be the real Caerwen – the one that I remembered singing over her cooking – laughing and throwing snowballs on Hampstead Heath – let her –

The little man had halted and he was holding up his hand warningly. We had come to the end of the straggling street with its occasional lighted window, and ahead of us was the darkness of the bush.

'Quiet now, mate,' he cautioned. 'The beak's compound is a couple of hundred yards ahead of us. You couldn't let us have the money now, could you?'

'For you to scarper with and leave me standing here like a gull?' I said. 'What do you take me for, you little rat?'

'I've got to have something to show 'em,' he whined. 'They won't come out else. The soldiers come up here sometimes with no rhino and try and get it for nix. The girls have got to know you've got something in your kick – be reasonable, mate.'

I gave him half-a-crown and rattled some more coins in my pocket. 'I've got quite a lot in my kick,' I told him. 'But I want a lot for it. I want them all out here – one at a time – so I can take my pick. Do you understand? *All* of them.'

'Sure – sure,' he gabbled. 'Don't you worry. They'll be here when I tell 'em you're holding quite substantial. You couldn't keep 'em off with your banjo. Just wait here, mate,' and he scuttled away into the darkness.

The first one came out ten minutes later – a shapeless bundle in the gloom, who demanded her money before proceeding further, in a voice which was, thank God, not Caerwen's. I gave her five shillings and thanked her as politely as the rather peculiar circumstances allowed, but declined her services, and she said, 'Bloody hell – the bastard's mad,' and ran off. The next two arrived together, probably for mutual protection – little wizened creatures who took their money and went back giggling and mystified. There was a pause of another ten minutes then, and I waited, sweating, with my nails digging into my palms. My guide sidled up beside me and said, 'Live and let live, mate, for Chri'sake. This isn't Pitt Street Sydney. There's only four of them.'

I said, 'Get out, or I'll break your bloody neck. Go on – wait on the road, you lousy little peeping Tom, or you don't get another stiver.' He went off like a frightened rabbit – and then the fourth woman came.

I couldn't see her face, but she was taller than any of the others, and my mouth and throat were dry and I couldn't speak. She chuckled softly and said, 'What's the matter, love? Having a bit of difficulty with it, are we?' and I was torn between relief and bitter disappointment, because this wasn't Caerwen either.

I found my voice and said, 'I thought there might have been someone here – someone I knew.' I handed her two half-crowns. 'I'm sorry to have troubled you.'

'Any time at all, love, on the same terms,' she laughed. 'Who was you looking for?'

'A girl called Morgan – '

'Oh – Ginger Taff? Yes – she's here, but she don't do it, the silly cow. Could be making a fortune – Hey! What's the matter? You sick?' She grabbed my arm. But I wasn't sick, although I was shaking like a leaf.

I said, 'Can you get in touch with her – *now?*'

'Sure, we're in the same hut,' she answered. 'But you'll get nowt off *her*, I'm telling you.'

'Just go and tell her that Neil is here, and bring her back,' I said, 'and there's a sovereign in it for you. But please – *please* – don't let anybody else know.'

'You needn't worry – her and me's pals,' she said. 'A quid? My God!'

Another ten minutes passed on leaden feet, then they came back together and I gave the woman her sovereign and she said uneasily, 'Go easy with her, mister. The shock's just about knocked her flat – and she's a good lass. If it wasn't for her me and me baby would have been underground. Go easy – you will go easy, won't you – ' and she kept on saying it, until Caerwen used the only dirty word I ever heard her utter, and drove her off, and then broke down into a storm of weeping interspersed with hysterical laughter and a jumble of Welsh and English and a spate of questions the answers to which she wouldn't listen, until at last I had to shake her, and the strength went from her legs and she sat on the ground, and once more she was crying, but softly now, and with pure happiness.

'But Neil?' she kept repeating. 'Big Martha said Neil, not Ross. Where did she get that from?'

'From me,' I explained. 'I said Neil because I thought you'd believe it more readily, knowing he was out here.'

'Have you seen him? Do you know where he is? Is he all right? He had the fever, you know. But you – ? What are you doing out here? Oh, Ross, boyo – you haven't been in trouble, have you?' Once more the questions were tumbling out, and it was a good half-hour before I was able to get some sense into her, trying desperately to make her keep her voice down, because I was conscious of 'Live-and-let-live' lurking somewhere nearby and eavesdropping. I left her for a time and went in search of him, and found him obediently waiting on the road, so I gave him ten shillings and sent him on his way and then returned to her, and by that time she was once more her own sensible self, and she not only understood the rough escape plan that we had drawn up, but was able considerably to improve upon it.

'Over to Penrith?' she said. 'Then we don't need to go back into Lithgow from here. There's a track from Hassan's Walls that leads to the summit. We worked in the vegetable gardens there when they were starting the zigzag road, and there was a big camp of soldiers and police at the top. We can miss Blackheath that way too – that's full of coppers. There's plenty of water and the men used to snare rabbits – and there's scrub turkeys there. We'll need some copper wire for that. Plenty of flour – and don't forget salt – you don't get the strength from food if you don't use salt – oh – and boots for me – I've only got clogs. The smallest man's pair you can find, with some rags and tallow for me to pack them with. And soap – *please*, boyo – lots of soap. That's the only trouble I've been in here – two beatings for stealing soap from the kitchen and going down to the river at night to bathe and wash my clothes. Oh, boyo – I'm going to wake up and find this is all a dream – I know I am – '

It was another hour before I could persuade her to go back to the compound. 'We'll be here at the same time tomorrow,' I promised. 'I must go now, Caerwen. Neil will be worried, and I'm scared that he might come looking for me. Be careful. That woman – ? Can you trust her to keep her mouth closed?'

'Big Martha? Yes, she's all right. She nearly died when she had a baby, and I helped her. The others might try to sell me for the reward after I've gone, but they'd have to admit that they've been out of the compound at night, and that's a flogging offence – and Big Martha would have the eyes out of them as well. No, I think we're safe enough as far as they're concerned.' She threw her arms around me once more. 'Oh, cariad – to see you both again – my heart's just bursting – '

'Get on with you, you silly bitch,' I said roughly. 'We'll be here tomorrow,' and I pushed her on her way back to the compound.

It was well after dawn before I eventually got back to the ledge, to find Neil in an agony of suspense, which resolved itself into a towering rage immediately I showed my face, and we nearly came to blows before I got it into his thick head that I had actually found her. Thereafter it was almost a repetition of what I had already experienced with Caerwen – unbelief, joy and endless questions – until I swore like a bullock driver at him and slept the sleep of sheer exhaustion until he roused me hours later with the handle of his Irish banjo in my ribs and told me it was getting on for sundown.

We had something to eat and, since I could no longer hold him back, we went openly into town and bought our supplies, then we went into the bush and waited for darkness.

She was already there when we reached the compound, and having had twenty-four hours in which to compose herself, she was the most sensible of the three of us and she wasted no time in extravagant greetings.

'Come on,' she said tersely. 'The soldiers have been paid today. They'll be swarming up here from the pubs before long,' and she led off down the track at a clip that had us gasping in less than a mile.

We halted on the bank of the river, which here ran very rapidly through the gorge, before tumbling in a high waterfall to a dark pool below.

'Careful,' she warned. 'There are stepping-stones across but they're slippery. A man fell in once and – ' She broke off and said, 'Dammo! That's an idea!' and started to strip her coarse grey gown off. 'They never saw him again,' she said.

We left the prison garments on the bank, to tell their mute tale, together with a piece of soap and a tattered towel she had stolen from the compound, and she got dressed in those we had brought, laughing at their lack of elegance but grateful for their warmth, because at this height the nights struck chill, then we pressed on, and any doubts we may have had previously about her strength and stamina were dispelled. She was as tough and agile as a mountain goat, but there was a grace with it as well, and it was a joy to watch her when the dawn came, moving along that narrow track ahead of us. We halted when the sun was well up and, as formerly, moved back into the bush to camp, and we made tea and damper and broiled mutton over the embers, then I wandered off because I knew they had much to talk about, and they had fallen into an awkward, tongue-tied silence.

Things fell into place after that, and the old easy comradeship was re-established. With her hair cropped and a wide-awake pulled down over her tanned face, and the rough miner's jacket and trousers doing at least something to mask the franker feminine contours of her splendid figure, she could have passed easily at a safe distance as a graceful but well-set-up youth, and we debated at length over the advisability of risking marching by day, because we had seen nobody on this track since we started.

'With Ross going ahead to give warning we could put an extra five miles a day on it,' Neil mused.

'With the track twisting and turning like this he'd be out of our sight most of the time,' Caerwen objected. 'And suppose somebody comes up behind us, moving faster? What then?'

'And what's the hurry?' I asked. 'Caerwen's right. We should keep it as it is.' And so we did.

Although the straight distance between Lithgow and Penrith was a mere forty miles according to the atlas, the windings of the track must at least have trebled it, and until we reached the summit of the range the climb was murderous, so it took us nearly two weeks to reach the Nepean, but the time sped by very happily. We snared rabbits on several occasions, and twice we ran down, killed and butchered a sheep from the semi-wild flocks that roamed the eastern slopes of the range, so, although we had to husband our supplies carefully, we fed well, with Caerwen performing miracles with our three billycans.

The days in camp were a sheer delight. We were usually lucky in finding waterholes or small streams in which we could bathe and wash clothes, and we would lie in the shade and relate our experiences since the time we had last been together, bowdlerized and expurgated no doubt, but always vastly entertaining – and at other times I would read to them from my beautiful copy of *Gulliver's Travels*.

Yes – if I had to choose, I would say for myself and the others that those days were the happiest any of us had ever known.

We had to make camp five miles or so downriver from Penrith, because several small farms clustered round it on both banks. I walked on into town after leaving the others in the bush, and replenished our supplies, and I was startled to read among other 'Wanted' notices outside the police station, one concerning Neil, who was described as desperate and dangerous, and the current reward of two hundred pounds was offered for information that would lead to his capture and conviction. I wondered why the notice should appear here in an area so remote from that in which he had escaped, but then I realized that they would have been printed in Bathurst and no doubt distributed by the daily mail coach. There was nothing concerning Caerwen there, I was relieved to notice, and I hoped that our ruse at the river had succeeded in hoodwinking them into the belief that she had drowned.

I went back to our camp realizing that we would have to be considerably more careful from now on, as we were moving into a relatively thickly populated area. We had discussed many plans regarding our progress downriver to Broken Bay and had finally decided to stick to our original method of marching at night and camping during the day as long as the banks afforded a path, but if they didn't then we would have to build a raft.

I explored downriver for a few miles alone on the second day. The path was easy – too easy, because it was well-trodden and obviously frequently used and I met no less than three people – two men and a woman – in the first hour. All were civil enough, but I sensed suspicion in each case, probably not of me personally, but rather the innate resentment of the settled farmer for the nomad. One man did, in fact, put it in so many words. 'Nothing round here for you blokes, mate,' he said. 'There never was any alluvial gold on these coastal plains, and it's no good digging, because you hit water at three feet. I'd push on over the mountains if I was you.' I thanked him politely and said I'd think about it.

We marched quite swiftly on the first two nights, but on the third the track petered out and we found ourselves floundering in endless mangrove swamps, so we retreated into the bush again to look for a more solid inland track, but found nothing going in the right direction. There was, how-ever, a great quantity of floating timber moving quite fast with the current, so, with Caerwen high in a tree keeping watch, Neil and I spent the next day collecting suitable pieces and steering them inshore on to the mud. We then bound them together with strong liana vines into a platform which, while not buoyant enough to support the three of us at the same time, did take one, together with our three swags and clothes, while the others swam and steered.

We pushed out into the stream, and let the current take us. Down here the night air was warm and languorous and the water was pleasantly cool in contrast, and we found that we could swim for an hour or so before feeling cold, so we rotated – two in the water, with one sitting on top snug in a blanket. We had no means of judging distance so it was with some surprise that we realized on the tenth night that the water was salt, and on the eleventh, after losing ourselves several times at places where other rivers joined with ours, we found ourselves out in an open bay, and Neil remembered some horrifying stories of the sharks that infested these waters, and we hurriedly beached the raft and scrambled ashore.

We headed north on foot the next night, along a well-defined though deeply-rutted road, and here we were passing small settlements and isolated farms, and although we had long used all our dry stores except the salt that Caerwen jealously hoarded in a bottle and carefully rationed, we were not short of food, because again the bush swarmed with sheep and we butchered one on an average every second night, and in addition to that we also passed orchards from time to time, and we helped ourselves to oranges, peaches and grapes.

The settlements ceased after the fourth night, when we reckoned we were about a third of the way to Newcastle, but we passed two stagecoach posts, at each of which there was a store, so I was able to walk in, safe in my guise of travelling fossicker, and buy supplies. We had butchered a sheep on that last day, and I had bought potatoes and gathered some fruit, and Caerwen had surpassed herself with a meal that I still remember, and while Neil and I lay back in the shade, full fed and torpid, she had gone down through the bush to the stream.

It was her scream that woke us. Neil leapt to his feet and swore. 'God damn her! I'm always telling her not to bathe after a heavy meal –' and rushed headlong downhill, with me hard on his heels.

But she wasn't in the water. She was on the bank, stark naked and fighting like a fury with one man, while a second leaned back against a tree doubled up with mirth. He swung round as we arrived and brought up a carbine and covered us both with a slight to and fro motion. He was sundried and bewhiskered, and he grinned widely at us, disclosing blackened, gap-toothed gums.

He said amiably, 'All right, cobbers. Share and share alike in the bush. You've had the lot up to now. We been following you.'

I checked, but Neil continued straight on at him, and the man fired and Neil went down. The other one released Caerwen and dived for his carbine, which was lying on the ground, but I managed to kick it to one side. The first one fired again and I heard the round go past me, but Neil was only foxing, and he grabbed the other's ankles and brought him down and I jumped on to the second man's back and flattened him. And now Neil was laughing – if it could be called laughter. It was perhaps more a roar of exultation. He had a handful of the other's beard and he was banging his head on the ground. The man underneath me whined, 'Fair do's, mate. We didn't mean no harm – just a bit of a joke like – '

I let him rise after I had picked up his carbine, and only then did I turn to Caerwen. She was lying on her side, and she moved slightly as I approached her. I think she was reaching for her clothes, which she had obviously washed and spread over a bush to dry. I dropped to my knees beside her and gathered her into my arms. There was a neat, bloodless hole between her breasts, but underneath her a crimson patch was spreading over a carpet of fallen leaves. She smiled and wrinkled her nose as she was wont to do when some small thing had gone awry. And then she died.

Neil had come up behind me. I did not dare look up and meet his eyes. He turned away and I heard one of the men scream, 'No, mate – no! I didn't harm her – it was *his* shot took her!' and the other was babbling incoherently. Then there were two more shots and the babbling had ceased.

Neil was sitting on the ground, and I hope to God I never hear a man weep like that again.

Chapter Five

We buried her in a glade of beautiful red-gum trees, and although I doubted the wisdom of it, Neil carved her name together with his own on a rough wooden cross and set it over the grave. The bodies of the two bushrangers we dragged some distance off and left in the scrub to rot. I think we must both have been in a state of deep shock, because I remember little of our onward march that first night, or indeed that of the next, but on the second day I had started to recover, and to worry about Neil. He said he wanted a drink, and I promised I'd buy beer in a billycan at the next store we came to, but he brushed my offer aside impatiently and insisted on pressing forward along the road in broad daylight.

I said, 'This is sheer foolishness. We're almost there now. Why risk everything?'

'I don't give a damn,' he said sullenly. 'I'm sick of skulking in the dark like a bloody rat. And I don't want beer. I want rum.'

'Not while I'm with you,' I said firmly.

'Then piss off on your own,' he told me. 'I'll not be dictated to by you or anybody else.'

'What do you think she'd say if she were here?' I asked him, and he hit me full in the face. I picked up my swag and walked off up the track, and after a time I heard him running through the dust behind me and he caught my arm and spun me round, and again he was weeping. He tried to say he was sorry but the words were sticking in his throat, so he wiped the blood off my mouth with his sleeve and we walked on in silence.

Things improved a little between us, but I knew that inside him was a deep void that would never completely cease to ache. The tragedy of it all was that even he had been unaware of the depth of his feeling for her, until it was too late. I was missing her warm, generous presence as a man would miss a well-loved sister – but he had had the heart wrenched out of him.

He gave no difficulty after that, but by unspoken mutual consent we took to the road openly for the last two days, which passed uneventfully except for one disquieting incident. It was very hot, and we came to a stream a few miles out of town, and we decided to have a bath and to spruce up a little. There was nobody in sight at the time, so we moved a few hundred yards off the road, stripped and dived into the water, and lay in the shallows, and I looked up and saw a man standing on the bank just above us. I muttered a warning to Neil, for his flayed back was towards the man, and he turned over and slid into deeper water, and I climbed out and pulled my trousers on and went towards the stranger. I don't know what I intended to do, but the thought of that two hundred pounds reward flashed across my mind, and I was certainly in no way prepared to let my brother be endangered, come what may.

The man stood his ground and greeted me amiably enough as I came up to him. He was middle-aged, bearded and sunburnt, and he carried a swag like ours together with an Irish banjo. He was obviously a fossicker and he looked as if he had travelled a long way.

He said, 'Hello, mate. That water looks good. I think I'll have a go meself. You come far?'

'From the north,' I lied. 'We're making for Sydney.'

'Mind if I tag along?' he asked. 'I've heard that there's a couple of bushrangers to the south. Three of us together would be safer than one on his own. You're not carrying shooters by any chance, are you?'

My mind was working furiously. I ignored his question about guns and said, 'Sure – tag along by all means – but have your swim first. We're going to camp here.'

'Thanks,' he said gratefully. 'My name's Jim Ward. Ticket-of-leave two year ago,' he added frankly, 'and I been scratching ever since. Had a bit of luck a couple of times, but I always pissed it up against the wall like a damn fool. Can't keep off the booze, you see – '

He stripped off, still talking garrulously, and waded into the water, and I saw that his back, also, bore the marks of the lash. Neil had come out by now and we hurriedly dressed, and under cover of collecting firewood we moved our swags into the bush and then made off quickly back to the road, and turned north and kept going, fast.

We walked for the rest of the daylight hours, lying low in the scrub at the side of the road from time to time to see if he was following us, but we saw no sign of him.

'I should have killed him,' Neil said, and the sheer matter-of-factness of his tone startled me, because he meant just that.

'For God's sake!' I protested. 'In cold blood? The man was probably quite harmless.'

'None of them is,' he said flatly, 'any more than I am myself. It doesn't take long for that hell to turn a man into an animal. For two hundred quid any old lag would turn his mother in.'

'You're talking like a fool,' I said angrily.

He shrugged. 'Maybe,' he said. 'But if that fellow does come after us I'm taking no chances. He'll go the same way as the other two.'

'That was different,' I said. 'I'd have killed them myself if you hadn't. But not some poor devil who has done us no harm – '

He shook his head obstinately. 'He knows I'm a convict on the run,' he said. 'Therefore I represent two hundred pounds to him. That and nothing more.'

'A convict perhaps,' I said. 'He saw your back – but why should he assume that you were on the run? His back was marked, too.'

'He told you he was ticket-of-leave, didn't he? They always do, as soon as you meet them – and they'll show you the ticket quite proudly. I didn't show *my* ticket, so that could mean only one thing to him – I hadn't got one. That's why he wanted to stay with us – so he could tip off the first trooper we met.' He was silent for some time, then he said,

'I'm sorry, Ross, but you've got to understand *now* – so it would not be a shock to you later, if I ever did something – something really bad – I'm different now. I can't help it – but I know it. I'm *different*.'

And, although I argued hotly with him, inwardly I had to agree. He *was* different, but it was only becoming apparent now that Caerwen had gone. She, I felt, could have held him. But only she.

We came at last to Newcastle, and I was amazed at its size and the bustle of its streets, because Neil had spoken of it as purely a convict station of bad reputation. It had, until quite recently, been known as Port Hunter, and there had been persistent rumours of tremendous gold strikes along the river of the same name that flowed into its spacious harbour, but they had never come to anything, although coal in easily worked seams had been found just below the surface. This was now being brought down to the wharves of Newcastle and shipped by sea the eighty-odd miles to Sydney, and engineers had come out from England to survey the route between the two cities, with a view to constructing what could well be Australia's first railway. Coal was also being sent all the way across the Pacific to California, and there were no less than six American clippers in port when we arrived, and I could feel my excitement rising, and Neil seemed to be shut of his evil mood of these last few unhappy days.

We found clean, if spartan, lodgings in a house some distance from the waterfront and, after a good night's sleep, we set out to explore the town. Our clothes had suffered in our passage through the bush, so we bought new outfits and had decent haircuts and I had my straggly adolescent beard shorn. Neil decided to keep his. It was a splendid affair, and when it had been trimmed by the barber I doubt if I would have recognized him had I come upon him unexpectedly. We had an excellent meal of fish and beef, two things the taste of which we both had almost forgotten, and afterwards we visited a music hall and then, tired but content, we went back to our lodgings. We had had a reckoning, and on counting our money we were pleasantly surprised to find that we still had a hundred and eighty pounds and some odd shillings left.

'There'll be no need to rely on whitebirders now,' Neil said. 'We can go to a proper shipping agency and book our passages in the ordinary way. They shouldn't be more than fifty or sixty pounds each.'

I made a round of the docks the following day. Only two of the Yankee clippers were alongside. I boarded both of them, but the first already had her passenger accommodation filled to capacity, and although we could have got berths on the second one at seventy-five pounds each she was calling in at Sydney before leaving for San Francisco, so I decided not to risk it, particularly since the mate asked me if our 'clearance papers' were in order.

'What clearance papers?' I asked.

'These God-damned passport things they've got going now,' he told me. 'All on account of gold at both ends and some pretty tough guys skipping from one place to the other. Your cops and ours have got a deal between 'em. No papers, no passage.' His right eyelid drooped just a fraction. 'It don't worry me none. I can always forget to ask for 'em until we're out at sea if it's any inconvenience to you.'

'Oh, passports,' I said. 'Sure – we've got those all right. They're back at our hotel. Fine – I'll talk it over with my friend and we'll come back later.'

'Don't leave it too long,' he said. He dropped his voice and glanced meaningly at a couple of men leaning idly on the rail at the head of the gangway. 'Some of these guys are getting a mite inquisitive about one or two of our passengers.'

I nodded and went down on to the wharf and felt rather than saw their appraising look as I passed them. Neil was waiting in the shade of the dock office and I walked past him without a glance and continued on along the waterfront until I was out of sight of the ship. He caught me up some minutes later and he knew without my having to tell him that something had gone badly wrong.

'Passports?' he said, dismayed. 'Damn and blast it. Just when things were going smoothly.'

We sat all that long afternoon considering this new and totally unforeseen problem, and in the end it was decided that I should go to the source of these wretched documents and find out how they were issued and, most importantly, what means of identification I should require.

'It would probably mean that you'd have to get some respectable bastard to vouch for you,' Neil said gloomily. 'That's a bit of a facer. We don't know any.'

'I do,' I said. 'Surgeon Palmer. His regiment, the Nineteenth of Foot, is in Western Australia.'

'It would take a bloody year to get a letter to him and an answer back,' he said, and my temper frayed.

'At least I'm trying to do something about it,' I snapped. 'If I could get a passport here, you could sail out on it, and then I could go down to Sydney and get another. Who's to know?'

He shrugged sullenly, and I could see that he was slipping back into one of his ugly moods, and I knew, even as I argued in its favour, that a wait of some months would shorten our chances of a clean escape proportionately, because he would not be able to stand the suspense.

'All right then,' I asked hopelessly. 'What do you suggest?'

'Only one thing for it,' he replied. 'Take up the mate's offer – and sail without passports. He'll want bribing, of course, but once he's taken our money he'll have to keep his mouth shut.'

'She's calling at Sydney,' I objected.

'Well, we just lie low on board while she's there.'

'I don't like it.'

'Neither do I – but it's better than waiting around here, with the chance of being picked up always hanging over our heads.'

And so it went on, until wearily I had to give way, and I went back to the ship in the evening, and by a fortunate chance ran into the mate on the wharf as he was making for the nearest pub.

'We're sailing on the tide tomorrow morning,' he told me over drinks. 'Come aboard tonight about eleven. But I'll have to see your passport, and the other guy's, before I collect your fares.' He studied the bottom of his glass and then swivelled his eyes round to meet mine, 'Unless you've mislaid 'em somewhere – in which case we might be able to come to some arrangement.'

'Such as?' I asked.

'Such as a hundred pounds on top,' he said flatly.

'I haven't got it,' I told him.

'Damn bad luck, stranger,' he said, and finished his drink, and I turned away hopelessly and went out of the bar, but he followed me into the darkness.

'What *have* you got?' he wheedled. 'The one-fifty goes to the skipper, but I'm the guy that takes all the risks.'

'Twenty,' I said. 'I can't bargain with you any further. I just haven't got another stiver in the world.'

'The other guy?'

'He hasn't either. Good night.' I walked off, but again he caught up with me.

'All right,' he said. 'But I'll want it as soon as you come aboard – the fares and the sweetener for me. No putting it off until we're at sea. Understand?'

'I understand.'

'Good. Eleven o'clock. That's six bells. When you hear them from the poop, come up the gangway – because by then I'll have invited the cops down to my cabin for a drink. If you don't hear the bells, don't come aboard, because the cops'll still be on deck. Just wait around in that case until I come down for you.' He sighed and said dolefully, 'Why am I always the God-damned mug in these deals, while the other guys collect the dollars?'

A fine rain was falling and a cold wind was making a chop on the surface and causing the ship to strain at the mooring lines. There was a dim lantern at the head of the gangway but we couldn't see if anybody was standing there. Behind us, in the town, a clock struck eleven and I held my breath waiting for the ship's bell and I could hear Neil cursing in an undertone. Then they came – six tinny chimes in three pairs, and Neil gripped my arm convulsively and we went forward and up, and the gangway was creaking beneath our weight. My left hand was clutching the money inside my pocket tightly and Neil was behind me with the carpet-bag I had bought to carry our belongings.

A figure loomed up in the lantern's faint glow, and the mate whispered, 'This way – and no noise,' and we tiptoed for'ard behind him. He came up to a deckhouse abaft the foremast. 'I'm going to lock you in the bosun's store until after we drop the pilot,' he said. 'Right – you got it?'

I handed the money to him and heard him catch his breath sharply at the thinness of the roll. 'You trying to be funny, mister?' he said menacingly. 'What the hell's this?'

'Three fifties and four fives,' I explained. 'Check it under the lantern if you don't believe me.'

He grunted and said, 'Take your word for it. Right. Keep it quiet until I come for you.' He closed the heavy storm door and we heard the key turn. Neil struck a match and we saw in its brief light that we were in a space about ten feet square, most of which was taken up by barrels and coils of rope, and there was a smell of paint and tallow that was almost tangible. We sat on the deck and waited.

Seven bells struck – half-past eleven – and then eight – midnight. We were cold and cramped after waiting in the rain and I was dreading the hours ahead of us. 'Until we drop the pilot,' he had said. We weren't sailing until dawn – that was about six o'clock. I didn't know how long the pilot would be aboard –

Footsteps were approaching along the deck and there was a low mumble of voices, then the heavy key turned in the lock and a lantern shone in our eyes so that we couldn't see anything beyond it.

A man said, 'Bail up and come out, both of you. No monkey tricks or we'll shoot.'

Neil said, in something between a snarl and a sob, 'You bastards. Come in and get us, if you've got the guts,' and I felt him shaping up into what I thought was a boxing stance, and I realized the hopelessness of it – and I certainly hadn't the desperate courage it would take to face bullets, so I said,

'It's no good, Neil,' and put my hands up. Other hands came forward into the light, holding handcuffs – then something flew past my head from behind and I felt a violent shove in the back and Neil yelled into my ear, '*Run!*' – and the instinct of a lifetime of obedience to him took over and I dashed forward. I cannoned into the man holding the lantern, and he dropped it. Neil had me by the arm and we continued our rush straight across the deck. The bulwarks loomed before us and I felt Neil tense and jump, and I jumped with him – up and outwards – and I seemed to hang motionless in mid-air – then I was in the water, and still that iron grip was on my arm. I struggled and my head broke the surface, and Neil muttered, 'Quiet, you bloody fool. Just drift,' so I dog-paddled beside him. Already the current had taken us clear of the stern and I could see a red glow amidships, and flames were leaping up towards her lower rigging. A voice screamed above us, 'Christ Almighty! The paint locker's alight. Pumps! Man the pumps, you fools!'

I would not have thought it possible had I not seen it with my own eyes, although looking back I suppose it was inevitable. A wooden deckhouse filled with paint, turpentine, tar and tallow, with the oil from the broken lantern flaming in its midst. The whole waist of the ship went up like a mighty torch, oil-dressed teak decks and tarred hempen shrouds, guys and braces. In a matter of minutes the main courses, loosened in their brails ready for sailing, were afire, and the flames were spreading to the other masts. The ship hadn't a chance.

We were clear of the light cast by the fire and drifting fast downstream. We could hear bells ringing ashore and they were being echoed from ships at anchor all around us.

Neil said, 'Well, even if we drown we'll have the satisfaction of costing the swine a hell of a lot of money.'

'What do you think happened?' I asked him miserably.

'Pretty obvious, isn't it?' he answered. 'The son of a whore guessed we were on the run and sold us to the cops. If I meet him again I'll kill him, even if I swing for it.'

My teeth were chattering. I said, 'If we don't land somewhere soon you won't live to swing for anybody,' and for some reason it struck him as funny, because he laughed and pushed my head under the water playfully and I spluttered curses at him, and somehow, absurd though it may seem now, it served to raise us both from the hopeless despair that had been threatening to engulf us. Penniless, adrift and on the run, but, for the moment at least, we were still free. And then, as if to match our momentary light-heartedness, we heard other laughter close by – and we bumped softly against wooden planking.

It was an anchored ship, and we were swept along its length, our fingers scrabbling for some sort of projection to hang on to, but nothing broke its slimy sides until, as we were resigned to continuing our seaward drift, we came up to a longboat moored amidships, and we scrambled over its low freeboard and lay gasping in its bilge. The laughing was shrill and high-pitched and it seemed to be very close to us, and I realized that the ship was a small one and the main-deck was only a few feet above us.

'Chinks,' whispered Neil as someone gabbled in a strange tongue. He fumbled around in the darkness. 'Let's see if there are any oars here, and they won't be so sodding happy in the morning when they find their boat gone.'

But there weren't any oars, so we debated the wisdom of casting off and letting the current take us where it willed, but abandoned the idea.

'A drifting boat is anybody's property,' Neil said. 'Somebody is bound to come and take it in tow. We had better swim on when we've got our breath back.' He stood up, steadying himself against the side of the ship and looked over the bulwarks for some minutes, then lowered himself down beside me again.

'They're looking at the burning ship – laughing their heads off,' he told me. 'This is a junk – that's a Chinese sailing boat. I've seen them once or twice in Port Jackson.'

Looking up, I saw a man's head silhouetted darkly against the sky and I gave Neil a warning nudge. I thought for a moment that the newcomer had seen us, but he obviously hadn't because he merely cast off the painter and towed the boat down astern and re-tied us to the rail of the high poop, and I was greatly relieved at this temporary respite because the very thought of getting back into the water appalled me, although I knew we would have to face it again before dawn. Neil seemed to sense my reluctance. He said, 'It's no good starting to swim again until we can see the shore, or we'll be finishing up as shark bait. Christ, I'm cold. I wish I'd held on to our bag instead of throwing it at the coppers. There was a bottle of rum in it.'

We must have slept then through sheer exhaustion, because the next thing I was aware of was the sun just appearing over the horizon ahead of us, past the hull of the junk, which was under way beneath the spread of her huge single, slatted sail, and we were bouncing and skipping at the end of a long towline. I sat up and gaped around. The coast was a low, misty blue line on the western horizon and the junk was standing away from it, close-hauled and sailing superbly on a brisk breeze. I woke Neil and he said tonelessly, 'A long swim if these yellow gents turn nasty,' and then laughed again, but this time without mirth.

They saw us after about an hour – first the helmsman who happened to glance astern, and then the rest of the crew who came tumbling up on to the poop at his startled yell. They backed the big sail and hauled us in alongside and beckoned us to come aboard and my throat went dry at the sight of vicious knives in the hands of most of them, but once they had seen how miserably harmless we obviously were, they seemed more amused than angry. A venerable old codger with a pigtail that came nearly down to his heels chattered angrily at the rest of the crew, and I thought that he was telling them to throw us over the side, but he appeared merely to be upbraiding them for lack of courtesy, because we were then offered water and immediately afterwards a colourless spirit that nearly burned the gullets out of us, and finally some rice and fish which, while strange to our palates, cheered us enormously for, as Neil muttered wryly, they'd hardly feed men whose throats they intended to cut. There seemed to be about ten of them besides the old man, to whom they all deferred, and one at least had a few words of broken English. He was a big, raw-boned man with a villainous cast in one eye which gave him a most sinister look which was, however, belied by a cheerful grin.

He said, 'Captin he say whaffor you come along this piecee boat?'

'Fall in water – make swim – make climb in boat – plenty dark,' Neil answered, miming the actions.

There was a long colloquy between the squinting giant and the old man, then came the next question.

'Captin he say maybe you get drunk – yes?' He went through the motions of raising a glass to his lips and staggering. I was virtuously about to deny this, but Neil murmured, 'Leave the talking to me. I've dealt with these buggers before,' then he nodded and felt his head gingerly and winced. 'Drink plenty too much,' he agreed ruefully. The big man translated again and what he said appeared to afford all of them the most exquisite amusement. The 'captin' spoke at length and the other turned to us and said, 'Captin, he say bad joss turn back. You come along us. All li'?'

'All li',' Neil answered and beamed upon the company. 'We come. Bring plenty good joss.' He slid his hands up each of his opposite sleeves and bowed several times to the 'captin', then to all of the crew in turn. This seemed to meet with general approval, and the bows were returned. Neil said to me, 'Copy me, you bloody idiot. Don't stand there gawping.' So I went through the same motions, after which one of them obligingly threw a couple of quilted mats down under the bulwarks and invited us to take our ease.

'But how did you know all about Chinese?' I asked Neil in awe.

He shrugged nonchalantly. 'Just a matter of keeping my eyes and ears open,' he said. 'There were some caves up in the mountains near Bathurst that were full of birds something like swallows. They used to make mud nests, and the Chinks were always after them, but they weren't allowed to go up there. We used to collect them on the sly and swap them for tobacco and food.'

123

'What did they want the nests for?'

'They used to scrape the slime out of them and make soup of it. There's no need to go green round the gills,' he added as I shuddered. 'It was very good. I've had some. They're very fond of soup. Down on the coast they used to make it out of sharks' fins and sea slugs.'

'That stuff we've just eaten?' I asked faintly. 'I mean – ?' I couldn't finish.

'It *tasted* like fish,' he said solemnly, 'but you can never be certain. Dogs, cats, kangaroo tails, anything that isn't actually shit – and I'm not absolutely certain about *that* – is food to a Chinaman. You must never refuse anything they give you to eat. That's a terrible insult. Sheeps' eyes and pigs' balls are regarded as a great delicacy – ' But by this time I was hanging over the bulwarks and heaving up my inside. Behind me I could hear Neil roaring with laughter.

We stood on north all the rest of the day, with the coast a good ten miles away on the port beam, and I marvelled at the simple efficiency of the junk's rig, that could be handled comfortably by two men, even when changing course. She had one great main mast stepped amidships, with very much smaller fore and mizzen masts, on the very tip of the bows and on the poop, respectively, which were unshipped and laid on deck when not in use. She looked very much like pictures I had seen of Elizabethan galleons – low in the prow and high astern, and it seemed that the only metal on board was in the knives the crew carried – the hull and decks being held together with wooden pegs. Her square sails were stiffened by horizontal bamboo spars from the ends of which ran impossibly slender lines that appeared to be no thicker than cobbler's twine, but which were actually of tremendous strength, and it was in the handling of these that the skill lay, because with them the sails could be trimmed to a nicety, and the seemingly clumsy craft could sail closer to the wind than any modern windjammer I have ever seen. The rudder was huge and could be raised and lowered vertically, so that when it was at its full depth it acted also as a keel, but when raised, either in shallow water or skimming along on a fair wind, it did not diminish the vessel's speed by its dragging action. All this, and more, I learned during the next few days as we stood steadily north. On that first day I was too busy eyeing the preparations the cook was making for the evening meal.

But I need not have worried. His equipment consisted merely of a chopping-block and two or three large pots, and all were kept spotlessly clean, and the raw materials, far from being slimy birds' nests or cats and dogs, were beautiful fish that they caught on trailing lines, and fresh meat and vegetables that they had brought from Newcastle. The squinter, who told us his name was Ho Chang, gave us each a beautiful little porcelain bowl and two slender bamboo sticks about a foot in length. 'Chow bowl, chopsticks,' he explained. 'You keep. No man take other man's bowl. That belong him – all time. All li'?'

The meal was served on deck, the crew squatting in a circle round a huge platter of rice and a series of bowls of various sizes from which they all helped themselves and, when they saw our diffidence, Neil and me also. We made a very clumsy showing at first with our chopsticks, but we persevered and got the hang of their use before we finished.

And then a curious ceremony took place. Each man produced a small lamp of peculiar design and a pipe unlike any I had ever seen before, with a long thick wooden stem and a diminutive bowl at the end, and they took blobs of treaclish substance on slender needles and twirled them in the flames of their lamps and then inhaled the smoke deeply down into their lungs. Only the helmsman and the old captain refrained, the latter seeming to disapprove of the whole thing. Ho Chang offered us each a draw at his pipe, but Neil politely declined on both our accounts.

'Opium,' he explained to me in an undertone. 'Most of them smoke it and it's supposed to kill them in the end. One or two of the convicts took to it at Bathurst. I tried it myself a couple of times but it made me sick. I think it's best left alone.'

One by one the crew seemed to lapse into a sort of coma

which differed from ordinary sleep in that their eyes remained open, as if they were watching with complete absorption something which they alone could see. They were peaceful enough, but I still found it vaguely frightening. Opium in itself was familiar – one bought it in London in pill form for stomach complaints – but this was something entirely different – and chilling.

On and on we sailed, due north on a following wind, and the weather got warmer by the day, and the coast remained a blue thread to the west, and we both found time hanging heavily on our hands. I would have given anything for some books, and I was bitterly regretting the loss of my beautiful copy of *Gulliver*, which had been in the carpet bag that Neil threw at the police.

For want of something to occupy our minds we started to pick up a few phrases of Chinese from Ho Chang, which was not easy, because we found that one simple monosyllabic word could mean as many as three totally different things, according to the tone of one's voice, but, again, we persevered. Ho Chang was a natural teacher, patient yet firm, and he was the only literate man in the crew. He had some beautiful scrolls rolled into bamboo cylinders, and he used to read to the others, holding their attention by the hour, and it was he who first aroused my interest in their beautiful calligraphy, where one character could represent a word or a whole sentence, an interest which remains with me to this day. We evolved a system of communication between us in a compound of his pidgin English and our newly acquired Chinese that was in itself a minor miracle of semantics.

'This Chinese talk no ploper talk,' he told me one day. 'This Canton man talk – *coolie* talk – ' he gestured contemptuously towards some of the other sailors. 'Ploper talk *Mandarin* talk – Peking talk. I teach you – you teach me ploper English talk.'

And so we started 'ploper' mutual lessons that lasted five or six hours a day, and his pidgin improved, although never could I break him of his national tendency to turn the letter 'r' into 'l' – and along with my instruction in Cantonese came that of Mandarin – the language of the Court and the scholar.

He, I gathered, was the son of a high civil official in the north and he had got himself involved in some political trouble and had found it expedient to disappear for a time. This, in itself, formed a sort of bond of friendship between us. They realized, of course, that we were fugitives, as Neil no longer bothered to hide the scars on his back.

'It all li',' Ho Chang assured me. 'Policeman our side bad man, same like policeman your side. We don't like – we don't talk. You all li' along us Hong Kong side.'

I had heard of Hong Kong as a small island off the South China coast that had been ceded to Britain after the war of 1841, but I knew little beyond that, although some of the sailors on the *Boadicea* had been there, and spoke slightingly of it. This, I learnt, was the junk's home port.

'Velly good place,' Ho Chang told me. 'Plentee business – you come my side – want foleign devil compladore make plentee money.'

I could never quite understand in those early days what he meant by 'compradore', although he had made the meaning of 'foreign devil' abundantly clear. It meant quite simply anybody who was not Chinese, and was not in itself a pejorative so much as a stressing of the difference between them and the rest of the world. Whatever he meant, however, it would appear that he wanted a European to go into business with him. I talked this over with Neil but he was not impressed.

'You can't trust them,' he told me flatly. 'Hong Kong is British – as British as New South Wales – and we'll probably find there's a reward for us out there too. No – the first port we come to we skin out, and jump the first ship sailing for a non-British port, even if we have to stow away.'

I didn't argue with him, but in spite of his slight prior knowledge of the Chinese I felt he was wrong in this instance – and I instinctively trusted Ho Chang.

Although the coast was still visible on our port beam one could feel that we had now entered the tropics. The water under our keel was lighter and clearer, and frequently one caught glimpses of coral beneath us – white, pink, green, in beautiful convolutions – with multi-coloured fish darting into the light from forests of seaweed. And then we saw land on our starboard side as well. First it was just one small palm-crested island of incredible beauty and it tapered off into a long coral reef which just broke the surface of the sea, and we could hear the roar of the surf the other side and see white spray rising high against the blue of the sky. Then came more islands, and more reefs, until they looked like pearls threaded on a long white string. I remembered seeing in the atlas the line of the Great Barrier Reef, which extended along the north-eastern coast of Australia for over a thousand miles, and I would have given my ears to have had that much-thumbed volume with me now, or anything else that had ever been written about it. As it was I could only look, and wonder, and store for future reference.

I had long been puzzled why this vessel had been so far south, and why she was now apparently returning to Hong Kong empty, but I had thought it impolite to question Ho Chang. It was explained one day as we came in close to one of the islands and the great sail was lowered for the first time, and the anchor dropped in crystal clear water.

'Tlepang,' Ho Chang said to me, and then added, 'Tlo-kus.' But neither word meant anything to me until he pulled a little mother-of-pearl amulet from inside his shirt and showed it to me. 'Tlo-kus,' he repeated, and pointed down into the water. 'Here we get. Velly good. Plentee money Hong Kong side.' That I understood, but not the 'tlepang', although he went into the pantomime of eating.

'Fish?' I suggested, but he shook his head.

'Bime-by I show,' he said, and went and helped to pull the longboat round alongside.

Three of the crew had now stripped to the merest wisp of cloth round their loins, and the knives from which they were never separated, and they had nets round their necks. They dropped over the side and we watched them swimming down to the coral. They were down for what seemed an unbeliev-ably long time, but we could not see what they were doing as clouds of white sand were rising from the bottom. At last they broke surface and handed their nets over while they rested with their hands on the side of the junk. Then they went down again, and again and again – six times in all – and their harvest was being sorted and appraised on deck. It consisted mainly of shells rather like enlarged cockles, but there were also a few others that I recognized as oysters, which were common enough in London markets. The rest of the crew were squatting in a circle deftly opening the shells with the points of their knives and swallowing the contents. The shells themselves they laid out in rows for the captain's inspection.

'Tlo-kus,' said Ho Chang again, picking up one of the bigger ones and showing the inside to me. It was pure mother-of-pearl – all blue-green iridescence that caught the full spectrum as he twisted it in the sun. He picked up some of the oyster shells and shrugged. 'These – no good,' he said, and tossed them over the side. So, tlo-kus for mother-of-pearl, oysters for eating, I concluded.

Then one of the divers brought up two hideous-looking objects that resembled nothing so much as three-foot-long black sausages that wobbled like jelly.

'Those are the slugs I told you about,' Neil said, and Ho Chang said, 'Tlepang.'

We went ashore as the sun dipped below the coastline and they made a fire of driftwood and boiled the horrible trepang in a big iron pot, then hung them in the smoke to dry. They seemed to value these highly, far above the trokus in fact, and I heard the captain upbraiding some of the crew for cutting pieces of the blubberlike flesh off and guzzling it. We all stayed ashore that night, and I saw, and tasted, my first coconut, and the cook broiled freshly-caught fish in the hot ashes. It was a brilliantly moonlit night and I heard Neil catch his breath and murmur, 'Jesus Christ, what wouldn't I give if Caerwen could have seen all this.'

I received further enlightenment from Ho Chang as we sat round the fire after our meal.

'Bling out Chinese food to Sydney – jinjah – lice – soya –

dly fish – dly duck – longtime egg – Chinese clothe – all thing Chinese people no can get Sydneyside. Take back to Hong Kong all thing no can get that side. Tlepang, shark fin, that all li' – soldier, police this side say maskee, don't wollee. Tlokus – no – they don't like – sometime send ship – big gun go boom-boom – we lun like hell. Wellee funny,' he explained at length.

'Poaching,' said Neil and looked worried. 'The navy gets after them, does it? I hope to God we don't run into a bloody cutter *this* trip.'

But we did, the very next day. She was sailing south, close-hauled against the stiff breeze that was behind us – a big fast sloop that ran up the white ensign and fired a warning gun, and my heart stopped. We were actually diving for trokus at the time and there was a pile of shells on deck and we could see an officer standing in the weather shrouds with a telescope trained on us.

Neil said tensely, 'Over the side and swim for the reef.' But the captain, completely unperturbed, had already given the order to hoist the big sail, and the anchor was coming up fast, and the divers, warned by hammering on the hull, popped up like corks and clambered aboard. The junk drove forward, and the sloop swung hard round on full helm and came storming on after us.

Ship for ship, starting from scratch, I think the junk would have had the legs of the other, but we had been halted, and the sloop had the advantage of a flying start and she was gaining on us hand over fist. She fired another round from her bow-chaser and the shot bounced and skittered over the surface obliquely across our bows. The old captain was standing beside the helmsman, calmly and unhurriedly giving him steering directions, and he caught my eye and winked like a mischievous Cockney schoolboy eluding a lumbering peeler. He twittered an order softly to Ho Chang, who chuckled throatily and relayed it to the crew, and they manned the light lines that ran from the ends of the flexible sail battens, then with a crash the helmsman swung the heavy tiller hard over and the junk buried her lee scuppers in a smother of white water as she heeled in a ninety-degree turn. The sloop, now a mere cablelength off our stern, tried the same manoeuvre, which was in effect the dreaded gybe that I had been warned about on the *Boadicea*, because she now hadn't the searoom to go about in the accepted manner, but it was too late and she went crashing head on to the reef, her boom thrashing wildly from side to side, jib and staysail blown out in ribbons and her bow high out of the water, pointing skyward, fastheld by the jagged coral just below the surface. The captain winked again and the wrinkled yellow parchment of his face split in a wide grin, and the crew, retrimming the huge sail to its former balance, chattered joyously, and I saw, and for the first time really appreciated, the wonder of that thousand-year-old rig that could stand up to this sort of treatment, where heavier modern spars failed.

'Wellee good,' Ho Chang grunted. 'Only one piecee gun-ship this side. Plentee tlo-kus now. No more boom-boom.'

'Thank Christ for that,' Neil said fervently, and breathed again. 'She's a fixture there now for all time. I hope the sharks get them.'

On we sailed, stopping to dive at spots where they seemed to know the shells would be plentiful as if by instinct, because they used no charts, so it could not have been by any fore-knowledge recorded from previous voyages. I asked Ho Chang about this, and he shrugged and tapped his eyes and then his nose. 'Make plentee look-see – talk to Wander Joss. All li',' he answered, and I was none the wiser.

The stops were more frequent the further north we travelled and I saw that the reef was closing in nearer to the mainland more every day, until towards the end we were sailing in a lagoon that was sometimes no more than a mile or so across. Trepang was more plentiful here and we had to make longer stops to boil it, which pleased Neil and me because here we could make ourselves useful collecting fire-wood and tending the pots, thus freeing the others for diving, and the opportunities it afforded for wandering over the islands and also through the bush of the mainland on occasion were a mixture of ecstasy and frustration. The wonders of the botany and marine life of the place were countless, but I had nothing with which to make notes or sketches. I remembered a book Neil had brought me to St Caldbec's that dealt with this very coast, and I would have given my right arm to have had it with me now. It was by Sir Joseph Banks, the naturalist who had accompanied Captain Cook in the *Endeavour* when this vast land had been claimed by the British in 1770, and who had, in fact, named their first landing place Botany Bay.

There were signs of life ashore now for the first time – stark naked savages who flitted silently into the bush on our approach, like black ghosts, and once one of the crew had a narrow escape when a spear came out from the undergrowth fringing the beach and nearly transfixed him.

Our holds were full at last, and the stench of the trepang was overpowering, but it seemed to send the Chinese into transports of delight. We spent a day filling the huge porcelain water jars from a spring, and another gathering fruit and coconuts, and we were about to weigh anchor when on what was to be the very last dive one of the men brought up a cluster of oysters, and as they opened them there was an excited outcry – and I saw my first pearl. It was the size of a pea, pale, translucent and beautiful, and even the captain was momentarily stirred out of his normal preternatural calm, particularly when, from the same cluster, another three came to light.

We stayed for some more days in that anchorage, until the whole of the bed was cleared, but we found no more. Ho Chang said, 'Wander Joss come like that – altogether one place – then no more good joss long time. Bad joss all time here every place.'

So on we went, and suddenly, dramatically, mainland and reef ceased, and we were in the open sea and the captain set off a string of fireworks and threw coconuts and fruit into the wake, while the rest of them beat brass gongs and blew into conch shells.

'Send away bad joss – bring good Wander Joss. Bime-by we go Hong Kong side,' Ho Chang explained.

They brought up a beautiful porcelain bowl then and lashed it to a projection in the deck in front of the tiller, and half-filled it with the colourless rice spirit that they had given us the day we came aboard, and I thought this was a libation to the good Wander Joss – but it had a more practical use than that. Into the spirit they placed a sliver of wood with a tiny piece of metal fastened to one end.

'All time stay one way,' Ho Chang explained, and spun the floating wood, and we watched it come back to rest with the metal tip towards the north. So this was our compass. I had been wondering how they would keep a course once we were out of sight of land.

We made another landfall after continuing to sail north for a further three days, then we turned to the west, keeping this new coastline on our starboard beam. I was hoping that we were going to land at least once to look for more trokus, but Ho Chang shook his head decisively. 'This place no good altogether,' he told me. 'Plenty black man go make chow – eat all men – chop-chop.'

Cannibals? Yes – that had been in Banks's book also. This probably was New Guinea then. God! How I longed for that atlas.

Then the land had ceased again and once more we had the horizon all around us. But the wonders had not ceased. There were dolphins that played around our prow, and once a huge whale that surfaced and spouted not a hundred yards from us, and flying fish, and an evil grey shark that followed us for some days, its triangular dorsal fin slicing the water like an inverted keel, until Ho Chang begged a chunk of trepang from the captain and they baited a hook the size of a small grapnel and let it bounce along in the wake at the end of long grass-line and a length of chain. The shark nosed up to it suspiciously, and evidently did not like what it saw and smelled, and we watched, fuming with impatience, until after half an hour it overcame its fears and took the bait with a rush and a half turn that showed its white belly and grinning underslung mouth. There was a homeric struggle after that until they brought it alongside and hoisted it inboard to thrash its life out bloodily under their knives and hatchets. The captain thriftily claimed the fins and hung them to dry in the rigging – 'Plenty money Hong Kong side,' according to Ho Chang – and we feasted royally on the rest of it.

All these things could no doubt have been seen from the deck of the *Boadicea* at various times during the voyage, but one had just not had the leisure to observe them properly, even when at the wheel, and in the all-too-brief four-hour watches below, sleep was the paramount necessity. Here it was different. The course was set, the sails trimmed, and there was time to watch and store and talk without the grating voices of authority continually driving one on in some often quite unnecessary task. This, I decided, was the way to live. The unhurried, undemanding way of the East. I said as much to Neil and he looked at me askance and said I could have his share.

'It's money *I* want,' he told me. 'That is the only really important thing in life. Money. Enough of it can guard you against *everything*. Don't let anybody tell you different, young Ross.'

'We haven't any now,' I reminded him.

'We will have,' he said with assurance. 'I've been talking to Ho Chang. Now I've got the hang of his pidgin English it's coming easier. This compradore business he keeps talking about. A compradore is a Chinaman who works for a white man. The white man has the power and the money – the Chinaman the knowledge of local customs and affairs – between them they make more money – and more – and more. Hong Kong is swimming in it. Ten years ago it belonged to the seagulls and a handful of pirates. Now it's a big town, and getting bigger. He wants a white man to work with him – two white men in this case. He'll supply the money and the local knowledge, but he has no experience of English business methods. I haven't either – but *you* have – and I can learn.'

'But you said you didn't trust him,' I said.

'I don't – any of 'em. Nobody in fact, except you. That's why we're going to make money. If you trust nobody you can't be rooked by the bastards.'

'Not much of a basis on which to found a business.'

'The *best* basis.'

'But I like Ho Chang.'

'So do I. You don't have to trust a fellow to like him.'

'A funny philosophy.'

'To hell with philosophy. It's business I'm talking about.'

We had many such talks, and it worried me. Yes, Neil had changed – and not for the better. But perhaps he could change again. Perhaps – if there was another Caerwen somewhere in this world – and the Wander Joss was kind.

Ho Chang said, 'Tomollow wellee big day.'

'What day?' I asked.

'Sea god day. We give it plentee money – tlepang – wine – coconut – fluit – make plentee bang-bang – have big show. Catch plentee good joss for long time.' He opened a carved teakwood chest in front of him and showed me piles of what I took to be Chinese money – both paper and coins – and some cheaply glittering jewellery – and I realized that there had been an air of expectancy over all the crew for two days past, but I had put it down to the change in the weather. It was much hotter now, and the brisk breeze that had brought us up the Australian coast had died, and the big sail was flapping lazily. 'Always same like,' he said. 'Sea god name Huang Hsi. Before his day he take wind away – no give back 'till you give cumshaw – that plesent. You see – tomollow plentee wind.'

By sundown they had Huang Hsi's 'cumshaw' laid out in the bows – the money, which was obviously counterfeit, fruit, coconuts, a jar of rice wine, and a large piece of trepang which the captain was loath to part with. Ho Chang tried to talk the shark fins out of him, but there he wasn't successful. The captain was no doubt as superstitious as the rest of them, but his thrift transcended all else.

There was an immense meal that day, and as the sun dipped below the horizon in a fiery red glow that made a path across the motionless surface of the sea, the cumshaw was thrown overboard to the earsplitting accompaniment of fireworks and gongs – then, inevitably, out came the opium pipes and lamps, and within an hour the helmsman, who was this day little more than a boy, the captain, Neil and myself, were the only fully conscious people on board – and that not for long, because we had all eaten heavily and drunk a greater or lesser amount of rice wine. I remember saying to Neil as I spread my sleeping mat near his on the high poop, 'I hope Huang Hsi keeps his half of the bargain. This calm is getting on my nerves.' But he was already asleep.

Somebody was shaking me violently and shouting, *'Tai fung! Tai fung!'* I sat up and saw it was the captain, his face greenish-yellow in the light of a paper lantern hanging from the rigging overhead. There was still no wind, but far in the distance I could hear a shrill piping that was coming nearer. The lad at the helm left it and grabbed a piece of rope from a belaying pin and tied it round his waist, and the captain, chattering with rage, jumped up and belted him with a length of bamboo, and then he ran round the recumbent figures of the rest of the crew, screaming at them and kicking them in the ribs, but apart from an occasional sleepy grunt they might have been carved from stone.

I woke Neil, and he listened for a moment and then said, 'Jesus! It sounds like wind. It used to happen down in New South Wales – Southerly Busters, they called them. All hell breaks loose when it hits – '

The captain was clawing at my arm and pointing to the big mainsail and going through the action of lowering it, then he rushed to the down-haul that was secured to bitts at the bottom of the mast, and tried to cast it off, but it was beyond his strength. Neil and I went to help him then, and we managed to get the sail down and make a rough stow of it. The captain literally pulled us both back on to the poop then and pointed to the small mizzen mast which was lying on the deck with the slatted sail wrapped round it, and dumb-showed the raising of it, which was simple enough because it fitted into a tabernacle, and we had seen it done often before. We got it up, and secured the guys that steadied it and tailed the slender lines out to belaying pins near the tiller, we supplying the brute strength it took, with the captain making the final delicate adjustments.

The piping had increased to a shriek that was getting nearer by the second, but still there was no stirring of the heavy air around us. The old man hustled us to the stern then and pointed to a long sweep. We hoisted it out between pegs on the bulwarks and, led by him, worked it back and forth to bring her head round in a full circle. The sky was perfectly clear and the moonlight was brilliant, and I realized that the old man had now brought us about until we were heading almost due south – and in the direction from which the shrieking was coming. Then he got more ropes and made us secure ourselves as the helmsman had done, and all four of us manned the ten-foot-long tiller – and waited.

It hit us like a solid wall – a mast-high wave that would have bowled us straight over on to our beam-ends and swamped us had we not been bow-on to it. As it was, it swept us from stem to stern and I thought all of us had gone overboard with it – but the body-and-soul lashings held, and I felt rather than saw that the four of us were still clinging to the tiller, for in that instant the moon had disappeared and we were in complete and utter darkness.

The big initial wave was followed by others almost as high. We rose up the side of them at an angle akin to that of a steeply-pitched slate roof – perched for an instant on the crest – then slid sickeningly down the other side, fighting every inch of the way with the tiller to keep her head on to it. And I saw then the reason for the mizzen sail. Compared with the mainmast it was the merest pocket handkerchief, but such is the magic that goes into the building and rigging of those wonderful craft that it served to keep us luffed, while the huge rudder, now lowered to its full depth, acted as a keel and helped us still further to hold her steady.

I don't know how long it went on for. Possibly no more than an hour or so, but it seemed an endless age of darkness – then, as suddenly as it had struck us, it ceased. The waves just stopped, and there was no more wind, and I could even hear a frightened chorus of sea birds overhead. I started to cast off my lashings and I said to Neil, 'We'll have to go and see if any of those poor devils are still aboard – ' but the captain, who was shivering like a half-drowned rat, grabbed my arm and somehow made me understand that there was more to come.

Neil said, 'You get the bloody things in two spasms. This is what they used to call the eye of the storm – a bit of calm in the middle – then the second lot hits you – '

And it did – just as he said, and the next minute we were fighting with the tiller again. But this time, although the waves were as high, and the wind shrieked just as hellishly, it wasn't as terrifying, because I had seen what the junk could stand now, and I was not so frightened.

Dawn came at last, and with it comparative calm, because the storm, as if in contrition, had left behind it a briskly fair wind. We unlashed ourselves, and the captain pushed his hands up his sleeves and bowed deeply and ceremoniously to each of us and we went down into the waist to get the mainsail hoisted again, to find that the devil – or sea god – had looked after his own, and the entire crew crept out from various holes and crannies and stood bowing sheepishly in front of the captain while he flayed them with language one didn't have to understand to appreciate.

Ho Chang, looking ruefully penitent, said, 'Opium wellee bad. Not take any more – any time. Captain say wellee much thank you. You not there, ship go down.'

'Huang Hsi no likee cumshaw?' I suggested, and he spat disgustedly.

'Huang Hsi no good,' he said. 'Only bloody Canton god anyhow.'

He had apparently been taking English lessons from Neil as well as from me.

Chapter Six

A light mist hid the shore but it ended abruptly a few feet above the junk's mainmast, exposing the tops of the high cliffs that close in on the eastern entrance to Hong Kong harbour. It was still dark at deck level, but high above us the dawn sun was turning the summit of a huge mountain to pale gold. The was no wind that one could feel, even with a wet finger, but the junk's slatted sail found and trapped what there was and we ghosted through Li Mun Passage as soundlessly and unerringly as a swan on a mill pond.

Ho Chang stood beside me in the bows. He said quietly, 'The Wander Joss has brought us safely home. We shall go ashore at Kowloon within the hour.' Six months unremitting study had made the use of pidgin no longer necessary, and we were now able to hold an intelligible conversation in Cantonese, and I even had a few honorific phrases in Mandarin.

I said, 'I am grateful for all you have done for my brother and me, Ho Chang, but we cannot impose upon your kindness any longer. When we go ashore we must learn to stand upon our own feet.'

He shook his head firmly. 'It is neither kindness on my part nor imposition on yours,' he said. 'You will both be men of modest wealth – '

'I know,' I interrupted. 'The pearls. We cannot accept them. What Neil and I did on the night of the storm was as much to save our own necks as yours.'

'The captain intends giving you one each nevertheless,' he said. 'In front of all the crew. If you refuse them he will lose face. Be sensible and accept them graciously. I shall take you to a hong who will advance you money on them – then you will be able to buy suitable clothes and our business will be upon a proper footing. As you are now, you are merely ship-wrecked sailors who would be arrested by the Company police and put aboard the first British ship to leave the port.'

Neil had joined us. His spoken Cantonese was not as fluent as mine but he had picked up sufficient to be able to grasp the gist of our conversation. 'Don't worry, Ho Chang,' he said. 'The gift will be accepted – with gratitude. Number Two Brother is number one piecee fool.'

I turned on him angrily as Ho Chang went off on ship's business, but I knew that they were both right. We had called at several ports in the East Indies on our way here, and we had seen enough to realize that Europeans as ragged and unkempt as we were at present were regarded with deep suspicion by the authorities.

The mist cleared as we left the entrance channel and turned into the harbour proper. I shall never forget that first sight of Hong Kong itself, which is simply a steep-sided mountain emerging starkly from the sea a mile off the mainland – an island, nine miles from east to west and five from north to south, sheltering a stretch of water that is one of the safest, and certainly one of the most beautiful, harbours in the world. The island belongs to Britain, ceded to her by the Chinese after the first Opium War of 1841. The busy town of Kowloon on the mainland opposite the island was at that time still Chinese, but even then the East India Company, which ruled the colony from India, was negotiating for its annexation. It was there that we landed after a gracious little ceremony on the high poop of the junk, when the captain presented us each with a pearl in a tiny red silk purse, after a short speech, and we kowtowed gravely with our hands thrust up opposite sleeves.

There must have been a dozen foreign ships at anchor in the harbour on that day, besides innumerable big seagoing junks, all loading and discharging cargoes into lighters that ferried between them and the Kowloon waterfront, on to which open the big warehouses that they call godowns. Ships and exotic cargoes were nothing new to me, but never in London had I ever seen the variety of merchandise that was piled on the warm stone paving of those wharves. Tea in teakwood chests, hides, baulks of mahogany and camphorwood, ebony, bolts of silk, porcelain, pottery, wool in bales, cotton piecegoods, mountains of rice and, guarded by armed watchmen, small wooden barrels of opium, instantly recognizable by its peculiar odour.

Ho Chang summoned three sedan chairs, each carried by four coolies, and although I would have preferred to walk and take in the sights, sounds and smells of that most fascinating of ports, I realized that the less we were seen in our rags the better, so we climbed in and drew the curtains, and were taken off at a jogtrot through a series of lanes and alleyways that contrasted sharply with the grandeur of the waterfront, until we were clear of the town and were crossing a wide sandy plain, then, ahead of us, I saw for the first time the Old City, with its hundred pagodas rising above the high encircling wall.

We trotted through an arched gateway into a narrow street which ended in a market place in the centre, with two runners preceding us and clearing a path for the chairs through the crowd with long staffs and much obscene language, and then we entered a courtyard and heavy gates were closed behind us and the chairs were set down. We climbed out, and I gazed around in wonder.

The courtyard was formed by a double-storeyed house on three sides and a high crenellated wall on the fourth which was pierced by the gate through which we had entered. There was a fountain in the centre with a black marble dragon spouting water through its mouth and nostrils, and beautiful flowering shrubs were set in enormous china urns, and there was a peach tree in full blossom in one corner. The facade of the house was arched and colonnaded and the ground floor appeared to be given over to offices and workrooms, because I could see people bent over desks and benches and hear the muted tapping of hammers. A flight of marble steps led up to a balcony, and a man was coming down them to meet us. He was Chinese, or so I thought, but he was dressed in cool white linen – trousers, frock coat and ruffled shirt – all cut in smart European style – and he had no pigtail. I guessed that Ho Chang had sent a message in advance, because we were evidently expected. They kowtowed to each other and Ho Chang spoke in rapid Mandarin which I could not follow, then he turned to Neil and me and said in Cantonese, 'This is Senhor Estavão Mascharenhas. Senhor, allow me to present Mr Neil Stafford and his younger brother, Ross.'

We started to kowtow, but the Senhor put his hand out in Western style and said in perfect though stilted English, 'Your servant, sirs. Welcome to my establishment.' We bowed and shook hands in turn, then he snapped his fingers and a man-servant came forward. 'Fan Lee will show you to your apartment, then, if it is agreeable to you, perhaps we could meet here for refreshments in an hour's time?'

I caught Ho Chang's eye. He nodded reassuringly and Neil and I followed the servant. He led us through a door farther along the terrace into a suite of large cool rooms that were paved in marble and furnished heavily with ebony. As we entered, two Chinese girls were pouring hot water into very English brass hip baths each side of an ornately carved screen and placing towels within reach. I had ceased to wonder by this time, even when the girl on my side started to help me out of my tattered shirt. I did balk, however, when her ministrations were extended to my trousers. The other side of the screen I heard Neil say, 'Jesus! This must be a knocking-shop. All right, my dear – very much obliged, I'm sure.'

I said sharply, 'Stop that!'

'Stop what?' he asked innocently.

'Whatever you're doing. We don't want to give offence before we've been here five minutes,' I told him.

'That one wasn't taking offence,' he chuckled. 'She *has* taken my clothes though.'

And so had mine, and we never saw those maltreated garments again, because when we had finished bathing, the girls came back with loose but comfortable shirts and trousers – and then a barber arrived and gave us each a much-needed shave and haircut, and we went along the terrace and found Ho Chang and our host sitting over tea and hot rice wine.

'Tea – or would you prefer brandy or beer, gentlemen?'
Mascarenhas asked hospitably, and we chose beer, which,
when it arrived proved to be best London export ale served
in magnificent cut-glass tankards.

Ho Chang left shortly after our arrival, as he had some
business to attend to, so I walked to the gate with him. 'The
Senhor will tell you what we both have in mind,' he said. 'He
has arranged for a tailor to attend to your needs. Please feel
at liberty to ask for anything you require. I shall return in
ten days.'

'Money?' I said anxiously. 'Could we dispose of these
pearls before you go?'

'The Senhor says it is not necessary to sell your pearls. He
will make an advance against your share of the business,
which will be adjusted later.'

'But damn it – there *is* no business yet,' I said. 'Ho Chang,
nobody could be more grateful than my brother and I for
all you have done for us – but now we begin to lose face. We
feel ourselves to be beggars.'

'There *will* be a business,' he assured me gravely. 'A
business that will bring much profit to us all. Let Mascarenhas explain the plan to you.'

'Who, and what, exactly is Mascarenhas?' I asked. 'He
looks Chinese, but dresses and speaks like a foreign devil.'

'He is of mixed blood,' Ho Chang explained. 'His father
was a Portuguese merchant from the island of Macao. His
mother . . .' He shrugged. 'Possibly a bond servant or concubine in his father's household. Foreign devils often make
that sort of arrangement when they take up permanent
residence in this country. Watch him, listen to him, learn
from him, but do not altogether trust him. That applies to
everybody you will meet in Hong Kong – including myself.'
He kowtowed deeply and left.

I woke early the following morning and went out on to the
terrace. My head was aching slightly because we had sat long
·er a colossal dinner which had been accompanied by
  uch wine. I hoped it hadn't loosened my tongue unduly,

although in justice I had to admit to myself that Mascharen-has hadn't seemed to be pumping either of us. I was worried, however, about Neil. He had drunk too much and he had talked about Australia, and Mascharenhas was apparently interested in trade possibilities with that country.

'Now that transportation is ending they will need labour out there – agricultural labour – and that will mean large-scale emigration from this country,' he had said. 'That, in turn, will mean an increase in trade from here. But this damned East India Company that has a stranglehold on both India and this colony must be kept out at all costs.'

'You can send all the Chinks – *Chinese* – you like there,' Neil had said owlishly. '*I* never want to see the stinking place again,' and I had kicked his shin viciously under the table, and thereafter he had sulked. I would have to have a serious talk with him, I decided, much as I hated the idea. As the elder, who had always taken the lead and had stood *in loco parentis* to me as a child, he naturally resented my advice, but the fact remained that he became utterly irresponsible when he was in drink.

He was looking rather bilious when I went in to wake him, but he obviously had no clear memory of the happenings at dinner, so I cravenly let the matter drop, and suggested a long walk through the colony after breakfast.

'Good,' he agreed enthusiastically. 'We were on that damned boat so long that I've practically lost the use of my legs. I'd like to cross to the island and see the British side.'

But when I told Mascharenhas of our intentions he firmly vetoed the idea. 'Kowloon, certainly,' he said, 'but I think it would be highly inadvisable to be seen in Hong Kong itself until your clothes are ready – which should be tomorrow or the next day. Europeans can wear comfortable shirts and trousers on this side and not appear *infra dig*, but in the purlieus of the sacred East India Company frock coats and grey top hats are *de rigueur* – for gentlemen.' There might have been the slightest stress on the last word, but there was certainly no mockery in his eyes. I wondered how much Ho Chang had told him of us. How much, indeed, Ho Chang himself knew for certain?

So we settled for a walk through the Old City in the first place, with perhaps a wider expedition down to the waterfront later. But even so, Mascharenhas would not let us go unaccompanied, and two huge bodyguards armed with steel-shod staves walked behind us.

'The hills behind the town are infested with bandits,' he explained, 'and they have a habit of coming down and mingling with the harmless peasants in the market place and attacking and robbing as opportunity presents itself. For that reason it is inadvisable to carry money on this side, so I have had these prepared for you,' and he gave each of us an exquisitely carved little ivory seal. 'They are called "chops". If you wish to make a purchase you stamp a piece of rice paper – so – and the shopkeeper will present it at my count-ing-house later and be paid the proper price for whatever you have bought – thus ensuring that he has not overcharged you.'

A convenient arrangement, I thought, but at the same time I felt a little irritated, because we were being cosseted and over-protected. But we thanked him politely and set off through the narrow lanes towards the north gate of the city, which he told us was the most interesting part.

The place teemed like an ant hill. At ground level were the open-fronted shops of the silversmiths, jewellers, apothe-caries, and the sellers of silk, jade and ivory. Above them, rising to two, three and four storeys, were the rooms wherein the bulk of the population lived, so closely huddled that two people leaning from windows each side of any of the alleys could touch hands. All law-abiding folk lived inside the walls, so Mascharenhas had told us, because it was too dangerous to do otherwise. A gun was fired and a gong was beaten at sundown, and the iron-studded teakwood gates were shut, and devil take any laggards who were left outside, because nobody was admitted thereafter until they were opened again at sunrise. The richer merchants had houses similar to his, surrounding the open market place, but the less wealthy deemed themselves fortunate indeed if they had as much as one room over a shop, or even a bed space on a flat roof.

'But why do they stay here?' I asked. 'Surely China is vast enough to allow them to live more spaciously elsewhere?'

'Money,' he replied. 'Here, in this cramped city, is concentrated more wealth than in Canton itself – so here flock the merchants, the bankers, the gold and silversmiths – and here they will stay until they are gathered to their ancestors.'

'But I should think they could make money in pleasanter surroundings?' I said.

He shook his head. 'Not as much and as quickly as here. The real wealth is held by the East India Company – over there, on the island. These people are like those in the Scriptures who crouch beneath the rich man's table and gather the crumbs. Money and face – the two main things in a Chinaman's life. One is as important as the other, and he will endure any hardship to acquire and hold them.'

Always this matter of 'face'. Face, Ho Chang had already explained to me, was a compound of honour, dignity and probity. One could sometimes lose one's wealth but still retain face, but having 'lost face' one's wealth was of little use.

We came to the north gate and walked through it on to the plain outside. For a hundred yards or so all round the perimeter of the walls the ground was cleared, but beyond that were fields that stretched right to the foothills of the surrounding ranges, dotted with copses of trees, and there were a number of little streams that flowed down into a large lake which seemed to be the main water supply of the city, because strings of coolies were filling huge brass pots and carrying them in through the gates. It was a pleasant sight, and one that put me in mind of a Chinese painting I had often stopped to study in a print-shop window in Blackfriars, so we sat on the tail of an empty ox cart and rested for a while, glad of the surcease from the noise and smells of the alleys behind us. I had once taken Caerwen past the shop and she had surprised me, as she so often did, by the extent and variety of her knowledge of the world outside her narrow ken of Welsh farm and London streets.

'Those fields are called paddies,' she had told me, studying the picture closely. 'The women wading in the mud there are planting rice. Those big black animals in that plough are not oxen. They're called water buffaloes.'

'How do you know all this?' I had asked her.

'There was a missionary who came from our village. He gave us a magic-lantern lecture once,' she said. 'Oh, *Duw anwyl*, boyo, how I'd love to see some of those foreign places. I wonder if they'd have *me* for a missionary?' And we had both laughed at the absurdity of the idea.

It was Neil's voice that brought me back with a start to the present. He said, 'Hello – something's happening, I think.'

A group of soldiers had come out through the gate behind us and had formed a ring to hold back the crowd that had followed them, and on the wall above the gate a brass gong was being beaten. Then came a straggling line of ten men, their hands tied behind them and wooden plaques covered in Chinese characters hanging from ropes round their necks. They were hustled into the centre of the ring and forced down on to their knees, and a soldier knelt in front of each of them and took their pigtails and pulled their heads forward until their necks were stretched and arched like those of gamecocks about to fight. An enormous Chinaman came from under the archway, and a hush fell on the crowd. He was bare from the waist up and the sun rippled on his sinewy arms and torso, and he carried a heavy curved sword over his shoulder. He stuck the sword point downward in the ground and spat on his hands and flexed his muscles, then took it up again and made a couple of lightning strokes through the air, making the blade whistle keenly. He stepped across to the first kneeling man then, bowed to him ceremoniously and curiously without irony, and the sword whistled through the air again and landed with a muted thud on the outstretched neck, and the head dropped to the ground but the body remained kneeling for an appreciable moment before pitching forward and wallowing in its own blood, with the legs jerking spasmodically. They were still jerking, in fact, by the time the tenth man had been decapitated.

The heads were gathered by the soldiers and tossed up to

the gong-beater above the gateway arch, who hung them from a beam by their pigtails, while the bodies were loaded on to the very ox cart on which we had been sitting, and trundled away.

Neil said drily, 'They ought to have had that bloke in New South Wales. I saw three convicts hanged outside Bathurst Jail once, and it took them over an hour to stop kicking.' Then he was violently sick.

I looked enquiringly at our bodyguards, who had been watching the executions without particular interest, and they kowtowed and said, '*Maskee daiman*' which means 'bandits', 'pirates' or 'soldiers' according to the tone in which it is said.

Our clothes were delivered the following day by the master tailor and no less than three 'makee-learns' as apprentices are called in the pidgin, but it was another two days before Mascharenhas would let us have them. To our eyes they fitted perfectly, but he was not satisfied, and insisted on stitches being taken in here and let out there, until the tailors were in tears.

'I'm sorry, gentlemen,' he said when we assured him that we could find no fault with them. 'This suit I am wearing is one of many that I had made last time I was in London. I will accept no lower standard from our own craftsmen.'

'London?' I said, surprised.

'Where I was educated,' he said with some pride. 'Both privately and at Westminster School. I have my father to thank for that very wise decision. English is spoken throughout the East – Portuguese only in Macao and Goa. Of course I regard myself in all respects, except domicile, as an Englishman –' He broke off as Neil tried unsuccessfully to stifle a giggle. 'You find that amusing, Mr Stafford?' he asked in little above a whisper.

'No – no, of course not –' Neil stammered, the corners of his mouth still twitching.

'I am glad to hear it,' Mascharenhas said, and added, 'What was *your* school, may I ask?'

'St Caldbec's,' I interposed hastily.

'Eton, Harrow, Winchester, Rugby, my own *alma mater*, and, of course, that educational pot-house of the East India Company at Haileybury – ' He counted on his fingers. 'These I know, but St Caldbec's – ? No – I am afraid I am not familiar with it. It is, I take it, one of our great public schools?'

'It was public all right,' Neil said solemnly, and then left the room hurriedly.

Looking back, I know that Mascharenhas's hatred of Neil dated from that moment.

We crossed the mile-wide harbour to the island in a smart clinker-built gig rowed by six magnificently liveried water-coolies, and entered yet another world, because Victoria, which is the name of the actual town of Hong Kong, could be likened to a piece of well-to-do residential London set down holus-bolus on the shores of the China Sea. The houses would not have been out of place in any square in the West End – porticoed, bow-windowed and adorned with a wealth of wrought-iron railings – and, as I noticed uneasily, the streets were patrolled by British police constables uniformed exactly as their Metropolitan counterparts. I exchanged glances with Neil as we landed on the wide esplanade that lay between the water and the steep streets running at right angles up the lower slopes of the Peak, and he smiled tautly.

Mascharenhas said sourly, 'The sacred groves of John Company, gentlemen. None but their superior servants and those they nominate may live here. Personally I wouldn't wish to. I prefer the freedom of Kowloon.'

'So do we,' said Neil with feeling.

'I am afraid in your case you will have to take up residence on this side,' Mascharenhas said. 'I don't know how much Ho Chang has told you of our plans – ?'

'Nothing,' I said. 'We understood that you were going to.'

He nodded gravely. 'I shall be happy to do so.' He led the way to a stone bench at the water's edge. 'Shall we sit here?

149

I usually discuss confidential matters in the open. In no building in China can one be absolutely safe from eavesdroppers. A good thing to remember, gentlemen. Right,' he went on as we took our places each side of him. 'Let me briefly explain the position of the Honourable East India Company in this colony. They are, as you undoubtedly know, the undisputed rulers of India. They control all its vast trade and raise their own armies to protect their interests. Fifteen years ago they decided to extend their activities here to China. Tea, silk and rice were the commodities in which they have been most interested – paid for not in other trade goods, and certainly not in gold and silver – but in opium. Opium which is produced in vast quantities at practically no cost in India, but which was forbidden in China under pain of death. Their agents introduced it here, secretly at first, among the peasants and coolies – actually giving it to them without cost. The habit spread like wildfire, not only among the labourers, but also to the upper classes, until the whole nation became debauched in a mere decade. The Emperor and his mandarins, those of them who were free of the vice, banned the trade and insisted on payment for their commodities in cash or goods of another kind, but the Company persisted in forcing their opium on to the markets of Canton, so the local mandarins, under the orders of Peking, seized their ships and burnt their cargoes. The Company riposted by sending warships and soldiers from India – and the Opium War of 1841 between China and Britain was the result. That was a tragedy, because Britain was never the enemy of China – it was just their damned, cursed East India Company – ' His clenched fist beat out the words upon his knee. 'Thieves, robbers, charlatans and hypocrites who have set themselves up here as our rulers – because, naturally, China lost the war and this place – Hong Kong – was ceded to them as part of the reparations at the resultant peace conference.'

'And the opium still comes in?' I asked.

'Not officially,' he answered. 'The Queen herself condemned the trade when she was made fully aware of it, but it continues to be smuggled in vast quantities to Canton, up the river from here. It never comes direct to Hong Kong itself, or to Kowloon, which will surely in the near future be ceded to Britain also, because there are British government forces here as well as Company, and they watch each other like hawks. The Company pretends to enforce the anti-opium edicts in their territories, but they turn a blind eye to the smuggling, and many of its officials are actively engaged in it themselves – and are making millions from it. Have you followed me so far?'

'Yes,' I said, 'but I don't understand how my brother and I come into it.'

'Let me explain further,' he said. 'This place – I mean this island itself – is, as I have said, absolutely Company territory. None may trade here except themselves and –' he paused and then stressed his next words – '*those to whom they grant licences.* These nominees, as they are termed, pay fifty thousand silver Mexican dollars for their licences in the first place, and thereafter a two and a half per cent levy on all business that passes through their hands. Do you understand?' I nodded though I was, in reality, still mystified. 'Very well,' he continued. 'We, that is my company, or hong, wish to nominate you and your brother jointly to represent us on the island.'

I was conscious of Neil looking at Mascharenhas with his mouth agape in amazement, and I realized that mine must have appeared the same.

'Fifty thousand?' I gasped. 'You don't think that we – ?'

'Have got that amount?' He shook his head. 'Of course not. As I understand from Ho Chang you have nothing but two pearls given to you in gratitude by the captain of the junk that brought you here. Keep them, and have cravat pins made of them. No – the fifty thousand dollars, which is rather less than fifteen thousand English pounds, will be put up by me – as will be the cost of the office and counting-house and godowns that you will have to establish here – together with your own not inconsiderable living expenses. All that will be found. There will be little or no profit on your first year's trading but after that we should make – um – two hundred to two hundred and fifty thousand pounds in the second year, of which your share would be ten per cent.'

I was making rapid mental calculations. 'You mean twenty to twenty-five thousand pounds – to us – ?' My head reeled.

'In the second year,' he confirmed. 'After that the profits should rise quite sharply to a not inconsiderable sum, in which case we might reconsider your percentage – say twelve and a half or even fifteen.'

I could see that Neil was past words, and I myself was in difficulties with a dry mouth and throat.

'I don't understand,' I muttered. 'Why *us*?'

He shrugged. 'You are not unintelligent,' he said. 'Ho Chang tells me you learnt good Cantonese in a very short time. The majority of these Company taipans don't pick up more than half-a-dozen mispronounced words in a lifetime out here, and they have to rely entirely on their compradores, and are accordingly cheated. That is one consideration, but not the main one.' He smiled bitterly. 'The main one, gentlemen, is that you are English. No Chinese, or man of mixed blood, can be a nominee.'

'I see,' I said thoughtfully. 'But aren't you taking a risk? I have a little experience – of shipping – but that was in London. My brother hasn't even that.'

'I can learn,' Neil said gruffly.

'You both can learn,' Mascharenhas said. 'The bulk of the business will be handled by Ho Chang and other members of my hong in Canton, in the early days – with myself in Kowloon exercising overall control. Only as you gain in experience will your responsibilities increase.'

'Fair enough,' Neil said, and put out his hand. 'We accept.' But Mascharenhas appeared not to see the hand. He shook his head slowly and deliberately.

'Your brother is hesitant,' he said. 'I would prefer you to discuss it further before committing yourselves. Once you have accepted there can be no drawing back.' He rose. 'I shall leave you now to talk it over. Let us meet here again in an hour.'

We watched him as he walked away, his tall figure dwarfing the stocky Cantonese who thronged the waterfront.

'Hesitant?' breathed Neil. 'God Almighty! Do you realize what he has just offered us?'

'Yes,' I answered, 'and it worries me.'

'But why?'

'The thing's too big. I feel he wants to use us as puppets.'

'He can use me for anything he likes, as long as the money is there.'

'And there's another thing –'

'What?'

'If we go into business on the scale that he is suggesting, we are going to be conspicuous. People will want to know who we are and where we've come from. This is a British colony – just the same as New South Wales. Don't forget that.'

He stared at me. 'I don't understand you,' he said. 'Where's your guts, boy? You've never jibbed at a risk before. Who the hell is going to connect me with a convict who went on the run at Bathurst over a year ago? As far as *you* are concerned you've never had a conviction anyhow.'

'Even so, I'd feel safer if we went on to California, as we intended originally,' I said. 'We'd have enough money if we sold the pearls. I counted four American ships as we crossed the harbour just now.'

'I don't give a damn if there are a hundred and four. I'm not sailing on any of them.' He got up from the bench and turned and looked towards the Peak. 'Those houses,' he said. 'Can you imagine what it would be like living in one of them? A crowd of Chink servants – horses, carriages – a boat like that we crossed in today – bloody peelers touching their hats to us. In one year – two years – or even ten – I could make twenty-five thousand pounds – and the world could kiss my arse. I'm staying, brother Ross. You do as you wish.'

And I knew I had to stay too. I said, 'All right. Have it your way. But remember this – you'll never be really safe, *anywhere*, under the British flag – so for God's sake be careful. One drink too many – the wrong word at the wrong time – something illegal in business – and somebody starts to make enquiries –'

'Fiddlesticks!' he laughed. 'I agree – we don't want to start kicking over the traces and attracting attention to ourselves unnecessarily – but the very idea that I'm likely to be recognized as an old lag, who has no doubt been listed as dead by now, is plain nonsense.'

But the feeling persisted, and I felt when we shook hands with Mascharenhas later that we had made the wrong decision.

Things moved quickly after that. A Mr McClintock came to dine the following night. He was a little wrinkled Scot who ate little but drank whisky prodigiously without any marked ill-effects.

'I'm happy to make your acquaintance, gentlemen,' he said as Mascharenhas introduced us. He consulted a piece of paper through a quizzing-glass. 'I have all your particulars here. Your father, now deceased, was Charles Stafford Esquire, merchant of Liverpool. He had several mutually profitable transactions in the past with Mr Mascharenhas, who is now holding fifteen thousand pounds sterling on your behalf which you wish to put up for a nominated trading concession under the Honourable East India Company in the colony of Hong Kong. Correct me if I'm wrong.'

I looked at Mascharenhas. His face was as blankly expressionless as ever. He gave the slightest nod.

'That's right, sir,' declared Neil forthrightly.

'Aye – guid,' said Mr McClintock. 'That being so, as a sitting member of the local Court of Directors I'll be delighted to sponsor you. The necessary papers will be ready for signature at eleven in the forenoon the day after tomorrow, at which time I'd be honoured if you'd be calling at my office in Victoria. And now, perhaps, just a wee dram to be christening the transaction – '

By the end of the following week we were installed in a villa on a ledge high above the town, which commanded a magnificent view of the harbour. It had four enormous rooms on the ground floor and the same number above – deeply verandahed and balconied and built of local sandstone and coolly limewashed.

I have but to close my eyes to see again the garden in which the house stood, in a riot of flowering trees and shrubs, none of which I knew by name then, but Mascarenhas, no mean botanist, pointed them out to me as bougainvillaea, azaleas, jacaranda and hibiscus. A small stream came out from the hillside behind the house and fell in a cascade to a stone-lined pond in which huge golden carp darted among cream and purple water-lilies. The house was reached by a narrow zigzagging path at the bottom of which was a stone shelter where four relays of chair coolies waited day and night to carry us and our frequent guests to and from the town.

Our offices and godowns were a mile away to the east, in a valley which ran back into the hills from the village of Wanchai. Our duties were anything but onerous. We had a large staff of clerks and compradores – Chinese and Macanese, with one or two Indian babus – who carried on quietly with their work without supervision other than an occasional visit from Mascarenhas and Ho Chang, which was as well, because neither Neil or I knew much about things in those early days. Forms, bills of lading, manifests and chalans came to us by the sheaf, in Chinese, Portuguese, Hindi and, only occasionally, English, and all we were required to do was to stamp them with our 'chop' and sign them on behalf of 'Stafford Bros: Importers and Exporters by Appointment to The Honourable East India Company (China)'. The goods themselves we seldom saw. They came and went into the godowns – barrelled, boxed, crated and palmetto-matting-wrapped – in the merest trickle at first, but increasing perceptibly over the months to a steady flow, and at times, when there were many ships in the harbour, to a veritable torrent.

The godowns were at all times liable to inspection by the Company customs officers, though in actual practice they troubled us little. They called upon us at irregular intervals, obviously by prior arrangement, because Ho Chang was invariably present on these occasions, and they would require us to open a proportion of whatever goods happened to be passing through our hands, and these were inspected for contraband – then, none being found, the boxes and bales would be repacked and sealed, and the customs chop would go on to everything in the godowns, and the officers would retire to an inner room with Ho Chang, to emerge later smiling happily and smelling strongly of Scotch whisky, to take their departure with much kowtowing.

Neil said to me after one of these visits, 'My God! Who would want to slave one's guts out in England? A customs officer back there would be overpaid at twenty-five shillings a week. These Chinks collect the equivalent of ten pounds in squeeze-pidgin every time they poke their noses into a godown. There are forty-three nominated companies here. Reckon it out for yourself. The bastards must be making more than the Lord Mayor of London. And they are only the small-piecee men.'

'How do you know that?' I asked him, and he winked and tapped the side of his nose with an extended forefinger.

'I *know*, little brother,' he said. 'I know a damned sight more about the dealings of Mascarenhas, Ho Chang and Company than you think. I make it my business to find out.'

'Be careful,' I warned him. 'They are treating us handsomely, but if you start prying into matters that don't concern you we are going to lose their trust.'

'Trust?' he jeered. 'Trust? Who the hell ever heard of a Chink trusting a foreign devil?'

'They trust us and they are treating us more than generously,' I said angrily.

'Of course they are,' he said. 'We are useful to them at present – but if ever they feel they can do without us they'll drop us like hot spuds. So it's up to us to learn the ropes damn quickly – and set up on our own – *really* on our own, and not as "puppets". *Your* word, old boy.'

'Listen to me, Neil,' I said. 'I didn't want to stay here in the first place, but you insisted and I fell in with your wishes. But now that we are committed *I* insist that we honour our side of the bargain.'

He raised his eyebrows. 'Of *course*,' he agreed. 'But you can't blame me for keeping my ear to the ground. I'll tell you something that I heard at the Club only last night – '

'Damn your bloody Club,' I swore furiously. 'You spend too much time there. You drink too much – and *talk* too much – '

'So you may think – but I listen as well – and I know how to carry my liquor. Now suppose *you* listen to *me*. The Company is under pressure from both London and Peking to abrogate the British monopoly on the island here. If that happens we'll be dropped – ' he snapped his fingers – 'just like that. And Stafford Brothers can go to hell.'

'They wouldn't do that to us,' I said, a little uneasily, because I, also, had heard this persistently repeated rumour from no less an authority than McClintock.

'Of course, there's no saying that *all* Chinese and Macanese backers will be sacking their British frontee-pieces,' he had said one night over dinner, fixing me with his beady little whisky-filmed eye. 'And in your particular case you ought to be all right. Mascarenhas thinks a lot of you. Ha' ye no' been up to Canton with him yet?'

'No,' I answered. 'Is there any particular reason why I should?'

'Ah, weel,' he said vaguely, filling his glass again. 'Time will tell – then you *would* be safe. A very fortunate young man – in more ways than one.' And he had winked and tapped his nose, just as Neil had done. A hateful gesture that I had always associated with thieves and blackguards – and convicts. How much did this little toper know? I had wondered.

'They'll do it immediately they require our services no longer,' Neil said, bringing me back to the present. 'And since I have no intention of being thrown on to *any* Chink's scrapheap, I'm taking a few simple precautions in advance.' He grinned and scuffed my hair. 'There's no need for *us* to fight though. Just trust your big brother.' And once more he made that horrible sign.

'For Christ's sake don't *do* that!' I shouted, and stormed out.

I really was worried about him – more so than at any time

in the past. Affluence such as neither of us had ever dreamed had gone to his head badly. We both belonged to the Club – that was a *sine qua non* for all Europeans of a certain status – but Neil was spending more and more time there, drinking and gaming, and I knew that he was also exploring the seamier side of Hong Kong and Kowloon with a coterie of the younger bloods. But it was no use my lecturing him. He resented it, and only acted the wilder. I just hoped that reports of this had not got back to Mascharenhas.

It was some weeks after this that I made my first visit to Canton. Mascharenhas sent word by Ho Chang that he would like me 'if it suited my convenience' to accompany him up-river the following day, and to be prepared for a week's stay in the city. The invitation did not include Neil, and I assumed, or perhaps hoped, that that was because he thought it desirable that one of us should remain in charge of the office – but Neil took it amiss.

'The good boy gets taken ta-tas,' he sneered. 'The bad bugger gets a kick up the arse.'

'I don't think that's the case at all,' I said unconvincingly. 'He just doesn't want us both away at the same time.'

'Balls,' he answered. 'Well, to hell with him. I'll go to Canton when I feel like it – at a time of my choosing.'

We sailed from Kowloon early next morning on Mascharen-has's yacht, which was a magnificent junk, low-prowed and high-pooped, with sails of 'wild' silk which were featherlight and impervious, yet, he told me, were stronger than the stoutest storm canvas of any Western ship. Her hull was finished with red and black lacquer, and gilded dragons embellished her bow and stern – and she was armed with six highly polished but very businesslike brass cannon on each side. She carried a large crew, all in the Mascharenhas livery and wearing cutlasses and heavy pistols in their belts. He saw me looking curiously at them and he said, 'Pirates. They infest the estuary all the way up to Canton itself – hence my warlike crew.'

He stood beside me pointing out the salient features of the harbour we were leaving, and the mainland on our starboard beam.

'Stonecutters' Island – there, in the middle of the western passage. The northern tip of Lantao Island beyond it. Lantao is bigger than Hong Kong but it has no water. I think the Company might try to annex it shortly, purely as a seaward fort to guard the harbour. That big mountain on the mainland there is Tai Mo Shan – '

'Great Mother of Mountains,' I translated, in order to parade my knowledge.

'That's right. I congratulate you, Mr Stafford. As I said before, you are one of the very few Europeans I know – other than our Jesuit Fathers – who have mastered any of the tongues out here.'

He had of late been extremely complimentary of my modest accomplishments. A well-read man himself, he took a great interest in the small library I was once again assembling, and had been kind enough to invite me to borrow from his own very extensive store of books, and I had overcome my initial suspicion of him and was genuinely sorry that Neil disliked him so.

We had a splendid run, against the current but with a strong southerly wind behind us. The Pearl River estuary averages ten miles in width in the dry season, increasing that by fifty per cent in the south-west monsoon, until, just short of Canton, it reaches a narrow gut between high cliffs which the Portuguese had named Boca Tigre, or the Tiger's Mouth, and here several forts had been built to protect the final stretch to the city. Although we had passed many trading junks proceeding both up and down river, we had not laid eyes on anything that remotely resembled a pirate craft and, boylike, I was disappointed. Mascarenhas laughed when I mentioned this to him.

'Any one, or dozen, of those peaceful craft out there could be pirates,' he said. 'It is that which makes the Chinese bandit so dangerous on land or sea – his chameleonlike propensity to merge into the background. At one moment he is a patient, hardworking peasant or fisherman – the next he is at your throat. One cannot afford to be off one's guard for a single moment in this country. In Europe one doffs one's hat in greeting and puts out one's right hand, which stems from the symbolic raising of the visor and proof that one is not concealing a weapon. Here we kowtow at a safe distance, never dropping our eyes from the other's face, and we keep our hands in our sleeves – on a hidden dagger – and not always symbolically.'

The last few miles were exciting, because the wide river was now compressed into a narrow pass. Junks coming south to the sea rode the swift current in the middle, sweeping past at a breathtaking speed, but we, the northbound craft, had to hug the banks, with tow ropes rigged to the bows and manned ashore by teams of toiling coolies, because the cliffs each side blanketed the wind.

We anchored off the city late in the evening. It was an imposing sight. The banks on both sides were completely hidden by junks and sampans moored four and five deep along a frontage of four miles, and forming a floating city in themselves. Behind them, on the eastern side, the city walls, brick-built, battlemented, twenty feet thick and rising to a height of thirty feet, were pierced at intervals by gates set in watchtowers. Pagodas and temples soared above the crowded roofs of lower buildings and, incongruously, a carillon was ringing the Angelus from a cross-surmounted steeple.

'The Catholic cathedral,' Mascharenhas told me. 'With the Carmelite convent beside it. It was built by the present Emperor's father as a gift to the Portuguese and French. The Chinese have a deep veneration for all religions.'

We were rowed ashore in a longboat manned by watermen in the Mascharenhas livery, and we landed on a jetty that had been kept clear of junks and sampans, where watchmen similarly dressed cleared a way through the crowd for our chairs.

I said, 'You seem to be as well established here as in

Kowloon, Mr Mascharenhas.'

'Considerably better,' he answered. 'My family has lived here for three generations, whereas our Kowloon branch has been opened by myself fairly recently.'

We were carried through the South Gate, which opened from a wide esplanade between the river and the city walls, and the grandeur ceased, because the streets were narrow, cramped and indescribably filthy, and the houses were meaner than those of Kowloon although there was here a greater number of temples, pagodas and mandarins' yamens, each in its own high-walled courtyard which gave a spurious impression of spaciousness to the city – spurious because entry to these open spaces could be gained only through gates that were jealously guarded by watchmen armed with huge swords, so that they did nothing to relieve the teeming congestion of the place since the common herd was excluded.

The street we were in ran arrow-straight from the South Gate to the wall the other side, bisecting the city and ending on an open parade ground at the North Gate, which was surrounded by a deep moat, thus forming an inner keep. There were trees and gardens and fountains here, though again there were guards to keep out the crowds, but they threw the gates open, saluted and kowtowed as the liveried footmen preceding us approached, and we wheeled to the right and halted under a marble pavilion from which steps led up to a terrace above.

Mascharenhas said, 'Welcome to my home, Mr Stafford. I trust you will regard it as your own whenever you come to Canton. I apologize for the squalor of the streets we have to traverse to get here – ' he shrugged – 'but this is China, where the extremes of wealth and poverty are never far apart.'

'But I thought that Kowloon was now your home,' I said.

'A *pied-à-terre*, purely as a business convenience. It was *here* that I was born – and it is here that my family live.'

Servants had come forward to take our luggage, all dressed in European clothes, although they appeared to me to be Chinese, but then I realized that they, like their master, were half-castes.

'You will possibly find all this a little confusing,' he said as we walked up the wide marble steps. 'My ancestors always tried to make the far corners of the earth another Portugal. Your people have done the same in Hong Kong, have they not? Some of those villas might have been lifted in their entirety from London and set down in their present locations, as you will probably have noticed. Therefore I hope my great-grandfather's efforts here won't strike you as in bad taste.'

We had reached the top of the steps by this time, and the whole bewildering prospect was before us. The huge house, which had until now been hidden by the overhang of the terrace, owed nothing to Chinese architecture. It was built of white and pink marble instead of the predominant mellow brick and carved sandstone of the rest of the city, and it put me immediately in mind of the palaces I had seen on the banks of the Tagus when the *Boadicea* called briefly at Lisbon on the voyage to Australia. In fact, I actually said, 'Just like Lisbon', which appeared to please him.

'I'm glad you recognize the style,' he said. 'That, incidentally, is its name – The Villa de Lisboa.'

It was more a palace than a villa, solidly rectangular in shape without the characteristic courtyard of the yamens we had passed on the way here, so that its windows faced outward, commanding a view of the beautiful gardens that surrounded it, and where the Chinese would have had gilded dragons guarding the terraces and the entrances to the house itself, here were lifesize statues in the classical style – Venuses, Minervas and Apollos mounted on plinths stretching all round the house and lining the pergolaed walks, with a somewhat out of place Poseidon and a group of landlocked tritons spouting water from a marble fountain.

'An architectural solecism, I'm afraid,' Mascharenhas said deprecatingly. 'But there you are. As I said, it was built by my forebears, all of whom, less my mother, were pure Portuguese. Some people no doubt would find it ridiculous.'

'I certainly don't,' I said stoutly. 'It is magnificent.'

'I'm glad you think so,' he said drily. 'I had a schoolfriend at Westminster – the son of a wealthy brewer – who used to invite me to his home during the holidays. They had a Highland castle, complete with moat, drawbridge, portcullis, arrow-slits and chutes for boiling pitch and molten lead. That, also, was magnificent – except for the fact that it had been built within the last few years – in a south London suburb. My friend always apologized to any guests that he took home, and used to poke fun at his father's taste, or lack of it. I despised him for it. Now I find myself reacting in exactly the same way.'

I was conscious of both embarrassment and wonder. Here was this powerful man of whom I stood in awe, apologizing to *me*, a workhouse-raised starveling who had arrived on his doorstep penniless and wellnigh naked only a few short weeks previously, and I was still fumbling for something tactful to say when we came to the big ironbound front door.

'Very well,' said Mascharenhas briskly, seemingly once more his normal assured self. 'Lobo will look after you. Let us meet for aperitifs in the drawing-room in an hour's time. Several people will be joining us for dinner later.' He went through a door, and a servant in a blue tail-coat bowed and said in perfect English, 'This way, sir, if you please,' and I followed him up a wide curving staircase to a suite of rooms on the upper floor, where already other servants had unpacked my bags and were laying out my evening clothes, while through an inner door I saw water steaming in a marble bath the size of a double bed.

'If you will ring, sir, when you are ready, I shall conduct you to the dining-room,' said Lobo, ushering the other servants out.

I bathed and dressed and found I still had some twenty minutes in hand, so I went out on to the balcony and stood looking back over the city towards the river. The short twilight was drawing in and lights were appearing in the streets beneath us and smoke from a myriad cooking fires was layered over the flat roofs of the huddled houses. I listened to the noises that came up through the evening air, noises that differed from those of Hong Kong and Kowloon where, night and day, there was always a breeze that tempered and mixed sounds. Here it was still, so that from the background hum one could distinguish the individual calls of street hawkers, the keening cry of a muezzin from a distant Mohammedan mosque, the barking of dogs, and from one or other of the six hundred and more temples, the booming of gongs. Every city has its characteristic sound, but of all those I have ever been in, only that of Canton has remained with me over the years – unchanging and instantly recognizable. It had a calming effect on me, but I was still vaguely troubled, and I did not know why. Neil, certainly, had something to do with my unease. We had quarrelled again the night before I left, and he had gone off to the Club and had not returned by the time I crossed to Kowloon next morning to join Mascharenhas. What an unbelievable stroke of fortune had come our way, I reflected – and what a heartbreaking shame it would be if he endangered it. I would have to talk with him again when I returned – seriously and without bitter argument. Either he accepted without equivocation the amazingly generous terms Mascharenhas had offered us, and worked wholeheartedly to make the venture a success, or it would be better if we decided to withdraw at the end of the year and go our way, either together or, if he preferred, separately. Whatever the outcome, I would not stay on here alone as I would feel inwardly that I had ousted him for my personal benefit.

Yes – that would have to be it. Pull together or split. I hoped it would not be the latter, but if it was, then I would go on to California.

The hour was up, so I went in from the balcony and rang for Lobo, and he led me downstairs and through the wide hall where several portraits looked down from the walls. They were of both men and women, ranging in period from wigs, paint, powder and patches to some of fairly recent vintage – and all were of Europeans. Mascharenhas's ancestors, I assumed – less his mother. I found myself wondering about her. Who and what was she? Some highhorn Peking mandarin's daughter, or a timid little concubine?

Lobo tapped at high double doors, then threw them open, silently but with a flourish, and I heard the sound of a piano being played softly. The room was large, with french windows opening on to the terrace on two sides, and it was brilliantly lit by candelabra hanging from the vaulted and painted ceiling, and sconces round the silk-hung walls. It seemed to be furnished entirely in gilt and ormolu, and I was conscious of my feet moving soundlessly over soft rugs. Once again there was a complete absence of Chinese atmosphere or influence here.

The playing stopped, and a woman rose from a grand piano at the far end of the room and came forward to meet me.

She was, without question, the most beautiful creature I had ever seen in my life.

Mascharenhas entered on my heels, and in a daze I heard him say, 'My dear, may I present Mr Ross Stafford? Mr Stafford, my daughter, Leonora.'

Chapter Seven

Looking back, I suppose that must have been the very first time I had ever been presented to a lady. I dimly remembered reading somewhere that one did not proffer one's hand unless the lady did so first, so I essayed a clumsy bow and stammered something unintelligible, and then Mascharenhas mercifully came to my rescue by taking my elbow and leading me across the room out through a french window to where another lady reclined on a chaise-longue. She was large and blonde, and her handsome gown was very *décolleté* and since she had a fan in one hand and a glass in the other, protocol was simplified. Mascharenhas said shortly, 'And this is my wife – Mr Stafford,' with a complete absence of warmth, and she looked at me over the top of the fan, stifled a hiccup, and said thickly, 'An Englishman? God help you in this cesspit of a place then.' She took a sip from her glass and evinced no further interest in me, and I wondered, even in those first few moments, how on earth she could be mother to the exquisite Leonora.

We went back into the drawing-room then, in time to greet some new arrivals, and since I had now had time to collect my wits I was able covertly to study the girl as her father introduced them. She was small and slender, and not even the frills and furbelows of her fashionable but over-elaborate evening gown could disguise the perfection of her figure. Her delicately moulded features were definitely European, only the slight upward slant of her eyes giving any indication of her Chinese blood, and even this was counteracted by the length of her eyelashes and the well-marked arches of her brows. But it was the eyes themselves that had me completely at a loss. They were dark and luminous – as are all Oriental eyes – but there was a difference here that I could not define.

A voice behind me said softly, 'Have you ever seen lapsang tea in a Sung cup, Mr Stafford?' and I turned to see McClintock grinning impishly behind me, and when I shook my head he went on, 'The tea is golden-brown and the cup greeny-blue – like the sea off the Li Mun Channel at sunrise. That's poetry for you – and no' so bad, either, for a man who's read only that of Rabbie Burns.'

'I don't understand,' I said.

'The eyes, man – the eyes,' he chuckled drily. 'A lucky bit of breeding there. Mascharenhas is half-and-half, with the Chinese uppermost, to his great sorrow. She's only a quarter, with the English on top. If she's served by the right buck her children could quite easily be blue-eyed, without the lapsang – and I hope without the gin that mamma has to take in vast quantities for a distressing kidney complaint.' He winked and tapped his nose. 'You're blue-eyed and fair yourself. I told you that you *could* be lucky, didn't I?' He moved away and I found myself disliking him very much indeed.

The room was filling now and I recognized several merchants from Hong Kong and, in a few cases, their wives. Mrs Mascharenhas had come in from the terrace and she and Leonora were greeting the latter. Mascharenhas crossed to me and said quietly, 'When the ladies have withdrawn after dinner, Mr Stafford, I would be greatly indebted to you if you would stroll casually round the doors and windows of the dining-room, *outside* – to make certain that we have no eavesdroppers. I have something very important to say to our guests.'

I remember little of the dinner itself, other than that it was long, tedious and magnificent. I sat between two wealthy merchants who talked over my head, and, since she was sitting on the same side of the table two or three places down from my position, I couldn't see Leonora. And I wanted to. By God, how I wanted to. That first fleeting glimpse of her had simultaneously both numbed and galvanized me. The man on my right leant back in order to speak behind me to the one on my left, momentarily widening my field of view, and I craned my neck sideways to catch sight of her, but she was looking the other way so all I saw was the curve of her bare shoulder and the sweep of her raven hair – and McClintock grinning the other side of her. He winked again and I wanted to murder him.

At last it was over, and Mrs Mascharenhas, on a signal from her husband at the other end of the table, had risen and was collecting the ladies. We got to our feet and converged on Mascharenhas after the door closed behind them. He caught my eye and gestured towards the french window at the other end of the room and I went through and made a circuit of the other doors and windows. Port, brandy and cigars were being passed when I returned, and Mascharenhas was on his feet.

'Gentlemen,' he said. 'Please accept my thanks for your presence here tonight, especially those of you who have come all the way from Hong Kong and Kowloon, and also my apologies for introducing business into what purported to be a purely social occasion, but the matter is serious, and it concerns us all.' He paused, and his eyes went round the table. 'So serious, in fact, that I could not risk broaching it in Hong Kong, where the spies of those inimical to our interests are always active. I will be brief, gentlemen. The subject is contained in one word – *opium*. In return for the word of the Company, that it would use all the wide powers at its command to put down the trade in this foul substance, China ceded Hong Kong to us, with the implied undertaking that she would at some time in the near future add Kowloon to the colony. She is keeping her side of the bargain – but the Company is *not*.' The negative came out like the crack of a pistol shot, and again his eye went round the table.

There was an uneasy movement among some of his listeners, and McClintock murmured, 'Ahem – er – not exactly the *Company*, old fellow. Perhaps one or two of the *nominees* – those present definitely excepted, of course. A venal comprador here and there may slip an odd catty of the stuff into an otherwise innocent bale – '

'The *Company*,' Mascharenhas insisted. 'I can answer for

the nominees. All nominees' merchandise is liable to customs search. That of the Company is not. An "odd catty" you say, sir? Would it surprise you to know that forty-five *tons* of prime opium came up the river in the first three months of this year?'

There was a gasp of amazement from the guests, quickly followed by an incredulous disclaimer from McClintock.

'Oh, come now, let us not ascend to cloud cuckoo land, or we'll be suspected of smoking it ourselves,' he said. 'Forty-five tons? Impossible. That would be at least India's entire production for a whole year.'

'Exactly,' Mascarenhas agreed. 'One whole year's production of India *and* Burma – collected and stored in Calcutta and sent out here in a *Company* ship, concealed in bales of cotton goods – landed in *Hong Kong*, not Kowloon – bonded in *Company* godowns – franked and thereby rendered inviolate to search by the *Company* chop – and then sent up here in *Company* junks, escorted by a *Company* gunboat, where it has gone *not* into *Company* factories, or those of reputable hong merchants, but into the godowns of Triad secret societies – criminal bands who distribute it throughout the length and breadth of the country.'

McClintock rose to his feet. 'You are not implying, I hope, sir, that the Company is in league with Triad?' he said.

'I am,' Mascarenhas answered quietly. 'In this connection at least.'

'Then you put me in a devilish awkward position,' said the other. 'I am a guest at your table – but I am also a member of the Court of Directors. I must ask your leave to withdraw, sir.'

Mascarenhas made a courteous inclination of his head and McClintock bowed right and left to the others and left the table. He paused at the door and looked back at Mascarenhas.

'I am bound by my duty to the Company,' he said, 'but I am also mindful of our friendship of these many years past. You may rely on my discretion on how much of this – er – misfortunate address I disclose to my superiors.'

'Thank you,' Mascarenhas said gravely, 'but I ask for no favours. The purport of what I have said tonight, in somewhat greater detail, is already on its way to Whitehall.' He rose. 'Shall we join the ladies?'

I followed them out, listening to their low-pitched, excited buzz of conversation. The Triad? I had heard of this unholy assemblage from Ho Chang. The controlling body of China's many hundreds of secret societies, more powerful, so he said, than the Imperial Court of Peking and all its mandarins. That and the mighty commercial empire of the East India Company in combination would be a force to be reckoned with. In fact, one of the merchants was saying just exactly that to Mascarenhas as we approached the drawing-room, 'My God, man – take on the Triad if your heart is pure and your arm strong enough – and even have a tilt at John Company, if your nerve is steady and your purse *long* enough – but not both together. I agree with everything you said in there. We all know it, but only you have had the courage to drag it out into the open. But I'm frightened. Frightened for all of us. That little Scotch bastard will be reporting this the minute he gets back to Hong Kong.'

'Quite so,' smiled Mascarenhas. 'Which is precisely why I asked him here. I want them to know, downriver, that I've sent a despatch to London – to Her Majesty's Government in Westminster, *not* to the sleek gentlemen who misrule us from the *City* of London.'

'Mr Mascarenhas,' another of the merchants said earnestly, 'as Spencer has just said, we all know this smuggling is going on – but as long as we ourselves are not engaged in it, does it really concern us? This surely is a matter for the Chinese and the Company. We are merchants, not policemen – or parsons.'

'If the Company, at best, turns a blind eye to it,' Mascarenhas told him, 'or, at worst, actively condones it, it will inevitably lead to another war between Britain and China, and that, gentlemen, will surely mean the end of all legitimate trade between our two countries and the ruin of everything we have built since Hong Kong was ceded to us.'

'*Our* two countries?' a man behind me said, and Maschen-has turned on him.

'*Our* two countries,' he flashed. 'I bear a Portuguese name but I was brought up, educated and *married* in England. I am English in sentiment and outlook, and when Kowloon becomes British territory I shall be English also by domicile and naturalization. Does any gentleman question that?'

There was a hasty murmur of approval from the others, and then we entered the drawing-room and I was trying to insinuate myself through the crowd to get close to Leonora, and the intrigues of the Honourable East India Company no longer seemed of any importance. But, alas, beyond a polite smile when the party finally broke up, the lady took not the least notice of me.

I stood with Mascharenhas on the terrace and watched the last of the chairs bearing the departing guests jog down the hill towards the waterfront, until the paper lanterns of the running footmen vanished in the maze of streets.

He chuckled drily and said, 'McClintock will not be the only one to be carrying tales to the Court of Directors. There were some very nervous gentlemen among our guests tonight. Not all of them have spotless consciences.'

'It is really as serious as you said?' I asked him.

He nodded. 'Every bit,' he answered. 'You see, by flouting our side of a solemn compact we are causing the Chinese to lose face. That is the one thing they will not tolerate, and the one thing these fools cannot understand. My only wonder is that the second Opium War has not already broken out.' He turned towards me and put out his hand. 'I am grateful for your help, Mr Stafford,' he said gravely.

I was both flattered and confused. 'It's the other way round, sir,' I said. 'Your generosity to my brother and me has been overwhelming – particularly since we know so little about the business –'

'You are learning fast, and in the meantime it is comfort-ing to have a man of integrity on one's side,' he said. 'I intend to remain here for another three days, during which time I shall introduce you to some of the hong merchants.

I am not one myself, of course. That, like full membership of the East India Company, is denied to me by reason of my mixed blood, but they, the hongs, trust me and have accepted my nominee, Ho Chang – just as the Company have accepted you – so I have the advantage of a vicarious foot in each camp, although, God knows, I would prefer to be wholly in one or the other. Some day I hope the Company rules will be changed, which is why I have chosen to be regarded as British. Those of the hong are immutable. They would never accept me as Chinese. Good night, Mr Stafford. I hope I have not wearied you.' He bowed and went, and I, who had known much loneliness in my comparatively short life, found myself beginning to understand this strange man.

He had gone further upriver when I arose next morning, leaving me a message apologizing for his absence and telling me that he would be back in the evening, so I breakfasted alone on the terrace with one eye cocked hopefully back towards the house, but there was no sign of the girl, although her mother appeared briefly at one of the windows, looking decidedly the worse for wear. I found my way to his library and spent a couple of happy hours there, but as the morning drew on I became restless and decided to see something of the town. Lobo wanted to send for a chair and bodyguards but I told him I would prefer to walk on my own, which appeared to worry him.

'With the greatest respect, sir,' he said, 'I think it would be advisable to take a chair and a couple of footmen. Canton is a strange place, and for a gentleman who doesn't know the language – '

'I thank you for your concern,' I said in Cantonese, 'but one sees little through the curtains of a chair,' which surprised but did not reassure him, and he muttered something about the master not liking it, and the possibility of trouble on the streets, so rather than argue further I pretended to drop the idea, then I slipped away and went down through the archway to the Northern Gate, and turned towards the centre of the town.

I was conscious almost immediately that there was something different in the atmosphere from that of the previous day. There were fewer people about, and many of the shops were boarded up and, significantly, there was a total absence of beggars. They have a saying – 'Beggars, the snowflakes; Trouble, the summer sun' – but the day was pleasant and a cool breeze was blowing from the river, so I went on downward to the waterfront, vaguely puzzled but not unduly disturbed. Mascharenhas's junk was still at anchor, as was an East India Company gunboat, the *Arrow*, which had been alongside the wharf the day before, but all the other shipping that had thronged the waterway on our arrival had departed. The wharves were piled with cargo, but no coolies were working, and there was a strange silence over the crowded sampans of the floating city.

It was becoming clear even to my conceited cocksureness that something was decidedly amiss, so I turned and retraced my steps to the Northern Gate, to find that the few people I had seen on the way down had now totally disappeared, and I was walking through a ghost city, with my footsteps echoing back from the walls on each side of the street, and I was conscious of eyes peering at me through the cracks of shuttered windows, and finally, as I passed a yamen gateway, a heavy earthenware jar came hurtling down from a window, narrowly missing my head. It took all my willpower not to break into a run over that last four hundred yards, and I was sweating and trembling by the time I got back to the house. I avoided Lobo, and the necessity of having to explain my absence, and went to the library and stayed there until my solitary dinner was served in the great dining-room, which had been the scene of such splendour the night before, but which was now silent and gloomy. To break the oppressive silence I asked Lobo when he expected Mascharenhas back.

'He said he would be here before sundown, sir,' he answered, and I could plainly see the anxiety in his face, in spite of the fact that, like that of his master, the features were more impassively Oriental than European.

'Do you know where he has gone?' I asked.

'I understand to Fahsu, sir – one of the smaller factories,

ten miles or so upriver. A messenger came for him early this morning.'

'The – er – ladies?' I said hesitantly. 'Won't they be dining – ?'

'In their quarters, sir. Mrs Mascharenhas is a little indisposed, so Miss Leonora is staying with her. Coffee and cognac, sir? Here, or in the drawing-room?'

'Neither, thank you,' I said. 'I shall go to my room to read. Call me when Mr Mascharenhas returns.'

But I didn't read. I realized that I was very tired, and I put out my light immediately I got into bed.

A hand was shaking me gently. I opened my eyes, then closed them again, because I thought I was dreaming. It was not Lobo who was bending over me. It was Leonora, her face pale in the light of the lamp she was carrying.

She said urgently, 'Mr Stafford – please – there is trouble outside, and all the servants have run off.' I sat upright and she went on, 'There are fires – and people are shouting in the streets.'

I heard it myself then, a sustained roar like wind through trees. I swung my legs out of bed and went to the window and threw back the shutters. The sky over the waterfront was a red glow, and flames were leaping above the city wall. I stared stupidly, still sleep-befuddled, and she said, 'It started two hours ago, and I thought at first it was just another festival among the water people – '

I peered down into the compound in front of the house. It was dark and deserted but I thought I detected a slight movement near the gates, where a dim lantern hung over the watchman's shelter, then I was certain that there was a group of men crouching in the shadows. I said, with an assurance I was not feeling, 'Whoever they are, I don't think they would dare attack your father's house.'

'They did when the Opium War broke out,' she answered. Her voice was steady, but I could sense her fear. 'Most of the merchants' houses were burned. This one was saved because the British soldiers arrived in time. But now there are no soldiers in Canton.'

'There are in Hong Kong,' I said.

She shrugged. 'That is ninety miles away. It could be days before the news reached them, and more days before they arrived up here. Do you know where my father has gone?'

'Somewhere upriver – Fahsu, I think Lobo said. I understood that he was to have been back by nightfall – ' I broke off as more dim figures came through the gate. 'Put that lamp out,' I told her, and as she did so I climbed through the window on to the terrace and looked down over the parapet.

There was a group immediately below us, perhaps half a dozen or so, and I think that they must have seen my head against the sky because I heard a soft warning whistle and they scuttled quickly back towards the gate. For a moment I was heartened, but only for a moment, because some more appeared then, carrying torches, and there was a parley by the watchman's shelter. The increase in numbers seemed to embolden them and they came forward to the steps leading up to the terrace, but a heavy wrought-iron gate held them for a time. I climbed back through the window and hastily pulled my trousers over my nightshirt. I could hear Leonora panting with terror in the darkness.

'Is there a way out from the back of the house?' I asked her.

'Some steps from the garden that lead to the top of the city wall,' she answered.

I swung the shutters closed again and bolted them, then I groped for matches and relit the lamp. The noise at the front gate was getting louder, and above the shouting I could hear a heavy pounding as they evidently tried to batter it down. I looked at the girl. She was doing her utmost to hold her panic in check, but I could see that she was trembling like a leaf. She was wearing a dressing-gown over her night attire and her feet were thrust into flimsy slippers.

I said, 'I think you had better get dressed as quickly as possible. If we can manage to get out and work our way down to the waterfront and on to your father's boat we should be safe. Where is your mother?'

175

'In her room,' she said as she made for the door. 'She is – is – *ill*. I may need help with her.'

I followed her along the gallery outside to a door at the end. She took a key from the pocket of her gown and opened it and we went through. The light of the lamp I was carrying fell on a large, ornately carved and draped four-poster. Leonora went up to it and shook a recumbent figure under the bedclothes and said, 'Wake up! Come on – *wake up!*'

The woman stirred, then heaved herself half upright and shielded her eyes from the light with an upraised arm. She moaned hollowly and said, 'What on earth – oh my God – ' and even from a distance of half-a-dozen paces I caught the stench of stale gin.

Leonora said, 'Get up and get dressed. Hurry! There's a mob outside trying to break in – '

'Leave me alone, you bitch,' said Mrs Mascharenhas, and tried to lie down again; Leonora slapped her sharply across the face, and the other started to snuffle. I stood holding the lamp, prickling with embarrassment, while the girl hauled her out of bed. She turned to me and said, 'If we have to go through the streets it would be better if we had amahs' clothes, don't you think?' and without waiting for an answer she snatched the lamp from me and darted from the room. In the darkness I heard Mrs Mascharenhas subside on to the bed again sobbing drunkenly. The noise outside was growing and I could hear cries of *'Sha! Sha!'* which means 'Kill! Kill!' and it sent shivers up and down my spine.

The girl was back in a matter of minutes with a bundle of the universal black cotton garments that Cantonese menials of both sexes wear. She dumped them on the bed and dragged her mother to her feet again. The need for reticence and modesty had gone by the board now and I helped to get the inert woman out of her nightgown and into loose pantaloons and smock, then Leonora changed quickly and covered both their heads with coarse woollen shawls. It probably would not have deceived anybody for long in daylight, but they would certainly be less noticeable now than in voluminous European skirts and petticoats. I tried some of the clothes on myself but unfortunately they were too small.

The wrought-iron gate had obviously given way under the onslaught, because we could hear the mob on the terrace, and there was a thunderous pounding on the front door. I looked at Leonora and I was relieved to see that her initial fear seemed to have left her now that we were embarked on a definite course of action.

'This way,' she said, and grasped her mother's arm. I blew out the lamp and took the other arm and went out on to the gallery, down some back stairs and through a rear door into a courtyard. The woman between us was walking mechanically and at first gave no trouble, but then the cold night air partially revived her and she started to struggle and to hurl abuse at us both until Leonora hit her again and she broke into maudlin tears. It was comparatively quiet on this side of the house, but from the front there was a crash of breaking glass and a howl of exultation as the mob broke in, and looking back, we could see torches through the windows going from room to room.

We crossed the courtyard and came to a flight of stone steps leading upwards. We stumbled up them with Leonora leading and myself in the rear pushing the woman, because they were not wide enough to allow us to walk abreast, and we reached a broad footway which I realized was the top of the city wall. We paused and I looked back over the roofs to the waterfront, which now was ablaze from end to end as far as the eye could see. I tried to pick out the anchorage where the junk would be lying, but the river was hidden in a pall of smoke. I judged from memory that we were diametrically opposite it, with the whole circle of the city between us and it.

I said to Leonora, 'It would be quicker to cross through the streets but I think we'll be safer if we stay on the wall,' so we started off along the footway, briskly at first, with Mrs Mascharenhas again walking mechanically and docilely as if in a cataleptic trance, but waking from time to time to scream at us both until finally we had to gag her with the shawl because, once away from the neighbourhood of the merchants' houses, the streets below were unnaturally quiet and her voice was strident and far-reaching. It was an unnerving and confusing experience. I had heard drunken women quarrelling and using filthy language often enough in London, but they were always of the same class and type, and their voices betrayed it, but this woman spoke with an educated, even cultured, accent, which made her vituperation the more horrible.

We traversed the first half of our semi-circle without incident, but then two coolies came out of a watchtower and barred our path. We might have managed to get by in complete darkness, but as luck would have it there was a burning building just below us lighting the area, and one of them realized that I was a European, and he made a swipe at me with a bill-hook. I managed to dodge it, and he overbalanced and fell flat. I grabbed the bill-hook and turned to face the second man, who was armed with a rough pike, and I jumped aside just in time to avoid being transfixed. I hit out at him as he lurched past me and I felt the bill-hook slice sickeningly into his neck, almost decapitating him. The prone man rolled to one side and made a dash for some steps leading down into the street below, yelling at the top of his voice, and there was nothing for it but to chase after him with the bill-hook and deal also with him. I rejoined the women and we grabbed Mrs Mascharenhas's arm and ran like the very devil until we were out of breath.

The next watchtower was unmanned, but after it came another brightly lit area of burning buildings and we felt as conspicuous as figures on a lighted stage as we ran along the wall, but fortunately the mobs below were more interested in looting than in us and we reached the waterfront without further challenge.

I saw the junk immediately. She was blazing fiercely from stem to stern – as was the Company gunboat alongside the wharf.

I looked at the girl and shrugged hopelessly. She didn't understand for a moment, then she said, 'Is that my father's boat – out there?' Past words, I nodded. 'What do we do now?' she asked.

Somehow I shook myself out of my feeling of utter helplessness and said jauntily, 'Oh, we'll – er – just get another boat. There are enough to choose from down there.' And there were – the whole four miles or so of the floating city moored along the bank, although how on earth I was going to steal one I had no idea, because it seemed that those of Canton's population who weren't actively engaged in looting and arson had taken to the water in blind panic, and they were slipping their moorings and pushing out into midstream. Then, through the flames and smoke, I saw one that seemed to have been abandoned – a small sampan, pulled up on to the muddy foreshore. 'Come on,' I said, and we hauled Mrs Mascarenhas, who had slumped exhaustedly to the ground, on to her feet and went along the wall to the steps that led down to ground level by the Water Gate.

In spite of their preoccupation with their immediate safety, several of the Boat People looked at me curiously as we pushed through the crowd, and I heard ominous mutters of 'foreign devil' – but I slipped as I waded knee-deep through the mud to the sampan, and when I struggled to my feet I was black, evil-smelling and indistinguishable from the rest of the mob.

The sampan was little more than a tender for a larger craft, and it was filthy and waterlogged, but fortunately there was a pair of clumsy oars lashed to the thwarts, together with a slatted sail wrapped round a stumpy mast. I shoved and heaved at it without budging it an inch until Leonora left her mother and joined me, and we managed to tip it on its side and empty it, then slide it into the water. Mrs Mascarenhas, now relatively sober and correspondingly terrified, refused to embark at first, and Leonora had to slap some sense into her once more, then together we got her through the mud and into the sampan, where she subsided wailing forlornly on to the bottom-boards, and we were afloat.

I took the oars and pulled out into the stream, intending at first merely to cross to the other side, which is called Honan and appeared from a distance to be peaceful, but suddenly I found that we were in the grip of the current and being carried sideways, with the burning city sliding past us at an alarming rate. I fought to hold the boat and to make lateral headway to the other bank, but I soon realized that with only one pair of oars it was hopeless, so I made virtue of necessity and, as the dawn streaked the eastern sky, I turned her head and let the current take us downstream.

Completely exhausted, the women lay on the bottom-boards and went to sleep, so I shifted my position to the stern and trailed a single oar to keep on a straight course, then I, also, dropped off.

The sun was high overhead when I woke. We had long left the environs of the city, though I could see a pall of smoke far to the north. Ahead of us rose the cliffs of the Boca Tigre that channel the broad river to a narrow torrent, and already I could feel that our speed was increasing. I recalled our voyage upstream and made a mental calculation. My watch had stopped but I judged from the sun that we had been afloat for some hours, and already we must have drifted the better part of fifteen miles. Three miles an hour, and that without any effort on my part. The overall distance to Hong Kong was just under ninety miles. If we continued at this speed, that only left twenty-four hours, which in turn could be considerably reduced if we picked up a favourable wind once we had got through the turbulent narrows in a craft as small and flimsy as this, but I thought that if the going became too rough I could always steer into slack water at the side and manoeuvre the empty boat at the end of a rope from the towpath until we came to broader and more placid reaches again. The only alternative to this would be to make for the shore before we reached the mouth of the gorge, and abandon the sampan. We could then be faced with something in the nature of a seventy-five mile walk over mountainous country of which I knew nothing – except that it most certainly would be bandit-infested – with two women. My heart quailed at the prospect.

I saw that Leonora was awake. She was wet and dishevelled, her hair was awry and she had picked up a not inconsiderable amount of black mud in our launching efforts, but she was still wildly beautiful. I smiled at her and she inclined her head gravely but did not otherwise reciprocate, and I found myself comparing her with Caerwen. The harder conditions became during our journey through the bush, the more that one enjoyed it. She would have been in her element here, bless her.

Leonora said, 'Do you know where we are, Mr Stafford?'

'Just coming to the Boca Tigre,' I told her, and then went on to explain my newly formulated theory, and the two courses open to us. 'I would like your opinion,' I finished.

'Stay with the boat, undoubtedly,' she said without hesitation. 'My mother would never survive the journey on foot.'

Her consideration for her parent, and the tone in which she expressed it, were at such variance with her Draconian treatment of the previous night that I must have shown my surprise, because she said, 'I'm sorry if you were embarrassed last night, Mr Stafford, but when she has drunk too much she becomes uncontrollable. The danger we were in seemed to justify my taking drastic measures.'

'It certainly did,' I said with feeling. 'And I assure you I was not in any way critical, Miss Mascharenhas.'

'I'm glad,' she said simply. 'I don't enjoy bullying her. Fortunately she will have no memory of it when she wakes.'

In fact she did wake at that moment. She sat up and looked about her in complete bewilderment, then she winced and closed her eyes again and shook her head tentatively from side to side as if the effort pained her, which I have no doubt it did. She was, in short, as acute a case of alcoholic remorse as I have ever seen.

She said, 'Where the devil are we – and how did we get here?'

'There was some trouble in the city,' Leonora said gently. 'Thanks to Mr Stafford, we managed to get away. We are going downriver to Hong Kong at the moment. You were unwell last night.'

'And still am,' her mother groaned. 'Get me a drink, for God's sake.'

'I'm afraid we have nothing in the boat – not even water. You'll have to scoop some from the river with your hands,' Leonora told her.

Mrs Mascharenhas did so and was immediately sick, then she cursed us both roundly and lay down and went to sleep again. I tried to avoid Leonora's eye, but she said quite frankly, 'There – you see our problem. She will be like this until the effects of the drink have completely worn off.'

'How long will that be?' I asked.

'It all depends on how much she had yesterday. I think it was quite a lot. These bouts usually occur when my father is away.' She was discussing it as if it was a matter quite outside her mother's control – like headaches or *la grippe*. 'She should be herself again by the time we arrive in Hong Kong.'

'Does it often happen?' The complete absence of embarrassment in the girl helped to dispel mine.

'Erratically. Perhaps two or three times in as many months, then she might go for the better part of a year without taking as much as a glass of wine.'

'Can't *anything* be done? I mean – some sort of restraint – '

'Lock her up? No – my father still loves her. So do I. We couldn't do that.'

'I meant the drink itself – keep it away from her.'

'That is impossible with Chinese servants. Even if every drop of alcohol in the house was kept under lock and key she could always send out for it.'

'But if you told the servants not to obey her – ?'

'That would mean loss of face, and that would be unthinkable. You've not been in this country very long, have you?'

'But surely – *something* could be done – '

She sighed. 'Only what we are doing at present – staying with her – watching over her – reasoning with her. The attacks can often be averted – but it means constant vigilance, with either my father or myself always being on hand.'

'I can sympathize with you,' I said. 'My father was a drunkard.'

She looked shocked. 'Oh, Mother isn't a *drunkard*,' she said. 'She was brought up very strictly. Her father was *my* father's tutor in London. She once told me that the very first strong drink that she ever tasted was a glass of sparkling wine at her wedding. But she was very ill after I was born and the doctors prescribed gin, and she became addicted to it. So you see – I feel partially responsible for it all.'

'I don't see how you can blame yourself,' I averred stoutly.

'I didn't say blame – I said responsible.'

Then, as suddenly as going through a door, we had entered Boca. At first the increase in speed was wholly exhilarating, because the surface of the river was smooth and unbroken and there was no fear of collision with the rocky banks, at least while we kept to the centre, but the strain on my arms and shoulders of holding the sampan on course with the clumsy steering oar was becoming greater by the moment. And, truth to tell, that was not the only strain I was under. There was a more mundane one on my bladder, but I was far too bashful to relieve myself in her sight, and I was certain that she and her mother would be grateful for a few minutes' privacy also, so I swung the oar across and made for slack water, and we fetched up under the lee of a huge boulder. I leapt out with the painter and made fast.

'I think I'll climb the cliffs to see what lies ahead,' I said diplomatically, and went up over the loose rocks like a mountain goat, until I came to a convenient cave.

I had intended staying away ten or fifteen minutes, but I heard the long-drawn-out scream above the roar of the river even while I was still communing with nature, and I peered out of the cave and saw a blackclad figure struggling in a smother of foam, with another standing immobile on the rocks by the moored sampan, and I raced down the almost vertical cliff-face at a speed that still makes me shudder in retrospect, cursing the besotted slut for standing and watching her daughter drown without raising a finger to help her – but when I reached the sampan I saw that the figure on the bank was Leonora and she was now trying to untie the painter. I snatched it from her and jumped into the boat and yelled to her to get right up in the bow ready to make a grab for her mother when we came level with her, then I shoved off into the stream just in time to see a hand and a black sleeve break the surface for a fleeting second before disappearing round the next bend. I caught sight of her again, minutes later, as I sculled frantically with the single steering oar. She was in the grip of the main current now, being swept along like a bundle of rags, not swimming, but managing somehow through her struggles to remain above surface. I tried to get alongside her, and actually succeeded twice, but the first time Leonora was unable to hold her, and when I left the steering oar and tried to reach her outstretched hand myself, the sampan broached to and nearly capsized and we were swept past her. Then she disappeared altogether.

We came out of the Boca two hours later, after fighting desperately with currents and whirlpools that spun us in circles like a piece of driftwood, and finally came to rest in a quiet backwater. I think I must have collapsed then through exhaustion, because my next clear recollection was waking with a burning thirst in the bottom of the boat, which had now grounded on the bank. Leonora had got out and was lying asleep on the sun-warmed rocks some distance away.

I knelt and took a long drink of muddy river water that was the colour of strong tea, then I wondered if I should walk back up the gorge to search for the woman, but I knew that I would only be doing so for the sake of appearance, and the only practical thing to do now was to push on to Hong Kong as quickly as possible. I turned as I heard a slight sound behind me. Leonora was now sitting up.

I went over to her and said, 'I think it would be futile, but if you wish I'll go back up the Boca on the off-chance – '

She shook her head, and I could see that she had been crying. 'Thank you, Mr Stafford,' she said, 'but I agree. It *would* be futile. She could not possibly have lived through that. Poor Mother.'

'What happened exactly?' I asked. 'Or would you rather not talk about it?'

'She woke just as I was getting out of the boat, and stood up and – and – just overbalanced, I think,' she answered. 'I didn't actually see it, as my back was towards her. I heard a splash, and then she screamed – then you arrived – ' She started to cry again and I knelt beside her and put my arm round her shoulders.

'You mustn't blame yourself,' I said. 'You did everything

possible to save her.'

'I should have been able to hold her when we reached her,' she said unhappily, 'but she was just wrenched from my grasp.'

'That was not your fault. It was beyond your strength.' I stood up and helped her to her feet. She leant against me for a moment and wiped her eyes on her sleeve, then smiled wanly at me.

'I don't know how to thank you,' she said. 'For everything.'

'Please don't try,' I told her. 'It's little enough I've been able to do – but if there is ever anything in the future – '

She took my hand between both of hers and pressed it gently. 'I know,' she whispered. 'Thank you. I'll remember that.'

We got under way again then, and there was quite a fresh breeze blowing, so I stepped the mast and set the sail and we made good progress down the broad estuary until, as the sun went down we saw, far to the south-east, the faint outline of the Peak against the sky.

I had been worrying over the danger of pirates, because Mascarenhas had told me that this particular stretch was infested by them, but as it happened we saw only two other craft the whole day – a large junk going the same way as ourselves which overhauled us and swept past at mid-afternoon, obviously making for Hong Kong at top speed, and later a naval gunboat going north under full sail and with clunking paddles churning the muddy waters into a café-au-lait foam. I tried to hail this one in the hope of getting food from them, but if they saw us at all they disdained to notice us.

We rounded the tip of Lantao and passed Stonecutters' Island as dawn was breaking next morning, and I headed for Kowloon Point and was fortunate enough to see one of Mascarenhas's compradores on the praya. He stared at us in amazement when I hailed him, then, when recognition dawned on him, he got us chairs and running footmen and we were whisked off to his master's compound. It was plain that something serious was afoot because the whole water-front was as busy as an overturned ant hill, with junks loading stores and ammunition, and troops, both British and Chinese, drawn up under arms waiting to embark – and then, when we arrived at the compound, we were met by Mascharenhas himself.

His head was heavily bandaged and his right arm was in splints, and he was pale and worn, but I will never forget the sheer joy that came to his normally impassive face as Leonora rushed towards him. I left them together and crawled into the room that was always reserved for me when I stayed here overnight, and hot drinks, a badly-needed bath and gloriously clean dry clothes were immediately forthcoming, and as I sat down to an enormous dish of bacon, eggs and kidneys and a pot of scalding coffee, Mascharenhas came in.

His momentary emotion was past now and he was once more in complete control of himself, although I could see that he was in considerable pain. He looked at me for some moments without speaking as if considering his words, then he said quietly, 'Leonora has told me what happened. I am grateful.'

'I'm sorry about your wife,' I said awkwardly.

'You did what you could,' he said shortly. 'I only regret that I was not there when I was needed. I had been lured upriver by a false report, and then attacked when I tried to return. I was unconscious when they put me on the last junk to leave the anchorage. I was just about to start back with the punitive column the British garrison commander is sending up.'

'I am afraid your house was under attack when we left, and your junk had been burnt,' I told him, but he waved it aside as if it was a matter of small consequence.

'Material losses can be made good,' he said. 'It is the destruction of the confidence of the hongs that is the tragedy. We gave them our bonded word, and we have broken it. What I said to those fools the other night has come to pass. They will never trust us again.'

'By *us* you mean the British?' I said.

'Unfortunately, yes. Specifically it is certain members of the Company who are to blame – but the hongs do not differentiate.' He appeared to totter, and I jumped up to guide him to a chair, but he shook his head. 'I am all right,' he said, and he turned to go out, then paused and looked back at me levelly, almost fixedly. 'Remember – whatever happens – I am grateful to *you* – personally.'

He went out, leaving me puzzled and disquieted. It was not so much the words themselves, but the way in which they had been delivered. Without doubt he *was* grateful for what little I had been able to do for Leonora, and he did not appear to hold me responsible for the death of his wife, but that apart, it seemed almost as if he had been giving me a warning about something. But what? Did he imagine that I had taken advantage of circumstances – and his daughter? Surely the very idea was ridiculous. The randiest Casanova this side of hell would hardly pause for dalliance when running for his life in front of a Chinese mob. Then what was it? That there was *something*, I was certain, but I was too weary to ponder over it then. I closed the shutters and went to bed.

The house was hushed and dark when I awoke some hours later. I rang for a servant and learned from him that Mascharenhas had collapsed earlier in the day and had been taken by litter across to the Company hospital on the island, and that Leonora had acompanied him. I dressed quickly and hurried down to the waterfront and crossed the harbour and was carried by chair up to the plateau on the slopes of Mount Austin where the hospital was situated, high above the heat and miasma of Victoria, and to my surprise I was greeted by Neil.

'My God! I'm glad to see you again,' he said, wringing my hand. 'All sorts of rumours have been coming down the river. I heard at one time that you and the whole Mascharenhas household had been massacred. You can imagine how I felt.'

'But what are you doing here?' I asked.

'I'd crossed to Kowloon for about the tenth time to try and get news of you,' he explained. 'Hildreth, the surgeon, was just moving Mascharenhas over here – and Leonora appeared distressed, so I thought it civil to come back with them, since you were safe and well – and sleeping like a log.' He winked and nudged me. 'Crafty old devil, you. What a lovely armful, eh? And the guv'nor's daughter to boot! I'd heard all about her from McClintock. Best education in London and Paris that money could buy, but she's fed up to the teeth out here because the Old Man keeps anything in pantaloons off with a big stick – but *you* ought to be all right now – I tell you, McClintock said – '

'I don't want to know what McClintock or any other of your foul-mouthed friends said,' I told him furiously, and he looked hurt.

'Hey! Draw it mild, old chap,' he said. 'I was only joking – and I assure you I wasn't trying to poach on your preserves.'

'That's all right,' I mumbled, feeling foolish. 'I'm tired and irritable. What's the matter with Mascharenhas?'

'Fractured skull, they say. He'd been clubbed. They're doing a – a – *trephine*, I think they call it. That means sawing a bit out of his napper. The poor devil has been under chloroform for hours – ' He looked past me. 'Ah, here's Leonora now.'

I turned to see her coming along the verandah towards us. Leonora? I thought bitterly. She was still Miss Mascharenhas to me.

My Adonis brother seemed to be running true to form, blast his bloody shallow charm.

She looked pale and deathly tired in the lamplight and I instinctively put out my hands to her, forestalling Neil, and led her to a chair.

'How is he?' I asked.

'They've completed the operation,' she answered dully, 'but he is still under chloroform. All we can do is wait now.'

'Stay here with her,' Neil said quietly, and went off.

'You should be resting,' she said to me, breaking a long silence.

'I've slept for hours,' I told her. 'It's *you* who should rest.'

'I can't,' she said. 'Not until he is out of danger. Those

beasts beat him unmercifully. *Papa* – who has always defended and championed them against the wretched Company. He has never cheated or acted dishonourably in his life, but he has more enemies than any other man in the whole Colony. In both camps now. He is very grateful to *you*, though. He feels he can trust you.'

'There is no need for him to feel grateful,' I said, 'but I'm glad of his trust. I'll try never to forfeit it.'

She reached out and took my hand, and we sat in silence until Neil came back with a servant from the Officers' Mess carrying a tray on which a light supper and a cool bottle of wine were tastefully set out.

He said, 'Now come on, Miss Leonora, I'm going to insist on your eating something. You must be famished.'

I felt a hot stab of resentment. Of course he *would* be the one to go off and organize things. Doors opened and wheels turned smoothly for Neil. She smiled up at him gratefully and under his urging picked at some cold chicken and drank half a glass of wine, and she even laughed at some stupid joke of his, and soon he had dropped the 'Miss' before her name, and was, in short, on easier terms with her in an hour or so than I had been after three days alone in her company.

We sat on long into the night, and I dropped off to sleep, and awoke as dawn was breaking to see that she, also, was asleep, with her head on Neil's shoulder and his arm about her. He motioned peremptorily to me not to disturb her, and suggested in a whisper that I should go inside to enquire after the patient – and I, seething inwardly but without the will or wit to argue with him, went. I saw an orderly who took me to two tired surgeons, still in canvas aprons and blood-and-pus-stained frock-coats, drinking coffee in an ante-room.

'He's come round,' one of them told me, 'but he's very weak at the moment, naturally. The prognosis is favourable, but he must be kept quiet for a very long time.'

'Can his daughter see him?' I asked.

He scratched his chin doubtfully. 'Hm – yes – all right – but only his daughter, and only for a minute or so.'

I went back to the verandah. She was awake now, and she jumped to her feet and ran through into the ward when I told her she could see her father.

Neil said, 'She thinks a hell of a lot of you, old chap. She told me everything that happened. My God, I am proud of you.'

'Bloody balderdash,' I snarled.

'What the devil's the matter with you?' he asked mildly. 'You seem to have it in for me. I've only tried to help.'

'There's nothing the matter with me,' I said sullenly.

'You don't think I'm trying to queer your pitch, do you?' he said earnestly. 'I'm not – I promise you. Damn it all, if you'd heard me singing your praises while you were asleep you'd be thanking me instead of behaving like a bear with a sore head.'

'Go to hell!' I spat at him, and then she returned, and her eyes were shining with tears of relief.

'He's going to be all right,' she told us. 'I'm going to light a candle to São Francisco Xavier, Papa's patron saint. Oh Ross – I just don't know how to thank you for everything.' And she stood on tiptoe and kissed me on both cheeks.

I felt a golden glow suffusing me from head to toe. A kiss – and my Christian name! I didn't know she even knew it. But then she turned and kissed Neil also, and the glow waned, because whereas I had stood blinking and blushing like a ploughboy, he had taken both her hands in his and gently returned the salute.

We took her down to the waterfront then, and back across the harbour to the villa. Ho Chang was there and he told us that the riots had been put down by the timely arrival of troops.

'But half the city has been burnt down,' he said gravely, 'and our losses have been tremendous.'

'What caused it?' I asked him. 'I mean, why did it break out at this particular moment?'

He shrugged. 'The same as last time,' he said. 'Opium. The Company promised that no more would be sent upriver, and that proper trade would be promoted, but it *is* going upriver

– and the only trade is that which comes *down*river. Good tea and silk and cotton – jade, fine leather – the best rice in the East, in exchange for poison which is killing a whole nation – poison which is produced in India for a few copper coins, for goods worth a thousand times as much – in gold.'

'But Company rules have forbidden it since the war of 1841,' I protested. 'And you yourself have seen their customs officers searching the bales and bundles going upriver. You are surely not suggesting that the Company itself and its reputable nominees are all engaged in flouting their own laws?'

He smiled fleetingly. 'The elephant and the little monkeys,' he said. 'The elephant is the Company – big – powerful – standing on guard in the gateway here. No, the elephant is not smuggling. But hidden in his shadow are the monkeys who scuttle past him, between his feet and even over his back – each carrying a little opium upriver – and coming back bearing fruit and sweetmeats, and each dropping a trifle under the elephant's trunk. Stop the monkeys going upriver and you stop them coming back – and elephants love fruit and sweetmeats.'

'Can't anything be done to stop it?' I asked hopelessly.

'Yes,' he answered. 'Get rid of the elephant and replace him with a lion. Lions do not eat fruit and sweetmeats. They prefer real meat – sometimes even *monkey* meat. I think that day is not far off.' He kowtowed and left me.

'What was Ho Chang bellyaching about to you in chop-chop?' Neil asked as we went back across the harbour.

'Elephants and monkeys,' I said shortly.

'You are a sulky bugger, aren't you?' he laughed. 'All right – keep it to yourself. Are you going to the Court of Directors' Ball next month, by the way? Our invitations have arrived.'

'No,' I snapped.

'You're getting old before your time.' He dug me in the ribs. 'Why not ask Leonora? She'd love it. With her old man safely in hospital the way would be clear.'

'Shut up, Neil,' I begged. 'For God's sake *shut up*!'

Chapter Eight

I plunged back into work the next day, and there was much to be done as our godowns were crammed with trade goods that had been held up by the trouble. The customs officers came as before, but it was plain that they had been badly frightened by the events upriver and the consequent furore that came blasting down from the Court of Directors, and they were now most diligent in their duties, searching and rummaging through every box, bale and bundle however small, and trapping much opium as a result, which was then burned under the supervision of a board of Company officers. I went to the hospital each day to enquire after Mascharenhas. The delicate and perilous operation, which had involved the cutting out and lifting of a small disc of bone from his skull and replacing it with a silver plate, had, as far as could be judged at this stage, been successful, but the surgeons told me that it would be many weeks before he would be completely out of danger, and they intended keeping him incommunicado in hospital for some considerable time.

I was seeing less and less of Neil as I was now spending more time at headquarters in Kowloon, and he rarely returned to our house until the early hours of the morning, by which time I was usually asleep. He had acquired a smart sailing sampan which he handled with great skill, and although he still put in an appearance at our godown on the island when it was absolutely unavoidable, he sometimes stayed away for two or three days at a time, which troubled me greatly. I finally sat up all one night and tackled him on his return after one such absence, just as dawn was breaking.

He tumbled out of his sedan chair and I could see as I waited for him on the verandah that he was dirty, dishevelled and obviously very weary, and I came straight to the point.

'Where the hell have you been?' I demanded.

'And what the hell has that to do with *you*?' he yawned. 'You're getting just a bit above yourself lately, young Ross.'

'It has everything to do with me, since I have to do your share of the work as well as my own,' I told him.

'Well, go and complain to your lord and master,' he retorted, and pushed past me. I grabbed his arm and he swung round on me. His fist was clenched and poised to strike, and for a sickening moment I thought that we were about to fight, but he took a deep breath and stepped back.

'Actually I've been fishing with a couple of my friends,' he said. 'As far as my share of the work is concerned, it cuts both ways. I've been doing a lot of yours – while you've been running Mascarenhas's errands for him. It's come to something when we start squabbling like a couple of bloody footmen about who carries the coal upstairs.'

'I don't want to squabble,' I said miserably. 'But I'm worried, Neil. We're supposed to be partners in this business, but we're drifting apart – and you've got in with a pretty questionable crowd.'

'I'm quite capable of choosing my own friends,' he said coldly, 'and I'm damned if I'm prepared to be spied upon. I think I'll go and live on my boat for a time. Don't worry about the work. I'll do my share – and more, if necessary.'

He went on into the house and when I returned from Kowloon later in the day I saw that he had removed his effects. I hoped that the split would not be lasting, and that after a while, when the air had cleared, he would come back and the wretched quarrel would be forgotten. But he had not returned by the end of the week, although he did appear at the godown more frequently, and he paid more attention to business. We saw each other from time to time, and at first were distantly polite, then the ice thawed a little and we almost got back on to our normal footing. Almost – but not quite – and, sadly, I felt the old days had gone for ever, and with them the unquestioning loyalty and trust that had hitherto unfailingly held between us.

In spite of the time I spent in Kowloon, I rarely saw

Leonora, and when I did it would only be fleetingly – just a glimpse of her on the terrace as I went to and from the counting-house or, once or twice, at the hospital when she was visiting her father. I did not feel that she was avoiding me deliberately, because on the occasions when I did come into contact with her she was gracious and friendly, so I put her seeming aloofness down to grief over her mother's death and anxiety for her father, and I respected her desire for privacy.

But then came the Court of Directors' Ball, over which Neil had teased me. It was the principal event of the social calendar, we had been told, attended by every lady in the Colony, magnificently gowned, bejewelled and befeathered, and the officers, civil, military and naval, of both Crown and Company, resplendent in full dress uniform, and all merchants above a certain degree. In spite of my peevish disclaimer I had, in fact, intended to pluck up courage and ask Mascharenhas's permission to invite Leonora, because I had clumped through the waltz, polka and mazurka often enough with Caerwen to be confident of not disgracing myself, although I could never hope to aspire to Neil's prowess on the dance floor – but I had abandoned the idea in view of her father's condition and the fact that she was wearing mourning.

I sat on the verandah of our house that night and listened to the distant music that came up from the Club, and watched the magnificent firework display that lighted the sky and the slopes of the Peak at midnight, and hoped wistfully that the position would have improved by next year. Then I went to bed.

I saw McClintock the next day. He had been somewhat subdued after the riots, but was now emerging from cover and sniffing the air, like a fox that has had a narrow escape from the pack, and he chided me with his usual odious bonhomie for missing the event of the year and my 'opportunities'.

'You mustn't let that brother of yours steal the prize from under your nose,' he said.

'I don't know what you mean,' I said shortly.

'The bonnie wee lassie, man,' he laughed, and dug me in the ribs. 'There at the Ball with that sly dog Neil – and no chaperon, either. I bet Mascharenhas would be spinning like a top in his sickbed, if he knew. He's a stickler for the proprieties. Aye, a wonderful sight for sore eyes she was too – dancing with him all night, and him keeping off the competition like a buck in rut. Wake up to yourself, laddie, or you'll be losing her.'

I said, 'Go to hell, McClintock. I'm busy,' and he went out of the godown laughing maliciously, and I left shortly afterwards and walked myself into a muck sweat up the Peak, raging like a madman against Neil, against myself, against the whole unjust world – against everybody but her. No, she was not to blame. I kept telling myself. It was he – the *bastard* – he who took everything with outstretched greedy hands – and gave nothing in return. He who dirtied everything he touched. And it was I – I who lacked the courage to approach her – who stood by gulping and gawping while he with his facile charm and fairground thimble-rigger's patter swept her off her feet. I had risked my life to deliver him from the road gangs, and he had stabbed me in the back. Me – his brother.

And so it went on – in an alternating frenzy of jealousy and a welter of self-pity – until the madness had worn itself out, and I crept back to the house exhausted.

He made no reference to the Ball when next we saw each other, nor to Leonora. I knew that they were now meeting frequently at the Club, at picnics and the newly opened racecourse at Happy Valley, and twice while crossing the harbour I saw them together on his boat, all very daring behaviour for a properly brought-up girl even had they been officially affianced and chaperoned, and I was positive that her reputation was being torn to shreds by the so-called ladies and gentlemen of the Colony, and there was nothing I could do about it, because I knew my brother well enough to realize that it would have been worse than useless to take the matter up with him, although I did tell McClintock that had he not been an old man I'd have horse-whipped him when he made a sly insinuation on one occasion. But it only afforded him amusement.

To my relief Mascharenhas had made a good recovery, but he was still very weak, and the surgeons gave Leonora specific instructions to see that he did not overtire himself when he returned to Kowloon from hospital. We took him home together, and Neil at least had the discretion to busy himself elsewhere that day. We got him comfortably settled in a long chair on the terrace and I gave him a brief résumé of the various transactions that had passed through our hands in the weeks he had been absent, and he expressed his thanks and satisfaction, then, while Leonora was absent for a while, he said, 'You have done very well indeed, Ross. I am not going to make the conventional remark of "I can never repay you for all you've done." I can and will repay you in a practical manner in so far as the business is concerned. But your service to me personally, and my family, is a different matter –' He broke off and was silent for some time, and I thought he had dropped off to sleep, but then he said, 'You're fond of Leonora, aren't you?'

I said yes, and held my breath, wondering what was coming next, but whatever it was it remained unsaid, because she returned then and insisted on his retiring to his room to rest in accordance with the surgeon's regime.

She walked with me down into the courtyard, and I was sorely tempted to warn her that she was being talked about, but I just could not find the words, and I was about to take my leave when, as she had done once before, she put her hands on my shoulders and reached up and kissed me on the cheek. It was merely an affectionate gesture such as might pass between brother and sister, and nothing more, but before I realized what was happening I had taken her hands in mine and was pouring out my feelings in an incoherent spate.

She gently withdrew her hands and shook her head. 'I'm sorry, Ross,' she said softly. 'I heard what my father said to you just now – and your answer. I am fond of you, too – but not that way.'

I said, 'Neil – ?' and could go no further. Her manner changed immediately, and something of the warmth went out of the evening.

'That is a matter I cannot discuss,' she said. 'Good night, Ross – and, once again, thank you.' And she turned and went back up the steps.

The stinging shock subsided to an acute ache, which in turn became a dull one, and then that, too, passed, leaving nothing but a sense of emptiness that fortunately could be filled with hard work and the interest of the things around me. Mascharenhas improved to a point where he was able to pay a short daily visit to the counting-house, and he was always available for advice or a snap judgment on a problem which I considered beyond me. I made mistakes, but he never once held me to blame, and, as time went on, the mistakes became less frequent – and there were even occasions when he, quite solemnly, would ask for my opinion on sundry matters. Leonora was as warm and friendly as ever, but I am sure that she must have made her feeling for me, or lack of it, quite clear to her father, because he never again broached the subject.

Neil had settled down to a steady routine, and the most captious of employers could hardly have faulted his industry and application. He had taken over my duties in the godown and I was more engaged with 'taipan pidgin country-more-far' as out-station business was called, and I travelled widely on Mascharenhas's affairs – to the rehabilitated Canton, Macao, Amoy and Swatow, and even on one occasion as far as Shanghai. Neil and Leonora continued to see each other, but they were now more discreet, and although there were still covert winks and leers between the gentlemen, and raised eyebrows and whispers behind fans among the ladies, they were no longer an active topic of malicious gossip at the Club.

And so one whole year went by, and it was hard to realize in our affluence how short a time had elapsed since we came up the Li Mun Channel penniless and near-naked. I was in ıact, thinking over the events of the year on the anniversary of our arrival, sitting on the verandah watching the sun go down over the hills of Lantao, when Neil came up the path in a chair. Now that I had got over my bitterness we were once again quite friendly, but he still lived on his boat – a larger one these days with two commodious cabins which, when he was not sailing in it, he kept moored at the Murray Steps.

I had not seen him for some time, as I had been away upriver, and it was clear from his face that something was amiss. I called to a servant to bring his favourite tipple – very cold beer – but he said he would prefer brandy.

'Has His Lord High Panjanderamship said anything to you about me today?' he asked sourly.

'I haven't seen him today,' I told him. 'I only arrived back a couple of hours ago and Leonora told me that his head was paining him and that the surgeon had ordered him to bed.'

'Did *she* say anything?'

'About what?'

'Me, damn it – *me*.'

'Not a word. Why should she?'

He took a long draught of his brandy and water before answering.

'I asked the bastard for Leonora's hand,' he said quietly, and I felt a sharp pang of the old ache.

'What did he say?' I asked.

'Nothing for a time. His face just went all Chinese, like one of those masks in the Wanchai market – then it was a very polite but very emphatic no.' He took a long black cheroot from his pocket, bit the end off savagely and lighted it.

'What did you say to that?'

'I told him I loved her, and that she loved me, which would have been enough reason for most men – but not for *him*.' His face contorted. 'He told me I wasn't to see her again.'

'And are you?'

'You can wager all you possess on that, my lad. I most certainly am.'

'Be careful, Neil,' I warned. 'He's a very powerful man.'

'Leonora is three-quarters European – this is a British Colony – and he's not Jesus Christ,' he answered.

I bit back, 'And you're an escaped convict – ' and substituted, 'She is not of age. Her father's word is therefore law.'

'That won't be for ever – and I can wait.' He turned and looked at me very directly. 'Yes, I can wait,' he repeated, 'and so can she. But in the meantime don't try to cut me out, little brother. You may be the apple of His Lordship's eye, but you're just a green and gangling youth as far as she's concerned. She prefers *men*.'

I got up from my chair. 'I was man enough to get you out of prison,' I said viciously. 'Sometimes I wonder whether it was worth the effort. Go and find somebody else to wail to, Neil – and don't bother to come here again.'

He sat on in his chair, his head drooping, then he looked up at me with all the misery of the world in his eyes. 'I'm sorry,' he said brokenly. 'I didn't mean that, old lad. Please believe me – *I didn't mean it*. I just wanted to hit out – to hurt somebody. I'm sorry – Christ, I'm sorry.'

I dropped my hand on to his shoulder, and I think we were both near to tears – then I said, 'Let's have some more brandy – and stop acting like a pair of old maids with the vapours.'

And we got right royally drunk.

The letter was on my desk when I went to the godown three days later to make certain that all was secure and battened down, because the local weather prophets, who were seldom wrong, had warned us that a typhoon was approaching. It was heavily sealed and was addressed to me in Neil's cursive script, and the compradore told me that it had been delivered by a coolie an hour previously. I broke the seals with some foreboding, because he hadn't been near the godown since the night of our carouse, and I had begun to worry.

My dear Ross, [I read]
I take up my pen hoping that this finds you in good health and will not be a shock to you. My darling girl and

I have decided that there is nothing in this place for us so we are leaving for Macao, from where we will take the first clipper to San Francisco. Should you ever wish to join us you know you will be as welcome as the flowers in May, and in that hope and to that end, I shall keep in constant touch with you. Leonora sends you her love, and the both of us give you our heartfelt thanks for all you have done for us jointly and severally, and it is our fervent hope that you will not judge us ungrateful.

God bless you, and may we meet again soon,

Yr affct. Bro.

Neil Stafford.

PS. Forgive me for clearing out our joint account at the Victoria Bank. My need is greater than thine at the moment and you will recoup in no time.

Such is the perversity of human nature that I remember that the shock of losing my half of our combined savings exceeded that of their elopement – certainly in that first hour. I hurried down to the bank and learned from the shroff that Neil had indeed made a foray on our finances the night before, to the extent of eleven thousand Mexican dollars in silver, which he had converted to English banknotes – leaving us in credit to the amount of one hundred and twenty-two dollars. I went on to Murray Steps then, to find that he had slipped his moorings and departed in the early hours.

I sat on a waterfront bench feeling sick, drained and empty. Mercenary considerations were assuming their proper proportions now, and were fading. The thing that really appalled me was having to face Mascharenhas in the knowledge that my brother had repaid his benefaction to us both in this scurvy and underhand manner, and I honestly believe that had any avenue of escape from the Colony existed at that moment, I would have taken it. But there was none, and I realized that the longer I left it the harder it would be to meet him – so I crossed the harbour to Kowloon just as the first deceptively gentle breezes of the typhoon were ruffling the surface.

Furious fathers pursuing daughters in headlong flight to Gretna Green were a popular theme in the theatre of those days, both in drama and comedy, and I think that if Mascharenhas had behaved traditionally it would have been easier to bear, but, although he looked dreadfully ill, his manner was as impassive and courteously restrained as ever. He greeted me with his customary handshake and even made some conventional remark about the impending storm, then he said, 'When did you first learn about your brother and Leonora?'

'He told me that he had asked your permission to marry her but that you had refused it,' I told him miserably. 'I had no idea that they intended to elope. I ask you to believe that.'

He inclined his head gravely. 'I do,' he said. 'You know, I take it, that they are now on their way to Macao?'

I felt a surge of relief, because I had been dreading the possibility of his *not* knowing, and therefore asking me their present whereabouts. I nodded, and he went on, 'I understand from Leonora's letter that they intend being married there, and then going on to California. If that were the only consideration I would accept the inevitable and withdraw my objection, but there are other factors, and I cannot allow them to marry – even if I have to arrange for him to be – removed.'

I stared at him, aghast. 'You don't mean – mean – ?'

'Killed? Yes, I'm afraid so,' he said, as emotionlessly as if he had been discussing the putting down of a sick animal. 'I hope it won't come to that, but if it *is* necessary, it would be only justice according to Chinese philosophy.'

'But damn it all,' I shouted, 'you pride yourself on being entirely European in outlook. Christ! You can't mean that – '

'I can and do,' he said chillingly. 'You see, I have already saved his life, so he is under obligation to me – and morally he could not complain if I called the bond in.'

'Saved his life?' I said. 'I don't understand.'

'Yes, saved his life,' he repeated. 'At the cost of losing face – and a quarter of a million dollars to the Triad. The opium that caused the Canton troubles went upriver under *my* chop.

I had the confidence of the hongs and my merchandise used to go through the Canton godowns without search – even when that of the main Company was suspect. I trusted you as I would never have trusted a Chinese – not even Ho Chang. I was still trusting you, right up to the morning I was summoned to Fahsu – and saw the evidence with my own eyes. Opium inserted into the bales after they had been chopped by Company customs in *your* godown – and then rechopped with my personal seal which I had entrusted to you two boys.'

'Oh, my God,' I gasped. 'You don't think that *I* – ?'

'That you were in the plot also? Yes. What else was I to think? I intended to have you both dealt with – but in the meantime you had put me under an obligation in respect of my wife and Leonora, so I held my hand – and then further evidence came forth which completely exonerated you – but not your brother. I had him warned – *and* McClintock, who was the instigator of it all, and the mischief has stopped.' His face was twitching. He dabbed his forehead with a folded handkerchief, and then leaned forward and took my wrist in his hand. 'I can't trust him, Ross – not with my daughter. You must see that – you *must*!'

'I do see,' I assured him. 'But to have him killed – no, not that.'

'That would only be as the last possible resort,' he said. 'Only if I am unable to stop her leaving Macao with him by any other means. Fortunately there is no ship leaving there for any American port for the next few days. Were it not for this wretched typhoon I would even now be on my way there. I shall certainly set out immediately it passes over.'

'Let me come with you,' I begged.

'By all means,' he agreed. 'I was hoping you would ask.'

Outside the wind was rising to a shrieking crescendo and, although it was not yet noon, the sky was as black as at midnight, and so it remained for a full twenty-four hours until the storm had blown itself out. We went down to the waterfront then, picking our way through uprooted trees and masses of tiles that had been scythed from the roofs by the fury of the wind, to find that the big junk that had taken the place of the one that had been burnt at Canton had been driven on to the rocks and badly holed, as had, in fact, a round dozen of Mascharenhas's fleet. He therefore selected the biggest of the craft that had survived – a swift sampan with a small cabin in the stern – and had it prepared for the thirty-eight-mile crossing of the estuary mouth.

'We will go the northern way,' he told me, 'through the strait between Lantao and Castle Peak. It's somewhat tricky, but we'll save nearly ten miles,' and to my surprise he ordered the two-man crew ashore after the sail had been set, and took the tiller himself, and I guessed it was because he wanted as few people as possible to come back and gossip about anything that might transpire in Macao. Mindful of his weakness and the strain he was under, I tried to take the steering over, but he shook his head irritably, and I took the hint and retired to the bow and did not thereafter try to make conversation.

I fancied myself as a helmsman in these spirited craft, but he could have lost me, and we bore away from the waterfront with every square inch of the sail drawing and our lee gunwale awash, screaming along on the lively breeze that was the legacy of the typhoon, and I reckoned that if the wind held we should get into the Portuguese port by sundown. There were few other boats about, those that hadn't been wrecked or beached mostly skulking in coves and inlets licking their wounds, and after the first hour they ceased altogether and we had the passage to ourselves.

We saw Neil's boat ten miles out from the harbour.

She was high and dry on the rocky beach at the northern tip of Lantao Island – unmistakable even at a mile away, because of the brass and brightwork with which he had lovingly bedecked her, and the red dragon he had had appliquéd to her slatted mainsail, which made her stand out from others of her type like a bird of paradise among crows, and which was still streaming in the wind.

I turned and looked at Mascharenhas. He had seen her also, and he put his helm over and stood in towards the shore, then he brought us up into the wind all-standing, a danger-ously close ten yards from her, and I dropped the anchor and lowered the sail. We peered at her without speaking. There was no sign of life about her, but in the hope that they might have been in the cabin I gave a shaky hail. There was no response, so I dropped over the side into fairly deep water and swam the few strokes to the shore. It was plain that she had been lifted bodily by the storm and had been set down heavily, because her planking was stove in the full length of the starboard side.

I clambered up on to her sloping deck and looked down through the hatchway into each of the cabins, but there was still no sign of them. Then as I ran my eye along the beach I saw a flash of colour against the pebbles a few yards in from the water's edge, and I jumped down and ran towards it. It was a blue-striped sailor's shirt of the type that Neil, in common with other young bloods of the Colony, always affected when yachting – and it had been spread out to dry and carefully weighted down with stones. I gave a deep sigh of relief and turned to wave to Mascharenhas, but he was already swimming one-handed in to the beach, his bundled jacket held high above his head. He came out of the water and joined me and looked at me questioningly. I pointed to the shirt, and he nodded curtly.

Without a word we walked across the pebbles to higher ground and scanned the bare, treeless shore back towards the low hills of the interior. Other than the screaming gulls over-head, there was not the slightest sign of life, human or animal, but half a mile or so away I could make out a small driftwood shack. There were many such along the deserted shores of the outer islands – built by Hakka fishermen for occasional occupation when away from their permanent villages. Mas-charenhas pointed to it and we set off across the rough ground.

I said, 'Don't you think you ought to rest? Let me go on my own,' which were the first words either of us had spoken since we left harbour. He shook his head and kept plodding on, and I could see that he was deathly tired.

There was nobody in the hut – but there had been, because

there were warm ashes in the rough fireplace – and a rumpled travelling rug on a pile of dry bracken.

We came out of the hut and stood peering round – and then I saw them. Two heads bobbing in the water between our boat and the beach. I cupped my hands round my mouth and yelled, just as the leading figure reached the boat and climbed out. I saw that it was Neil. He held out his hand and helped Leonora over the gunwale and then stood up, steadying himself on the rigging, and waved to us in acknowledgement of the hail. Mascharenhas had already started to stride back towards the beach.

We were still only halfway there when we saw the sail being hoisted. I raced ahead and by the time I was knee deep in the shallows Neil had got the anchor up. He dived back to the tiller and hauled in on the sheet and brought the boat round in a tight circle and headed for the open strait.

I can see him now, legs astride, braced against the tilt of the deck, tiller and sheet in one hand as he waved the blue-striped shirt overhead with the other, his bare torso glistening in the sunlight, and his mouth open in a bellowing laugh.

'Sorry old laddie – and you, sir!' he shouted. 'I'll send the boat back from Macao.'

And then there was a shot from behind me – and Neil stood for a moment with a look of slight surprise taking the place of that of sheer joyful exultation. Then he crumpled at the knees and pitched head first over the stern into the water. I turned and stared in horror at Mascharenhas, who was standing with a smoking pistol in his hand.

The boat, lacking a hand on the helm, swung round into the wind and lost way, and I swam frantically towards it because I could see Neil in its shadow, his hand fumbling feebly at the planking. I reached him and got him under the armpits and screamed to Leonora to drop me a rope. She did so, and together we somehow got him aboard. He looked up at me and grinned sheepishly as he did so often when I took him to task, and said, 'Sorry, old laddie – I meant no harm. Where – is – she?'

I said, 'Shut up, Neil. You're hurt. We've got to get you

back.' Leonora was bending over him, her long hair streaming loose and covering his face, and he coughed, and blood trickled down his side on to the deck, and he twitched once, and then was still.

Mascarenhas climbed over the gunwale. Leonora looked up at him expressionlessly and dry-eyed, then slowly she raised her left hand and pointed it at him, with forefinger and little finger outstretched and the others folded tight against the palm, and slowly and very distinctly she said in Cantonese, 'For the family honour I murdered my mother. This is *my* punishment. For yours, may dogs defile the graves of your ancestors back to the beginning of all time.'

For me it was just one more horror – the twisting of a knife that was already deep in the wound. For Mascarenhas it was the end. He stood looking down at her for a time, his face as expressionless as hers, then he shivered convulsively and fell forward, prone on the deck, and I, in my grief and hatred, did nothing to assist him – or her, and hours later we were still in the same juxtaposition – she cradling my brother's head and rocking gently to and fro, Mascarenhas motionless and apparently dead, I hunched numbly in the stern unable to act or even think coherently, all of us like figures in some grotesque Greek tragedy.

Finally a semblance of reason returned to me, and I realized that if we took Neil back to Hong Kong there would of necessity be an inquest, and awkward questions of identity would be raised, and the matter of the bullet wound would have to be explained, and I couldn't face any of it, so I told Leonora curtly what I intended to do, then I swam ashore and scratched a shallow grave. She made no protest as I took the body from her and floated it to the beach. I buried him and then rolled stones over the grave, and I gathered some dry brushwood and piled it in the cabin of the stranded boat and set fire to it.

I swam back then. She was still hunched in the same position, gazing out to sea. I said, 'If questions are asked you must say that we left my brother in Macao. Do you understand?' But I doubt if she heard me. She was entirely Chinese now. Grief is something they brood over deep within themselves, to the exclusion of all else.

I went to Mascarenhas, intending to arrange his sprawling limbs into a more seemly posture and to cover him with a sheet, and it was only then that I discovered that he was still alive – if one could call it life. One side of his face was frozen into a twisted grimace, with the eye fixed in an unblinking stare, and a trickle of saliva came from the corner of his mouth. But there was recognition and a dumb pleading in the other eye, and he tried to speak but only a hoarse mumble escaped him. He was cold and paralysed down one entire side, and there was but little voluntary movement left in the other. I managed to get him into the shelter of the cabin and I covered him with a rug, then I set about getting the boat under way, and headed back for Hong Kong. Behind us the burning boat was a pyre, and there was a pall of smoke above the inlet.

I told Leonora to sit with her father, but again she didn't answer.

I said bitterly, 'I have cause to hate him. He killed my brother. But whatever he did, it was for *you* – and you've cursed him and put the sign of the evil eye on him. Isn't that enough?'

But it availed nothing, and she was still crouched in the same position, staring into the distance when we came at last into harbour.

The surgeons came across from the island in response to my urgent summons, and I told them a cock-and-bull story about taking Mascarenhas out in the boat to inspect storm damage, and this attack coming upon him suddenly. They accepted it without question, and deliberated over him, and entered into abstruse professional argument and finally pronounced it to be a cerebral stroke directly stemming from his original head injury, but, of course, not in any way due to their trephining – and they bled him as a matter of routine, and said that he would eventually recover, or he would not.

He lay like a log in his bed thereafter, completely immobile except for an occasional slight movement in the fingers of his left hand, but, terribly, in full possession of all his mental faculties less that of speech. That he could hear and understand was made evident by the fluttering of his fingers – one movement for an affirmative, two for negation, three for a request for repetition of something that had been said to him but which he had not understood. He was, in short, a man incarcerated and held almost incommunicado within his own moribund body.

I grieved over the death of my brother, but, after the initial shock, I found I no longer hated the man who had killed him. It was not a matter of Christian forgiveness, because of the Mascharenhas I had known there was now nothing left to hate – except this pathetic hulk.

In regard to Leonora, my feelings were completely chaotic. She had emerged from her almost cataleptic trance and had assumed the full responsibility of nursing her father – competently, tirelessly but quite emotionlessly – and when we met she was polite but unsmiling and withdrawn. There were times when I was impelled to offer her some sort of sympathy and reassurance – to take her hands in mine and try, however clumsily, to comfort her, but that awful confession – 'I murdered my mother' – kept ringing in my ears, and I would become completely tongue-tied. I tried to convince myself that it had been pure hysteria – an unjustified self-accusation because she had *failed* to save her mother that had grown into a morbid belief that she had actually *caused* her to drown. But then a doubt would emerge – a doubt that had been in the back of my mind to where I had thrust it, ever since the day of the 'accident'. She *was* standing motionless while her mother struggled in the water – and she *had* managed to reach and hold the drowning woman's hand – but then, inexplicably, her grasp had loosened.

I wondered if Leonora realized that I had heard and understood that tortured cry in Cantonese over my brother's body. If she did, she showed no sign of it.

I stayed on in Kowloon for two weeks, and then, realizing

that there was nothing more I could do there, and finding
the very atmosphere of the place now unbearable, I returned
to the island – to discover that it was not only the Kowloon
house that oppressed me – it was the whole Colony, and I
knew I had to leave.

I called on McClintock the next day and told him I was
winding up the affairs of the nominated company, and asked
for an auditor to scrutinize the accounts. To my surprise, he
offered no objection – in fact I thought he looked somewhat
relieved. He nodded ponderously and said, 'Aye – I think
you're wise, laddie. A man can stay out here too long. The
ways of these wicked heathens get into him, and he often
finds himself thinking – aye, and *acting*, like them. With
some the poison works quicker than with others.' He cocked
an eye at me from under his beetling brows, and lowered his
voice. 'I take it you've learned that the Triad have got you on
their "Makee run or makee die" list?'

'I don't know what you're talking about,' I told him, and
again came that hateful sign of the wink and the tapped nose.

'Quite right,' he said. 'I'm talking nonsense – but many a
true word is spoken in jest. I understand that Neil took the
hint and got out in time. Of course you've had the protection
of Mascharenhas, which he hadn't – but now that Mascharenhas is *hors de combat* you're just a wee bit exposed.'

'I still don't know what you're referring to,' I said. 'And
for Christ's sake don't tap your bloody nose again.'

'Oh, come now,' he smiled. 'You mean to say that you're
as snow-white and Simon Pure as all that? Mascharenhas –
the so-called leader of the anti-opium faction – sending the
stuff upriver by the ton, and using you two innocents as a
blind – and the Triad not getting their proper squeeze-pidgin
as a result. But your brother is not such an innocent after all,
and he not only clips the Triad of their just dues, but he tries
to bilk Mascharenhas himself, and then the fat's in the fire,
and half Canton goes up in flames. You need a long spoon
to sup with the devil. Your brother's a clever young bastard,
but not experienced enough to take on a Chink-Portuguese
halfbreed – '

I stood up and grasped the edge of his large flat desk and heaved. It toppled over on him, knocking him out of his chair and pinning him beneath it. He stared up at me, white-faced and speechless.

'You're wrong,' I told him. 'Utterly and entirely wrong. Repeat that story once again before I leave the Colony, McClintock, and I'll kill you.'

I pushed my way through the cluster of compradores and Indian babus the noise had brought to the door, feeling lighter than I had for a long time, as if my foolishly violent act had been a catharsis which lifted the weight of guilt, doubt and chicanery from my shoulders. I would probably never know the truth of the matter now, but at least I felt I had stopped one murky fountain of lies and calumny, temporarily at least.

I overhauled my personal account and found I had just short of two hundred pounds after I had sold a few possessions, because the money that Neil had taken from the bank had vanished – no doubt in the flames of his boat – and, curiously, I was glad. I only wished to leave this place, and having done so I wanted no tangible links leading back to it.

The tea clipper *Asturias* was sailing for London, via the Cape of Good Hope, in three days' time, and I was able to secure a cabin aboard her. I went to see Mascharenhas for the last time. He obviously understood when I told him I was leaving, and there was no reproach in his eye, although there was a mist in mine as I left his room. Poor Mascharenhas, most generous of men. My brother and I had brought him and his nothing but sorrow, and the tragedy of it was that neither of us had meant to.

Leonora listened unmoved as I stumbled through my farewell to her, then she nodded gravely, shook hands with me and wished me well in the future. Ho Chang came to the ship just before we sailed and I begged of him to watch over them both.

'Have no fear,' he said. 'He has been as a father to me, and his daughter as a sister. Family bonds are the strongest things in life to our race.' He held out his palm. 'Give me a coin,

Ross,' he asked, and I handed him a silver dollar. He looked at it and murmured something in Mandarin that I did not understand, then he threw it over the rail into the harbour. 'You will come back now,' he said, and when I shook my head he smiled and said, 'It is written. Two things bring us Chinese back to this country from the four corners of the earth. Money left behind us, and to be buried with our ancestors.'

'I am not Chinese,' I reminded him.

'Not by birth certainly,' he said. 'But look about you – ' then as I turned he caught my arm – 'no, not that way. With the sun – from Li Mun, in the east – south, over the Peak – keep turning – Lantao – on to Tai Mo Shan – Kowloon – Kai Tak – and so back to Li Mun. Tell me – are you not leaving something of yourself here?'

And in that moment I felt I was, and much of the revulsion of the last few weeks left me – but I shook my head again.

'You're trying to put a spell on me,' I laughed. 'You should be ashamed of yourself – an educated man indulging in fisherman's superstition.'

'You will come back,' he said positively. 'The Wander Joss has spoken.' And then an officer on the poop was calling on visitors to leave for the shore, and t'gallants and headsails were being shaken loose.

I watched the Peak fading in the evening mist – and wondered.

Chapter Nine

The *Asturias* was a fast and well-found ship, and we made
an excellent passage south through the China Sea to the
Strait of Malacca where we swung round to the north-west
and into the Bay of Bengal, for, having been unable to obtain
a full cargo of tea in China, the captain intended to call at
Calcutta to fill his holds with the less costly but more readily
available Indian varieties. There were only six passengers for
London besides myself, and since she was not a Company
ship, none of them was an official, for which I was thankful.
I had brought a box of books with me, and with these and
the general interest of the voyage through the tropical seas
with its myriad islands, I did not find time hanging heavily
on my hands. I thought little of what lay ahead of me in
England, possibly because I thrust the subject to the back of
my mind. It was not a particularly attractive prospect when
considered in contrast with the excitement of the last few
years, marred by tragedy though some parts of it had been.
I would have to find immediate employment, of course, but
then I determined that I would try to obtain an overseas post
somewhere.

We arrived at Diamond Harbour on the twentieth day out
from Hong Kong and picked up a pilot for the difficult eighty-
mile passage up the Hooghli to Calcutta, most of which was
made with the assistance of two paddle-wheel tugs. We
warped into the docks at Kidderpore late in the evening, and
it was only then that our captain learned, greatly to his
wrath, that a ship which we had passed outward bound in
the river that afternoon, had cleared all the tea in the port,
and no more was expected down from the gardens of
Darjeeling until the following season. Cursing at this completely wasted and extremely expensive detour, he told us

over dinner that he intended sailing at first light next morning in the hope of overhauling the other ship and beating her into Colombo, where, hopefully, Ceylon tea would be available. I asked him if there was anything of interest ashore that would make an evening excursion worthwhile, and he growled something about there being nothing but niggers, pox, filth and stinks. The other passengers therefore settled down to their eternal whist and bezique, and I retired to my cabin to read – but in the absence of a fresh sea breeze the air was heavy, hot and humid, so I decided that in spite of the captain's denigration I would go for a walk.

I saw the mate at the top of the gangway, and he grinned sourly as I passed.

'Be careful, sir,' he warned. 'The Old Man is sailing on the tide at the crack of dawn, come hell or high water. So if it's the ladies that you're looking up, be certain that you're out of bed and back aboard before five o'clock at the latest.'

I waved airily and said I doubted if I'd be ashore more than an hour at most, and that he had a filthy mind, and then I set off along the docks towards a massive grey pile I had seen in the daylight a mile or so upriver, and which one of the officers had told me was Fort William.

But there was little to see when I got there, except for a native sentry standing under a guttering guardlamp the other side of a raised drawbridge, so I bore right across a dark plain towards a group of lights which I judged marked the outskirts of the city itself.

I can remember little after that, apart from hearing a slight rustle behind me in the darkness of the plain, and catching the merest glimpse of white before being struck down by a heavy blow on the head.

I was lying on bare stones in almost complete darkness, and somebody was singing 'The Rose of Tralee' in a cracked quaver. I sat up and heard a squeak and a patter, and something ran across my legs. I tried to get to my feet, but my head spun in circles and I toppled backwards and measured my length on the stones. I lay still and tried to collect my scattered wits, and again something soft and furry brushed over my leg. I kicked out, and once more there was a squeak and a patter, and I realized I was stark naked. I started to yell, and the singing stopped, and from somewhere above me a voice said, 'Oh, so you're back amongst us, me boy, are you? It's lucky you had me for company or the rats would have been eating you in real earnest instead of just playing.'

I looked around, but couldn't see anybody in the gloom.

'Where am I – and how did I get here?' I groaned.

'Where the hell else but in the fort – the fort called for that murdering bastard that was after killing me countrymen at the Boyne, and whose name I wouldn't be befouling me tongue by uttering,' the voice went on. 'As for getting here, you were brought back by Sergeant Sloan, the lousy Orange son of a whore. What a blind you must have been on,' he added admiringly.

My eyes had become adjusted to the gloom now and I could make out a head silhouetted against a barred window above me. I tried once more to get to my feet, and this time succeeded, although I had to lean against the wall for support. The other man was standing on a stone bench, and he moved slightly to one side and held his hand out to assist me.

'Come up alongside me here,' he invited. 'It's no cooler than down there, but at least you'll be getting what fresh air there is, if there was any, which there ain't, if you see what I mean in a manner of speaking. Don't take any notice of me running on like this. It's always the same when you've been in the Hole for a bit on your own. This is me fourth time – twenty-eight days, fifty-six days and now a hundred-and-bloody-twelve days, which are coming to an end, praise be to God. I'll be getting you a drink of water.' He made a long arm through the bars and brought back an earthenware jar. 'I keep it up here,' he explained, 'because the bloody rats are after drinking, swimming and pissing in it on the floor.'

I grabbed it from him and drained it. The water was luke-warm and evil-smelling, but it eased my burning thirst. The man took the empty jar from me and pushed it back through the bars.

'Gul Mohammed, you whiskery heathen,' he called. 'Be after getting this filled again, jaldi-jaldi, or I'll be kicking your black arse when I get out of here.' He turned to me and grinned puckishly. Standing beside him I was able to see that he was a little gnome of a fellow who barely came up to my shoulder. He had a wrinkled, yellowish face, bright black eyes like shoe buttons, and he was toothless except for a single discoloured fang which protruded over his lower lip. His scanty hair was tangled and matted with filth, and he was badly in need of a shave.

'Please – what is this place?' I begged.

'The fort, as I told you,' he said. 'This particular bit of it is what has been known as the Black Hole, for the last hundred years. Bad enough for two of us, but think of a hundred and forty-six poor bastards squashed in here by that *soor-ka-bacha* Suraj-ud-Daula. Can't you see it now? Choking and groaning and dying – until only twenty-three got out alive in the morning – '

'The Black Hole of Calcutta?' I gasped in horror. 'Good God! But what am *I* doing here?'

'Meditating and sorrowing over the wickedness of your military ways – and vowing to mend 'em in the future, thereby earning the good opinion of your kind and generous benefactors, the officers – God rot 'em. That's what you *should* be doing. Actually you're leaning against the slimy wall, shivering and shaking and wondering what in the name of Christ ever made you go a-soldiering.'

'But I'm not a soldier!' I said.

'Standing there bollock-naked, with a lump the size of a goose's egg on your napper, there's many as would be inclined to agree with you – particularly sergeant-majors – but having rashly taken their shilling and signed a contract with the Honourable East India Company to serve the Governor-General, the Court of Directors and their officers set above you for the term of your natural life or such lesser period as may be decreed by the said Governor-General, *but not by you*, you bloody *are* a soldier, me bonny bucko – and you're in the Black Hole for sodding off without leave and getting pissed. I hope that sets matters aright for you.' He grinned disarmingly and took the stump of a cheroot from behind his ear and reached up to the window. 'Gul Mohammed! Bigli do!' he yelled, and a black hand came into view the other side holding a smouldering length of tow. The little man drew deeply and lit the stump and then proffered it to me. 'Take a pull on that, me old half-section. You'll feel better.'

I shook my head. 'Look,' I said earnestly. 'There's some terrible mistake. I'm *not* a soldier. I never have been. I am a passenger on a ship to England. I came ashore for a walk. I think I must have been attacked and rendered unconscious. Please – I must speak to somebody. The ship is sailing early –'

He looked at me sympathetically. 'Don't be taking on too bad about it,' he said. 'You was probably drinking sharab – real panther piss it is, not to be taken lightly by the newly arrived. Gives you all sorts of ideas. Hallooginations the doctors call it. We had one young feller – your type to a tee – talked like a real gent he did – got a skinful of the old mocker aboard, and reckoned he was Hannibal, and he pinched an elephant from the Nawab's stable and started to ride home over the Alps – only it was the Himalayas, and they say he's somewhere in China at the moment.'

'I've just come from China,' I said wildly.

'There you are!' he said triumphantly. 'What did I tell you? But it will pass. Another couple of hours' sleep and you'll be your own man once more. Just tell the adjutant when you go up in front of him that you didn't mean it, and it'll never happen again – and you'll get a few days in here to larn you, and maybe a one-rupee fine – and no hard feelings. Happens to the best of us at times.'

'Damn you! Get out of my way,' I shrieked at him, and grabbed the bars and shook them. 'I want to speak to somebody in authority! Call an officer! *Immediately!*'

A bearded native soldier in white breeches, scarlet jacket and tall shako, looked at me in mild surprise from the room on the other side. The little man called past my ear, 'Achcha, Gul

Mohammed. *Sahib thora nashi hui.* Little bit pissed, eh. He'll be all right – but don't call the sergeant-sahib for Christ's sake – or he bloody *won't* be all right.'

I slumped down weakly on to the bench and held my aching head in both my hands. 'Oh, God!' I moaned. 'Can't you realize? The ship – the *Asturias* – it's sailing at five in the morning – '

'Which morning?' he asked.

'*This* morning, you fool!'

'Well – it can't make much difference one way or the other now, can it?' He held up a warning finger as a distant bugle call and a roll of drums came to us. 'There you are. Just sounding Retreat. Sundown – six p.m. Visiting Rounds any minute now. Get up off your arse and stand to attention when the officer comes to the door, or that'll be another charge on your crime sheet.' He looked at me critically and then took a sweat-soaked kerchief from round his neck. 'You better be covering your conjollickers with this,' he said, 'or they'll be having you for indecent exposure as well.' There was a clacking of footsteps from outside, and a rattle of bolts and the heavy door swung back. A young boy in a white uniform stood revealed in the light of a lantern held by some dimly seen soldiers behind him. He pressed a handkerchief to his nose.

'Faugh! What an unholy stink,' he said.

I hastily draped the damp cloth in front of me and went forward. 'Please – I must speak to you urgently,' I implored.

He stared at me in pained distaste. 'When I give you leave to,' he said. 'Until then, shut your mouth and look to your front.'

'I am *not* a soldier,' I shouted.

'One can see that with half an eye,' he said disdainfully. 'But by God you'll be one when you leave here – or a corpse. The choice is yours – about the only one you'll get.' He pointed to the little man with a betasselled cane. 'You, drummer. Any complaints?'

'Nary a one, sir – begging your pardon,' the little man answered, standing rock still and staring fixedly ahead of him. The youth pointed at me. 'Now, you – any complaints?'

'Please – I'm trying to tell you – ' I began.

'Feller's still drunk,' said the boy, and stepped back into the passage. 'Right – carry on.' The door slammed to and I rushed at it and hammered on the wood impotently with my fists.

'You stupid jackanapes!' I howled. 'Will you listen to me – '

The little man grasped my bare arm with surprising strength. 'You can fart against thunder all you wish,' he said savagely, 'but not at *my* expense. Conduct to the prejudice of good order and military discipline, they call that, and they're as like to stop our supper for it as not – so sit down and bloody well compose yourself, or it'll be a drummer's salute for you.'

And since there was nothing for it, I sat, in sheer black despair.

Our food came shortly after that – a large flat brass tray piled with rice and various vegetables that were totally unfamiliar to me, and there were two bowls with a savoury concoction of meat so highly spiced that I could hardly hold it on my tongue – but it was surprisingly appetizing none the less, and I was young, healthy and hungry, as I had not eaten for over twenty-four hours by this time. My companion chuckled approvingly and said, 'Ah! Grub from the sepoys' cookhouse, thank God. If it came from the European lines it would have been the only bad thing that ever came out of the Distressful Country, bar me – Irish stew, and be damned to it.'

He chattered on incessantly while we ate, and I learnt that he was one Drummer Aloysius O'Hehir, of the 3rd European Infantry, Bengal Army, and he had been in India for eleven years. I asked him how much longer he had to serve, and he said, 'Until I can no longer stand unaided and bate me drum. I didn't know that a poor feller enlisted for life, all to be served in this country, when he took the Company shilling. To tell you the truth, I didn't know anything much on that black day. Some bloody rogue I was drinking with in Cork told me he could get me into the Fenian Brigade to fight the

British for fifty shillings a week and a golden guinea for every damned red-coat you sent to hell. Good money, in a year when the potato crop had failed for the third time. I woke up at sea, on me way to Brentwood.'

'Why there?' I asked.

'The Depot – Warley Barracks, damn it. Don't act the greenhorn with me, young feller. You must have been there yourself.'

'As God is my judge,' I said earnestly, 'I was never there. I was a passenger on the *Asturias*, bound for England from Hong Kong. I'm telling you the truth,' I finished desperately.

He looked at me closely in the dim light that struggled through the bars from the guard lantern the other side.

'Be damn,' he said thoughtfully. 'You know, I'm inclined to believe you. You certainly don't look like a deserter on the run from one of the Royal regiments – though you *may* be a broke officer fleeing from his debts. Hm – a civilian, you say? Then unless you're a real big bug, *and you can prove it*, you're in a prime fix, me lad.'

'Why?'

'Why? Because the Company has got its talons into you now, that's why, and they're not going to let you go without a hell of a lot of *tamasha*. Recruits are hard to come by.' He shook his head commiseratingly. 'I heard Sergeant Sloan reporting to the Orderly Officer out there in the passageway when the picquet brought you in, that you were Private Muir Dalrymple – there's a fine name for you – a recruit that had just landed with a draft from London, and who had gone adrift after drink and women. Picked up naked on the Maidan, you were.'

'I can prove I'm not,' I said indignantly.

'How?'

'Well – er – how can they prove I *am*?' I countered.

'They don't have to. The onus is on you. This is India – where the game is played strictly by the rules – and the Company makes 'em.'

'Damn it! The real Private Whatever-his-name-is – when he's found –'

'I'll give you five to one in quarts of beer that he won't be.

The draft went through here a week agone. If he was still alive he'd have been picked up by now. Strangled for his uniform and boots, poor bastard – that's what's happened to *him*.'

'They've only got to get somebody from the draft to confront me – '

He laughed hoarsely. 'Somebody from the draft?' he cried. 'North of Allahabad that lot was bound for – marching on foot up the Grand Trunk Road, all twelve hundred miles of it. Then they'll be split up over hell's half-acres from there to Meerut and beyant. Half the poor sods'll be dead come the monsoon, anyway.'

'But surely they can't just give me somebody else's name and draft me into their wretched army without investigation?' I insisted.

'There's only one thing they can't do to you in the army, me lad – and that's put you in the family way. And that's not for want of trying, either.' He slapped at a mosquito. 'Investigate, did you say? Oh yes – they'll no doubt do that if you make a big enough fuss about it. Letter back to Warley Barracks, Brentwood – six months – answer, a further six months – buggering about at each end, another six months or so on top of that – two bloody years rotting in the Hole here in the meantime. Sooner you than me, cocker.'

'Then what do you advise?' I begged.

He grinned again. 'An exercise in military strategy,' he said, 'which for the likes of us means standing with your heels together and toes turned out, thumbs in line with the seams of your trousers and a look of supreme unintelligence on your mug, and saying "yes sir" and "no sir" when given permission so to do – and not a bloody, blind word more. That way you'll get a "First Drunk" on your sheet and you'll be out of here in a week. Then, if you *are* who you say you are you can set about proving it.'

He was still talking when I went to sleep on the bare stones, worn out and in the depths of despair.

They came for me next morning. A corporal threw a bundle

of coarse white canvas garments and a pair of clumsy boots through the door, and the drummer helped me to put them on, then I was pushed out into the passageway and fallen in between two soldiers, and the corporal bellowed, 'Pris'ner and escort! Quick march! Lep' ri' – lep' ri' – lep' ri' – pickem up for Cri'sake – ' and we sped along to some stone steps and out into the open.

I remember that it was early morning, and the air still held an illusion of freshness, and there was even a hint of dew on the gold mohur trees. We crossed a wide parade ground where separate squads of European and native troops were drilling, and went into a doorway in the outer casemate under the frowning battlements of that grimmest of all forts. We were halted in front of a table at which sat two officers – one of them the youth I had encountered before, the other only slightly older.

The corporal said in a gabbled monotone, 'Sir! Adjutant's Orders – absentee apprehended by town patrol on Maidan on twenty-third instant improperly dressed and in drunken condition.'

The elder picked up a sheet of paper and read in languid tones, 'Seven, nine, six, three, Recruit-Private Dalrymple M. Absent from the place of lodgement appointed by his Commanding Officer from Retreat on the twenty-second until apprehended by the patrol at dawn on the twenty-third.'

'Stark naked, pissed as a whelk and probably poxed to the eyebrows,' yawned the other one. 'Disgusting feller. They must be dragging the gutters for them at Home.'

The first one said, 'Anything to say?' then as I opened my mouth, he added, 'Shut up! Will you accept my award or do you elect for trial by court martial?'

Again I opened my mouth, and they both said 'Shut up!' and the corporal dug me sharply in the back and growled, 'Shut up, like the officer told you, until you're spoke to.'

'Award accepted by accused,' the officer said, picking up a pen and scribbling on the paper. 'Seven days to cells, and to be fined two rupees and placed under stoppages of pay for loss of uniform, kit and equipment. Watch yourself in future, my good man. You've made a bad start. March him out.'

It was too much. I shouted, 'Look here! I *have* got something to say – '

The officer raised his eyebrows and said, 'Indeed? So have I. *Fourteen* days to cells. Away with the fool, corporal, before he hangs himself.'

'Rogues' march! Hup! 'Bout turn! Double!' snapped the corporal, and I found myself grasped by the elbows, spun round and rushed at a smart trot by my escort back across the square, down the steps and into the Hole again, and never once in that swift passage did my feet touch the ground.

The corporal said, 'Give him a fatherly talking-to, drummer. Got off light and then starts to argue – and ccps fourteen. More mouth than Bridget O'Reilly has pussy.' The door slammed and the drummer stood looking at me reproachfully.

'There – what did I tell you now?' he said. 'Fourteen days is it? And it could've been seven if you'd heeded me – ' and he went on in the same vein, day and night, until he was released a week later.

But not all his verbosity was profitless, because he gave me a great deal of information that was to prove useful in the future, and he even showed me some elementary drill – how to fall in on parade – to dress to the right – to stand at ease, and to attention – to recognize the different bugle calls from the parade ground outside, and, above all, how to salute my officers.

'Forget your name, the colour of your sweetheart's eyes and the prayers you learned at your mammy's knee, if you will,' he said. 'But for Christ's sake never forget that. Hup! One – two – three – Down! – and a look of utter adoration even while you're hating the bastard's guts. There's nothing the young gentlemen dislike more than to be ignored. And they *are* young, even if some of 'em may not rightly be blessed with gentility. Packing 'em out here from Addiscombe at fifteen and a half now.'

'What the hell's Addiscombe?' I asked.

'The Academy where the little bastards are trained,' he told me. 'Just south of London. The Royal army officers come from Sandhurst, and have to buy their commissions, and they

only serve ten years out here. Our jewels are with us for life
– but they get a whole year's furlough every ten, which is
more than us poor sods get. Thirty years for a pension for us
– if we live that long, which damn few do. We get more pay
than the Royals, of course. Twelve rupees a month for a
private, as against about nine for them. Unfortunately we
can't be flogged, which the Royals can.'

'Why unfortunately?' I asked.

'Because the drummers always do the flogging in a British
regiment – strong arms and wrists, see? – and they get extra
pay for it.'

'You horrible little bastard!' I said, and he laughed merrily,
and went on with my instruction.

I was sorry to see him go at the end of my first week in the
Hole, but he came to the guardroom on most days and left
something for me each time with Gul Mohammed, the regimental policeman who was permanently stationed there –
fruit, native sweetmeats, a cheroot, and once even a tot of
murderously potent army rum.

They let me out on the morning of the fourteenth day, and
I was marched to the Quartermaster's store and issued with
the miscellany of garments that made up the European
soldier's uniform of that day – a bewildering collection of
jackets, coatees, shirts, breeches, helmets, neckcloths, boots
and a double armful of straps, buckles and pouches. The
quartermaster-sergeant pushed a document across to me and
said, 'Put your mark on that,' and I was about to sign 'Ross
Stafford' when I noticed at the top of it he had already
written the name of the missing recruit, so I quickly changed
my signature to 'Muir Dalrymple'. He looked at it for a
moment or so, then nodded approvingly.

'Quite a good fist,' he said. 'Man of education gone wrong,
eh? I could do with a clerk in here since the last one drank
his bloody self into the grave. Get through your recruit
training and I'll keep it open for you. Meantime you can help
out with the kit ledgers in your spare time, and it'll be worth
a few rupees to you. You're going to need it after paying for
that lot.'

And thus the wind was tempered to the shorn lamb, and, truth to tell, I did not find the next few months until I was dismissed the square quite as irksome as I might have feared. The drill was hard and monotonous, but not unbearably so, and I quickly mastered it to the satisfaction of the drill sergeant and his two corporals, and there were parts that I even found enjoyable, particularly the days spent on the musketry ranges at Dum Dum. I had done a little wildfowling in Hong Kong, and I had a naturally true eye, so it was no hard task to qualify for the coveted crossed muskets of the Marksman on my sleeve, which would bring me another two rupees a month when I started to draw pay.

Our quarters in the fort, although spartan, were adequate, and as comfortable as any could be expected to be in that dank and humid climate, as they were set high above the river where they caught the breezes, and when there were none, we had *punkahs* – large fans suspended from the ceilings and put in motion by a coolie sitting on the verandah outside pulling a long cord. We were spared most of the degrading menial fatigues that so marred the lives of soldiers in the Royal regiments because we had coolies to perform most of them – sweepers, watercarriers and washermen – or *mehtars*, *bhistis* and *dhobies* as they were called in Hindi. We even had barbers who shaved us in bed before reveille, and boys to clean our uniforms and equipment, all for the paltry sum of two annas a month, which was one-eighth of a rupee, which in turn, was then a fifth of a pound sterling.

There were no more than a hundred European rank and file in the fort at that time, the rest of the regiment being in permanent quarters at Barrackpore, fifteen miles up the Hooghli from Calcutta. We were mainly employed on staff and administrative duties – signallers who manned the heliographs and semaphores on the turret high above the main bulk of the fort, and also the very new electric telegraph that was then beginning to spread its tentacles throughout lower India – and there were clerks and writers, and orderlies for the Governor-General at the nearby Residency, with, inevitably, the provost-sergeant and his men. In command of us

224

were four officers, two of whom were always absent on leave in the cool hills to the north. The two who were present when I arrived, were the Assistant Adjutant, Lieutenant James Law, who had sentenced me, and his youthful companion-at-arms, Ensign the Honourable Piers Ingoldsby-Moreton. The former was relieved by Captain John Kelso in my first month – a slight change for the better – but the Honourable Piers remained to try us. He was, I learned, the younger son of an impoverished peer. He was about my own age, fair and good-looking – with a frank, open countenance and, to belie it, the meanest and most spiteful disposition it has ever been my misfortune to encounter.

Because of the nature of our duties the majority of the men were at least literate – in fact many of them were highly educated. Some of them had taken Indian wives, and lived with them in cheap lodgings outside the fort when not on duty, the progeny of such unions usually being baptized by the missionaries, after which they were educated at Company expense for ultimate employment as overseers and subordinate clerks. We numbered in our ranks, to my knowledge, at least three 'broke' officers from Royal regiments, a struck-off physician, an unspecified number of absconding bank employees, a defalcating lawyer and an unfrocked parson.

'Bloody rogues the lot of 'em,' Aloysius told me over beer in the canteen one evening, 'but middling good soldiers none the less for that. The Company recruiting sergeants back in England are always on the watch for them, the cunning bastards. They don't wear uniform like the Royal army recruiters, and they work from quiet little offices in London, Liverpool and Bristol – and one in Edinburgh, and, of course in the Distressful Country – at Cork and Newry. They sit around in pubs near the police courts – nice kindly looking buggers with eyes like hawks – on the watch for gents down on their luck, and they're ready with a little sympathy and a pint or two with a tot of gin in it, and marvellous tales of the Rajah's life all white men live out here, and the fortunes just waiting for smart fellers to pick up, and before you know it you're on your way to Warley Barracks, with some tough-looking sod travelling with you to make sure you get there.'

So passed my first six months. I had the advantage of being thoroughly acclimatized by my two years in Hong Kong, and since I didn't drink to any extent, had the digestion of an ostrich, and didn't frequent the bazaars, I escaped the fever and cholera that all but halved our numbers that summer. There was some talk of sending me upcountry with the next draft, but since I was by this time making myself useful to the quartermaster-sergeant, my name was removed from the list and I carried on with guard and provost duties, apparently to someone's satisfaction, because I was marked for promotion to lance-corporal – and I worked on various ledgers in the cool of the evening. I made enquiries about the *Asturias* at the three main shipping agencies in Calcutta, but without success. She had come in late in the afternoon and had sailed with the dawn, and apparently there had been no report regarding a missing passenger, so I mentally wrote off the loss of my books and luggage, and began to think seriously of my future, because, although I was not in any way unhappy with my lot at the moment, I certainly had no intention of spending the rest of my life soldiering for the Company in another man's shoes, at the behest of a couple of fools who consigned me to their damned dungeon without giving me a chance to explain. But, at the same time, I was in no overweening hurry to return to England. There was nothing for me there that I knew of, while the fascination that strange lands had always held for me was once more stirring in my blood. As Ho Chang had said, 'The Wander Joss had spoken'.

There was an excellent public library in the city, and I made full use of it, and read widely, and I also started to pick up a few words of the local languages. There were three main ones – Urdu, the lingua franca used by the army in all parts of the sub-continent of India, and thus by far the most useful of them – Hindi, the civil version of it – and Bengali, spoken only in this province. I therefore decided to concentrate on the first, and found it to be considerably easier than

Cantonese, in so far that it was not tonic, and had a difficult but understandable Persio-Arabic alphabet, and a regular grammar – and I made reasonably fast progress in it.

And then we were relieved at the fort by another company, and posted to our parent unit at Barrackpore. I welcomed this because I had explored Calcutta and its immediate environs to the full, and was more than ready for a change of scene.

We marched the fifteen miles upriver in one day, with Ingoldsby-Moreton riding a spirited charger at our head and showering us with dust, but I enjoyed it nevertheless, in my new glory of one stripe, supplementing the rat-tat-tap of Aloysius's drum with a most professional 'Lep – ri' – lep!' and comparing the landscape each side of the road with that of Hong Kong and the overland route to Canton, and feeling, strangely, a certain nostalgia for the latter.

In Barrackpore the whole tempo of military life changed, and I was sent to a Horse Artillery Battery to be trained in elementary field gunnery. Naturally I was not consulted in this, nor was the strange metamorphosis explained to me, but I gathered that there was a new experiment afoot. Artillery, costliest of all military branches, was perennially thin on the ground in the Company army. The smallest tactical unit in the field was normally a battery of six guns, each manned by six gunners and drawn by six horses – each pair of horses being controlled by a driver, making a detachment of nine men under a sergeant per gun – a total of sixty men plus twenty supernumeraries to handle ammunition and supply wagons, with altogether, over a hundred horses per battery. Infantry, on the other hand, was largely self-supporting except for a baggage train, but, without artillery protection, very vulnerable on the line of march. It had been decided, therefore, to equip each infantry company with one gun, and to train a detachment of its own men to handle it.

No doubt because of the novelty of it, I found the experience very interesting. The gun selected in our case was a muzzle-loading nine-pounder, an extremely manoeuvrable weapon which, properly handled, could hurl its nine-pound shell, loaded with high explosive, over two miles.

With six European privates and three Indian drivers, I reported each morning to the Master Gunner, and we were put through a strenuous programme of gun drill and equitation, because not the least attraction of the proposition was that the whole detachment was to be mounted. In the afternoons we were instructed in ballistics, gunlaying, fuse-setting and range-taking – and at the end of three months I sat a practical and a written test, was passed as efficient, promoted to corporal, and appointed bombardier in charge of the company gun. With my rank pay now sixteen rupees a month, plus another four efficiency allowance *and* the right to swagger abroad in smart Hessians and spurs in place of the infantryman's heavy boots, life took on a renewed interest, particularly since, added to all this, by custom and tradition artillery took precedence over foot soldiers, and we had the inestimable privilege of riding with our gun at the head of the column when on the march, with only the company commander in front of us. That this last named functionary was the loathsome Honourable Piers, now promoted to lieutenant, rather dimmed my personal enjoyment, but at least, I told myself, I was now on a level with him and no longer had to trudge on foot at his damned horse's heels. Of such small things is military satisfaction composed.

The monsoon was over, and what passed for the 'cold weather' in Lower India was upon us – which meant that the mornings between dawn and nine o'clock were wholly delightful, with just a hint of a nip in the air, and the nights were cool also. This was the season for marches – twenty miles between sunset and sunrise – with the heat of the day passed in the camping grounds, each set a day's march apart, usually in a mango tope in which a well was invariably situated.

Never a whiff of wood smoke comes to me to this day, without my thoughts going back to those marches. The rows of bivouacs under the cool, glossy-leaved trees, with the officer's tent separated from the lower orders by a seemly interval, the cooks' fires gleaming brightly, the horses, watered, groomed and fed, drowsing on their picketing lines, the baggage wagons in laager, with the bullocks munching contentedly on their cuds. These were only practice marches, five days at a time, to condition us for sterner stuff to come, for the regiment was to move to Faraqbagh, a small but important town on the River Ganges, roughly halfway between Lucknow and Cawnpore, and our company was to form the advance guard, marching two days ahead of the main body – with 'my' gun proudly leading the way.

We set off on a brilliantly moonlit night, with the band playing us off the Barrackpore square and out of cantonments to the strains of *'Jan Kampni Ki Jai!'* (John Company for Ever), a lively march to which the troops had set some highly irreverent and obscene verses. The Colonel, who was to proceed with regimental headquarters more comfortably by river transport, had taken up a position five miles along the Grand Trunk Road to see us started on our way, and, as we passed him, the Honourable Piers, riding at our head, gave a resounding 'Eyes Right!' and a sweeping sword salute, unfortunately just as the band ceased playing, and the Colonel bellowed to the adjutant, 'Captain Kelso! Tell that bloody boy that swords are not drawn nor compliments exchanged after sundown!' A ripple of laughter ran through the marching ranks, and some wag started to sing, 'And a Little Child Shall Lead Them'.

But we paid for our fun in a variety of small ways thereafter. I was the first to be dealt with. The Honourable Piers turned in his saddle a mile farther up the road and snarled, 'Take that filthy tin can to the rear, damn you,' and thereafter we suffered the full dust of the column, and my beautiful gun was debased most days to the uses of Field Punishment Number One, when sundry unfortunates would be strapped spreadeagled to its wheels, to swelter in the sun for various trifling sins of omission or commission.

On the advice of an old soldier I had bought a battered but serviceable sporting gun for ten rupees, and for the first few days I used to go out after we had halted at the end of each march to catch the early flights of duck along the river bank, as did one or two of the sergeants, and, of course, our little tyrant himself. With the advantage of a pair of magnificent guns and the services of two Indian beaters and a trained red setter, and, in justice, because he was no doubt a much more experienced shot than any of us, he normally brought back a commensurably bigger bag, but on one occasion his luck was out, and mine was in – and I came face to face with him when he was returning empty-handed to camp, while I was carrying a treble brace of ducks and a magnificent jungle fowl. He caused an order to be read out that night, forbidding private shooting by the rank and file – on the grounds that most of us were unused to the sport and were likely to cause casualties among ourselves – and our delicious game stews were at an end. There was no singing in the ranks as we marched thereafter, and Aloysius, greatly daring, often tapped out the Rogues' March, with the beat coming down on the right instead of the left foot – to which the Honourable Piers riposted by stopping our evening rum issue. And so it went on – childishly and spitefully – but nevertheless I enjoyed every minute of the march itself – not the least being my first sniff of powder fired in earnest.

It came in the fourth week, when we had covered nearly half of the eight hundred miles to Faraqbagh. The country we were traversing at that time was in sharp contrast to the jungles of Bihar, which lie on the northern boundary of Bengal and through which our route had run for the first two hundred miles; now it was barren and strewn with outcroppings of rock, with scant scrub and brushwood, and few trees. But people lived here in isolated villages, and scratched a bare existence from the impoverished soil, and it was from them that we bought the few meagre supplies that we needed to supplement our iron rations of salt beef and biscuit – eggs, chickens, the occasional goat for slaughter, and fodder for our animals. Because I was by now reasonably proficient in Urdu and Hindi, the quartermaster-sergeant usually detailed me to accompany him on these missions, and this day we had gone up the road in advance of the company, in a light wagon drawn by two of my gun horses, to a village which was shown on our highly inaccurate map to be five miles ahead. As expected, the village was not where it should have been, but we could see smoke rising from behind a low hill the other side of the river, so we crossed by a ford.

The road ran across dried paddy fields and through brakes of sugar-cane, so that one did not see the village until right upon it – and when we did arrive we found it to be deserted, and the smoke that we had seen from across the river rose from burnt-out huts. We sat and gazed around us in dismay, and only then did we see the bodies – men, women and children – among the ashes and in the surrounding jungle, which came right up to the trampled palisade that enclosed the huts and empty cattle compounds.

'Bloody Pindaris,' the quartermaster swore. 'And probably not far off. Come on – back to camp – and quick.'

I swung the horses, who had now smelled blood and were restive and frightened, and an old man staggered from behind a hut and fell prone in our path, and the wheels missed him only by inches. I threw the reins to the quartermaster, jumped down and went back to him. He had a deep sword slash down the side of his face and across his shoulder, and his torn shirt was soaked with blood. He moaned for water and I gave him a drink from my canteen, and he recovered sufficiently to be able to gasp out his story.

'Pindaris,' he confirmed. 'They came in the night while we slept, and were upon us like tigers. They tortured the village elders until they disclosed the hiding-place of our few rupees, raped, pillaged and slaughtered, then drove off our cattle. I received this wound and fell outside the circle of firelight, and I managed to creep into the shelter of the undergrowth.'

'Ask him which way they went off,' the quartermaster called, and I translated the question to the old man.

'Back across the river,' he told me. 'Their camp is opposite our position here, about a mile inland.'

The quartermaster consulted the map. 'Christ,' he said. 'If the chap is right, and this bloody map is not too far out, that puts them within two miles or so of *our* camp.'

'What are Pindaris?' I asked him.

'Every damned thing,' he told me. 'Rag, tag and bobtail of all the disbanded armies in India – Marathas, Jats, Sikhs, Pathans – there must be thousands of them roaming the countryside, although John Company is supposed to have finished them off twenty-five years ago. They band together in gangs of about fifty in the first place, but they are apt to snowball, and the fifties become hundreds and eventually a thousand or so at a time – well armed with military training and discipline behind them. Ordinary bandits and dacoits we can deal with one-handed – but if this is a big band properly led, our hundred-strong poor little company under me-laddo the bloody Honourable Piers, could be in for a rough time! Come on – let's be moving.'

'What about the old man?' I asked.

'Bring him if he wants to come – but for Christ's sake hurry, boy. Our duty is to them back there.' He shook the reins impatiently. But others were creeping back from the jungle now, and the old man thanked us courteously and declined my offer.

The quartermaster decided not to recross the river at this point. 'We'd be sitting ducks if they came down on us in the middle of the ford,' he said wisely. 'We'll stay on this bank until we're opposite our own camp and swim the horses over, and recover the wagon later.'

So we went in from the bank and followed a cattle truck that gave us a certain amount of cover from the river, but lengthened our journey by a couple of miles – and we were still some distance away from where we judged our camp to be when we heard the first burst of firing. We lashed the horses into a gallop and arrived at a thick copse of trees where we picketed them and then went forward in bounds from one patch of cover to the next, until we arrived on the bank directly opposite the camp. We sank down breathlessly behind a screen of water-rushes.

It was still early morning and the troops had not yet settled for the day after the long night march. Many of them were strung out along the river, where they had been bathing and washing clothes, and they were now crouching under the bank, taking cover from fire that was coming from hidden marksmen in the scrub, and I could see that there had been casualties from that first fusillade – three figures lying prone and still on the mud, and some others feebly stirring. In the camp itself the troops had instinctively formed a square, front rank kneeling, rear standing, and Aloysius's drum was beating the 'Alarm and Rally'.

The quartermaster ran an experienced eye over the scene, and said, 'There's dead ground at river level between us and the other bank – see where the splashes of their bullets begin? Avoid that patch there – and that one. Wait for the next lull and then make a dash for it. If we can get that gun of yours into action with a few random rounds into the jungle it ought to flush 'em out.'

I nodded, delighted that my toy was to be given the chance to prove itself, and not yet in those opening minutes having had time to be frightened.

The quartermaster said sharply, 'Now!' and then, as we started to rise, he grabbed my arm and said, 'No – wait', and pointed.

Across the river a small boat was creeping along under the shelter of the bank – a tiny one-man affair that I recognized as the Hon. Piers's duck-shooting punt, although at that distance I could not make out who the occupant was. We watched it until it disappeared round the next bend of the river, temporarily at least, out of immediate danger. I turned and met the quartermaster's eye, and it was plain that we were sharing the same unspoken thought.

'I'd like to think it was the little bastard,' he said, 'but much as I hate him I don't think even *he* would skin out and leave his command in the shit. Probably one of the youngsters who hasn't developed a stomach for it yet. Best keep quiet about it, lad. It's a serious thing to accuse an officer of cowardice without cast-iron proof.'

We crossed then, and although in my fevered imagination I felt that every bullet that whined overhead as we swam was especially aimed at me, we gained the camp without mishap, and I managed to assemble three of my gun crew. We unlimbered and swung the trail round in a half-circle until the piece was pointing roughly in the direction from which the bulk of the firing was coming, then, as Number Two and Three placed and rammed the charge, as per the gun-drill manual, I loaded explosive canister and made the last fine adjustments to the lay, swung the portfire round my head in the approved manner, and clamped it down on the touch-hole, and a most satisfactory roar resulted and the shot scythed murderously through the scrub. We traversed three degrees right and left and got off another two rounds, with two more totally unnecessary ones to clinch matters, because the firing had stopped after the first shot and we could hear yells of panic, and a bugle was sounding a ragged 'Withdraw' – then the sergeant-major gave the order to fix bayonets and charge, and it was all over, because they were already in disarrayed retreat.

We came out into the open through the scrub to find a total of fifteen dead and nearly twice that number wounded, which the sergeant-major and two other non-commissioned officers went round and despatched with single pistol shots. The quartermaster must have seen my look of horror, because he shrugged and said quietly, 'All right, lad – what's the alternative? Twenty-seven extra mouths to feed for the next month or so, with half our strength struck off to guard them. They've just slaughtered a villageful of their own people, and they'd have cut the throats of every one of *us* if things had gone the other way – all for our arms, ammunition and boots. These bastards never took a prisoner in their lives, so why should we give them quarter?'

Our commander had now reappeared, looking relieved and euphoric. He strode round the battlefield sword in hand, brave, benevolent and paternal, scattering praise and encouragement right and left – even to me.

'Well done, corporal,' he said. 'I'm glad you kept your wits about you. Those shots were just in the nick of time – otherwise it might have been a damned close-run thing.' And he

234

ordered the quartermaster to make an immediate issue of rum, which was unfortunate, because Aloysius, true to form, managed to secure for himself a full pint, with tragic consequences. He staggered up to the Honourable Piers and hiccupped, 'Well, me little cock-o-lorum – and what was it you were after downriver in your wee boat? Ducks, fish or just a little decent privacy in which to change your soiled breeches?'

The officer went scarlet, then white, and he turned to walk away, and it might have ended there, but the drummer reached out and caught him by the arm and spun him round, then struck him full in the face with his clenched fist.

I heard the quartermaster groan, 'Oh my God! That's a hanging matter,' and then the sergeant-major and the provost had Aloysius in their grasp, and they tied him to the tail of the supply wagon.

I saw the quartermaster that night, and indeed many more times in the fourteen days that elapsed before we reached Allahabad, but always the answer was the same.

'I know how you feel, lad,' he said sadly. 'I feel exactly the same, and we both know that it *was* the craven swine we saw in that boat, although neither of us could swear to it – and even if we could it would not make a tittle of difference. One of the rank and file has struck an officer in full view of the company – and for that there can be but one answer – a fair trial, and the rope.'

'But he was drunk,' I protested.

'Offering violence to an officer is the one crime for which due allowance for drunkenness is not taken into mitigation,' he quoted. 'Christ, boy, don't make me spout the bloody book at you like a damned barrack-room lawyer. He'll hang, I tell you, and maybe all the quicker for your interference, if you're fool enough to put your oar in.'

So we buried our four dead, and the Honourable Piers read the funeral service, and waxed eloquent over their bravery and sterling military virtues, although he had had all four tied to my gun wheels at some time or other on the march, and we bound the wounds of a dozen casualties – two of whom died subsequently on the road to Allahabad, which we reached a week later.

A General Court martial was hastily convened here from the officers of the garrison, and the still-visible traces of the assaulted lieutenant's black eye and the word of the sergeant-major and two other specially selected witnesses was deemed sufficient evidence by the prosecution. There was none from the defence beyond a plea for mercy and a promise of exemplary behaviour in the future, which the court did not consider sufficient reason for the exercise of clemency.

And so we were drawn up in hollow square one dark morning, and as dawn lightened the eastern sky, Aloysius, preceded by the Catholic chaplain, was slow-marched from the guardroom to the gibbet which had been erected over-night in the centre of the parade ground, to the muffled beat of a drum and the tolling of the garrison church bell. As his feet left the ground and he was hauled aloft by the drummers of a Royal regiment, a sibilant whisper reached us from the rear of our ranks, 'All right, drummer – the cur dies the next time we are in action.'

I turned my head, and the quartermaster, blank and ex-pressionless in the serrefile behind us, said mechanically, 'Look to your front, that man – and stand steady.'

There was a sharp intake of breath from the Honourable Piers, on parade in front of us, and I thought I saw the tip of his drawn sword waver just a trifle.

Allahabad and Faraqbagh were linked by telegraph, so news of our arrival had preceded us, and we were met by a regimental band five miles outside cantonments, which played us in to a heroes' welcome – the brave little company that had beaten off and defeated with heavy losses a far superior force of Pindaris. It was a 'family' station, which meant that many officers and civilian officials had their wives and children here, and they turned out in force to cheer us as we marched on to the parade ground, and the Honourable Piers, riding at our head and seemingly once more restored to his full *amour propre*, returned the ladies' waves right gallantly.

After the garrison commander, an elderly and very portly full colonel, had greeted us with a short but laudatory speech we were allotted our quarters in pleasantly situated thick-walled and therefore cool barracks, and excused duty until medical inspection the next day.

I marched my small detachment to the hospital after early stables the following morning and we joined the end of a line of troops that tailed along the verandah and turned into a doorway, moving forward one space at a time as each man was inspected and dismissed. I had been on many such parades in my short military career. They were usually very perfunctory affairs – a cursory survey by the surgeon for any of the more obvious signs of disease, a question or two about the state of one's bowels and other bodily functions, and, whatever the answer, the inevitable massive spoonful of treacle and brimstone doled out by a hospital staff-sergeant, and the all-but-vomiting soldier was sent upon his way at an average rate of thirty seconds per man. But this time it was different and we appeared to be suffering under that bane of military life, a conscientious doctor, and the parade was taking much longer than usual, and the men, with thoughts of breakfast dominating those of health, were muttering blasphemously.

At last my turn came, and in answer to my name and rank, I stepped through the door and came face to face with Surgeon John Everard Palmer, whom I had last seen being rowed ashore in Western Australia nearly five years previously.

There was instant recognition on both sides, but Mr Palmer said quietly, 'I did not catch that name,' and the sergeant-major, who was reading from the muster roll, repeated, 'Corporal Muir Dalrymple, sir, Third Bengal European Infantry.'

'I see,' said the surgeon, and proceeded to tap and prod me all over while he asked the routine questions. Finally he felt my right shoulder and said, more to himself than to me, 'Hm – you seem to have had a fracture of the clavicle here –

not recently, I should say – possibly within the last four or five years. Does it give you any trouble?'

I had had time to collect my wits by this, so I said, 'No, sir. I was fortunate enough to have it set by a good surgeon.'

He nodded slowly and said, 'I see – but even so I think I should make a closer inspection of it. Wait outside, corporal, until I have seen the rest of the men.'

There was no cordial reception when I went back. He looked at me unsmilingly and said, 'You seem to have been through some strange vicissitudes since we last met, young man – and many changes of identity. I am disappointed in you.'

I bridled and said, 'Through no fault of mine, sir. The change of name came about through my being picked up unconscious from the Maidan in Calcutta. I was a passenger on a ship bound for London, and I was attacked – '

'A long and no doubt convincing story, I am sure,' he said drily, 'but I was referring to much earlier incidents than that. A burnt ship in Newcastle, for instance – an escaping convict by the same name as yourself, or at least the name by which I knew you previously.'

I stared at him speechlessly, and he went on, 'A book I once gave you, which we, as a family inscribed on the flyleaf – "To Ross Stafford from his friends on the *Boadicea*" – and my name and regiment, and the place and date – Albany, W. Australia. Do you remember?'

I gulped and nodded. '*Gulliver's Travels* – I remember only too well – '

'Found by the police in a half-burnt carpet-bag on an American ship, together with a miner's licence in yet another name. They were in pursuit of two escaping convicts as they thought at first. They got in contact with me and questioned me closely. I told them what little I knew, and added that whatever the circumstances I was sure that *you* had not been involved in any criminal activities.' He broke off and walked to the window and stood looking out.

'That was good of you, sir,' I said, genuinely touched. 'Actually I was *not* involved in criminal activities as such.

My brother had been transported and I came out to effect his release if it were possible.'

'And it was, apparently. He made good his escape from a road gang, I believe.'

'That is right. Near Bathurst. We walked over the Blue Mountains to Newcastle. We had money for our fares to California, but we were betrayed.'

'So I gathered.' He spun round and faced me. 'But is that the whole story?'

'Not by any means,' I told him. 'But it would take a long time to tell. We were picked up by a Chinese junk and landed many months later in Hong Kong. We were taken into business there by one of the local merchants, and did well for a time – but there was trouble, and I had to leave.'

'Where is your brother now?'

'He – was killed –' The words were sticking in my throat and I was floundering in that most awful of all morasses – when one is speaking the literal truth and it sounds a tissue of lies even in one's own ears. 'I'm sorry if it all appears unlikely,' I finished lamely, 'but that is just what happened.'

'But that is still not the whole story,' he insisted.

I felt my confusion giving way to impatience. 'Of course it's not,' I retorted, 'but you can't expect me to cross all the t's and dot all the i's in the space of a few minutes.'

'Two dead men – left in the bush – and a woman buried under a cross inscribed "Caerwen Stafford". All shot,' he said. 'How do you account for them, Ross?'

I shrugged hopelessly. 'I *can* account for them,' I said, 'though I don't expect you to believe me. The woman, Caerwen, was entirely blameless. She was my brother's sweetheart – mistress if you prefer it – and she was involved in the burglary he was transported for – through no fault of her own – and was transported also. My brother refused to leave without her, so we rescued her from the place in which she was serving her sentence. The men were two bushrangers who came upon us on the way to Newcastle. One of them shot her, possibly by accident as he tried to kill us. We fought – and they too were shot. I hope you have no more questions, sir, because I'm damned if I'm going to answer them. I've told you the truth – all of it.' And I found myself weeping.

He crossed to me and put his hands on my shoulders. 'I'm sorry, my boy,' he said gently. 'But I had to know. I spoke up for you without hesitation when the police first approached me. It seemed quite obvious to me that your brother's escape was your sole object in going to Australia – and in my heart I admired you for it – but when later they stumbled on these graves, quite by accident, I naturally began to have my doubts. They are resolved now, and I believe you – but by gad! What a story! I must hear it all, every word – from beginning to end.' He pointed through the window. 'That bungalow over there – the white one. That is ours. Come across this evening, about six. My wife will be delighted to meet you again.'

'How is she, sir?' I asked. 'And Miss Judith?'

'Very well, the both of them,' he said. 'The regiment was only transferred here from Australia six months ago, so they haven't had a full summer in the country yet.' He walked with me to the door. 'Right – until this evening – and, of course, you know without my having to tell you that you can rely completely on my discretion.'

I dressed with care in my best white uniform, but I felt self-conscious as I crossed the lines to the officers' quarters later, because I had been long enough in the army to know that a gulf existed between commissioned and non-commissioned ranks, and nowhere was this gulf more unbridgeable than in India. But their welcome was warm and sincere. Mrs Palmer threw her arms around my neck and kissed me on both cheeks as I came into their drawing-room – and then a young lady entered. She was as elfin and pretty as before, but those five years had made a vast difference – a difference that had me completely tongue-tied and awkward for the first few minutes, but she had changed not one whit in disposition, which was as happy, kind and completely unaffected as it had been when she was a thirteen-year-old hoyden on the ship.

We sat talking about the experiences we had passed through in the intervening years, greatly bowdlerized in my own case, but it was plain that Mr Palmer wanted to hear my story in detail, so he eventually ejected them both, kindly but very firmly, and I began at the beginning – omitting nothing – right from our early days in London – and never once did he interrupt or ask a question. Bearers came with lamps, and Mrs Palmer sent in sandwiches and coffee, but still the tale went on.

There was a long silence between us when I finished, dry-throated and somewhat hoarse. He refilled our glasses, and then he looked at me and said, 'So now what?'

'So now I'm a soldier,' I said. 'I didn't want to be, but it seemed that I had no option.'

'And do you intend to remain as such?' he asked.

I shook my head. 'No. Had I enlisted in the ordinary way I would have stood by my bargain, but as it is I feel I have every moral right to call it off at a time of my own choosing.'

'You mean to desert?'

'An ugly word, sir – but yes.'

'You realize that desertion is a capital offence in the East India Company army?'

'So we are told, frequently. It is read out to us on parade at least once a month.'

'We don't hang for it in the Royal service,' he said, 'but the punishment is almost as severe. A hundred and fifty lashes and seven years' penal servitude – which very few men have been known to survive.'

'Yes – I've heard that too.'

'But it doesn't affect your decision?'

'No.'

'How on earth do you think you could escape from a station like this? A white man in a black country – over a thousand miles from the nearest seaport – a price on your head, and every man's hand against you?'

'All bridges to be crossed as and when I come to them, sir,' I told him. 'But as I've already said, when I go it shall be at a time of my own choosing. Until then I shall do my duty to the best of my ability. To tell the truth I am not finding conditions at all disagreeable at the moment. I delight in seeing new countries, different people, strange sights.'

'I realize that,' he said. 'While you keep those interests alive, and exercise your powers of observation, and abide by a few simple rules for the safeguarding of your health, you should come to no harm. But unfortunately not every man does that in places like this. I have seen some sorry sights in my short time here. The hospital is full of men brought low by drink, opium and the terrible venereal diseases they contract in the bazaars. I don't want to preach, Ross, but for God's sake be careful, boy. Tell me, do you still read as voraciously as you did on the voyage?'

'When I have the chance, sir,' I said. 'Unfortunately my collection of books went on with the ship when I was left in Calcutta, but if there's a library here – '

'There isn't,' he said bitterly. 'At least not for the so-called common soldiers. That is the main evil of the system. There is absolutely nothing for them in the way of recreation, except those I have just mentioned.' He waved towards his well-stocked bookshelves. 'But please regard yourself as free to make full use of those.'

'That is kind of you,' I said. 'But I realize the delicacy of our respective positions here. I can't visit your house openly.'

'I've been thinking of that even as we talked,' he smiled, 'and I have a solution for it. I am, of course, with a Royal regiment, but the Company have no medical officer on this station at present, so I do duty for both services. I intend asking for an intelligent non-commissioned officer from your unit to assist me in keeping your medical records in order. That will be sufficient reason for you to come to the hospital and also here from time to time.'

I took my leave of them and walked back to barracks through the night, in a welter of mixed feelings – sheer happiness at having met these sincere and genuine people again, and thereby the lifting of a weight of loneliness from my shoulders, but, at the same time, I felt a resentment forming within me at the absurdity of a social system that could keep friends apart except by the exercise of subterfuge.

That first six months sped past rapidly. The hot weather came, and with it the fevers and agues that were our dreaded but inescapable lot, with long days and even longer nights spent sweltering under the punkahs that did little to relieve the merciless heat, when all outdoor activities ceased after early morning parades and a little perfunctory drill, until guard-mounting in the evenings – but in my particular case I was kept very busy indeed, and that was no doubt my salvation. I was sent with my gun on attachment to a battery of Royal Horse Artillery, and we used to practise for one hour before, and one after, sunrise each day on a gunnery range outside cantonments, and I became, in my own estimation at least, a master gunner of no mean ability. I also had charge of the company horses – the six in the gun team and my own mount – which had to be groomed, fed, watered and kept exercised by my three Indian drivers, under my supervision – and between times I really did work in the hospital office and at Mr Palmer's bungalow – all of which gave me a complete exeat from routine company duties, and made me more or less my own master – so much so that when two deaths through cholera and one suicide caused vacancies, I was promoted sergeant.

But there was the inevitable fly in the ointment. The Honourable Piers. His roving eye had lighted on Judith and he took to haunting the bungalow and making himself most agreeable to the family, and commensurately disagreeable to me. Judith used to ride most mornings, accompanied by her father, but the latter, ironically, had become afflicted of that painful and humiliating complaint, piles, which kept him out of the saddle, so, on mornings when I was not on the firing ranges, he had deputed me to acompany her, which, of course, delighted me. But my *bête noire* found out, and made it his business to detail me for various duties which kept me in barracks. Mrs Palmer quite liked the lout, while the surgeon seemed to reserve his opinion, and I had enough sense to realize that I would not improve my standing with them by denigrating him, as it would undoubtedly have appeared to be personal spleen on my part. But Judith, I am happy to say, could not stand him, and after suffering his company for some days, she gave up her morning canter, and we used to meet privily on the edge of the cantonments in the cool of the evenings when the Honourable Piers usually played polo, and we would ride along the river bank and return to her home by a roundabout route which kept us out of the view of the club and the surrounding playing fields where most of the officers and their families used to foregather to take what air there was and listen to the regimental band.

But he must have become suspicious, because twice in one week he intercepted us. The first time he was correctness itself. He returned my grudging salute and said, quite amiably if condescendingly, 'Very good, sergeant. You may return to your duties. I will see Miss Palmer back to her home.' And, fuming, I had no option other than to rein back, wheel, and gallop off.

The second time it was different. He rode up to us with a face like thunder, and I heard Judith mutter angrily, 'Oh, this pest again. I shall give him a flea in his ear –' and I just had time to say, 'Don't. That will be sufficient excuse for him to confine me to lines –' before he halted in front of us.

He said coldly, 'You are wanted in barracks, sergeant. Report to the sergeant-major and tell him I sent you.'

Once again I saluted and rode off.

The sergeant-major, taking his ease over a pot of beer, cocked a quizzical eye at me when I arrived. 'What have you been doing to that bloody rear-rank runaway?' he asked. 'He has given me orders to find you a job every night and morning, and also not to allow you to exercise horses without his express permission.'

'I know what I'd *like* to do to the bastard,' I growled.

'It's not worth it, lad,' he said wisely. 'They've got power of life and death over us in the safety of cantonments. Just leave nature to take its course.' He winked. 'There's always the chance of a quick bit of action in these parts with the

Pindaris, bless their dirty shirts and black arses, and something tells me that there are a few ounces of lead resting in a pouch or two – with his name on 'em.'

'Let's hope he hasn't got a boat handy next time,' I said.

'If he has, it'll have a bloody big hole in its bottom,' he chuckled. 'Someone'll take damn good care of that.'

Mr Palmer saw me when I went to the hospital next morning. 'That whippersnapper of an officer of yours had the confounded impertinence to advise me not to let Judith ride with you again,' he said furiously. 'I let him have a piece of my mind, but I am afraid that it will not make matters easier for you, my boy. Take care not to give him the slightest reason for putting you on report for some trumped-up offence, because Judith, also, has given him his *congé* in no uncertain terms.'

So, sadly, our rides were at an end – until a few days later, just as we waited breathlessly for the monsoon rains to break, and I was returning on horseback from the artillery lines one evening, and I saw her in the distance, and I could not forbear to canter up to her, because she was on foot leading her mare. She greeted me delightedly.

'Oh, I'm glad to see you,' she said. 'I think poor Mina has picked up a stone. She seems to have gone awfully lame in her off-fore.'

I dismounted and picked up the mare's hoof and removed a flint with the picker on the end of my lanyard, and we stood talking for a few minutes, because the Honourable Piers's *ukase* was now in force and I hadn't seen her for some days – and we didn't hear his horse until he was right upon us.

I said quickly, 'Please go, Judith dear. This is not going to be pleasant.'

'I shall do no such thing,' she retorted indignantly. 'What right has he – ?'

'*Please*, Judith,' I begged, and helped her to mount – and she rode off slowly, with many a backward glance, until she was lost in the gathering gloom.

He waited until we could no longer hear her mare's hoofbeats, then he said venomously, 'You are under arrest, Dalrymple.'

Something snapped and I said, equally venomously, 'Go to hell, you son of a whore,' and his riding whip whistled through the air, and caught me across the face. I grabbed his foot and wrenched it from the stirrup, and heaved, and he went over the other side out of the saddle, and landed on his back – and then I had his whip in my hand, belabouring him, and I can hear his screams to this day. My horse had galloped off, but his had stood, and I remember throwing his now -broken whip into his face and saying, 'I'm not hanging for *you*, you bastard!' and mounting.

And then I was galloping wildly across cantonments and down to the river.

Chapter Ten

I had no clear objective in the early part of that ride, other than to put as much distance between myself and the East India Company as possible. The monsoon broke as I galloped along the river path, suddenly and dramatically, with a blinding flash of lightning and a deafening clap of thunder, and the rain came down in a solid sheet. The path narrowed and became a river of mud in which the horse could not keep its feet, and it fell twice, so I tied the reins to the near stirrup and turned its head back to cantonments and let it go, and I staggered on in the pitch darkness until, like the horse, I couldn't keep my feet either. I blundered into a banyan tree, so large and overhanging that it gave a certain shelter from the rain, and I sat shivering, soaked to the skin, confused and, as sanity returned slowly, terrified.

What in God's name was there ahead of me now? I wondered. Court martial and a shameful death if I were captured, for absolute certainty on the one hand – almost equally certain death from starvation and fever if I were not. 'Almost'? Was there not the slightest chance that I *might* get through – somehow? Through where? Through the jungle – to Calcutta, the nearest seaport. And once there? Obviously on to a ship – to stow away – a ship to anywhere. Impossible. A thousand miles of jungle – wild beasts – hostile tribes – military patrols – penniless – unarmed. And yet, I had escaped before – through the Australian bush – and again from Canton. Yes, but conditions were different – And so it went on through half the night, my thoughts running through my tired brain in a chaotic jumble. But one thing remained clear and fixed. Come what may I would not be recaptured. Not even if it meant suicide.

That being arrived at, I certainly could not remain on this

path which, apart from the Grand Trunk Road running through the town, was the only practical route out of Faraqbagh, so both were bound to be searched.

I came out from the shelter of the banyan tree. The first fury of the rainstorm had abated a little and a half-moon shone fitfully through ragged clouds. As so often happens in India, where a dried creek can become a raging torrent in the space of an hour during the monsoon, the river was now in full spate, putting paid to my intention to cross to the other side. There was nothing for it, therefore, but to plunge into the jungle that bordered the path and remain hidden until I felt it safe to return to it.

Unfortunately the river at this point ran through a steep-sided gorge, and the slope, combined with the tangled undergrowth and ankle-deep mud, made progress both slow and painful, but at last I came to the top just as dawn was breaking. The rain had stopped now, and clouds of steam rose from the valley beneath me. I rested for an hour or so, grateful for the warmth of the sun as it climbed higher and cleared the mist, and sure enough I heard the unmistakable sound of troop movements from below – a clinking of accoutrements and an occasional sharp order, and I thought for one heartstopping moment that they were halting right underneath my position, but the sounds died away towards the south, and I got up and continued to push on to the east.

My intentions were now beginning to crystallize, and some sort of plan was taking shape in my mind. This river, here called the Dilhwa, was a tributary of the Ganges, which it joined a few miles to the north of Allahabad. The Ganges flowed arrow-straight across the central Indian plain to a point just above Calcutta, where it split into a many-mouthed delta, the westernmost mouth being the Hooghli, which ran through the city itself. Theoretically, therefore, all I had to do was to follow first this river, then the main one in its course to the sea – just as I had done in New South Wales, and, indeed, Canton. I might even be able once again to steal a boat or construct a raft, floating swiftly with the current by night, and lying low under cover in daylight.

Food? Well – I was a soldier, wasn't I, used to 'living off the country', as stealing was euphemized in the army? It shouldn't be too difficult, even though I was unarmed. The poor devils of farmers and villagers were timid enough in my experience, and were used to being bullied and robbed. Yes, that was it – the mixture as before. Move by night and hide by day – and hope to God that tigers, panthers, bears and poisonous snakes, of which I had heard some terrifying old soldiers' stories, would not be too numerous. No – it shouldn't be impossible – in theory.

I sat on through the rest of the morning, watching the storm clouds gather once more for the daily downpour which would persist off and on for the next three months of the monsoon. At least I would not suffer from thirst during my journey, I reflected wryly. But hunger was beginning to make itself felt, and my belly was rumbling cavernously – so much so that I decided to break my self-imposed rule and travel in daylight, on this first day at least, in the hope that strenuous activity would help to keep my mind off curry, salt beef, hard tack and similar delicacies. I got to my feet and pressed on.

The mist had cleared now and I could see down the slope to the path that I had left, and to the river beyond it, and I had to exercise the greatest care to keep below the skyline when moving from one patch of cover to the next. I was worried by the party that had passed unseen earlier in the day. Sooner or later they would be returning over their outward route and unless I was careful I might easily meet them face to face.

I would have given a lot for a quick scrutiny of a map of this area, inaccurate as they were known to be, and I cudgelled my brains to remember the salient geography of the Ganges basin. This, the eastern side, to the best of my recollection was thick, well-nigh impenetrable jungle for hundreds of miles, right to the foothills of the Himalayas. The other side was flat and more open, and was dotted with villages and patches of civilization. That would be the obvious choice of a fugitive, if only for the fact that food would be easier to come by on that side, therefore that would be the side they would patrol and ambush. So, logically, the obvious thing for me to do would be to remain on this inhospitable side, crossing only to forage at night, then returning to travel on down the path for the remaining hours of darkness, and to lie low during the day. It would slow my progress down badly and would be hideously dangerous, because the river, swollen by the daily downpour, was now constantly in spate – but of the two alternatives it seemed the safer.

And so I kept doggedly on for the rest of that day, tightening my belt and trying to keep my thoughts off food, until suddenly I found myself at a village.

It was little more than a collection of about a dozen huts huddled together in a clearing, with some plots of growing maize and a thornbush enclosure for a few head of cattle, with a well in the centre, round which a group of greybeards were squatting and smoking a communal *huqar* – the 'hubble-bubble' pipe of India which holds half a pound of rank, locally grown tobacco, the smoke of which is drawn through a container of water by means of a flexible tube.

They stood up and stared at me as I approached, and one of them said nervously, '*Salaam aleikum*', which means, peace be unto you, and I felt greatly relieved, because that told me that they were Muslims. In the towns one could usually tell the different religions apart, by certain peculiarities of dress, but not out here in the jungle, where the custom was to wear the irreducible minimum of loose shirt and loincloth, and so it was possible to make mistakes and sometimes give offence.

I answered, '*Wah aleikum salaam*' – (and to you also be peace), and put out my hand, which they all shook in turn. Hindus do not shake hands, as the touch of one not of the same caste can defile. They were studying my torn muddy uniform with some curiosity, so I said, 'I have strayed from my regiment in the storm, and become lost, and I have a great hunger, my brothers,' and since the Indian peasant is the kindest of creatures there was an immediate outcry, and women came from the huts with brass trays of steaming rice and hotly curried chicken, and gourds of milk – and fortunately I knew enough of their customs to take water from the well and wash my hands and mouth, and remove my boots before sitting down on the ground to eat with my right hand, because the left is never allowed to touch any vessel containing food. They ate with me as hospitality decreed, in the sensible Indian way of complete silence, selecting the best bits from the bowls and trays and piling them on my plate – and I stuffed myself until I was near bursting point, belching loudly from time to time, which, as I had learned from our sepoys, is their way of expressing appreciation of good food.

After the meal the huqar was brought out again and placed down in our midst, and the tube was passed round from one man to another, including myself, each of them delicately wiping the carved amber mouthpiece on the hem of his shirt before passing it on to his neighbour. Only then did conversation break out, but, such is their natural courtesy, nobody asked me any awkward questions, although I could see that they were curious about me, so I lied shamelessly, telling them that my regiment had been on an exercise in which I represented a fugitive who had to get through the enemy lines, unarmed and unequipped. This intrigued them greatly and they offered me much advice about the terrain and the various paths through it, some of which I found useful later. They invited me to stay overnight with them and I was sorely tempted to accept, but I felt that the wisest course would be to press on and get out of this area as quickly as possible, so I declined politely and prepared to leave, whereupon they insisted on sending a boy with me to show me the best way out of this part of the jungle, which unfortunately lay in the opposite direction to that in which I wanted to go. To have insisted on going my way would have been to contradict all I had already told them, so I thanked them and set off with the boy back along the path I had already come, with the intention of shaking loose from him as soon as possible.

But he proved the very devil to lose and insisted on taking me down to the river by a hidden side path that led off from the main one, at the bottom of which was a rocky ford that gave access to a road on the other bank.

'If you cross here, sahib,' the boy explained, 'you will save many miles, because the river forms a great loop.' And he drew a rough map in the mud with a pointed stick, and I saw what he meant. It was as if the river was the letter U and he was showing me the way across the gap at the top in preference to walking the whole way round it. I thanked him solemnly but flatly refused to let him come any farther, then I made the crossing alone, and very difficult it proved to be, because the current was swift and the rocks were slippery, and many were completely submerged. The boy stood watching my progress until I crawled out on to the opposite bank like a drowned rat, then, thank God, he waved, turned about and went on his way back to the village through the gathering gloom.

I waited until he was well out of sight, then, cursing, I made my laborious way back over the ford and set out to regain the distance I had lost, determined this time to make a wide detour round the village, but darkness had fallen now, and I was almost on to it before I realized it – and, suddenly, I heard English voices. I dived into the undergrowth and crept away from the path and found myself hard up against the back of one of the huts. Peering round a corner I could see a group of soldiers in the firelight, and I recognized a sergeant from one of the British regiments. He was confronting the old headman and bellowing at him through an interpreter, an Indian munshi of our own unit.

'Tell the old bastard that I want to know *which* way the man went, and how long ago,' the sergeant said, and added, 'and I want the truth, or I'll be putting my belt across his back.'

'Don't be frightened of this fool's braying, old one,' the munshi said gently in Hindi. 'Which way did the soldier go, and when?'

'As I told the great one,' the old man quavered. 'Along the path to the river, which he crossed with difficulty, just as the boy has said.'

'Shabash! Well done. *When?*'

'When the lower edge of the sun touched the upper edge of the trees – '

'At what *hour*, old one?'

'Have I a clock? As long ago as it would take a woman to milk three – possibly *four* cows – '

'Just before sunset, sergeant-sahib,' the munshi translated. 'The boy took him to the ford, and saw him cross it.'

The sergeant hauled a turnip of a watch from his sweat-soaked tunic pocket. 'Sunset? That's about half-past six, ain't it?' he mused. 'How far away is the ford?'

The munshi translated again and the headman told him that the same woman could milk a cow and possibly a goat as well in the time it would take a young man to walk it.

'Half an hour's walk,' the munshi told the sergeant, and added untruthfully, 'He says the ford is dangerous at night and it would be better to camp here until morning.'

'I'm damned if we will,' the sergeant swore. 'There's a thousand rupees on this bugger's head. Come on, you idle pack of brothel sweepings – up on your feet. Our man's a couple of hours ahead of us. He's bound to lay up overnight, so, with luck we should be able to nab him at dawn. *Up*, I said – *Move* – Get behind them, corporal – '

I lay in the darkness with my heart pounding as the sound of the marching patrol faded. This, I decided, would be the party I had heard moving along the river path that morning. Obviously some limit had been set for them, and they had reached it and were now returning to cantonments by this upper path. With luck that would mean that there were no more searchers south of me, though it would be rash to take that for certain, but at least I had the comfort of knowing that they were now on a wild goose chase the other side of the river. My ruse had worked – for the moment.

I retreated into the jungle and circled round the village, determined in future always to follow the same practice – that of approaching all habitations from the opposite direction and leaving as if continuing that way. I would have to be doubly careful now that a reward of a thousand rupees had been put up for me. Indian peasants, charitable and compassionate though they may be, were only human, and a thousand rupees would be more than most of them could possibly hope to earn in a lifetime.

I continued on doggedly through the night, but I was fast coming to the conclusion that I could not keep this up indefinitely. Marching along a proper road in the company of a hundred other soldiers, with a good meal beneath one's belt and the comforting prospect of another in the morning, was a vastly different thing to being alone, unarmed and hungry, on a jungle path, fearing that every rustle in the close-crowding undergrowth presaged the spring of a tiger or a panther, with the yelping of jackals and the insane laughter of hyenas chilling one's blood. No – now that I had put a manoeuvrable distance between myself and Faraqbagh I would have to risk marching by day and somehow finding food and a safe shelter at night.

I was lucky that second morning in finding a mango tree in full bearing, not yet stripped by monkeys, and although there is nothing sustaining in the fruits, they were delicious and refreshing, so I stuffed myself on them, paying for it later with severe collywobbles and looseness of the bowels.

I rested for some hours under a banyan tree, sheltering from the brief but heavy monsoon showers that were now occurring every couple of hours, and I held a review of my resources. I had two silver rupees and eleven copper annas, a useful jack-knife, and the flint, steel and tinder in a stoppered flask that all soldiers carried in lieu of sulphur matches that quickly became damp and useless in that climate. My clothing consisted of a once-white drill tunic and breeches, now torn, sodden and filthy, peaked forage cap with attached neckcloth, and Hessian riding boots. I regarded these last with some anxiety. They had been stout enough originally, but as a result of constant soaking, the soles were showing signs of coming apart from the uppers, and I resolved to buy a pair of heavy native chaplis with my rupees at the first opportunity.

I climbed a high nim tree as the sun went down, and surveyed the countryside and found it to be completely deserted, with never a wisp of smoke to mark the cooking fires of a village, so I resigned myself to going supperless to bed, and cast around for another banyan. These remarkable trees start life conventionally enough as a single trunk with outspread, thickly foliaged branches, from the ends of which they drop tendrils to the ground. These tendrils take root and become trees in their own right, so that, with the passage of time, they develop into a small forest, all remaining attached to the parent tree by the branches.

I found one, and pushed in through the overhang with a wary eye cocked for snakes, and I flushed out a jungle fowl which squawked and tried to fly past me. I struck out at it with a heavy stick I was carrying, and by a lucky fluke knocked it to the ground. I pounced on it and wrung its neck, then plucked, cleaned and roasted it in the ashes of a small fire that I risked making. And so ended the third day.

The country was changing now, becoming flatter and more open, and, as I saw with mixed feelings, more populous. Food might be easier to come by from here on, but the need for caution would be proportionately greater. I could not rid myself of the fear of the telegraph. The whole countryside could be alerted and on the lookout for me, I thought gloomily, and they would know that I would be forced to make forays on villages and isolated farms to live.

Yet, curiously, as time went on the depression and fear of the earlier days started to lift from me, and I thought more and more of our journey through the Australian bush, and much of the primitive lore learned then but forgotten since, came back to me. Fires, for example. No matter how the rain poured, and sodden though twigs and branches might be, I remembered the knack shown to us by Caerwen, of stripping the outer bark right down to the dry pith, and I found myself instinctively knowing which type of wood smoked and which didn't – and how to make a tiny but very hot fire in such a way that it could not be seen from even a few feet away if correctly screened. I was fast learning, also, to be an expert plunderer of chicken runs, stealing eggs and, on occasion, a chicken or two themselves, and, after finding a gourd which I thereafter carried with me, I sometimes even milked cows in the village compounds.

I arrived in the vicinity of Allahabad on the tenth day, avoiding the city and adjacent cantonments and making for the confluence of my river and the Ganges, which I remembered was just to the north of it. But when I got there I stared in dismay, because when I last saw it on our way to Faraqbagh my river had been a mere trickle through a series of dry sandbanks, and the Ganges was scarcely more impressive. But now the whole basin, which stretched from the centre of the city, where yet another river, the Jumna, joined the Ganges, to a fort five miles to the south, was a swirling torrent of brown and white water at least two miles across, down which uprooted trees and rafts of flotsam swept in an unending train. This put an end to my plans of stealing a canoe here, because it was plain that no boat could live in that maelstrom. So, once more cast down, I proceeded along on foot.

A further ten days had now elapsed, and I had made little real progress south, because I was continuously coming to tributary streams which flowed into the Ganges, necessitating long detours away from the main river until I found a reasonably safe crossing point. There were no villages or farms on this, the eastern bank, and I would have starved had I not come across a crate of a dozen drowned chickens washed up on to the bank. I camped for a whole day and a night and cooked them all and gorged myself sick, then I carried the rest on with me until they putrefied a day or so later.

I was now in a sorry state, ragged, hungry and bereft of hope or even the will to survive, but still fiercely determined not to be captured, which was the only reason why I still pushed on, the distance gained becoming less each day, until one morning I woke under a banyan tree at dawn and found that the hunger pains which had been cramping my guts had ceased, and I felt light and clear-headed and supremely comfortable on my bed of leaves – so much so that I made no effort to rise until hours later thirst drove me to seek a pool, and I found I was too weak to move. I accepted my fate happily and went to sleep.

A man was standing looking down at me, and I was in no

way surprised because I had been suffering from hallucinations for some days now, and creatures born of hunger and fever had often appeared to me in that period between sleeping and waking before consciousness has fully returned. I therefore looked up at him without particular interest, expecting him momentarily to fade. But this one didn't – instead he said, 'The de'il and all. Mon, you're the sickest-looking gomeral without being actually deid I ever saw in my life. A John Company sojer, and a sergeant, forby, by the remains of those stripes on what was once a tunic. Now who, I wonder, left you out in the rain to get in this shape?'

But I had drifted off again. I remember being carried along a jungle path in a litter – and somebody gave me a drink of fiery spirit that burnt my throat – then came more darkness.

I came to in a dark room, and the first thing I saw was a barred window in front of me, and I think I began to weep weakly, because it had all been for nothing. But then a voice said gently, *'Fiqa mat karo, sahib. Ap mahfuz hain,'* (Do not worry, sahib. You are safe), and I was partially lifted and a glass was held to my lips, and, somewhat reassured, I went to sleep.

How long I remained in this limbo I don't know, because I wasn't conscious of the passage of time, but I was told later that it was over a week.

When I finally came to full consciousness it was to see my original Samaritan standing looking down at me again, and for some moments I thought I was still hallucinating, because a weirder character I have never seen, before or since. He was immensely tall – six feet eight inches, I learned subsequently – and from his fiercely combed and upswept beard, elaborately wound turban, and steel circlet on his right wrist, he was a Sikh. He had an enormous nose, hooked and predatory as a king eagle's beak, and fierce ice-blue eyes under beetling brows. He was wearing a red tunic plentifully embellished with gold bullion, with the insignia of a major-general on his epaulettes, and, strangest of all, a Highlander's tartan plaid fastened with a cairngorm hung from his left shoulder – then, as I stared at him in sheer unbelief, I saw that he was wearing a kilt and sporran and a fearsome basket-hilted broadsword. Awed and frightened, I tried to wriggle into the position known in military hospitals as the 'lying attention' but he put out a huge skeletal hand and pushed me back on to my pillows.

'Whisht now,' he said, surprisingly softly. 'Dinna fash yoursel', laddie. Ye've a lang road to gang before ye're your mon's mon again.' He patted me gently on the shoulder and turned to a group of Indians behind him and told them in fluent but ungrammatical Urdu to look after me well and see I had every comfort, and not to fail to call him when they thought I had regained more of my strength. Then he left, and I lay wondering just what sort of lunatic asylum I had landed myself in. It certainly did not seem to be a prison, although it was some sort of military establishment, because I could hear bugle calls and the rolling of a drum outside, and from time to time the sound of marching men.

One of the Indians brought me a feeding-cup of soup, and supported my head while I drank it, and I asked him in Urdu who my visitor had been. Had he been a Christian I think he would have crossed himself before answering. As he was not, he whispered in reverent tones, 'General Jock Singh-sahib,' which left me in greater bewilderment than before. The 'Jock' fitted the accent and the tartan, and the 'Singh', which is a title all Sikhs attain on initiation to manhood, was of a piece with the turban and bangle, but together they made a wildly incongruous pair. I puzzled over it for some time, and I tried to question the Indians further, but the effort was too great for me – so I once more relapsed into sleep.

I made fast progress after this. Small but nourishing meals were brought to me at frequent intervals and my strength started to return, and a few days later, the fever having passed, I was able to leave my bed and sit in a long chair on the balcony, from where I was able to study the geography of this strange place.

It was a fort of sorts, surrounded by a high wall, pierced by a heavy arched gateway. In front of the building I was in, which was obviously the hospital, was a wide parade ground with barracks to one side and a very handsome palace the other.

Outside the walls of the fort was a small village and a bazaar which always seemed to be in a bustle of activity, as indeed was the fort itself, because there was much coming and going, sepoys were constantly drilling on the square, and guards were mounted regularly in a very smart and creditable manner.

The general came to see me again two days later. I was lying on my long chair on the balcony and I started to rise, but he put me at my ease and told me to sit down again, and he took a chair facing me and regarded me steadily for some moments in silence, and I began to feel very uncomfortable. Then, without preamble he said sternly, 'Muir Dalrymple? A guid Scots name, but from your speech I'll wager you've ne'er been north of the Tweed in your life. How d'ye account for that?'

I felt myself going cold all over, but I managed to mumble, 'I was born in England – but my mother was a Frazer,' hoping to curry a little favour with the fierce old devil, while I racked my brains for some reasonable story to explain my presence here. I had no papers or any other means of identity on me, so where had he got my name? Then it occurred to me, and I cursed inwardly. Of course – it was marked inside my forage cap.

'A Frazer, eh?' he said. 'Poor but prood – and a mickle too much intermarried with the bloody Campbells – but no' bad people for all that. But what are *you* doing here?'

'I – er – had a little trouble in my regiment, sir,' I faltered. 'I'm afraid it's a long and very involved story – '

'Which you can tell or withhold as you wish,' he said. 'I'm no' an inquisitive mon, in spite of the length of my beak.' He held out his hand. 'You can drop the "sir". I'm Alastair McMurtrie, late pipe-major of the 40th Hielanders – presently major-general of the forces of His Serene Highness the Rajah of Kandapore. I would have been full general long since, but I canna get my hands on the proper badges of rank.' His beard and moustache split in a wide grin. 'I'm prood to shake the hand of a mon with the spirit and guts to horsewhip an officer on his own parade ground – but that would no' save your neck here if you were ever of a mind to repeat the pleasure.'

I had risen to shake hands, but now my knees gave way under me and I sat down again heavily. He laughed heartily and said, 'Aye, I know all about it. The news was here the very next morning.'

'In God's name how?' I gasped. 'It happened in Faraqbagh, the better part of a month ago – and I've been travelling ever since.' Then, as a thought struck me, I added forlornly, 'I see – the telegraph? Yes, I had been fearing that.'

'Telegraph be damned,' he scoffed. 'The junglies have older and quicker means of sending news through this wilderness than that. Don't ask me how, because I couldna tell you – any more than Alexander the Great could, when he was using the same means two thousand years ago. Tell me, where were you making for when I picked you up like a grassed salmon?'

'Calcutta,' I said miserably.

'You were gey slow,' he chuckled. 'Faraqbagh is a wee bit over fifty miles from here.'

'I don't believe you,' I said indignantly. 'I was moving slowly towards the end, admittedly, but I swear I was making twenty miles a day for at least the first fifteen.'

'Aye, nae doot – but in a circle.'

'I couldn't have been. I followed the course of the river the whole way.'

'Which explains it. The Ganges runs due south-east hereabouts only in the dry season. It bursts its banks in the monsoon and curves right round to the north in a hundred-and-fifty-mile sweep.'

'Oh God,' I groaned, and he relented a little.

'Dinna fash ye'sel', laddie,' he said. 'If you're still of a mind to go south when the rains are over, I'll help you on your way. In the meantime I'll be glad of your company. I'm fond of these wee heathens, but ten years without hearing or speaking one's mother tongue is an awfu' long time.'

'Ten years?' I stared at him open-mouthed.

'Aye, and a little more,' he answered. 'I came out of the guardroom of the Red Fort in Delhi, pausing only to collect my pipes, which were my ain property – oh, aye, and the sergeant-major's wife – and we were away doon the Jumna. It was a court martial, ye ken – and I was certain to lose my four pipe-major's stripes, and as like collect a flogging as well. She was a bonny wee thing, an Indian Christian lass from the convent in Nawapet – little more than a child – and he was a Glascae keelie, a black-hearted ignorant bastard with the manners of a pig and the carcass of an ox – nigh as big as mysel' he was. He used to take his belt to her when in drink, which was most of the time, and flog the hide off her. I took the belt from him one day and beat the living hell out of him in front of the whole regiment – with them cheering me on – and I've heard since that he was invalided from the service as a result. I dare say the sympathy of every officer and man on the station was with me – but there can be only one answer to striking your superior officer – pig, ox, bastard or whatever you like to call him – so I didna wait for it, any more than you did.' He shook his head sadly and sighed. 'But it gets awfu' lonely at times.'

'What happened to – to – the lady?' I asked.

'I dropped her back at the convent, with a few words in season to the Mother-Superior about the inadvisability of handing over wee creatures like that to sweaty brutes of soldiers, even if the union *is* blessed by the Holy Church – and I continued on my way. Like you, I was making for Calcutta – ' he grinned wickedly – 'but I was making a better fist of it, although I was pretty hungry and footsore by the time I got doon to these parts, and I was sitting on the river bank in the gloaming, playing a pibroch to hearten mysel', and I found I was surrounded by a crood of ragged catch-'em-alivoes with muskets and fixed bayonets, and I thought my number was up, but all they were doing was listening to the music. Mon, how these blackamoors love the pipes. I had a few words of the language even in those days, and I managed to make them understand that I'd play the better for a full belly – so they brought me back here – and here I've been ever since. The Rajah's very old now, and the state is the size of two parishes and a bit, with the army but fifty sepoys, and all of it badly run doon. In return for my keep I became court musician, prime minister and commander-in-chief – and I've drilled these hairies until at least they *look* like soldiers, and we've managed to keep the Pindaris back – at least until now, though I have my doots how much longer we'll be able to hold out.'

'The Pindaris?' I said.

'Gangs of disbanded soldiers – ' he began.

'Yes, I know,' I told him. 'We fought, and routed, a small party of them on our march to Faraqbagh.'

'It's the *large* parties we fear,' he said. 'They're getting bigger all the time. They go to ground in the monsoon, but then when the rains are over they come out like lice from an Untouchable's blanket, and this is one of the first places they make for on their march to richer parts – to steal food and powder and shot. Before I came, the Rajah used to pay tribute to them – and these poor devils would starve for the rest of the year – but I managed to put a bit of heart into them, and we now get the villagers inside these walls and close the gates and hold them off with musket fire from the walls – but as I say, more of them come each year. If we get above a couple of hundred this time, and they use battering rams on the gates – ' He shrugged hopelessly.

'It's a pity you haven't any artillery,' I said. 'We were taken by surprise and heavily outnumbered – in the open without cover – but a few rounds of canister had them running like rabbits.'

'We have artillery,' he said. 'A nine-pounder, but nobody knows how to use it – and it's possessed of a devil. The damned thing has killed two men – '

'How?'

'It stands on its nose when it's fired – and the trail has dropped back and crushed the sepoy who touched it off. None of them will go near it now.'

'Where is it?' I asked excitedly.

'Under cover behind the barracks – '

'May I see it?'

'You may – but little good it will do. You're an infantry-man, like the rest of us – '

'I am also a trained gunner,' I told him, and he stared at me.

'Mon,' he whispered hoarsely, 'you're not gammoning me?'

'I am not,' I assured him. 'And the nine-pounder is the gun I know best.'

'Get your strength back,' he said earnestly. 'If I was a religious man, this is what I would be praying for.'

The rains had still not ceased a week later, but the skies remained clear for longer periods each day, and the heavy afternoon downpours had lessened to a drizzle, and it was plain that the monsoon was all but over. I had tried constantly to get Jock, as he had told me to call him, to let me see the gun, but he adamantly refused until he was satisfied that I was really fit again, then I crossed the square one morning feeling, in spite of my own six feet, a veritable pygmy beside him, and not a little self-conscious, because he had insisted on my wild and unkempt hair and beard being neatly dressed in the Sikh fashion and had provided me with a turban and a travesty of a native officer's uniform.

'But these people will still know that I'm a European,' I protested. 'What the devil else could I be with tow-coloured hair and blue eyes?'

'Of course they'll know,' he snorted impatiently. 'They'll take you for a *badal dalna*, like me.'

'What's a *badal dalna*?' I asked.

'Convert or renegade, according to which way you look at it,' he explained. 'God knows there are enough of us – run-away soldiers like ourselves in the main. Most of us choose Sikhdom, because caste Hindus regard us as Untouchables, while embracing Islam involves a gey uncomfortable re-arrangement of a mon's private affairs – carried oot with a rusty knife and a mort of praying.'

I had been fearing that the gun would prove to be a locally cast piece with some inherent fault in its construction, but, viewed from the rear it looked sound and stable enough, and it had obviously been well looked after in spite of its sinister reputation. The brass piece itself was polished, and the trunnions were oiled and free of rust, and I was reassured by the crown, broad arrow and Woolwich Arsenal mark on its massive breech. Its drag-ropes were neatly coiled beside each wheel, and the rammer and piassaver swab were resting across the trail in the regulation manner. I pushed a straw into the touch-hole and felt it go smoothly into the chamber. What then, I wondered, could be the matter with it?

I asked Jock to detail a squad to run it out on to the parade ground. They obeyed quickly enough, but they were unhandy with it and I noticed one or two of them covertly making the sign to ward off the evil eye.

'Have you ever seen it fired?' I asked him.

'Aye – four damned times. I touched it off mysel' once.'

'What happened exactly?'

He put his hand on the muzzle and I noticed it dip slightly, and then, as he removed his hand, return of its own volition to the horizontal. 'This part went doon – and that part –' he pointed to the trail – 'kicked upwards like the hinds of the dominie's donkey with a bee up its arse – and came down on the man who had fired it, and killed him. It had happened once before I came here, so they told me. It would have had me, the wicked de'il, if I hadn't been ready for it and skipped smartly out of the way.'

'Do that again,' I said.

'Do what again?'

'Put your hand on the muzzle, and press.' He did so.

'Good. Now remove it.' I knelt down and looked up from underneath it – and, as I suspected, saw that the four hard oaken wedges, that should have been in place, two each side of the cradle under the trunnions, were, in fact, missing, and the piece, that is, the actual barrel, was therefore free to swing up and down like a see-saw.

'Has anything been removed from the gun since you fired it last?' I asked him.

'Not that I know of. These people wouldn't come near the damned thing if they weren't more frightened of me than it.'

'I think I know the trouble,' I said. 'I want some very hard wood – and a carpenter.'

'*Lakri mistri!*' bellowed Jock, and a little old man came running from the timidly curious crowd that had gathered round the perimeter square, and salaamed profoundly. 'Best bloody carpenter in India,' said Jock, 'but as thick as one of his own planks unless you explain what you want very clearly.'

'Let me have a pencil and a large sheet of paper,' I said.

I drew the wedge, partly from memory, but mostly by guesswork – approximately eight inches long and three inches wide, tapering from two inches down to nothing, and told the little man that I wanted four of them in the hardest wood he could find – and he produced them in lignum-vitae within the hour. I put them in place and tapped them lightly until they were just gripping – then I bore down heavily on the muzzle. It was now immovable.

'There you are,' I said triumphantly. 'When the gun is fired, half the force of the explosion goes behind the projectile – the other half is taken on the inside rear of the breech – Newton's theory of action and reaction. Do you understand?'

'No,' he said flatly. 'All I want to know is if the bloody thing is safe to fire?'

'There's only one way to determine that,' I told him. 'Have it run on to the plain outside – and show me your powder magazine.'

I found that they had an ample store of powder, and a hundred solid round shot, but no canister, or shrapnel as it is now called, so I got Jock to set sepoys to the task of making up canvas 'sausages' of musket balls, then I went out to the gun and laid it on to a small tree three hundred paces away, loaded it, breathed a silent prayer, and touched it off. It roared and recoiled healthily, and when the smoke cleared I saw that although the tree was still standing, both it and a clump of bushes some distance farther on were torn and shredded. I made certain fine adjustments to lay and elevation, and tried again, with better results, until, after five more rounds I had it bearing accurately. I drove the wedges in firmly and we ran the gun back into the fort – and Jock and the sepoys breathed freely again.

Between us we selected six intelligent men, whom I formed into a detachment, and we drilled tirelessly for the rest of the day, and for days thereafter, until I felt I had a gun crew that was at least the equal of any I had commanded previously – and, in the evenings, I sat long with Jock devising a plan of action against the day when the Pindaris made their next unwelcome visit.

'It never varies,' Jock explained. 'They turn up – a bigger party each year – and they camp out there on the Maidan a mile or so away, and the villagers behave like chickens when there's a hawk poised overhead, and they run inside the walls here, and bring their cattle and goats – and we bar the gates and double-man the firing slits – and just wait, with conditions getting worse by the day. Then they send in a party under flag of truce to parley. They want powder and shot, and meat and grain and oil, and always silver rupees. It was five thousand the year I came here – it was twenty thousand last year – it will probably be thirty this time. I tell them to go to hell, and they salaam politely and leave – and that night a house in the village goes up in flames – and the next night another one – then two together – and the wailing inside here gets louder, and the poor old devil of a Rajah, who hasn't left his sickbed in the last four years, sends for me and tells me to give them what they want so they'll leave his people in peace. But each time I've disobeyed him, because I know that if I open those gates their demands will grow bigger, and they'll be after the women as well as the cattle.'

'But you *have* held out?' I said.

'Aye – but only at the price of much misery. They've always tried to storm the gates as a last resort, and we've killed a few of them in the attempt – but we've suffered losses ourselves, and cholera broke out in here last year. They have to withdraw in the end, because they work to a set plan

266

and have to rendezvous with other parties in different parts of the country – but I know that this year, next year, or the next, they're going to overwhelm us – unless we can do something to stop them once and for all.'

'You mean they'll mount a successful attack?' I said. 'What form do you think it will take?'

'There *can* only be one form,' he said impatiently. 'If you'd soldiered as long as I have, you'd ken that.'

'Tell me.'

'For every man I've got on the walls with a musket, they'd have to have three – one firing, one waiting to fire, one reloading. Each three attackers concentrates on one defender and pins him down under sustained fire. That would mean a hundred and fifty of them, with a minimum reserve of a further fifty. In addition to that they'd need another fifty to man a battering ram – with a hundred more standing by as a storming party ready to rush in when the gates gave way. Three hundred and fifty of them all told.'

'How much warning of their arrival do you normally receive?'

'They come when the monsoon has ended. It has ended when we have three clear days without rain. It's a four-day march from their camp in the hills, so they arrive on the fifth day, as regular as clockwork.'

'As you've just remarked,' I said, 'I haven't soldiered as long as you, so I dinna ken any bloody thing, but if you're not too proud to listen to a recruit's suggestion – '

He glared at me. 'What?' he grunted suspiciously.

'This,' I said, and went into preliminary details.

They came as he had prophesied, on the fifth day after the rains had ceased, and the skies were once more clear and brazenly hot, and they made a brave show as we watched from the walls, with drums beating and bugles sounding, wearing, it seemed, the remnants of every uniform in the Company army. They bivouacked on the Maidan, well out of musket range, and a party of ten came forward unarmed and under a white flag. Below us, in the fort, the villagers were silent and cowed.

The party halted in front of the gate, and one of them, a typical Bengali munshi – half soldier, half babu – called up to us softly, 'Oh, General, sahib-bahadur, most munificent giver to the poor, light of our eyes and father and mother to the hungry, open for us. We come in peace, bearing greetings from our commander.'

'Jackal shit – spawn of the camel louse,' Jock spat at him in sweeper's Urdu. 'Tell him to go to hell, and take his rabble with him. You get nothing here. Go!'

'General-sahib,' the other said reproachfully. 'At least in other years you have opened for us and we have discussed matters like sensible men – '

'*Phengto – gira do*,' Jock snapped, and an Untouchable beside us hurled the contents of a latrine bucket down into the upturned faces of the envoys.

There was a scream of rage and horror, and they turned and scuttled out of range.

Jock chuckled grimly. 'That will be costing them a thousand rupees apiece to the priests, to get their caste back again,' he said. 'But dear God help us if they *do* get in.'

The night was hell. They crept into the village and set fire to a couple of houses, and they sent showers of arrows over the wall with wads of smouldering tow attached to them which set several heaps of cattle fodder alight, and the animals stampeded in terror, trampling down the flimsy shelters the villagers had constructed round the parade ground, because no Indian, however hot and dry the weather, will ever willingly sleep out in the open.

With dawn they withdrew, and through a telescope we could see a council of war going on in the lines of their bivouacs.

'All grouped together like bugs in a rug,' Jock said wistfully. 'Could we no' be trying a shot at them with the gun? It would surely reach them?'

'Canister would be too dispersed at that range to be effective,' I told him. 'And a single round-shot is destructive only to that immediately in its path.'

'Ah, to hell with your drill manuals and book-learning,' he growled, but he didn't press the point.

Then we saw parties of them stringing out and taking up positions in the scrub at almost extreme musket range, and sporadic firing began, and two of our sepoys, crouching behind the parapet on top of the wall were hit immediately, the almost-spent bullets inflicting horrible wounds. Jock grabbed a musket from one of them and brought down a Pindari running between two points of cover with a magnificent shot. I tried to outdo him with a bead on a man who momentarily presented a good target, but a bullet slapped into the stonework beside my loophole, within inches of my head, and Jock caught my arm angrily and pulled me down behind the parapet.

'You damned young fool,' he swore. 'Can't you see they're only trying to draw our fire, so they can mark the loopholes that are manned? You're no' dealing with bare-arsed savages. These are trained soldiers. Never fire at an easy target, for it's three chances to one they're waiting to nail you.'

The firing went on through the morning, and two more of our men were hit, one being killed, and it was obvious that the tactics that Jock had explained to me earlier were now being employed, because it was impossible for any of the sepoys to fire without an immediate, well-aimed response, and even a quick peep with the telescope was becoming hazardous. Then, halfway through the afternoon, we saw a huge tree-trunk being brought in from the jungle, and the firing became fiercer and more concentrated until it rose to a crescendo from a position right opposite the gate. Risking a look from a loophole to one flank, we saw the battering-ram moving down the approach road to the fort like an ungainly centipede – which it was, literally, because a party of some fifty Pindaris was bearing it in a shuffling trot straight for the gate, and such was the curtain of firing over their heads from the group behind them that it was impossible for our men to risk their heads above the parapet.

Jock said, 'This, I think, is the moment you've had in mind, laddie.' And I dashed down the steps from the wall to where the gun was trained on the gateway from behind the barricade we had erected over the last few days. My detachment were already in position, as were the two parties detailed to open the double gates on my command. I bellowed, 'Kholo!' (Open) above the din, and as the holding bar was whipped away and the gates swung open on their well-greased hinges, I banged the portfire down on the touch-hole, just as the butt of the ram appeared in the archway.

I had double-charged and shotted with a murderous twenty pounds and more of musket balls, nails and bolts which blasted the rammers, and the musketeers who had been firing over their heads, into nothingness, and the doors were swung closed again almost before the reverberations had died, and we had reloaded, and I hammered in the wedges to increase elevation.

Jock looked down on us from the arch above the gate and said in an awed whisper which reached me easily in the stunned silence which had followed the explosion, 'Jesus! Gey near a hundred of them – and I don't think it missed a one.'

I went up on to the wall again, and the sight that met my eyes nearly turned my stomach. The approach road, which was banked on either side, thereby forming a tunnel from the gateway, was a charnel-house of blood, shattered limbs and dismembered trunks. Of the party with the battering-ram it was plain that not a single one had escaped, while some yards beyond it the few dazed musketeers who had survived the holocaust were stumbling back towards their lines, and our sepoys were busily picking them off. In the bivouacs the remainder of the Pindaris seemed to be making preparations for a speedy departure, so I hurried down again and ordered the gates to be opened, and we ran the gun forward through the shambles on to the higher ground at the end of the approach road, and I tapped the wedges in to give the piece even more elevation and we gave them a further peppering, though, as before, it wasn't really necessary because they were by now a beaten rabble in full disordered retreat.

Jock came down and joined us, and somehow we managed to organize a party of Muslims and Untouchables to clear the approach road and the village of the bodies, because no caste Hindu could be persuaded to come out of the fort until this was done, and then we ran the gun back in and reset it in its place behind the barricade – again charged, shotted and ready.

I slept the sleep of sheer exhaustion that night, but Jock, cast in sterner military mould, insisted on prowling the battlements, playing his pipes and keeping the sentries on the alert, although we were now confident that it had been a complete rout and there would be a long period of wound-licking before we were threatened again.

The river had gone down to its normal level and the blessed relief of the 'cold weather' was with us once more, and my strength had returned fully – and I was restless. I told Jock that it was time for me to move on, and although he raised no objection I could see that he had been hoping that I would stay longer.

'You must do as you think fit, laddie,' he said, 'but I would counsel you to think well on your plans before committing yourself to any definite course of action.'

'I have no plans,' I told him, 'other than to go to Calcutta and get aboard a ship.'

'For where?'

'England, naturally.'

'What opportunities are there in England for a young man of your talents?'

I shrugged. 'I don't know, until I get back there. It may not even be England. If there is a ship going the other way – say to California – I might take it.'

'Footloose and fancy free,' he said. 'For God's sake, why not stay here? It's no' such a bad life. You can take an Indian woman if you have a mind – as I have done.'

'In this country I will always be a fugitive,' I said. 'If I'm ever taken I'll be hanged. To hell with that for a life.'

'You're safe enough here.'

'Perhaps – but I don't want to stay cooped within twenty square miles for ever.'

'Well, stay until the spring, anyhow,' he suggested. 'The tea crop comes down from the hills then, and you'll have as many as a dozen ships in port to choose from. At any other time you may not find one for weeks on end – and Calcutta is no place to kick your heels in for long.'

And that seemed sensible – so I closed my ears to the Wander Joss and helped Jock to consolidate his victory, and we strengthened the defences, and I drilled the gunners and practised firing until they were near perfection.

And then came the *chapatti.*

Chapter Eleven

In India there are, for all practical purposes, three seasons – the Hot Weather, from April until July, the Rains, July until October and the Cold Weather, from October to April. 'Spring' if such it could be called, is a term used only by Europeans, and it falls for a short period towards the end of November. I had planned, therefore, to leave Kandapore in October – by boat, and disguised as a zemindar, or poor and peaceful farmer. Jock, although loath to see me depart, had proved generous in the extreme and had insisted on paying me for my services, so I could count on some two hundred gold mohurs which, when exchanged in Calcutta, would yield about four hundred English pounds.

'Get yoursel' some good English clothes, and stay at the Bristol Hotel,' Jock advised. 'If ye canna find a berth in the fo'c'sle of a foreign-bound ship ye'll have enough money to pay for a passage. The army is not likely to be worrying you – Sergeant Muir Dalrymple will have been written off as dead by this – but you'll have to be on the watch for Company police agents who might be taking an interest in a lone European, so have a good story always ready if you should ever be questioned.'

We mulled long over this, considering and rejecting such roles as Company writers, engineers or other civilians returning to England on leave, as being too easily checked by the authorities.

'Missionary?' he mused. 'No – ye're not lang enough in the jib for that – and ye're as like as not to be coming oot with a resounding "bloody hell" at the wrong moment.'

So we finally decided upon an academic guise as tutor to the Rajah's grandchildren, since I had, in fact, often given them lessons in English, and I had a long and eulogistic letter written in beautiful Persio-Arabic script by the munshi, thanking Mr Ross Stafford for his services, and regretting his departure – franked and embellished most imposingly with the State seal, and rolled into a scroll holder.

But the rains were late in ceasing that year, and the Ganges was still in full spate on the day I had set for my departure, so I postponed it for a week – and in that time word had come to Jock that a hundred of the new Enfield rifles lately issued to East India Company troops had been stolen from an arms convoy by the Pindaris who, for reasons best known to themselves, were offering them for sale to the highest bidder at Nerbanda, a small town outside the Company area, some three weeks' journey away, and nothing would do but that he should go down and chaffer for them. So, in decency, I had to volunteer to hold the fort until he returned – then, when he did, the better part of two months later – the journey and the transaction both taking more time than he had estimated – I had to remain to help him train the sepoys in their use.

I found the rifle a great improvement on the smooth-bore musket it was replacing. It was lighter and far more accurate, and its effective range was twice that of the older weapon, and, although still a muzzle-loader, its rate of fire was much greater, as it used a composite bullet and cartridge in place of the cumbersome loose powder, wad and ball, all of which had to be rammed separately. Jock and I were like schoolboys with a new toy, and we happily blasted away a lot of ammunition in order to familiarize ourselves with it before introducing it to the troops.

The round consisted of a soft lead slug set into an oiled paper cylinder which contained the powder and a percussion cap, the whole thing being heavily greased to protect it from dampness – and the end of the cylinder had to be bitten through to expose the cap to the firing pin after being pushed down the barrel with the ramrod, and we had the drill set to a five-beat rhythm of 'cartridge from pouch – bite – ram – aim – fire' until we could almost have done it in our sleep.

It was a fine cool morning on the day we paraded at the

rifle range. We made a brave show as we came out of the fort, now one hundred strong, since Jock had doubled the army after the last Pindari raid. We marched as Light Infantry, with the rifles at the trail instead of shouldered, with Jock in front – surely the only major-general in history personally to lead his troops with the pipes – and myself with the drummers behind him.

We halted on a mound two hundred paces from a row of targets I had set up the evening before, and I demonstrated the five-pointed drill several times, and then Jock and I dropped to the prone position and snapped off five rounds each in quick time, scoring with every one. Then, somewhat puffed up with my own prowess, I opened a fresh box of ammunition and stepped up to the first man in the ranks and held out five rounds to him. Looking distressed, he shook his head and made no move to take them. Thinking that perhaps he was suffering from some passing bout of sickness, I told him to fall out and sit down, and I moved on to the next man – to be met with a similar refusal. I turned and looked at Jock in bewilderment, and I heard him mutter, 'My God! The *chapatti* –'

Prem Singh, Jock's oldest serving *havildar* (sergeant), recently promoted to *jemadar* (ensign) was standing to a flank looking downcast and miserable. Jock beckoned to him curtly and he came forward and saluted.

'When did it come, jemadar-sahib?' Jock asked quietly.

'Two days ago, jinral-sahib,' the old man answered, and I saw tears trickling down his bearded cheek.

'Where is the messenger now?'

'He has gone on, jinral-sahib – perhaps to Faraqbagh, or back to Lucknow, where the cursed thing started.'

'You know it *is* a cursed thing?' Jock said.

'I know, jinral-sahib – and I have betrayed my salt and am ashamed – but I cannot touch the cartridge, nor can any man on this parade – Hindu, Sikh or Mussulman.'

'Why?' Jock snapped grimly.

'The jinral-sahib knows,' Prem Singh said. 'They are greased with that which is untouchable to men of all castes.'

'Am I a liar?'

'God knows the jinral-sahib is not.'

'Or an Untouchable?'

'Let it not be said.'

'You have seen me bite the cartridge? You have seen the colonel-sahib bite it –' Jock jerked his head in my direction.

Prem Singh squirmed and looked down at his feet. 'Both the sahibs are *Isdis* (Christians) to whom such things do not apply,' he said.

Jock touched his steel bracelet, then his turban and finally his beard. 'What are these?' he demanded angrily.

'The marks of a Sikh,' Prem Singh answered. 'We are proud that you have seen fit to wear them – but the jinral-sahib is not a *born* Sikh.'

'I see,' said Jock. 'You honour me by inviting me into your brotherhood, then blacken my face by denying me. Order the sepoys to ground arms, jemadar-sahib, then march them back to barracks. I shall find women's work for them to do – then I shall go to the hills to recruit *men* in their place – to protect them when the Pindaris attack again – *next time with these same rifles*. The Pindaris are our enemies, but none can deny that there are good Hindus, Sikhs and Mussulmans in their ranks. *They* bite the cartridges.' He turned to the men. 'You are dismissed,' he called out. 'But hear me before you go. These cartridges are greased with the oil of the coconut, which gives offence to no man's religion. I myself have watched them being prepared in the Company's arsenals. The story that the fat of cows and pigs is used is a lie spread by the enemies of the Company in the hope that these rifles will not ever be used against them. I, Major-General Jock Singh, swear it on my honour, on the honour of my father, on my sword and on the grave of my mother.' He spat. 'Take them away, jemadar-sahib. They shame me.'

We stood in silence as they marched away towards the fort, then Jock turned to me and said savagely, 'That damned pancake. I'd like to ram it down the gullet of the bastard who cooked it.'

'What damned pancake?' I asked, completely mystified.

'The chapatti. They've been threatening John Company with it for so long that nobody pays heed to it nowadays. But it seems to be going the rounds all right.' He shook his head gloomily. 'God knows where it will stop now.'

'I don't understand,' I said.

'You wouldna. You've no' been in the country long enough. The chapatti is their unleavened bread – the one thing that all religions can eat without damage to their castes – so their bloody gurus and saddhus and mullahs and other trouble-making de'ils use it as a symbol. They say that when one is sent by hand from one station to another, with the words *"Bande Mataram"* – that means "Motherland unite" – Hindus and Mussulmans will join together and rise against the white man.'

'But what has that to do with our rifles?'

'Somebody has told them that the new cartridges are smeared with cow and pig fat, to make outcastes of the soldiers – and so prevent the army and the civilians uniting. A clever ruse – but it's no' working.'

'In any case you've just sworn that the cartridges are *not* smeared with cow and pig fat,' I said.

He grinned sheepishly. 'Aye – by the honour I've never pretended to, the father I never knew, and the sword I stole from an officer's bungalow. Swearing's easy enough. I only hope my old mother is not spinning in her grave.'

'You mean they *are*?' I said, shocked.

He shrugged. 'They could be. That fat wee besom of a Queen of ours and her long-faced missionaries have been trying to make Christians out of these blackamoors ever since she came to the throne. The Pindaris think they are. That is why they sold me the rifles cheap.' He punched his fist into the palm of his other hand. 'God damn and blast it to hell!' he fumed. 'What does it matter one way or the other? All I know is that with a hundred of these weapons in the hands of trained men on our side, and the Pindaris not using them on theirs, we need never fear them again.'

'You've still got the cannon,' I reminded him.

'Aye – but one day they'll bring one too, and that will

277

cancel out our advantage. No – the odds are on the side with these beauties.' He stood combing his beard with clawed fingers, regarding the lines of rifles in the dust where the sepoys had grounded them. 'I've got one shot left in my locker,' he said thoughtfully. 'Stay here until I come back – praying hard the while.' He turned and strode towards the fort.

They were back in less than an hour, with the pipes skirling and drums beating, and they wheeled and formed on their rifles, and took them up on the jemadar's command, and Jock gestured to me to issue the cartridges. I thought I saw one or two hesitate momentarily, but all finally took them – and bit them – and loaded, and fired – and after the first rounds a frenzy of achievement seemed to descend upon them, with each man trying to outdo the other and to wheedle more ammunition from me, and the targets at two hundred paces were shattered, so Jock increased the range again and again until they were firing at six hundred paces, fast and accurately – and we marched back to barracks, tired, dust-and-powder-stained, and very happy, and Jock made an *ex gratia* payment to them of one hundred rupees, which they expended upon a great feast that night, with much of the murderously strong liquor the villagers distilled from the sap of the coconut palm.

'How on earth did you manage it?' I asked him as we leaned on the battlements and looked down on the revels, and he winked and grinned slyly.

'Two years ago,' he said, 'the Pindaris had us cooped up in here for three months, and we'd eaten every damned thing in the fort and we hardly had the strength to climb up here to the firing slits. I risked my neck and stole out through their lines in the darkness – and swam the river, and rounded up some sheep and goats. There was no way of getting them back on the hoof, so I slaughtered and butchered them that side and ferried the meat across in a canoe – and a couple of the women, who have a damn sight more sense than their menfolk, helped me cook it up into a gey big stew that just aboot saved our lives. I reminded them of that. "Your damned castes didn't stop you filling your bellies then," I told them – and they had to agree.'

'But sheep and goats are lawful food for both Hindus and Mussulmans,' I said. 'Only pork and beef are forbidden.'

'Aye – but this afternoon I told them that two of the sheep happened to be fine fat pigs from the Untouchables' camp, and one of the goats a calf. I'd kept the secret like a gentleman, I said, and would continue to do so, *if we had no more trouble over the cartridges.* They looked a bit doon their snoots for a while, and I wouldn't have been greatly surprised if some of them had taken after me with their bayonets, but fortunately old Prem Singh has a fine sense of the ridiculous, and he started to chuckle into his whiskers – and the chuckle grew to a belly laugh, and soon they were rolling on the groond and howling with the sheer glee of it and calling each other pariahs and reckoning how much it would cost them to be purified if their priests ever found out.'

'So really their caste means nothing to them?' I said.

'It means everything,' he corrected. 'Or almost everything. Saving face is just that much more important. Their faces are safe for only as long as I keep my mooth shut – and they know it. Actually there was no pig or cow in that stew – and damn little sheep or goat either. It was mostly drowned dogs and jackals I'd picked up along the banks – with a few dozen rats to make weight – and the buggers know that too.'

'You're a wicked old devil,' I told him.

'Wicked, aye – and de'il maybe – but old? Och awa' with you! I've yet to reach my thirty-fifth birthday. It's these damned whiskers that do it.' He was suddenly serious. 'But the chapatti *has* gone roond,' he said. 'There was rape, fire and bloody murder in Meerut not a week ago. Half the garrison wiped out while the British troops were on church parade – and the women and children slaughtered. And there will be worse to come round here, in Lucknow, Cawnpore and Allahabad, where the sepoys outnumber the Europeans twenty to one.'

I stared at him aghast. 'Oh my God,' I said. 'Faraqbagh – ?'

'Aye – nae doot it'll go the same way – and Delhi too, I'm told.'

'But how do you know all this?' I asked him urgently.

'Damn it, mon,' he answered. 'You speak the language as well, if not better, than I. Go out there into the village and ask for yoursel'. The whole place is a-boil with it. The news came this afternoon.'

'What are we going to do about it?' I demanded.

'*We?*' he said. '*We* stay here, laddie. The trouble is in the East India Company cantonments. Trouble the bastards have been storing up for themselves these many years. Och aye – *we* stay here.'

'While white women and children are being murdered?' I shouted. 'You bloody coward – '

I flew through the air and came hard up against the stone parapet, then slid down on to my behind. He came forward and helped me to my feet.

'I'm sorry, Ross,' he said quietly. ' "Bastard", "son of a whore" – anything you like – but never "coward" to a mon of a Hieland regiment. The response is a matter of instinct.'

'I have friends in Faraqbagh,' I said miserably.

'An officer and his family – aye, you told me.'

'A doctor – and not a Company man – and he's never shown me anything but kindness in all the years I have known him.'

'I hope he gets out, and his wife and the wee girl – aye, I know how you feel – but it disnae make the slightest difference, Ross. There's naught we can do aboot it – except sit here and *watch*. Damn it, you saw what happened this morning.'

'But that trouble has passed.' I was shaking in every limb.

'Aye – for the moment. The chapatti has come and gone, but there's no saying it won't come back again – and next time it may not be a laughing matter, followed by a *ramsami* and a few drinks. We're sitting on the lid of a boiling kettle, laddie, and from now on we don't sleep at the same time – and when we do it must be behind locked doors with a couple of pistols to hand – and the keys of the magazine must be hidden in a different place each night.'

'Jock,' I pleaded, 'I've got to go to Faraqbagh.'

'And get your throat cut if the sepoys have already risen – or be taken and hanged if they haven't,' he said angrily. 'Dinna be a bloody fool, boy.'

'You've just knocked me down for calling you a coward,' I said. 'How do you think *I* am going to feel, every waking moment, knowing that I am one in actuality?'

'I've got little enough education, Ross, God knows,' he said, 'but I've learned over the years that there's no real difference between a coward and a fool. A coward is a mon who is afraid to do what's right. A fool is one who does what's wrong, because he's afraid to be called a coward. So to throw your life away needlessly is both wrong *and* cowardly. Don't you see – ?'

'No, I don't,' I said obstinately. 'All I know is that I have friends in Faraqbagh who are in danger, and if I don't at least *try* to help them I'm going to call myself a coward every day for the rest of my life.'

'All right then – *how* would you help them?'

'I don't know – yet.'

'Well, suppose we stop shouting at each other until we've considered the matter.'

'I ought to go there and see what the position is, and if it's bad, make contact with them and bring them back here.'

'He's a good man, you say – and forby a doctor?'

'I've already told you so.'

'Then do you think he's going to drop his duty and scurry off to save his skin?'

'Maybe not – but there's his wife and daughter – '

'And they'll leave him to face the danger on his own? I canna see it – not if they're the people you say they are.'

'I've still got to go and see for myself,' I insisted, and surprisingly he gave way.

'All right,' he shrugged. 'If you must, you must. You're certainly no use to me here in your present frame of mind. I'll send someone with you.'

'I don't need anybody.'

'For a mon who took two months to cover fifty miles – '

'That was in the monsoon, and I was sick. Things are different now – and I know the ground.'

'I'm still sending somebody, if only for him to come back and tell me what happened when you get your throat cut.'

'But who could we trust?'

'One blackamoor in the whole damned garrison. Bundoo.'

'You mean – the *mehtar*?' I said in astonishment.

'Aye. Him that threw the bucket of shit over the Pindaris *at my command*, knowing that if ever he is caught by them it will take him a long time to die, hanging from a hook in the back of his neck.' He shook his head slowly. 'That poor wee black bastard has got more courage and honesty than any six of those damned high-caste, so-called bloody warriors of ours, yet because *they* call him an Untouchable, *we*, the equally so-called Protectors of the Poor, treat him as one also.'

'But does he know the jungle?' I asked.

'Better than *you* – or me.' He grinned. 'And you'll feed a gey sight better than you did last time. His wife was one of the cooks of that stew I was telling you about.'

We left after dark the following night – both dressed, and smelling, the same, because Bundoo had anointed himself and me with cheetah fat, which, when blended with garlic and pounded dung-beetles, is one of the most potent stinks in the East.

'Do I have to have this damned stuff on?' I had wailed plaintively to Jock, as he watched with a critical eye while we prepared ourselves for the journey.

'Aye, if *he* says so,' Jock had answered mordantly. 'With that on your hides no living creature, from mosquitoes to tigers, will willingly come nigh you. You can walk through a village at night, and the dogs will slink away without a whimper.'

We wore loincloths and tattered, filthy shirts, with wisps of rag tied round our heads. Bundoo was, as always, barefooted, but the concession of chaplis was grudgingly allowed by the little man in my case. I had given myself a coating of all but indelible anatoo stain, but it was hardly necessary, as I was sun-blackened almost to his colour. We each carried a bundle containing a little gram, or parched barley, half a dozen large and leathery chapattis, and flint, steel and tinder, and we wore knives in our waistbands, while I, in addition, carried concealed in my rags, a pistol and twenty-five rounds of ball. All this had been done in an empty hut well outside the village, so, we hoped, our guise and departure were unknown to the troops.

There was no ceremony. Jock gripped my hand and grunted a gruff 'good luck' and then turned to Bundoo and held out his hand. The other, through force of agelong conditioning, salaamed and stepped back quickly to avoid giving offence by contact, but Jock growled in Hindi, 'Shake hands like a man, my brother, for that's what you are,' and I saw the look of doglike fidelity in the outcaste's eyes as he grinned delightedly.

We slipped into the jungle, and although I could not see a path, there was obviously one there because the little man never as much as brushed against a tree or bush, but he kept jogging silently ahead of me at a mile-eating trot that, strangely, once I had fallen into the rhythm of it, seemed to take no effort to keep up.

It is remarkable what company will do for one's courage in the jungle. Travelling on my own I had started at the sound of every night bird, frog or taktu lizard, while a rustle in the undergrowth would have my scalp prickling and my nerves stretched like fiddle strings, but with a companion they passed unnoticed, even when, while resting for a few minutes, we heard a coughing snarl close by, and Bundoo said casually, 'Bara sher' (big tiger).

We halted at dawn and ate a chapatti, probably about as indigestible a comestible as ever to assail the human stomach, yet remarkably sustaining. We drank from a stream and then slept – at least I did. Bundoo seemed able completely to dispense with any form of rest, because when I awoke some time later, he had gathered a stock of wild bananas and ten large eggs. I looked at the latter with some puzzlement, because we had no means of cooking them, but he neatly sliced the top off one of them, presented it to me and told me to drink the contents. I did so, although my gorge was rising, and found it to be delicious, so I swallowed another three, and only then did I think to ask him what sort of bird had laid them, because they were larger than goose's eggs. He smiled and pointed through the undergrowth towards the river, and said, 'Magar', (crocodile).

We came to country I recognized on the second morning, approaching it from a different direction from the one by which I had left so hurriedly, and finishing on a wooded hill that looked down upon the cantonments – and I saw with relief that both the Union Jack and the Company standard were flying from their staffs in front of the Commandant's headquarters.

But there was an unwonted stillness about the place. Normally, in the first two hours of daylight, troops would have been drilling on the vast parade ground, officers and their ladies would have been exercising their horses on the bridle-track that bounded it, and the bazaar at the far end would have been bustling with the fruit and vegetable sellers who brought their wares in from the surrounding farms each morning. But now there was no movement except for a guard of twelve files marching round the perimeter to relieve and change sentries – and although the distance was too great for me to distinguish details, I could see from their forage caps and white neckcloths that they were Europeans. I would have given a lot for a telescope, because now I could make out many changes in the scene since I had last seen it. There were earthworks round the European barracks and the officers' lines near by, with a sap connecting the two enclaves thus formed. I looked in vain for the guns of the Horse Artillery battery. They were not on their gun park – and then I saw that their stables were empty, and I wondered if the guns were deployed out of sight in the surrounding jungle.

I could see the Palmers' white bungalow, and I strained my eyes for a long time in the hope of some sign of life there, but I saw none. More guards were being relieved now. I counted nine parties, each of twelve men under a non-commissioned officer. A hundred and eight sentries, I reckoned in amazement – almost a fifth of our under-strength regiment. Usually we never had more than twenty mounted at any one time. Obviously this was a garrison under threat of siege. But the most significant and frightening thing was that there were no Indian troops whatsoever in sight, and there was no smoke from their cookhouses, as there would have been at this hour on any ordinary day, even during festivals, when they were excused duty.

I lay on my belly peering through the undergrowth, in an agony of indecision. My every instinct was to rely on my disguise and go down into the cantonments and try to make contact with Mr Palmer, either at his home or at the hospital, but that in itself presented difficulties. With a garrison so obviously on the *qui vive* as this, it was highly unlikely that they would permit an Indian of any type or description to enter without interrogation, and although my disguise might have passed unchallenged in a crowd, I doubted very much whether it would stand close scrutiny in daylight. Perhaps if I waited until dark and tried to slip between two sentry posts – ? I shivered at the very thought of this, because of the troops' pronounced tendency to fire at suspected intruders first, and challenge afterwards. If I knew where all the posts were it might be different – I turned as I felt a touch on my shoulder. Bundoo was squatting on his heels beside me, his head cocked to one side like that of a hunting dog, with all senses on the alert, listening.

He said, 'The sepoys, sahib. They are coming.'

'How do you know?' I asked him.

He touched his ears and his nose and signed to me politely but firmly to be silent, then he pointed in the direction of the native town, which we couldn't see from this position.

'They come, sahib,' he said positively. 'Many of them.'

I strained my own ears, but I heard nothing for a long time, then, faintly on the breeze, it came to me. The unmistakable sound of marching men – and in the distance we saw the head of a column arrive at a point far up the valley where the road emerged from the surrounding jungle.

They came on, marching to the beat of drums – company after company – twenty of them, each of over a hundred men – two thousand in all – under strict discipline, with their jemadars marching in serrefile beside them, but no European officers at their head, and as we watched we saw the leading company break to half-column and swing round to the north of the cantonment, with the next to the south, and so on alternately until they had cordoned the whole area, with the head and tail of the column meeting below our position where they then established a field headquarters on which all the jemadars converged, seemingly for a council of war. It was a perfectly executed drill, in precise accord with the manual of arms, as I had seen it carried out many times on manoeuvres, and it had obviously been rehearsed, because I could see from our coign of vantage that they had taken up position just outside musket range from the perimeter earthworks where the European troops were now standing to.

We were too far away to hear the council, but it was clear that an attack was imminent, because we could see the sepoys crawling forward under the concealment of the undergrowth to find individual firing positions. I guessed, wrongly as it turned out, that they would put the assault in at dusk, probably under heavy curtain fire, probing with skirmishing parties until they found the weak spots in the defence, prior to charging in strength at dawn.

But no attack went in. Instead their *bawachis* (cooks) came up to the headquarters and prepared their eternal chapattis with huge pots of rice and curried meat and vegetables, which had the nostrils of both Bundoo and myself twitching as the savoury smells were borne upwards on the evening air, and the encircling sepoys came back in small parties from their firing positions to eat, and then return again. We could see European officers inside the perimeter studying the besiegers' dispositions through telescopes, and the sound of drums came to us as more troops paraded and then went out to strengthen the defences yet further, until it seemed that the whole garrison was standing to round the earthworks. There would be little rest for any of them tonight, I reflected, or on any subsequent night until this force withdrew – or attacked.

The sepoys below us, now full fed, seemed inclined to settle down to rest, and although we could see the jemadars going round in the half darkness kicking a man here and there into wakefulness, nature began to have its way with most of them, and after a time all activity ceased and we could even hear snoring from some of the nearer groups. Bundoo and I withdrew half a mile or so and dined frugally on some of our parched grain, washed down with water from a stream. He found some fat white grubs in a rotting tree trunk, which he generously offered to me, but I told him that raw grubs always disagreed with me so he ate them himself with every sign of relish.

I lay awake for hours, in a quandary, unable to face the prospect of returning to the fort without in some way trying to assist these people, but knowing full well that there was absolutely nothing practical that I could do for them.

The sound of heavy firing woke me at daylight, and we went forward again and saw that the besiegers were making attacks at several points round the perimeter. Assault parties were rushing forward and trying to break in through the earthworks at the point of the bayonet, under heavy covering fire from behind, in exactly the same way as the Pindaris had tried with us. Their losses were heavy, as the defenders kept up a well-directed fusillade in return, and the sepoys withdrew, leaving at least twenty dead and wounded on the ground.

But the defenders hadn't had it all their own way, as we saw half a dozen or so being either carried or helped into the hospital, and for the first time I thought I recognized Mr Palmer among the men who came out to attend to them – and I also saw some European women, though only fleetingly, in the entrance to the hospital, where they appeared to be helping with the wounded.

There was a long period of inactivity after this, broken only by brief outbreaks of desultory firing from both sides. One of the jemadars in the encampment below us was killed by a stray bullet and two bawachis were wounded as they took food to the firing positions. Inside the perimeter I saw three European soldiers hit during the course of the morning, one apparently fatally, as they crossed a piece of open ground to fill buckets at a well.

The pattern of the siege was beginning to take form. The sepoys, overwhelmingly outnumbering the defenders, would merely keep up a harassing fire during daylight hours, with probably a frontal assault in the two periods of half light at dawn and dusk respectively, and feint attacks in the dark, all of which would be designed to undermine the courage and resolution of the latter, and so make it only a matter of time before, with food and ammunition running lower by the hour, they would either have to capitulate or make a sortie that, as things stood at the moment, would be a counsel of utmost desperation – unless, as in the case of the Pindaris, the tables could suddenly be turned on the besiegers.

And there was only one possible way that could be brought about. The gun. We had to get it here – though God knew how. Jock would have to be persuaded in the first place, then it would have to be dragged along fifty miles of jungle track – without horses. It was impossible – doomed to failure before I even started. But I still had to try.

I stirred Bundoo, who was curled asleep under a bush.

'We return,' I told him, 'pausing not for food or rest until we reach the fort.'

He grinned cheerfully and started down the path ahead of me at his customary jogtrot. I fell in behind him, and I remember little of that journey thereafter. First we were in filtered green daylight, then dusk, then darkness when I could see nothing but the blur of his loincloth bobbing like a rabbit's scut before me – then it was light again, and at no time was I conscious of the transition. I was conscious of nothing towards the end except the pounding of my heart, the gasping of my lungs and the agonizing ache in my legs. We drank from streams, kneeling and lapping like dogs, and once or twice I tried to countermand my own orders and insist on resting, but when that happened he took my arm and continued on, even when I struck out at him weakly and tried to lie down on the path. I had no watch, but calculating later I believe we covered that fifty miles in something just over twelve hours.

I came to in my own bed in the fort. Jock was sitting on a chair nearby regarding me solemnly.

I said, 'How long have I been here?'

'Long enough,' he said shortly. 'How do you feel?'

'All right now,' I assured him. 'Listen, Jock – please listen carefully. I must tell you how things stand in Faraqbagh –'

'No need,' he said. 'I've had it all from Bundoo. They've got it tight ringed, he tells me.'

'Yes, about two thousand of them. They're playing a waiting game –'

'Just as they did in Cawnpore.'

'Cawnpore? Is that invested too?'

'Aye – and Lucknow, Allahabad, Delhi, Jhansi – every station in the Central Provinces.'

'Oh, God! What's going to happen to those people?' I groaned.

'The worst,' Jock said. 'It's already happened in some cases. Cawnpore couldn't hold out, because of sickness and lack of food. The garrison commander parleyed with the bastard who is at the head of them, the Nana Sahib, they call him. He promised them safe conduct to Allahabad if they laid down their arms. They did so, because there were three hundred women and children in the fort – then they slaughtered the men on the banks of the Ganges as they embarked in boats – and dragged the women back to the cantonments. Then when they'd finished with them, they threw their bodies down a well – hacked to pieces by Muslim butchers from the bazaar.'

I felt my head reeling with the horror of it, and for a long time I couldn't speak. I sat up and started to climb out of bed.

'Stay there for a while,' he said. 'You'll be needing your strength.'

'I can't,' I told him.

'So what are you going to do?'

'God knows – but I've got to do *something*.'

'Well, it's no use doing it at half-cock. How many of them are there at Faraqbagh – our people, I mean?'

'It all depends on what you mean by "our people",' I said bitterly. 'You're one of *them* now, aren't you?'

He said quietly, 'You're in a sick bed the noo, so I canna be giving you a skelp across the gob like last time – but don't try me too far. Ye ken what I mean. How many Europeans?'

I was beginning to see a gleam of hope. 'I don't know for certain,' I said. 'About forty women and children, at a guess – and the strength of the European regiment plus the Royal Horse Artillery was about six hundred, all ranks – but the artillery seemed to have gone.'

'Aye, a whole battery, plus a company and a half of the infantry. The commander thought they were safe, so they sent them upriver to help relieve Lucknow, which was under heavy siege. Now they've lost the lot.'

'How have you been able to obtain all this information?'

'The usual way – by listening to all the gossip brought down the river and through the jungle, piecing it together and throwing half of it out, then sifting through the rest for a grain of truth here and there. It all seems to agree. The whole of India is up against us – from Madras to the Punjab, north and south, and Calcutta to Bombay, east and west. A few Sikhs have stood true to their salt, and they say that the King of Nepal is sending an army of Gurkhas down from the hills to help. We have about twelve Royal regiments, horse and foot, plus some guns – but they are scattered over the whole damned country.' He rose. 'Well, I suppose the only thing we can do is to try and get the women and bairns out of Faraqbagh and bring them here – though God knows what we'll do with them then. When the de'ils have sacked all the big garrisons they'll be turning their attention to the tiddlers and mopping us up one by one.'

Again I was finding difficulty in speaking. I climbed out of bed and crossed to him and took his hand, but he shook me off impatiently.

'Time enough for bloody heroics when we've done something,' he growled. '*If* we can do anything – which I doot. Have you any ideas in that so damned clever heid of yours?'

'The gun –'

'Aye – so I've been thinking. But Lord God, it'd be a hell of a job to get it there.'

'How far can you trust these men of yours?' I asked.

'Quite a way – while they're doing something and I keep the whip hand on them. It's while they're sitting on their arses in barracks that they get up to mischief. I've been telling them that there are fifty thousand British troops with heavy guns being landed at this moment in Calcutta. Some of them believe it. While they do, we've got a chance.'

'Fifty men on drag ropes,' I said, 'with fifty clearing the path in places where it gets too narrow –'

'It will have to be less than that,' he said. 'We'll need a couple of wagons as well, for ammunition and rations –'

'Once the gun is through, the way will be clear for bullock carts –' I was gibbering with excitement.

'Aye,' he agreed grudgingly, unwilling to concede too much too soon. 'If it comes to that, we can yoke some of the bullocks to the gun itself. I believe we can raise twelve span all told – but that will mean yet another cart for their fodder. Still, the more carts the better. We'll be needing transport for sick and wounded and the children – *if* we get that far.'

And so it went on right through the night, adopting and discarding, weighing and considering, until, by dawn, we had a plan drawn up that would probably have sent the Duke of Wellington into a nervous decline, but at least it provided a starting point. I had the gun limbered up and we practised drawing it round and round the parade ground, with four men on the pole and what we considered the optimum number of twelve each side on the drag ropes, with a relief team marching behind, ready to throw their weight on to another set of ropes to check its progress on downward slopes and to push when the path rose. And from our own resources, together with those of the village and a couple of the nearer farms, we were able to muster a total of fourteen bullock carts.

Since I had so recently been over the ground, Jock put the advance guard of twelve troops under my command while he stayed with the main convoy, and we started out at dawn on the third day.

The path was a bare three feet wide to the gun's four feet, but for the most part we were able to push through the undergrowth, serious checks occurring only when two or more tree-trunks crowded close together on either side, but even then somehow we managed to get through, and by nightfall we estimated that we had covered fifteen miles.

We made equally good progress in the early part of the second day, until we came to a stream which crossed the path. I was then some two miles ahead of the main party, and I set my advance guard to felling trees to make a causeway over the mud, while I scouted on further with Bundoo and two Muslim sepoys, who were not as pernickety in the matter of Untouchability as the Hindus, even to the extent, until I intervened, of graciously allowing him to carry the bulk of their heavy equipment.

We had just rounded a bend in the path when we found ourselves, without warning, face to face with a party of five sepoys in single file.

For a moment it looked as if they had accepted us as fellow mutineers – in fact the leading man threw up his hand in greeting – but the one behind him yelled, '*Ferenghi top-khanawala!*' (the European gunner) and fired his musket past the other one's ear, the bullet whistling harmlessly over our heads. We three fired simultaneously, killing the two in front. The others turned tail and raced back along the path. I dropped the rearmost one with a pistol shot and continued on after the remaining two and, being longer in the leg and less heavily equipped, overhauled the fourth man and brought him down. He fought and writhed under me like an eel, and he had produced a knife from somewhere and I was cut in several places before I managed to throttle him. I got to my feet, cursing, because I thought that one had got away to raise an alarm, but Bundoo had slipped on ahead of him through the undergrowth and had tripped him with a bamboo thrust between his flying feet, and then despatched him messily with his knife. We dragged their bodies into the jungle and went on cautiously, fearing that they, like ourselves, had been an advance guard for a bigger party coming down the path towards us, but we saw no others, and things were still quiet when Jock caught up with us some hours later.

'Foraging party, most like,' he pronounced as we discussed the event that night. 'I've had the word that they're scouring the countryside like locusts, murdering and robbing their own kind as well as the Europeans. But that's no' to say that they *may* not break off their action against Faraqbagh if the resistance is too strong, and come this way. I think you and I had better reconnoitre forward a mile at a time from now on, before moving the gun.'

We did this all the following day, slowing our progress down to a degree that became wellnigh intolerable to me, although I could see the wisdom of it, until faintly on the evening of the third day we heard the sound of heavy firing in the distance. Jock and I hurried ahead then, with Bundoo guiding us through the darkness unerringly – right to the spot where he and I had hidden previously. The firing had stopped now, except for an occasional shot from both sides, but two buildings inside the perimeter were burning furiously and lighting a wide area.

The outer line of earthworks had been breached and it appeared as if the whole garrison had now retreated into the hospital block, while the besiegers had advanced right up to the inner line, a bare hundred yards away from them. It must have been like an oven inside the building, because all the windows were blocked and barricaded except for loopholes. As we watched there was a sudden burst of sustained fire from the flat roof of the building, which was answered by the besiegers, and a party of European troops carrying buckets came from round a corner and made a dash for the well. I counted eight of them – and four had dropped and lay still in the first few yards. Two more were shot on the way back, and finally only one man, obviously badly wounded, staggered the last few steps into cover with his pitiful bucket of water. The firing, which had been meant as a curtain for the carrying party, ceased then, and a mutineer called mockingly, *'Tunda pani pina ki waste! Tumlog hamara ijasat hain.'* (Cool drinking water! You have our permission to take it.)

When morning broke we saw that the slopes below us were no longer occupied, as the bulk of the besiegers seemed now to have concentrated into an area immediately in front of the hospital, shielded from the defenders' fire by a long row of outbuildings and the gutted walls of the European barracks. Dead littered the ground in every direction, mostly in European uniform – along the breached line of the outer defences and in the enclave that had been linked to the hospital by a breastwork, where it appeared they had made a desperate stand to keep the well within their defences.

As the sun rose the firing broke out again from both sides, and we could see the besiegers massing for what was obviously to be a final frontal assault, and we were grateful for it, because it masked the noise of our last frantic run-up with the gun to this position that commanded the whole of the cantonment below us. I loaded with canister as Jock fell in his storming party and gave his final orders.

'The gun will speak three times, my brothers,' he explained. 'Those of the enemy that are not killed will scatter like chaff before the wind. Then we make our charge – straight down the hill and across to the hospital – there – and we bring back the people that are inside – and if it is done quickly we will not lose a man, because then the colonel-sahib will make the gun speak again and again – and your children's children will tell in the years to come the story of your skill and bravery – ' and a lot more in the same vein.

I waited, with the portfire smoking in my hand, my eye on Jock, and only then did I notice that he was carrying his

294

pipes, and I remember wondering how he proposed to defend himself with both hands engaged, and giggling nervously at the strange figure he cut with his tarnished military finery, kilt and absurd turban.

Then he nodded, and I touched the gun off, and we had swabbed, reloaded and fired again twice, before the first blast had torn into their backs – so fast, in fact, that the three reports were almost merged into one.

Then, in the unearthly silence that followed, Jock screamed *'Charge!'* and was away down the hill with the pipes skirling wildly, and I had to wait, fretting and sweating, for the full ten minutes it took them to reach the hospital. I watched through the telescope as he yelled up to the defenders, and my blood ran cold for a moment as a couple of shots were loosed off at him. I couldn't hear at that distance what he was saying, but it was sufficient to persuade them to open up for him.

Only then, as he disappeared inside, did I scan the ground that had been raked by the gun. Here and there a figure jerked grotesquely, but for the most part they were still, and even at that distance I could see that the ground was crimson-soaked. The other side of the hospital, and therefore screened from the spreading canister, a small party of stupefied sepoys seemed to be gathering and I yelled fit to burst my lungs to Jock, but he was out of earshot, but Prem Singh, re-mustering his troops who were showing a tendency to a little private looting among the dead, had seen them also, and one volley was sufficient to send them bolting.

But I still couldn't believe it, much as I wanted to. Three rounds of canister had surely not decimated two thousand men? There must be others nearby, waiting to attack – and I was half insane with anxiety and impatience when I saw Jock reappear at the head of a pathetic column, men, women and children, the fitter supporting and carrying the weaker, making in the first instance for the well, hauling buckets, drinking, pouring water over themselves, the women, as always, seeing to the children and the wounded before taking any themselves. And Judith was among them, though I didn't recognize her for quite some time, because her hair was wrapped in a shawl, her face was streaked and stained, and her clothes were in tatters, as indeed were those of all of them. I recognized Mr Palmer then, as dirty as any of them, and even at that distance I could see that he was reeling with fatigue, but he remained steadfastly with the wounded, adjusting bandages, covering the helpless against the sun, and organizing carrying parties. I longed to go down to help, but I knew that I would face Jock's righteous wrath if I did, because my place was up here with the gun.

Then at last they came up the hill, and the tally was twenty-two gaunt but unwounded men, thirty-three sick and wounded, of whom eleven were still capable of walking, eighteen nominally fit women, seven seriously ill, and nine children. They staggered up the slope and some of the men raised a ragged cheer as they saw the gun, and they slapped its butt affectionately, and one cheerful scarecrow even kissed it, and all, without exception, pressed forward to shake the hands of Jock and myself, but he sternly put down such demonstrations.

'Time enough for that later, gentlemen,' he admonished. 'The noo we'll be better employed getting back to safety.'

We loaded the non-walkers and the children into the carts and started back immediately, halting after an hour to cook chapattis and boil rice for the sick, and then we pressed on, the carts and the walkers in front, and the gun bringing up the rear.

And in all this time I had not been recognized, even by Mr Palmer when he shook my hand, because I was heavily bearded and skinnier and browner than I had ever been before. The temptation to reveal myself to Judith was overwhelming, but I decided against it because, although she was a 'walker', she was obviously exhausted and I did not wish to subject her to a shock.

It was not until we halted for the night and Jock had put out a screen of sentries against possible pursuit and I had trained my loaded gun down the path behind us, that I sought out the surgeon. He had not spared himself for an instant during the march, but now he was sitting on the ground under a tree, with his head bowed forward on his chest, and I hesitated to speak to him in case he was asleep, but he looked up when I halted in front of him.

I said awkwardly, 'Hello, sir. I am Ross Stafford.'

He didn't appear to take it in for a moment, and I was about to repeat it, but then he peered up at me through the darkness and said, unsteadily, 'Hello, my boy. Somehow I knew you weren't dead.' He reached up and grasped my hand and tried to rise, but I pressed him back and sat down beside him.

'I've seen Judith, but haven't spoken to her yet,' I said. 'How is Mrs Palmer?'

'She was struck by a stray bullet on the second day of the siege,' he said dully, and for some time we sat in silence; then, to give him time to recover his composure, I told him my story in as few words as possible.

'You certainly seem to have a guardian angel, young Ross,' he said when I had finished.

'A series of them, sir,' I said. 'Not the ast of them being the Palmer family. I am glad to have been able in some small measure to balance the scale.'

'You have certainly done that,' he said. 'But we must give some urgent thought to your own position now.'

'Don't worry about that,' I told him. 'I haven't been recognized by anybody so far. We are taking you to a place of comparative safety now, and when things have quietened down I intend going on my way to Calcutta – and out of the country.'

'You must not do anything precipitately. I fear it will be a long time before travelling will be safe again,' he said. 'This mutiny has spread throughout the length and breadth of India, and only the arrival of massive reinforcements from England will be capable of putting it down.'

'Rumour has it that they are already on the way,' I said.

'I wish I could believe that. The army at Home was allowed to run down badly after the Crimean War, and now they just haven't the troops to mount an effective expeditionary force – ' He broke off and said, 'But enough of that for the moment. Let us revert to yourself. Quite apart from the debt of gratitude we all owe you, you are in no immediate danger. I understand your *bête noire*, Ingoldsby-Moreton, is dead, as, indeed, are most of the officers and men of the Third Europeans. They were sent up to Lucknow when trouble first broke out and were overrun and cut up in that first terrible attack. These people with us now are mostly convalescents drafted in from the Twenty-seventh at Allahabad. You yourself – I refer to Sergeant Muir Dalrymple – were posted as "missing, believed dead", nearly a year ago. In the present turmoil I hardly think the authorities will still be looking for you. So all we have to do is to think of a feasible story to account for the timely presence here of one Ross Stafford, should anyone enquire.'

'That has already been seen to,' I told him. 'I have had a document prepared for use in Calcutta, stating that I am the former tutor to the grandchildren of the Rajah of Kandapore, on my way back to England – under my own name.'

'Very wise,' he said. 'But I'm sure nobody is going to trouble you.'

'Probably not,' I agreed. 'But I'm worried about Jock. He's a very conspicuous figure – not easily forgotten.'

'Jock?'

'The "General", save the mark. He is a deserter also – from a Royal Highland regiment – in much the same circumstances as my own.'

Mr Palmer chuckled drily. 'Praise be for the gallant deserters then,' he said. 'Never fear. By the time all this is set down for posterity his name, and yours, will be inscribed in the halls of fame – and deservedly so.'

'God forbid,' I said fervently. 'After this, all I want is a quiet corner somewhere, in which to live in peace – without constantly looking over my shoulder for some damned policeman or soldier with a warrant or a gun.'

'In peace, I hope,' he smiled. 'But in a quiet corner? Never. You, and those of your kind, are the winds which blow the cobwebs from quiet corners.'

His voice trailed off and his head drooped forward, and I realized again how desperately tired he was, so I sat on beside him, not wishing to disturb him by moving, and after a time someone approached through the darkness, and Judith said softly, 'Father – I have brought some food. You *must* eat – '

I stood up and whispered, 'He is asleep. Go and rest, yourself. I'll stay with him. Don't tell me you've forgotten me already. Ross – '

I managed to catch the bowl of rice as she dropped it, and I said, 'Careful, you little bufflehead, this stuff is scarce !' And then she was in my arms, crying wildly.

Chapter Twelve

We reached the fort twenty-four hours later, without further incident, although, sadly, three more of our sick and wounded died on the way and for a time Mr Palmer, himself very ill, feared that cholera had broken out among the refugees. In vain Judith and I pleaded with him to rest on arrival, but he drove himself to the limit of human endurance, and seemingly beyond, organizing cookhouses and a supply of milk from cows and buffaloes that Jock had rounded up from nearby farms, and administering the pitifully small supply of medicines that he had carefully husbanded through the siege – until finally he collapsed and lay for days in a coma, devotedly nursed by Judith and some of the other women who took over the hospital, while we men foraged for supplies and strengthened the defences, because word was daily reaching us that bands of marauding mutineers had joined the Pindaris and were roaming the countryside, looting, burning and murdering.

We beat off several small attacks in that first month without difficulty, because now, in addition to our own hundred sepoys, we had forty-five fit Europeans, with only seven still incapacitated, one of whom was the sole remaining officer, a Captain Arthur Shelton, whose right leg Mr Palmer had to amputate on arrival at the fort. He was a magnificent man, who, in spite of his ghastly wounds and terrible operation without anaesthetic, still managed to maintain authority over his men from his hospital bed, although he had sensibly handed over their command to Jock. But supplies were running very short because we now had the refugees to feed in addition to our own people and the villagers, who could not any longer remain outside the walls.

But even more serious than food was the question of

ammunition. Jock and I checked our remaining stocks of powder and shot after an attack which had lasted three days and nights. He combed his beard with his fingers as I made a calculation.

'Twenty-five roonds for each Enfield rifle,' he said thoughtfully, 'and six full charges for that damned gun of yours. We'll no' stand another hammering such as the last – unless we can get our hands on some more. By God, every mon that squeezes a trigger from now on had better be hitting something – or he'll be getting my foot up his arse.'

But then we had a long quiet period, which put me in mind of the unholy calm that one experienced at the centre of a typhoon, because stories of strife all around us persisted, and although we made full use of the time to harvest grain from the neglected fields and paddies, and round up stray cattle along the river banks, we lived on our nerves, feeling that unseen forces were massing for a final, decisive assault. Even the news that Cawnpore and Delhi had been relieved, and that Lucknow was under heavy attack by a strong column of British under General Havelock, failed to rid us of the heavy apprehension that lay over our small garrison. The death of the old Rajah about this time further dampened our spirits, for although he had been senile for many years, he was held in great affection by his subjects – which his eldest son, the heir, was decidedly not. This latter was an ill-natured nonentity who hated Jock and had constantly striven in the past to undermine his authority.

'If it wasn't for that wee bastard I'd be awa' to Allahabad with a small but fast column to look for victuals and ammunition,' Jock said gloomily one night. 'But I know he'd be making mischief the moment I turned my back.'

'Let me go,' I suggested.

'Risky,' he said doubtfully. 'We don't know if the place is still occupied.'

'No more risky for me than for you,' I said.

'I dinna like letting anither body take over a job I should be doing mysel' – '

'Oh, nonsense,' I said impatiently. 'Your place is here.'

He let me go in the end, albeit reluctantly, and I picked a party of twenty of our own sepoys in preference to any of the European troops, as being less conspicuous in the event of Allahabad still being invested by the mutineers. I cravenly avoided Judith before leaving, because she used to worry greatly if I went any distance from the fort. She and the other women were working far beyond their strength, cooking our meagre rations, mending clothes which were for the most part past repair, nursing the sick and keeping the children amused and instructed in a small school she and her father had instituted.

Her father walked with me to the gate at dawn and enjoined me to be careful. 'God knows we need food,' he said, 'but not at the expense of your neck. Don't do anything rash, my boy.'

'I won't,' I promised, as we shook hands. 'We'll be back in three days, with *something*, I hope. Look after yourself, sir — and Judith.'

We marched up the river bank, keeping a sharp look-out, but we didn't see a living soul all that day, although there were many dead coming down with the sluggish current, but whether these were the sorry harvest of battle and famine or the corpses that were normally semi-cremated at the burning ghats and then cast into the sacred Ganges by the Brahmin priests, we had no way of telling.

We camped that evening in a mango tope a bare two miles from the outskirts of the city, and when darkness had fallen completely, Bundoo and I went forward to reconnoitre. I had noticed the little man lurking at the edge of the parade ground before leaving that morning, and I had ordered him to remain behind, but he had bobbed out of the jungle ahead of us an hour later, grinning broadly, and thereafter he appointed himself as our guide, leading us unerringly to the best crossing points and saving us many miles as a result.

While there was little I, personally, could see in the darkness, we at least were able to establish that the actual approaches to the city were completely deserted, although Bundoo assured me that there were many people still inside the walls of the fort which dominated the confluence of the Jumna and Ganges in the centre of the town itself. This was too much for my credence, in spite of my faith in him as a scout.

'How can you tell me that?' I demanded. 'We are at least two miles from the fort.'

'I *can* tell, sahib,' he said simply. 'Many people – and they have food – much food. The *buniyas* and merchants have returned and the bazaars now do business. I can smell rice and meat, and the smoke of their cooking fires.' And so positive was he that I had perforce to believe him, and greatly cheered we returned to the camp to snatch a few hours' rest.

We moved up as dawn was breaking, and sure enough there were signs of life round the fort. Bullock carts were creaking across the drawbridge, and women were carrying baskets of grain and crates of chickens on their heads, but, although I had a considerable sum in silver rupees with me, they flatly refused to do business with us outside the town, so I followed a group of them in through the arched gateway, telling my troops to stand to their arms until I returned.

The entrance, in common with all Indian forts, took the form of a covered passage which bent at right-angles at two places, in order to stem a rush should attackers manage to cross the drawbridge, and both the inner and outer gates were made of heavy teakwood planks liberally studded with spikes to deter elephants being used as battering-rams. I was conscious of being watched through loopholes as I walked along the dark passage, so I was not unduly surprised when I was sharply challenged in both Hindi and English as I emerged into daylight at the inner end, and a bayonet was thrust unwaveringly to within an inch of my throat. I put up my hands, smiled disarmingly and said, 'Friend!'

'Advance, friend, and give the countersign,' somebody said behind me, and turning my head I saw a European sergeant in the door of the guardroom.

'I'm sorry,' I said. 'I haven't a countersign or password. I have only just arrived in this area.'

'British?' he queried, looking at the scratch collection of

garments I was wearing.

'Yes.'

'Regiment?'

'Temporarily attached to the Rajah of Kandapore's State Forces,' I answered with some slight hesitation, cursing inwardly that I hadn't already got my answer pat for this totally unexpected encounter.

'I see,' he nodded. He was a short but powerfully-built man, like myself, clad in a miscellany of tattered military uniform. 'Name?'

'Stafford,' I said, and he nodded again as if satisfied.

'What would your business be here, Mr Stafford?' he asked.

'We are in search of supplies,' I said. 'We have a large group of refugees from Faraqbagh at the Rajah's headquarters, and we've been besieged several times by mutineers. Of course we're prepared to pay for anything you could let us have.'

The sentry in front of me was still holding his bayonet to my throat and I was beginning to feel distinctly uneasy, but the sergeant nodded again quite affably and came up to us, and then, without warning, his fist crashed full into my face, and the sentry brought the butt of his rifle round and drove it into my stomach.

Things were somewhat blurred after that, and remained so until I came round propped up against the guardroom wall, held by several European troops, all of whom seemed motivated by a desire to thump, cudgel or kick me.

'For God's sake!' I yelled. 'What do you think you're doing? I'm English, damn you – '

'Dirty renegade bastard,' the sergeant said venomously. 'Stafford my arse! You're *Hunt* – Corporal Bloody Hunt – Fourth Bengal Cavalry. Running with a bunch of nigger Pandies – murdering your own kind – or what *was* your own kind. By God, you'll – ' The rest of his tirade was drowned in a volley of rifle fire from the ramparts above us.

'That's dropped five of the swine,' somebody shouted. 'The rest are scuttling off. Shall we give chase, sergeant?'

'Stand fast,' the sergeant called back. 'You never know

how many more are lying up under cover.' He turned back to me. 'You better start praying to your nigger gods, because it'll be a short court martial and a bloody long rope for *you*, you son of a whore, as soon as the captain arrives. Shove him in the cells.'

'Sergeant – listen to me – *please*,' I pleaded. 'You're making a terrible mistake – '

He drove his fist into my face again and my head cracked back against the wall behind me.

I was being dragged out into the open, and brilliant sunlight was blinding me. Somebody was shouting, 'Give the officer your name, rank and regiment!'

I tried to say 'Stafford', but only managed an incoherent mumble, and again that fist crashed into my face.

'It's no use doing that, sergeant,' another voice said. 'I want some information from the wretched fellow. Throw some water over him.'

A couple of buckets were tipped over me and the water revived me a little. My eyes were becoming accustomed to the light and I could dimly make out a white-clad figure in front of me.

'My name is Ross Stafford,' I croaked.

The figure came forward and I could sense rather than see him peering closely into my face.

'Say that again,' he said softly.

'Ross Stafford – ' I began, but he cut me short with an upraised hand and turned to the sergeant. My vision was badly blurred and I could not clearly make out the features of either.

'Have you, personally, ever seen this man Hunt, sergeant?' asked the officer.

'Not me personally, sir,' said the other. 'But the description fits.'

'I have the description here,' the officer said. 'Five feet seven inches – eyes brown. This gentleman is a good six foot, and from what I can see of his eyes, they are blue. I think you may have been a little over-zealous, sergeant.'

'Oh, Christ,' said the other, deeply dismayed. 'But we was told to look for him around here – and he *was* leading a bunch of hairies.'

'Don't let it worry you unduly,' the officer said kindly. 'Mistakes can always happen, and I'm sure Mr – er – what did you say the name was, sir?'

'Ross Stafford,' I said again. 'And I wish to lay a serious complaint against this non-commissioned officer.'

'It shall be investigated, I promise you,' the officer said. 'Sergeant, send for the medical orderly and a barber, and see that Mr Stafford is restored in some measure to his normal comforts.' He bowed to me. 'We shall meet again later, sir.'

He went off and I could feel the sergeant's mounting anxiety.

'Sorry if there's been a mistake, sir,' he said apologetically. 'I'm afraid the men's all a bit jumpy, like. We've seen some terrible things. Women and little children murdered, and all that. That well at Cawnpore – oh my God! Here – this way, sir. Let's get out of the sun.'

He led the way back into the guardroom and solicitously installed me in a chair, then set about chasing various members of his guard off for food, drink and the medical orderly and a barber.

'Won't be long now, sir,' he beamed on me paternally. 'Mistakes can happen in the best of families, as the colonel's daughter said when the kid turned out to be a nigger. Ha, ha!'

But I was not to be mollified. 'I understand that you shot some of my men,' I said coldly. 'How many, exactly?'

'Er – yes – a bit unfortunate, that – but the guard have their orders, see? Any armed parties approaching the sally-port – well, you know what it's like, sir.' He was sweating copiously, and it wasn't all due to the heat.

'How many?' I insisted.

'Er – six, I believe.'

'Wounded?'

'None. They was all killed.'

'In other words, if there *were* any wounded, you slaughtered them?'

'Oh, just a minute, sir. Fair play – if you'd seen what we've seen –'

'Shut up, you bastard,' I spat at him. 'Those men had all fought valiantly to save *our* women and children. By God, I'll see you answer for this.'

'Only trying to do my duty, sir,' he mumbled. 'Life's hard enough in the Company army, God knows, without gentlemen trying to make it harder.'

I drank some water, because I was parched, but I wouldn't accept any of their food, nor, at first, the ministrations of the barber, but my beard was filthy and matted with blood, and I weakened in this last particular. I washed in warm water and sat back in the chair while the Hindu *nai* (barber), in the expert way of his craft, clipped my beard to the skin and then gently shaved me and cut my hair.

The medical orderly dressed the worst of my facial injuries with unguent, and, in spite of myself, I felt considerably better. I looked into the mirror that the man held in front of me, and received a shock, because the face that looked back at me was totally unfamiliar, for I had not seen it unshaven since I had escaped from Faraqbagh. It was like looking at an old portrait of oneself. It was *my* face – in spite of the badly blackened eye, slightly askew nose and missing tooth in front – and yet it was that of a stranger.

'That's better, sir,' said the still solicitous sergeant. 'Now how about a little something to eat – and maybe to drink?' And I was about to weaken and accept when the sentry outside gave a warning thump of his rifle on the paving and said, 'Officer approaching, sergeant.'

'Stand to, the guard,' ordered the sergeant, and went to the door and saluted. 'Guard – *attention!*' he snapped – and through sheer force of habit I jumped to my feet and stiffened like a ramrod, then remembered, and relaxed a little. But it was too late. Both the officer and the sergeant were regarding me closely from the doorway.

'Splendid,' said the officer. 'I'm glad to see that you haven't entirely forgotten your military manners.' He came up to me and looked into my face. 'Yes, I thought so,' he said softly. 'Congratulations, sergeant. You've caught an even bigger fish than the elusive Corporal Hunt. Let me present Sergeant Muir Dalrymple – a candidate for the gallows these last two years. Put him back into the cells and enter "remanded for summary court martial" in the log.'

The room was spinning before my eyes, but one thing stood out clearly. The face of the Honourable Piers Ingoldsby-Moreton.

I was in the cells for thirty-six hours before I was visited again – this time by a captain of the Bengal Horse Artillery who informed me of the charges against me, and my somewhat illusory 'rights' in the matter.

'You are accused in the first instance of desertion from the army of the Honourable East India Company,' he explained. 'That, being a capital offence, entitles you to call for the services of an officer to defend you, should you decide to enter a "not guilty" plea. In the second instance, you face a charge of unprovoked bodily assault upon your superior officer, also a capital charge but one which will not be proceeded with unless the first charge fails. There could be yet a further count – that of leading mutineers against the forces of the Company – but that is still under investigation. All in all, my man, you find yourself in an extremely parlous position. I think you would be well advised to plead guilty to the first charge and cast yourself upon the mercy of the court – and hope to God the third one is dropped.'

'A hell of a lot of good that will do me,' I said bitterly. 'Mercy? From *you* people?'

He shrugged. 'The option is yours, of course. At least, if the worst came to the worst you would be hanged without further ado – but if the third charge is proceeded with, and proved, you would qualify for five hundred lashes before what's left of you is blown from the mouth of a cannon – the statutory punishment at present being meted out to the ringleaders in this wretched business. I would give it careful consideration if I were you, Dalrymple.'

'That is not my name,' I shouted.

'It is apparently the name you enlisted under,' he said, 'and that is all that concerns us.'

'God damn you!' I stormed. 'I never enlisted in this or any other army. Will you please listen to me?'

'I see,' he said thoughtfully. 'Lose of memory – insanity. Um – you *could* try that, of course. It *might* conceivably save your neck – but the alternative of the rest of your life in the Calcutta Lunatic Asylum is not one I would care to contemplate myself. Still, that's entirely up to you. The thing I've come to see you about is your defence. There are only two officers at present in this fort – myself and Captain Ingoldsby-Moreton. He certainly couldn't defend you as he is the principal witness for the prosecution. So that leaves me. I'll try for "guilty but insane" if you insist, but it would be risky. Your best chance would be as I have already advised – "Guilty – mercy of the court" – and I'll put in a strong plea in mitigation of the death penalty. You were sick – lot of fever at the time – no animus against the officer you attacked, et cetera, et cetera – didn't know what you were doing, and so on. Do you follow me?'

'No,' I said gloomily. 'It seems that whatever I say or do I'm to hang.'

'If Captain Ingoldsby-Moreton has his way, yes,' he admitted. 'But there you are – I'm assigned to your defence, should you care to avail yourself of my services, in which case I'll do my best for you. I'd be wrong to hold out much hope for you, though.' He walked to the door, and then turned. 'Think it over carefully, Dalrymple,' he said. 'We have either to wait for three field officers to arrive here before we can conevene a court, or we must send you to Cawnpore – so there's no undue hurry.'

I believe it was Dr Johnson who once said that nothing was calculated to concentrate a man's mind more than the prospect of an early hanging. But it certainly did not apply in my case, because I lay for hours in a weltering torment of terror and indecision, unable to think clearly. What, I wondered, would my sepoys have done after they had been fired upon here? Would they have scattered and perhaps joined one or other of the many bands wandering the countryside – or would they have returned with all speed to Kandapore? Pray God that it was the latter, because then I knew that Mr Palmer would already be on his way here to plead for me. But what real purpose would that serve? He could clear me of the last, and most shameful charge of renegation – but there still remained two capital charges on the sheets against me. His evidence might possibly, of course, ameliorate the severity of the sentence from death to life imprisonment – I shuddered, because there was so little to choose between the two.

I stood on tiptoe in the darkness and tried each of the four bars on the cell window, and felt a slight looseness in one of them as I pushed and pulled against it. With one bar out I could possibly squeeze through, I thought. It was a slender hope indeed, but at least it gave me something to occupy my mind. I took the buckle from my belt and rubbed it on the stone window sill until I had sharpened one corner of it into a spike, then I started on the mortar round the base of the bar. I did not accomplish much that night, nor the next, but on the third I had loosened the bar considerably, but then the spike, worn to paper thinness, had broken, and I had to grind another out of the remaining metal, and dawn had overtaken me.

But I was beginning to hope, and the craven confusion that had been enveloping me was in some degree dispersing. I had weathered disasters, if not worse, at least as fearsome as this, before, and managed to survive. I was *not* going to founder – not without a supreme effort to save myself. Just let me get out of this cell. One more night's work – but then my hopes were blasted again.

The artillery captain came to see me that morning. The court martial had been convened in Cawnpore, he told me. 'They can't spare three field officers merely to make the journey down here and back for a single case,' he said. 'So you will go before the standing board up there. We leave within the hour.'

I tried to tell him about Mr Palmer – to beg of him to send a message to Kandapore – but it was in vain. He waved my pleas aside airily and said, 'Don't worry, Dalrymple – I'll do the best I can for you, but you're not making it any better for yourself by constantly changing your story. Get the escort fallen in, sergeant.'

We marched as before – twenty miles between sundown and dawn – a thirty-man party, with the two officers riding ahead, and myself in fetters and roped to the tail of the supply wagon, and it took us five weary, hopeless days, each merging into the other, until I was unaware of the passage of time – unaware even of the constant stream of abuse of the soldiers who marched either side of me and who broke the monotony of our progress from time to time by driving their rifle butts into the small of my back.

I was lodged in the guardroom on arrival, and the next morning I was shaved and generally smartened in appearance, and provided with clean fatigue uniform. The memory of that march from the cells to the assembly hall of the Residency, where the court martial was held, will never fade from my memory, and to this day I sometimes wake from my sleep in a cold sweat of sheer terror as I recall the hate in the faces of the soldiers who had relieved the garrison some weeks earlier and had seen the pitiful remains of the massacre in the Well, over which already a memorial plinth was being erected, because it had been beyond their endurance even to think of raising the mutilated bodies of the women and children who had been thrown down it. Several times men broke through the cordon around me to strike and spit upon me, and once I was beaten to my knees and kicked.

I stood between my escort of two Highlanders and faced the court, which consisted of a colonel, a lieutenant-colonel, two majors and an ensign, ranged along a line of tables, with a robed and bewigged Judge Advocate-general sitting behind them, and I was on the point of pleading guilty in order to get it over with, but since this was a standing court martial, and newspaper correspondents were present, strict protocol had to be observed, and I was not allowed to speak until the full indictment was read and evidence of identification sworn to by the Honourable Piers – in all, a lengthy procedure, at the end of which my defending officer entered a plea of 'Not Guilty' without consulting me.

Then the Honourable Piers was on his feet again, and I heard without particular interest, and certainly without hope, the full story of my misdeeds unfold. I had been a nuisance and a disgrace to a proud regiment of the Company – a regiment now, apparently, represented entirely by this gallant young officer, himself at one time reported dead, and me, most dastardly of creatures. I had given trouble ever since my enlistment in Edinburgh, the Honourable Piers was able to recount from his memory of my record. I had attempted to desert in Calcutta on arrival in India; I had skrimshanked and proved wanting in the face of the enemy during an encounter with Pindaris and, worst offence of all, I had tried to force my attentions on a *lady*, the innocent daughter of an officer on the station, who had been saved from a fate worse than death by the timely intervention of the witness, who thrashed the blackguard, only to be foully struck down with a heavy club from behind as he was assisting the lady, said blackguard then stealing the witness's horse and deserting the Company's service, being absent for any months thereafter until apprehended at the head of a party of mutineers attempting to break in to Allahabad Fort. At this point, there being no further prosecution witnesses available, or indeed necessary, the court adjourned until the afternoon, and I had to run that terrible gauntlet again back to the cells.

But I was aware of a change of atmosphere when I returned. One of doubt mixed with suppressed excitement now seemed to be overriding that of implacable official prejudice, and in the faces that turned towards me as I entered there was a certain curiosity in place of the cold contempt that had been there before.

I came to a halt in front of the court, and my defending officer rose from his seat to the left of the long table and said, 'With the Court's permission, I call Mr John Everard Palmer, surgeon to Her Majesty's Nineteenth Regiment of Foot, previously stationed at Faraqbagh. I regret that this witness's name was not submitted with the summary, but he arrived on the station only half an hour ago, having proceeded here from Allahabad with all speed, and not inconsiderable risk, on hearing of the accused's plight.'

I stared at Mr Palmer as he advanced to the table, his back now towards me, and took the Bible in his hand and was sworn.

'Mr Palmer,' said the defending officer, 'were you acquainted with one Sergeant Muir Dalrymple of the Third European Regiment, H.E.I.C. Army?'

'Closely,' answered the surgeon. 'He was my medical clerk for some time in Faraqbagh.'

'Do you see this non-commissioned officer in court now, sir?'

My breath and, I think, my heart stopped as Mr Palmer turned and ran his eye over me, then my escort, then past me to a line of court orderlies, then on along the two rows of spectators. He slowly shook his head.

'No – I don't, sir,' he said quietly but distinctly.

'You are sure of that, sir?'

'Most certainly.'

'But the accused? Will you look at him again, please.'

'I am doing so.'

'And you say you do not know him?'

'I know him very well – but he is not Sergeant Dalrymple.'

'You swear to that, sir?'

'I am already on oath, sir,' Mr Palmer said sternly.

'Then may I ask you who in your opinion the accused *is*?'

'He is the tutor to the children of His Serene Highness the Rajah of Kandapore – Mr Ross Stafford. I have here a document pertaining to the gentleman –' he held up a scroll – 'issued under the seal of the Rajah. I have known Mr Stafford for some years – long before coming to India, in fact.'

'When did you last see him?'

'Eight days ago, as he started out from Kandapore with a party of the Rajah's troops in search of rations for the garrison. Some of the troops returned two days later, telling us that they had been fired upon outside Allahabad Fort, and six had been killed, while Mr Stafford was being held there. I started out for the fort immediately, with Captain Shelton, of the Twenty-second Native Infantry, in order to make enquiries, but owing to this officer's disability we had to travel slowly, and Mr Stafford had already been brought on here when we arrived at Allahabad. We followed on with as much haste as possible.'

'Mr Palmer, would you be so good as to tell the Court, briefly, what you know of this gentleman?'

'With the greatest of pleasure, sir.' Mr Palmer took a deep breath and turned to face the president. 'Mr Stafford, in company with the commander of the Kandapore State Army, led a party of loyal sepoys to Faraqbagh at the beginning of August and, although heavily outnumbered by the mutineers who were besieging us, vigorously engaged them, and extricated us from what was a desperate situation, and then brought us – men, women and children, the majority sick and wounded – back through the jungle to Kandapore, fighting a brilliant rearguard action most of the way. They have cared for us and protected us since – ' The president checked him with an upraised hand and stared first at me, then at the defending officer.

'Then, if this witness's evidence is to be believed, how in the name of heaven has all this come about?' He shot an unwavering finger at the completely flabbergasted Honourable Piers. 'You, sir! Stand up, sir. Face the Court, sir. *Who* do you say the accused is?'

'Sergeant Dalrymple, sir. I – I am certain of it, sir – ' stammered the Honourable Piers. 'You see – I – '

'I do *not* see, sir,' said the president coldly. 'I am endeavouring to, sir. So is the whole Court, sir. You – surgeon – what's your name? – yes – Mr Palmer – You say you are equally certain that the accused is *not* this Dalrymple scoundrel, eh?'

'I am *completely* certain that this is Mr Ross Stafford, sir,' Mr Palmer answered steadily.

The president breathed heavily through his rather rubicund

nose. 'One against one, eh? Is there no other evidence of identity?'

'May it please the Court, I would like to call Captain Shelton,' said the defending officer. He seemed to be enjoying himself, confirming an impression I had gained on the march that there was little love lost between him and the Honourable Piers.

There was a thudding of crutches from the back of the room, and Captain Shelton, white and haggard but still erect and soldierly, came to the front of the Court, steadied himself, and then saluted and was sworn.

'Get a chair for this officer,' said the president kindly. 'Shelton? Twenty-second N.I.? I think we met in Jhansi, didn't we?'

'Yes, sir – the year before last,' Captain Shelton answered.

'Of course. Well, Shelton, my dear chap, will you take a long hard look at the accused – there, behind you. No – the accused will come forward and face the witness.' I moved round in front of Captain Shelton. 'Now,' went on the president, 'will you kindly tell the Court who the devil he is?'

'Mr Ross Stafford, tutor to the Rajah of Kandapore, without the shadow of a doubt, sir,' Captain Shelton said unhesitatingly. 'I have the honour of knowing the gentleman very well indeed. I owe my life to his bravery and that of the men he led, as do the rest of what is left of the Faraqbagh garrison.'

There was a suppressed ripple of applause from the spectators, and the president rapped the table for order.

'Thank you, sir,' he said. 'The Court is extremely grateful to the both of you for preventing what could have been a grave miscarriage of justice. Well done, gentlemen.'

He turned a basilisk eye on the Honourable Piers. 'And now, you, sir? Have you anyone here to support you in your contention that this gentleman is, in fact, Sergeant Dalrymple?'

'Not – not here, sir,' the wretched youth mumbled. 'The regiment was badly cut up, and what survivors there are have been scattered and reposted and then there was –'

'Yes, yes, yes,' interposed the president impatiently. 'So it's a case of your unsupported word, or rather opinion, against that of these two responsible and highly respected officers. I see. Well, I hardly think we need withdraw to consider the verdict –' The collective heads of the Court came together for the briefest instant, then they looked at me and the president was smiling broadly.

'The verdict is "not guilty" of course, Mr Stafford,' he said, 'and the court wishes to express its heartfelt regret for this unfortunate mistake on behalf of the sole prosecution witness, who no doubt was sincere in his belief and did what he conceived to be his duty – but whom we would counsel to be very, very, *very* certain before making accusations of this nature in future.' He rose. 'I declare this court martial dissolved.'

Mr Palmer was in front of me wringing my hand, and outside, the crowd which had been spitting on me an hour before was now cheering, but I saw and heard little of this at the time because there was a mist before my eyes and I was conscious of tears of relief and gratitude rolling down my cheeks.

We lost no time in returning first to Allahabad and then on to Kandapore by fast river craft, travelling swiftly with the current under the overall command of Captain Shelton, who, in spite of the loss of his leg, had been appointed to oversee the evacuation of women, children and the disabled from this area.

Twenty large country boats were finally assembled at the confluence of the Jumna and the Ganges, each manned by twelve oarsmen and carrying some thirty evacuees under thatched awnings amidships. A river gunboat escorted the convoy and a barge carrying a half-company of British troops brought up the rear, while Mr Palmer, who was to be in medical charge, was provided with a separate boat equipped as a mobile hospital, yet small and handy enough to be able to move up and down the waterborne column as required. Judith and I travelled in this with him – she still nursing the sick, I making myself generally useful.

I sat with Jock the night before we left, trying to persuade him to come with us.

'To go where – and do what?' he growled. 'I canna go back to the army with a price on my head, and I'd be no use as a civilian. I may as well stay here.'

'Not with this Rajah,' I said. 'Once the present trouble is past, and he feels safe again, he's bound to do you some mischief or other. Come with us, Jock,' I begged. 'There's the whole wide world to choose from.'

'Aye – and to starve in. I tramped the roads with my pipes, playing for my supper long enough before I took the Queen's shilling. I'm no' going back to any of that,' he said gloomily.

'You don't need to,' I said. 'I'm thinking of California. Let's try it together.'

'And what aboot the lassie?'

'What lassie?'

'Ye ken well what I mean. It'll no' be California for *you*, my lad. You'll be getting married.'

'To Judith?' I said. 'Yes – I hope so – eventually. But not until I have something behind me.'

'You'll be having *her* behind you, not to mention her father, if you try to skedaddle before calling the banns,' he grinned.

'What damned nonsense,' I blustered. 'I haven't even asked her yet.'

'Then you're a fool. Her father tells me he's leaving the army and putting up his shingle in London. Why don't you get him to take you on as an apprentice? There's gey good money in sawboning.'

'Not for *me*,' I said flatly. 'Look – at least come with us as far as Calcutta. There won't be a price on your head once your part in the relief of Faraqbagh is fully known. Leave it to Mr Palmer and Captain Shelton and the rest of these people who know the true story.' And I kept on at him without surcease for half the night, until in sheer weariness, and, indeed, because I knew he was secretly dreading being left alone up there in the wilds, he agreed.

The journey, which took fourteen days, passed without further incident, although we saw the smoke of many burning villages on both banks, and on three occasions we picked up parties of refugees who had been in hiding in the jungle, until, when we arrived at Calcutta, the boats were crammed to the point of suffocation, and once more Mr Palmer was near to exhaustion.

There was a huge tented camp on the Maidan for the reasonably fit, as the hospitals were filled to overflowing with the more seriously ill and disabled, and we thankfully handed over our charges to the medical authorities, then, having seen Mr Palmer and Judith into the officers' lines at Fort William, and fought off their invitations to stay with them, Jock and I went off in search of accommodation for ourselves and, more urgently, seemly apparel for the former, as he was still wearing the tattered remnants of his General's finery, and attracting a lot of embarrassing attention thereby.

Suitably clad in white duck suits after bathing, and receiving the attention of a civilized barber, we managed to find beds at the Bristol Hotel in which, after an enormous dinner and the better part of a bottle of Scotch whisky that brought nostalgic tears to Jock's eyes, we slept the sleep of the bone-weary for, in my case at least, some fourteen hours.

I crossed the Maidan in the cool of the following morning a prey to anxiety, dreading the parting with Judith, which I knew must come, because however favourable to my suit her father might be, I was determined not to make a declaration until I had something to offer her. I loved her, and I knew she returned it, but here I was once again, rudderless before the wind, possessed of nothing but a lucky knack of survival, a certain sharpness of wits and something that I was trying to tell myself was pride, but which I knew was really nothing more than a painful self-consciousness.

But it had to be done. I would see Mr Palmer, and thank him for his great kindness to me, and tell him of my feelings for his daughter, although I knew he was already aware of them, and ask his permission to approach her at some un-specified time in the future, if she was still free and I had succeeded in earning a competence.

This feeling of noble renunciation had reached divine afflatus proportions by the time I arrived at their lodgings in the fort, but I was not able to deliver my carefully composed speech, because Mr Palmer said angrily, 'Where the devil have you been? I've had patrols out looking for you since last night.' But when I tried to speak, he went on, 'Never mind now – we've no time. We're due at the Governor-General's ante-room at eleven.'

He grabbed me by the arm and steered me downstairs and across the parade ground that held so many memories for me.

'But, sir, what on earth – ?' I stammered, trying to hold back.

'Come on, come on,' he commanded. 'Lord Canning – the last Governor-General and first Viceroy, as his office is to be known henceforward, is holding a levee. The Queen takes over now, and the damned Company is finished – '

I stopped dead in my tracks. 'But what has that to do with *me*?' I demanded.

'His official thanks for your part in the relief of Faraqbagh,' Mr Palmer answered. 'You're famous, my boy. The story of our deliverance and your subsequent wrongful court martial has been published in the *Indian Gazette* – a most eulogistic account.'

'But what about Jock?' I asked.

'It only refers to him as the commander of the Rajah's State forces. They seem to think he's a Sikh,' he told me. 'It's best left at that for the moment.'

'Then be damned to it,' I said firmly. 'I'm not being patted on the head by anybody, unless he is there also.'

'By all means, if you think it wise,' Mr Palmer agreed. 'But where is he?'

'At the Bristol Hotel.'

'Then let's pick him up on the way. I have a gharry standing by.'

But Jock was adamant when we saw him. 'Not on your life,' he swore. 'Aye – it'll be all cheering and clapping the noo, but the next thing will be a sergeant's hand on my collar and I'll be clapped into a guardroom. Ye dinna desert from a Hié'land regiment with impunity. Nae – I'm keeping my gab closed and my heid doon until I'm shut of this country.'

'Nonsense,' Mr Palmer expostulated. 'What about Ross? He's been completely cleared.'

'Aye, because you were able to swear that he wasn't Dalrymple – but I'm still Alastair McMurtrie for all to see and recognize. No, thank you, sir. I'm biding here.' And nothing we could say would move him.

So on we went to Government House in the Belvedere, and we joined on to a long line of people who were being thanked officially, including Judith, who was already waiting there, suitably chaperoned by some colonel's wife – and my Lord Canning had a few amiable words for each of us – and out we came into the courtyard, where my hand was grasped and pumped vigorously and my back slapped violently by none other than – McClintock!

I stared at him open-mouthed as he yelled above the babble that surrounded us ' – every lawyer in the East looking for you – advertisements in the papers here and in England – another two years and you'd have been presumed dead and the damned convent would have got the lot – only by the merest fluke – saw your name in the list – '

'What in the name of God are you talking about?' I shouted at him.

'Mascharenhas's will, you fool – half to his daughter – half to you. Come on – got to get you sworn before a notary – '

In vain I search my memory to recall in detail the events of those last madhouse days in Calcutta, but they remain a blur – the scurrying round to find a lawyer who was still functioning in that sadly disrupted city – the signing of reams of documents, the affidavits sworn by myself with Mr Palmer and McClintock as referees, the latter a most interested party determined not to let me out of his sight for one moment, because it appeared that there was a standing reward of five thousand pounds to anybody who succeeded in tracing me, and he, having lost his directorship in Hong Kong and being hounded by creditors, was now greatly reduced in circumstances.

And then, overriding all else, was the stormy scene between Judith and myself in which she turned me down flatly when I formally proposed.

'But I thought – I mean – you once said – ' I stammered miserably.

'That I loved you?' she said coldly. 'Yes, I thought I did – right up until our arrival here, and you started avoiding me.'

'Only because I had nothing to offer you. I was about to explain to your father – '

'The matter is one between ourselves. I am not one of your Indian women to be bought and sold. Go back to Hong Kong, Mr Stafford, and I wish you the joy of it.'

'Not without you.'

'Then go to Timbuctoo for all I care. *I* am certainly not coming with you – *anywhere.*'

'But you would have married me if I had nothing?'

'Had you asked me – yes. But now you are putting me in the position of a fortune-hunting strumpet.'

'Don't use such language,' I said sternly.

'I'll use whatever language I choose, and be damned to you,' she spat at me, and then broke into a storm of weeping which enabled me to take her in my arms and thereafter things arranged themselves without further upset between us, and we were married two days later by the Residency chaplain, a few hours before sailing for Hong Kong.

We tried, jointly, to persuade her father to come with us, but he insisted on accompanying his regiment back to England before resigning his commission, although he promised to join us later.

Which left only Jock. 'I'm no' coming with you just because you've come into a few bawbees,' he growled.

'Oh, God preserve me from the prideful,' I swore. 'There's a big business up there, and I want your help.'

'What use would I be pushing a pen in a counting-house?'

'You'd be worth your keep as interpreter alone. The place is full of bloody Scotchmen cutting each other's throats – MacKinnon, MacKenzie – Jardine Mathieson – and all the other princely houses – there's room for a Stafford and McMurtrie.' And so it went on for hours, but at last he gave way.

Ho Chang came up the pilot ladder as we ghosted through the early morning mist of the Li Mun Channel. He kowtowed deeply and I returned it, and took his hand in Western style, and for a long time neither of us spoke. Then he said simply, 'We knew you would return. The Old Master's house stands ready.'

'Miss Leonora – ?' I asked.

'Is well, and sends her felicitations and welcomes you back,' he said. He turned and pointed up towards the Peak, where a long white building was catching the rays of the rising sun. 'She is Sister Josepha now, of the Carmelite convent.' He held out his hand. 'Another coin, please,' he asked, and I gave him a five-mohur piece, which in Calcutta they called a pagoda.

He weighed it in his palm. 'Pure gold,' he pronounced softly. 'Fruit of the Pagoda Tree. This will please the Wander Joss, and now he will hold you here.'

He threw it far over the water, and we watched the rings widening from the splash, and Jock yelped in dismay at the sheer wanton waste of a guid bawbee.